AQUAVIT

The Aquamarine Sea Series ~ Book 1

Bon voyage!

Karen Stensgaard

Aquavit is a work of fiction. Any references to historical events, real people, or real places are used fictitiously and not intended to refer to any living persons or to disparage any company's products or services. Names, characters, places, and events are products of the author's imagination and any resemblance to actual events, places, or persons, living or dead, is purely coincidental.

Published in the United States by Sandefur Metz Publishing Company, Philadelphia, Pennsylvania, USA

ISBN: 9781521210512

~ DEDICATION ~

For Xena & Petra,
Our beautiful, spunky and furry girlfriends,
Who bravely fought the big C, not once but twice.
Your time with us ended way too soon,
And you'll always be in our hearts.

~ INSPIRATION ~

"I always have a comfortable feeling that nothing is impossible if one applies a certain amount of energy in the right direction. When I want things done, which is always at the last moment, and I am met with such an answer: 'It's too late. I hardly think it can be done;' I simply say: 'Nonsense! If you want to do it, you can do it. The question is, do you want to do it?'"

From Elizabeth Jane Cochrane's memoir, *Nellie Bly's Book: Around the World in Seventy-Two Days,* published in 1890. Ms. Cochrane was one of the first American women investigative journalists. Despite some competition, she unexpectedly won and beat Phileas Fogg's fictitious 80-day journey in the novel, *Around the World in Eighty Days*, and met the novelist, Jules Verne.

AQUAVIT

1 ~ *Willfully Blind*

Friday nights weren't normally like this, but in a few hours, it should all be over, and I could finally plan my escape from New York City. I took another big sip of my pink pomegranate margarita to let the coldness give me a slight brain freeze matching what I felt all over. Charles, a ruggedly handsome guy, sat across from me behind a glass of whiskey. My first real date in what seemed like forever, and he wouldn't notice.

He droned on about what an expert he was in investment banking with his predatory Wall Street company. Not only was Charles lucky and smart, he apparently ran a close second to Gotham's own Batman. But I only wanted an ordinary guy, not a superhero.

Charles said, "My division grew exponentially this year. The fees we've negotiated are unheard of in the industry." He was proud and puffed up like a balloon for the Macy's Thanksgiving Day parade.

I couldn't resist a quick jab to bring him back to earth. "Yeah, well, someone must pay those exorbitant fees, and it trickles down from the company to the shareholders and anyone who buys the stock - even one share."

"It's the capitalist way, Kathryn." His greenish eyes narrowed while he pushed his rebellious brown hair back with his hand intent on convincing me.

I stared back wondering why his personality took such a drastic turn for the worse. He was charming, even alluring, during the first twenty minutes. Somehow that guy disappeared, and now I faced the typical, condescending executive I often audited.

"I fully support the capitalist system, but I don't like ripping people off Charlie."

I intentionally didn't use the overly formal 'Charles' and reminded him again. "It's Kat, not Kathryn."

I knew Wall Street, and the games he and his buddies liked to play. Always chasing revenue to feed their egos and massive bonus pools, and it was never enough.

In what felt like eons ago, I'd suggested meeting here at my favorite neighborhood place, Rosalee's Mexicana. The upscale restaurant was festive and warm and reminded me of my hometown, San Antonio, Texas. If I hadn't promised to meet him, and my dating prospects nonexistent, I would have left by now. But I was fascinated and eager to see what would happen next, and that stubborn part of me that didn't sensibly quit when the going got tough made me stay. Besides, I couldn't bear another lonely takeout dinner and boring TV.

Our mutual girlfriend Susan had raved about Charlie, so maybe we got started wrong. Susan had insisted, "Kat, he is the only guy out there who meets all your criteria - unattached, employed, mid-forties to fifties, lives in Manhattan, and no kids."

Tomorrow I must adjust my criteria and add two new ones, kind and modest, or put out a permanently unavailable sign and avoid the whole issue. I found the perfect guy once and married him. I knew the odds. This wouldn't happen twice.

Months ago, we'd set this up but rescheduled twice. I canceled last month when I lost Xena, my best friend and four-legged furry soulmate. I was her human more than she was my cat, and the ache would never leave.

Behind Charlie, a woman leaned against the bar and watched me. She was cozied up between two young hunks, but I didn't recognize her. I dabbed my mouth and chin with my napkin in case I'd dribbled red pomegranate juice. But she still looked at me and gestured in our direction.

Charlie was busy boasting about his famous neighbors in his building on Central Park West, adding details about a famous musician, and name-dropping other wealthy one-percenters. Ironic, after he bragged about how rich he was, we were still here in the downstairs bar instead of getting a table in the restaurant upstairs. But I was glad we hadn't since that would drag things out, and I preferred the casual bar.

"Are those friends of yours?" I asked, pointing behind him to our trio of gawkers. I pushed my hair back and wished I brought along a hair clip to keep it off my shoulders.

"Yeah, they're part of my old due diligence team. Checking up on me, I guess. I don't do blind dates." He waved for them to come over.

"Neither do I." And, I swore under my breath, "My first and last."

Due diligence teams did in-depth research for senior bankers like Charlie. I shifted in my seat uncomfortably. Did they investigate me for the hell of it to impress their boss? I took another sip of my drink but told myself not to worry since I had nothing to hide.

I glanced down at my newly manicured nails and admired my handiwork, even though I was out of practice. My blonde hair, transitioning towards brown, was trimmed and highlighted last Saturday. I even dressed up my usual jeans with a new silk top. But the extra effort to spiff up wasn't necessary with the way things were going.

To get through this date, I needed something stronger than a fruity margarita. I ignored the overhyped mezcal tequila with the requisite dead worm, a fate I wanted to avoid. But I couldn't pass up a tequila at Rosalee's with the most extensive list I'd seen this far north of Mexico.

The waiter came by, and Charlie ordered some appetizers without asking me what I wanted. I hoped he was being courteous, not egocentric, and didn't object since I liked everything on the menu.

Before the waiter left, I ordered a tequila and practiced my nearly nonexistent Spanish. "*Uno Patrón reposado por favor.*" This brand from the patron saint brand of tequilas was my favorite, and reposado tequilas were aged with a smoky taste.

"Make that two tequilas, please," Charlie added glaring at me.

Charlie swiveled around to greet his three young friends and introduced me. They lingered to chat and hovered around as if he smelled irresistible. It must be the nasty smell of money. Based on where Charlie lived and his job, he probably earned more than many third-world countries ever would.

While they discussed clients and what might be confidential deals that I shouldn't hear about, I scanned the immediate area. The jam-packed bar was noisy with pulsating music muffled by the spirited and lively crowd before the theater rush. I envied that sense of anticipation for a weekend. I hadn't looked forward to anything for nearly two years. Back before my husband received his death sentence.

The waiter returned with our tequilas and a cart to custom-blend our guacamole, so his friends drifted off. The waiter asked for our spice preference and how hot he should make it.

I couldn't help responding first. "Bring it on. Extra jalapeños, por favor."

After our waiter had made the guacamole and left, I apologized to Charlie. "I grew up on Mexican food. I hope you're okay with spice."

Charlie nodded. We sipped our tequilas, and I savored the sweet hint of smoky citrus and vanilla. Just what I needed, and the cold, soft burn tickled my throat.

We started in on the chips and spicy guacamole, fiery even for me. Charlie probably didn't like it since he stopped eating after a brief taste.

"So, Kathryn, I mean Kat, do you have any questions?"

I laughed being reminded of a job interview when managers go on and on, and at the end, remember they should have let the applicant speak. Dates were so much like job interviews. Everyone tried to present their best side.

"Have you ever been to Richmond?" I wanted to steer the conversation to a neutral topic and away from work and New York City real estate.

But I was distracted and busy with an important job to do. Since Charlie stopped eating, I was responsible for finishing off the guacamole waiting in a large stone molcajete bowl. Not even a teaspoon would be left behind.

"Richmond, Virginia?" After a pause, he said, "No, why?"

"Isn't your last name Richmond?" He must be curious about a city not far away that shared his last name. Didn't he have a sense of adventure?

"No, I've never been to Richmond. No reason to so why would I? I spend my time off at my beach house in the Hamptons. And I'm in London at least once a month for business. Thinking about buying a flat there, but their prices make New York look cheap."

Boring but at least Charlie wasn't talking about work.

Our waiter checked in, and I ordered a second margarita while Charlie demanded another Jack Daniel's whiskey. Didn't he know this was a Mexican joint? I shrugged but was beyond caring. He could eat or drink whatever he wanted.

Our mahi-mahi fish tacos and carnitas pork quesadillas arrived with more drinks. When we finished eating, I would say a polite goodbye and leave. I savored the gourmet dishes and picked out hints of cilantro and tried to do the impossible: distinguish the flavors of habaneros peppers from poblanos.

I didn't have any more questions for him since I was busy eating, but he broke the silence. "It's a shame your consulting biz is closing down."

I was so surprised I nearly choked and swigged down tap water to regain my focus.

He needed no urging and continued. "All that fame with the FBI, being in the New York Times, meeting the mayor, and then -"

"How did you know that?" I cut him off and put my water glass down shakily. We only told our existing clients and close friends last week that my business was closing.

"Well, it was broadly known. In the paper and all that."

"No, I mean about closing." My consulting business was the realization of a dream come true. I'd earned it and paid the price fighting dangerous money launderers and clients of my former employer. My fifteen minutes of unwanted fame.

"I'm in the business to know who I associate with."

"But this is not business-related, so that's not an acceptable answer." I wanted to reach over and pull the information out of him. But he was a professional negotiator and used to getting his way.

"Now Kat, I never reveal my sources. Besides, firms don't want someone like you poking around and looking at their business and clients. They pay you and all the other auditors to look the other way."

"It's not my fault everyone has something to hide, and no

one wants to do the right thing. That's the whole problem."

Waves of frustration reverberated across my tequila-soaked brain. Internal auditors fought a losing battle trying to do what's right and not only find, but fix the problems. We were never liked, respected, or well paid.

I shifted uncomfortably on my bar stool and leaned on our small table to find an escape route. Being trained to evaluate business disaster plans, I should have already done this. But the bathrooms were upstairs with no exit, and Charlie faced the front door. I reminded myself not to worry since I can leave at any time. But I'd stay to the bitter end and set him straight.

"Perhaps. But I'm sure your last employer, the global bank, was thrilled when you gave your notice."

At that bank, with help from a few brave colleagues, we identified an active drug-dealing account. Untold millions flowed through it unhampered since the founding of the bank in the 1860's. The resulting scandal reverberated throughout the industry and temporarily brought the bank to its knees. Charlie was right. The bank was probably thrilled, but I didn't need reminding.

Charlie focused on drinking more of his whiskey. When he looked at me again, his eyes changed color to a darker green. His gaze was so direct as if he was trying to bore a hole into me. "Internal auditors don't create or provide anything of value. The only reason your kind exists is to keep the regulators off our back."

"That's your uneducated opinion." He knew nothing about what an internal auditor did or why they were important, and how every company could benefit from an in-house evaluation. But I wasn't going to bother educating him.

He looked at me as if still trying to read my thoughts, but his eyes were less focused. All those whiskeys must be taking a toll. I glanced at our half-eaten dishes to avoid his scrutiny and felt the warmth from the tequila coursing through my veins.

"Filing Chapter 7 bankruptcy must not be much fun. But you'll get through it. Haven't been there myself, but my clients do it all the time." He patted my hand sympathetically.

I pulled my hand back as if bitten. "What? My firm isn't bankrupt. I'm shutting down because I've had enough. I'm planning to do something else."

"Oh, really?"

"Yeah, really. Your sources are wrong. Dead wrong." I motioned to his colleagues, the three stooges and likely the guilty party, still hanging out at the bar. "All expenses were and will be paid in full. We aren't walking away from anything."

Every expense, that is, but my salary. Despite some success, I wasn't good at promoting, selling or pricing our work high enough. If I didn't shut down the business my nest egg and retirement savings, which kept the firm afloat, would disappear.

"Yeah, and whoever your sources are, they need to do better homework because that offends me."

Charlie resumed eating as if nothing happened. These mistakes probably occur all the time. He gets his facts wrong and brushes it off. The more I considered his spiteful, condescending, and inaccurate comments, the angrier I got. The scrumptious Mexican treats served on colorful plates now resembled pulpy, brown masses.

"If you, or any of your sources, spread this lie around, I will consult with an attorney."

"Now, Kat, no need to get all bent out of shape. My apologies. I will talk to my team."

I sighed with relief. Charlie took a big bite of a fish taco, and the juice and salsa slid out and stuck to the corner of his mouth. I wanted to shift the conversation to anything else, even back to hearing about his incredible success and wealth. He stared at me and might have sensed I was suffering because I'd stopped eating.

"Well, think of it this way. Now you can do something more productive and valuable. Adopt orphans from Africa. Do some charity work. Scale a mountain. Cure a disease."

I was shocked, but before I could reply, he added, "Of course, that takes money and lots of it. My ex went through it faster than I could make it. My advice to you: find a rich guy."

He slurred his words this time, and when he mentioned his ex-wife, heat radiated from his hatred. I couldn't endure this date anymore. I was a career woman, and to him, my entire life's work was a waste of time. Maybe I hadn't stopped world hunger, but I'd tried to make a difference. And the idea of needing a sugar daddy sickened me.

Now that I was soon unemployed and nothing was holding me back, I was going to do something unique. A once in a lifetime bucket list worthy trip that would get me back on track. An adventure to be proud of and astonish and surprise my friends. I'd already imagined returning full of optimism, recharged, and happy again. I just hadn't figured out exactly what I'd do or where to go, but I would this weekend.

Charlie sat back and sipped his drink grumbling incoherently about women. I picked up my water glass, now just half full, and tossed the contents at Charlie. The water might eliminate his evil smirk, wake him up to the 21st century, and how he should treat women.

The water hit his chin and neck and then dribbled down. Charlie stood stumbling back in surprise, but when he realized it was only water, he sat down again.

I was still seething, but a smile crossed my face, pleased for once I fought back. I fumbled around in my purse for my wallet and tossed some twenties on the table. "Here's my portion," while I slid off my bar stool.

He dabbed the water off his face with a napkin and grinned. I did him a favor since the water removed the taco sauce, but his eyes looked bloodshot. He must be drunk to act like such a moron.

"I'm sorry, Kathryn. I was rude and deserved that. Please stay."

"Nope. This isn't working out." I gave Charlie plenty of chances to redeem himself, and I didn't see the point of staying for more verbal abuse.

Before I could stand, Charlie clamped his hand down on my wrist and held it firm against the tabletop. His soft, cold hand made me recoil. I tried pulling my hand away, but he pressed down harder. For a split-second, I visualized the terrible image

I couldn't believe this was happening, but I didn't want to scream or cause an embarrassing scene. "Let me go! Now," I demanded in the most forceful but calm voice I could muster.

Charlie shook his head and mumbled something about calming down. I stood, but it was awkward. I leaned towards him with my right-hand stuck under his on the table. My left hand covered the gap in my low-cut blouse. I wasn't about to let him see any more of my skin than necessary. But that was a minor problem. How could I get away?

I noticed the silverware next to my plate, grabbed my dinner knife, and waved it above Charlie's hand to threaten him. At the flash of silver, he jerked his hand away.

"Crazy bitch!"

2 ~ *Crossing The Line*

I grabbed my belongings and dodged people pushing my way out the front door. Adrenaline-fueled, I wanted to run but forced myself to walk not stopping to pull on my blazer. The calm, crisp October night air cooled me down from the fight. I hurried north on Columbus Avenue passing slow-moving pedestrians and the well-lit Lincoln Center Plaza with its centerpiece fountain.

"Relax," I chanted. You're safe and free again. My mood swiftly changed from fear to being exhilarated and on top of the world. As if I'd escaped some near disaster and emerged magically alive. The feeling I experienced on my last day at a miserable job. My last one, at the bank Charlie so kindly reminded me of, only lasted six months. After two short years with my own consulting business and a taste of real freedom when I could call the shots, it was all coming to an end on Monday.

Maybe I should do something more meaningful like Charlie said. Whatever it was it would be my decision, and a challenge while I was young and healthy enough to do it. My own personal Mount Everest that doesn't involve hiking.

"But what?" I tried again to imagine something.

At the busy intersection of 65th Street, the traffic forced me to wait before jaywalking ahead. I was several blocks away from the restaurant but looked back, worried Charlie might be following me.

I reassured myself that was nonsense. I'll probably never see him again, and if I did, we could ignore each other. I mumbled, "I showed him."

I would never have stabbed him or anyone for that matter. The knife was only a threat. No one will take advantage of me, but then again, no one will want to go on a date with me either. I'll just have to get used to being alone while I bit my lower lip not savoring the idea.

The sound of squealing brakes and an angry car's blaring

horn came from out of nowhere. I froze and saw the blur of a yellow taxicab. The cabbie yelled out the window, "Damn fool. Watch out," and shook his fist at me.

I stepped back on the curb and bumped into some people standing behind me. "Sorry. Excuse me."

Focused on what to do in the future, I'd blindly followed other pedestrians across a vast stretch of Broadway against the light without checking for traffic. I didn't look at the others standing around me, not knowing what to say or how to explain that I'm not normally this careless or suicidal.

While I waited on the curb, people around me made a few gasps and murmurings. "That was a close call. Holy crap. Geez." And worst of all, "Glad I didn't see that."

I let the crowd pass by when the walk sign flashed and waited for the next one. What a perfect end to an awful week. But when you're dead nothing matters, and I wasn't ready. A month ago, I'd say sure but not now. I had forward momentum and a trip to plan. I'll find my mojo out there somewhere and drag it back for a much happier life.

I trudged the last few blocks to my apartment. I missed my husband, Axel, but I had lots of friends. Except for tonight's failed attempt, I hadn't dated. Not even a one-night stand. But I didn't want another husband. A fun-loving guy to date once a week would be perfect. After my trip, maybe I'll try again.

I unlocked the door to my empty apartment wishing Xena, my little tabby cat, was there to greet me. She was a real New Yorker, abandoned and rescued from the Bronx. More of a seven-pound dog wearing a cat suit. Somehow, Xena always knew when I was coming home and waited at the door for me.

Losing her this past month after ten years of spending every night nestled together added more unbearable heartbreak. My chest tightened up again as if I wouldn't be able to breathe, and I tried to think about something else.

As I glanced around my apartment, I realized nothing but memories of what I'd lost kept me here. I didn't want to forget but needed some distance to heal. Inside the hall closet, I pulled out one of Axel's favorite hoodies and wrapped myself in it inhaling his faint smell.

"You're safe now," I said to my empty apartment while I wrapped my arms around myself in a straight-jacket hug. I wasn't crazy, but I missed Axel, and not just tonight, all the time.

I picked up Axel's coffee can with its label hidden by photos and reminders from our trips around the world. His final wish was to have his ashes recycled and stored temporarily in an old coffee can.

We bought gourmet coffee in bags so I'd argued, "At least make it a better class of coffee."

I ordered a fancy can of Café Du Monde chicory coffee from New Orleans. But at that point, he was too sick to drink it.

I flicked on the radio to drown out the sound of emptiness. The song *Beyond the Sea* surrounded me, and I reminisced about some of our trips, the easier ones, where we threw our stuff in a cabin, free to explore the ship and ports of call. One photo was from a cruise through the Norwegian fjords, and in late May, we had a snowball fight in the mountains.

"We had some good times, didn't we Axel? I miss our trips. Soon we'll go traveling, and I'll take you home to Denmark."

I needed to get out, take a chance, and make new memories instead of replaying the old ones. A hoodie, scarf and a few other things were all I had left. My assistant Mel insisted on a serious house cleaning six months ago, so almost all his personal belongings were donated to Goodwill.

And now after a year, I should scatter his ashes. I'll start in Denmark, Axel's birthplace, and have a ceremony with his brother. And then scatter him in some other places. I couldn't go anywhere before when I was running my business, or leave Xena when she got sick.

"Axel, I'm afraid I need another drink. It was a rough week. Any suggestions?" I didn't want to mention the details about my first and last blind date.

I didn't hear him or feel any communications coming through and didn't believe in it. Axel was an atheist and believed in caring for animals and the environment. After all that I'd been through, I wasn't sure if a God existed. Now I was unofficially agnostic and hedging my bets since no one made me chose.

The Beatles' *Eleanor Rigby* song started playing on the radio. "Axel, I don't want to end up like her. Why did you have to go and die?"

But whining was a waste of time, and I forced myself to do something productive. I confirmed in about a second that the fridge was still nearly empty. Our eclectic liquor collection was long gone. Turned into all sorts of strange concoctions when friends came by before and after he died.

We used to have Scandinavian aquavit, known as the 'water of life' in Latin, in the freezer. With the high alcohol content, it never froze. Digging past bags of frozen veggies, I found two bottles, one Danish and another Norwegian, wedged in the back. After I had placed them on the kitchen counter, a thrill went down my spine. I rubbed my hands together to warm them, while not losing eye contact with my friendly elixirs, eager for the tasting to begin.

The bottles were frosty, but like most Scandinavians, they were used to the cold. I plunked my favorite shot glass from Sweden on the counter and poured my first shot, a small one, unsure how it would mix with tequila.

I started with the Danish aquavit in honor of Axel. While I poured, I recalled the Danish warning that one drink, or shot, went to one leg. To avoid being off balance, you must have a second drink for your other leg. But I was already tipsy, so one tiny shot from each would have to suffice.

The liquor's smooth herbal flavor wafted up, and I inhaled deeply. The label said it was seasoned with coriander, cilantro, and dill.

I confirmed to whoever might be listening. "Not bad. The dill is light and not noticeable. After all, we aren't making dill pickles." I giggled at the idea.

I stared at the Norwegian bottle with an unusual story behind it. Barrels of this aquavit crossed the equator in ships known in sailor speak as 'crossing the line' not once, but twice, before bottling. I knew all this, but I picked up the semi-defrosted bottle to read more. The tradition started by accident.

Barrels of the aquavit were shipped to Asia but didn't sell. After returning to Norway, the liquor had acquired a unique flavor from being jostled on the ship while crossing two equators.

I admired the beautiful drawing of a sailing ship on the label and wished I was onboard. The label said you could track your bottle's sea journey with the date on the back. The song playing on the radio was appropriate, the Beach Boys' *Sail on Sailor.* I didn't know all the words but sang the chorus out loud while I googled the company's website on my phone. Find your Bottle popped up with instructions, so I plugged in the date my newfound friend began his journey.

"All right buddy, let's see where in the world you went. Perhaps, somewhere I haven't been." I stopped to sing the song's refrain wishing he could sing along too.

While waiting for the details, I threw back a small, second shot to stay balanced. The Norwegian aquavit tasted smoother than the Danish version. Must be the hell it went through to get here.

When the journey flashed up on my screen, I clicked from port to port as the ship's route went around the globe: Oslo, Brooklyn, Sydney, Hong Kong, Yokohama, Cartagena and back to Oslo. I was impressed with my little friend, a world traveler. Was it twice or three times it crossed the line? Trying to follow the ship on the company's website made me dizzy.

"Your adventure sounds like fun," I said to the well-travelled bottle. "I've been to all those places, but I've never crossed the equator on a ship, only on planes. Might be worth doing on a beautiful sailing ship like yours."

I rubbed the label trying to feel the ship's billowing sails and the force of the wind. The bottle stared at me as if it was waiting for more conversation. Were all those people who talked to bartenders talking to bottles instead?

I'd swear someone said, "You go girl." Or something to that effect, but I wasn't sure since the bottle probably spoke Norwegian.

When I was having a conversation with a bottle, even if he was a gentleman, I'd better call it a night. I was a one, or maybe two, drink social drinker, and tonight I'd passed my max. I kicked off my boots and stumbled into bed not bothering to change. My bedroom rocked as if I was at sea while I drifted off.

~ ~ ~

The phone rang, and I fumbled around on my nightstand and grabbed the phone, but it slipped, missed the area rug, and banged against the wooden floor. Not giving up, I retrieved it from the floor and croaked out a hello.

"Kat, are you okay?" I recognized Melanie's familiar voice. She was my soon to be former assistant since our last work day together was on Monday.

"What's up, Mel?" My voice slurred while I wondered where I was in the darkness. The room swayed as if I was in the cargo hold with the aquavit. Wishful thinking, when I recognized it was my bedroom.

"Sorry to call so late, but I've been texting and emailing you for hours. You haven't responded."

I swallowed hard and scanned my brain for what to say. "I'm fine but worn out. Can't this wait?"

"I guess so."

That was all the assurance I needed. As I hung up, Mel said, "But I should warn you -"

I was too tired to listen. Mel was a night owl and meant well, but it was probably some gossip that could wait. I tried to put the phone back in its cradle, but it fell to the floor. This time, I left it there.

My throat ached dehydrated from my alcohol binge. I dragged myself to the bathroom for a drink of water, and on the way, I discarded my clothes from last night. The liquid was refreshing and a real aquavit. New York City's tap water was one of the world's best.

Refreshed, I flicked on the bathroom light and groaned at what was reflected in the mirror. My face was smeared from carefully designed, heavier than usual, glam eye makeup for my date last night with Mr. Rich & Attractive. Unfortunately, he was Mr. Rude & Arrogant. I looked awful, like a zombie with dark, sunken eyes.

My blondish, shoulder-length hair always had a life of its own during the night and flared out from my scalp in all directions. My stomach was queasy, but I didn't feel that rush of water like I'd throw up. Maybe I'll be lucky for once. I hadn't over indulged for so long, not since Axel's death. Splashing my face with water, I washed off the worst of it, threw on a nightgown, and crawled back under the covers eager to re-board my dream ship and delay the start of another weekend.

3 ~ *Going Viral*

"I'm coming," I yelled to the incessant knocking and doorbell ringing while swinging my feet around to the cold floor.

"Who in the hell could be here this early on a Saturday?" I grumbled and glanced over at my clock radio. Shocked, it was already after 11 a.m., so I should get going.

I pulled on my robe while I stumbled across the living room to the front door. Peering through the peephole, Melanie, my faithful assistant, and partner-in-crime waited. Everyone called her Mel, and even though she was technically my employee, we worked as a team, and I respected her judgment completely.

Our friends teased us about running 'the Kat and Mel show' since we complemented each other so well. The past two years in consulting and beforehand at the bank were entertaining. Sometimes too much so. Now she could tell me whatever it was she called me about last night. I was surprised to see her since she lived in Brooklyn, and we shared a passion for sleeping late.

Her eyes were intense, and she wasn't smiling. My heart pounded so loud I was sure she could hear it.

"Mel, what's wrong?" Something awful must have happened for her to be here.

"I was in the area and wanted to see how you're doing. You weren't answering your cell or home phone."

"Nothing's wrong?" Relief flooded over me. But then why was she here? "I'm fine just didn't hear the phone. It fell on the floor after you called, and my cell is turned off. Just sleeping late. Come on in."

I stepped back to let her in. She was my height, but there the similarities ended. Her skin was pale, and she had red hair and carried about an extra hundred pounds. But if her weight bothered her, she never mentioned it, and I didn't either.

She carried a grocery bag from Whole Foods, and I

followed her into the kitchen.

I decided to confess about last night even though she would say I told you so. "I survived my first and last blind date last night. The guy was a complete jerk and drank so much he was wasted. I should have trusted my instincts and listened to you. I can't believe Susan insisted we'd be perfect together."

"Yeah, well, I can see you didn't exactly hit it off."

"Who told you that?" Did Charlie or his friends already tell someone she knew?

But Mel didn't answer. She picked up the strange aquavit bottles still on the kitchen counter one by one to read the labels. "Party last night?"

"Yeah, but just me. The date was so devastating. Axel must have sent me a subliminal sympathy message since I didn't remember these bottles were in the freezer."

Sitting on a bar stool at the kitchen counter, I tried to smooth down my wild hair. At least, I'd washed off most of the heavy makeup. Too bad I couldn't save that scary look for Monday night's Halloween party and my annual witch transformation.

"Mighty fine of him." She grimaced at the coffee can covered with his photos. She was tired of hearing about him, especially when I said how great he was or talked about him as if he was still alive. She'd never liked him much.

Mel looked at the bottles. "Aqua vitae. That's Latin for water of life. Does it work? Bring you back to life so to speak?"

"Yeah, well it did for me." I picked up the Norwegian bottle of aquavit with the ship logo holding it up to show her. "And isn't this the most spectacular, beautiful ship you've ever seen? The bed rocked, so I dreamed I was onboard a ship like this last night."

She glanced at the bottle again while she shook her head tired of my vivid imagination. With that reaction, I changed my mind about offering her a drink. No need to waste any of my valuable life-water on her. Besides, it was too early, and the bottles weren't frozen anymore.

"You may wish you were," she said in her serious, business-like voice. "Here, you have to see this." She handed me her smartphone with a video playing.

Mel wasn't the type to share stupid animal videos. Could it be a friend of ours in trouble? The video showed a blonde woman in a turquoise shirt trying to stand up, and then a glint of silver in her hand.

"But that's me from last night. What in the hell happened? How did it end up online?" I hadn't said anything when this happened and let the knife do all the talking.

She reached out to take her phone back, but I shook my head holding it out of reach. "Wait. I must see this again. I still can't believe it."

The clip started right after Charlie sat down after I splashed him with water. My actions must have captured his friends' attention, and they videotaped what happened next. I was trying to leave and stand and looked crazed, waving a knife around. The video didn't show how Charlie held my hand down on the table against my will.

Being well acquainted with my kitchen, Mel took out coffee and a filter and started a pot, while I watched the video over and over mesmerized. You could only see Charlie's back, not his face, and the video zoomed in on me.

"It's on Facebook, and you were tagged by a mutual friend of Krista O'Neil's with the comment 'Blind Date Gone Bad.' Saw it last night. That's why I called."

I slumped down on my bar stool. Mel sat on the other stool and patted my shoulder.

"And this morning, it went viral on Twitter, YouTube, and some blogs. A slew of discussions too," Mel added calmly, which I found odd under the circumstances since I wanted to yell and fight back or punch something.

Mel grabbed her phone back and brought up one of the other websites to show me. Some comments were positive, how I was protecting myself, but others said I looked like a deranged, serial killer, and should be locked up for psych treatment.

She poured me a cup of coffee and added a splash of skim milk. After years of working so closely together, she knew me better than anyone. I inhaled the comforting pumpkin spice wafting up from my cup and took a sip.

Mel sighed in frustration. "Totally sucks how with all the shit going on that women treat other women, part of their tribe, like this. Especially in this fricking testosterone fueled city."

"But why would she do this to me?" This wasn't funny and to be reminded and have the whole world see it. "How could anyone be so spiteful?"

"Yeah, Kat, I googled her. This Krista bitch works at that vile investment bank Levittman. Do you know her? It's a quirky, twisted video, so people are naturally eating it up. It's striking a nerve with both men and women. She probably didn't realize how many views it would get."

"Krista must be the woman I met at the bar last night along with a couple of others. They work for Charlie. Part of his due diligence team, but they acted like a groupie entourage."

I explained to Mel what happened and why I was forced to pick up the knife as a threat. She nodded as if it was all normal and reasonable.

Mel looked in the nearly empty fridge. "I don't see how you live like this Kat."

"I don't like cooking and just buy what I need."

She emptied her grocery bag - a carton of eggs, veggie sausages, and a bagel and started to make breakfast.

I zoned out still in a daze that this happened while I was sleeping or drinking. The two stoic liquid culprits, whom I mistook for friends last night, were guilty. But I quickly forgave them and picked up the bottle of Norwegian aquavit and displayed it to Mel to stop thinking about the damn video.

"Did you know the contents of this bottle were in a cask on a ship from Oslo, went practically all over the world, past two equators, before being bottled and sold to end up here?"

She shook her head and grabbed the bottle from me as if I was going to have another drink.

"Oh, Mel, don't worry. I had enough last night." I laughed. "But at least something good came from last night. I've finally decided. I'm going to do what the aquavit did. Go on a cruise on an old sailing ship. Take a few months off and find a job next year. Starting my search now is a total waste of time."

"Great. I keep telling you to take some time off and go somewhere. You need a break from all this bullshit. But first, we need to respond to this. Human Resource staff and headhunters look at digital media and web stuff before hiring anyone, particularly someone senior like you."

I knew that all too well. People lose not only jobs but entire careers over bad internet publicity, and I was at the managing director level in financial services, a publicity-shy line of work.

"Was Charles or Charlie Richmond tagged too?"

"Nope, I googled him too. He doesn't have a Facebook or other online accounts. Not any I could find."

"Smart. Charlie's firm probably tells him not to. Should I shut mine down?"

"You could, and I'll un-tag you on Facebook, but the video will still be out there for the world to see. I think it's better to fight back. Tell the world what happened after brunch."

Mel made herself at home and fried the sausages and seasoned and blended up the eggs in a bowl. The smell of a real breakfast cooking made my stomach growl, and I patted it to calm down. My overindulgence last night wasn't making me feel sick, and I was eager for this special meal.

When the eggs were cooked to perfection, she filled our plates with the sausages, scrambled eggs, and a toasted dark pumpernickel bagel.

"Yum. You are such a good cook. Will you marry me?" I teased and after a few mouthfuls started to feel better.

Mel knew how to make scrumptious eggs – moist and sloppy. I didn't like to bother with cooking especially not for one. And eggs weren't easy to master. I savored my last delicious mouthful hating to finish so soon. The last time I'd had eggs this delicious was at the buffet on a Royal Caribbean ship. Another reason to plan a cruise.

We debated an appropriate on-line response. Mel insisted I identify him by name.

"He insulted our profession. And he has that ridiculous old-fashioned, macho Wall Street attitude about how women must fill their days with kids, nannies, and society parties."

"Mel, I can't write that. If I do, it will hurt my future career worse than the video. Besides, I don't think he meant it all. He was pretty drunk."

"But, Kat, you can't let that bastard get away with this."

I considered how best to explain to her all the inappropriate advances, rude comments, and jokes teetering on the obscene, that I'd experienced first-hand or heard from my friends. Leaning in might work in the cyber-space Silicon Valley bubble, but on Wall Street, it often ended by getting your head chopped off. Particularly the employees who occasionally wore skirts.

"Sometimes I've encouraged women to report these distasteful, but not illegal situations. They backfired and hurt the women more than the original incident. Things got worse, and I regretted getting involved."

"But, Kat –"

"I know Mel. It sucks, but trust me on this. If I do something publicly, the old geezers filling the boards of directors and audit committees may hear about it, or see it, if I put it out on the internet. They'll never hire me."

"One of these days, we should let them choke on their damn cigars and martinis."

"Yeah, but not by me, or with Charlie and this video. That idiot woman Krista is responsible."

We agreed on a polite but watered down comment per Mel, and I posted it as my official response. I scrolled through the slew of Facebook likes on the video, which didn't seem appropriate. Should you like a video of someone getting robbed? I copied the message on Facebook too, so at least my friends wouldn't think I was dead or rotting in jail.

I had a slew of emails and texts, more than normal, and several from Charlie. I showed Mel one of his messages, pretty much all the same thing, briefly begging me to call him.

Mel glanced at it but got right to the point. "I trust you are going to delete his ass."

"Sure am. Gone." I hit the delete key. But secretly, I was glad he'd contacted me. Maybe he knew he was wrong and should apologize. There was even a tiny chance Charlie might behave better on his next date. Poor girl.

We scrolled through our devices laughing at some ridiculous posts related to the video. My Facebook page was more active with my West Coast pals viewing it. I added another post limited to my friends, "Still alive and fighting," with a happy face icon.

Mel started cleaning up my kitchen.

"Leave it. You've done enough. Jen must be missing you." I pulled her by the arm to the front door so she'd go home and spend time with her girlfriend. "I'll see you on Monday in less than 48 hours."

We stood in the small entry way, but she refused to leave.

"Why don't you come over tonight? I know you don't like the trek to Brooklyn. Jen and I will make you a nice dinner. Get your mind off things."

Things like men she meant. But I wasn't wired like her, and I still hoped to find a decent guy to date. If I hung around her, I'd worry about Monday and get more depressed. I didn't want her to feel guilty about the company closing. I was the one responsible for bringing in business.

"Don't worry about me. I'm off to the Metropolitan Art Museum to unwind. A special exhibit on Turner and his seascapes ends tomorrow. Besides, I've made it through much worse. At least no one shot at me."

She looked dubious but frowned remembering. "Yeah, at least you weren't dodging bullets."

After Mel had left, I climbed into my shower and let the steamy hot water pelt down jabbing my skin. I wished I could burn away the images from the video and date last night. The radio serenaded me with the upbeat Beatles' song *Here Comes the Sun.*

I poured some bath gel on my wooden brush and scrubbed my back hard to scrape off my stubborn grimy worries. A fusion of coconuts and sea salt filled the air. Letting me imagine a day at the beach without all the hassle of traveling. The next best thing to being there.

4 ~ Met With Inspiration

I held my breath staring at the painted ship battered on all sides by waves and threatened by rocks. Such spectacular works of art created with a brush.

"Thank you, Mr. Joseph Mallord William Turner," I mumbled his full name appreciating his genius with a brush.

A man said, "My sentiments exactly," but it was impossible to tell who said it.

A mob of people craned their necks and maneuvered around each other to push in for a view. I arrived at one of the worst times, mid-afternoon on a weekend. Since the exhibit was closing, getting anywhere near the paintings was a challenge.

I turned to move away and give others a chance to see them up close, wondering who had agreed with me. But anyone would since Turner's art was the closest to being at sea while on land.

I glanced around and saw an older man with gray hair. He caught my eye, and I smiled but didn't say anything. I circled the gallery to see each painting again but wanted to observe the huge canvases from a distance.

I sat at one of the marble benches in the gallery supported by carved clawed feet with four gnarled nails. My feet and all ten toenails were grateful for the break. Even though the floors were wood parquet and easy to stand on, I'd been on my feet for hours after walking across Central Park in the misty rain and through the Metropolitan Museum of Art.

I checked my phone and texted Abby, my neighbor down the hall, confirming brunch tomorrow. She was my best friend and close to my age with similar interests - watching movies, eating out, and drinking wine. Tomorrow we'd complain again about the lack of decent men. Ironic, in a city of over eight million, there weren't at least two out there, one for each of us.

I glanced around the room at the dramatic paintings. All the seascapes were so lifelike, but not all were pleasant. Turner showed the wild, stormy side and worst case scenario when passengers and crew faced death at sea.

The gray-haired man sat on the bench next to me leaving a polite gap of about four inches between us. He looked casually elegant and reminded me of older Europeans on an Italian cruise ship who were so well dressed. Even though he was older, he was attractive and fit. If only I could age like that. Axel used to reassure me that I was aging like a bottle of fine red wine, even though small lines started to show around my eyes.

My body began to radiate heat from the inside out. I took off my leather jacket and cashmere scarf. I hadn't bothered to check them since I wasn't patient about waiting in lines. The scarf was Axel's and invaluable.

"An impressive collection," I said into the air ahead unsure if he wanted to chat. If he did, it would be a short exchange. In crowded New York City, you were surrounded by people but usually strangers. People I would never speak to or see again. Never alone, but lonely.

"I'm glad you think so. The museum staff worked months to orchestrate this." He waved his hands around as if each painting was a musician playing in a concert.

I'd seen many of these large-scale paintings at Yale's art museum north in New Haven, Connecticut. Those wouldn't be hard to obtain, but many were from anonymous private collections which must be difficult to coax out of hiding.

"My favorite is that one." I pointed to a medium sized piece with beautiful colors and sails filled to capture not just the wind but my imagination.

"One of my favorites as well." He nodded and looked at me surprised. Perhaps since I picked a more modest painting.

"Kind of the owner to lend it out." What I wouldn't give to own one of these masterpieces. They'd be way out of my budget, even if I won a million dollars, since they must be worth twenty or thirty times that. And any sudden windfall had to refill my paltry, retirement nest egg.

"Yes, good of him to do this, but art shouldn't be hidden away. It should be shared."

"Exactly. But it might have been a her." But I knew it was probably a him. A wealthy, hedge fund guy with the rare combination of money and taste.

He picked up on this. "Or a him and a her."

I smiled knowing I could play this game too, but curious to see if I would press the wrong button and offend him. "Or a him and a him."

He laughed, threw his head back, and leaned over whispering, "Or a her and a her."

"Touché." He won this one since there weren't any other combinations unless I went into weird kinky couplings.

I was ready to leave, and this was the awkward part, saying goodbye to someone you never met and never would see again. Often people walked away not saying a word, but this seemed rude.

Some commotion and beeping started on the other side of the room by some paintings. A visitor must have gotten too close to the knee level rope barriers skirting the perimeter of the room to protect the artwork.

The man jumped up from our bench. He must be an employee or volunteer since he was dressed so well and knew so much about the exhibit.

The alarms sounded by the painting called *The Snowstorm*, renown from the recent film about the artist. In the 1840's, Turner had himself tied to a steamship's mast on a stormy sea to visualize and later paint these turbulent scenes from his memory.

Now was the perfect time to leave. I whispered, "Goodbye," into the air and walked to the adjacent gift shop. The small room was filled with Turner giftware and reproductions to encourage patrons to spend some money and bring home memories of the extraordinary display of Turner's art.

I picked up a miniature wooden ship model and admired the craftsmanship and intricate sails and felt a strange affinity for the little ship even though the price was ridiculously high. I will put this money towards a cruise on an old sailing ship like this. Create new memories and move ahead, as Axel urged me to do before he died. No more delays. I'll start my search tonight and won't give up until I find something.

I began to put the fragile, wooden ship back on the glass shelf careful to not disturb the glass and breakables surrounding me. While I was doing this, a loud, commanding voice behind me said, "Just a moment, Madame."

The voice rattled me so much I placed the ship only halfway on the shelf. It teetered and fell to the floor with a loud shattering echo. I stared down in dismay at the poor broken ship worried this might be a bad omen and hurt my chances of finding my ship.

Behind me stood a security guard in an official dark blue suit. His dark brown eyes and face looked stern and upset. I should pick up the broken ship and offer to pay for it. But I froze and wondered what he wanted and why he unnerved me. He squatted down and picked up the pieces. I blinked and swallowed hard still speechless but kneeled on the floor to help.

The guard stood and towered over me with the broken ship fragments in his hands. "Apologies, Madame. My fault. I caught you off guard."

"Oh, no. My fault. I should have been more careful."

One of the shop's clerks joined us, and the guard handed her the fragments broken beyond repair.

"I'm sorry. I can pay for it."

"No need," the sales clerk said to me. "I would have dropped it too if I'd been startled like that." She glared at the guard for being so menacing in her delicate shop.

I glanced at the guard since he hadn't explained what he wanted. "Thank you. I am truly sorry." I clenched my jaw and thought about the video last night. But how would last night be related to visiting an art museum?

"What did you want to ask me?"

"I wanted you to stay here. Mr. Overton is looking for you."

"Mr. Overton? Who in the world is that?" I was annoyed to be delayed for someone I didn't know.

"Me. I'm Greg Overton." The gray-haired man from the Turner gallery peeked from behind the guard at me.

"Oh, you."

He handed me my scarf. "You forgot this. You might need it. It's cold today."

"Yes, thank you. It has enormous sentimental value." The scarf and hoodie were the only two articles of Axel's clothing I'd kept.

He was probably in his 60's but still had a young, boyish look. As if he was refusing to age, or maybe he didn't care.

He thanked the guard while I knotted my scarf around my neck so I wouldn't lose it again.

He reached out, and we shook hands. I introduced myself and used my official name, Kathryn Jensen, as I did with strangers. The handshake was an ancient sign of friendship since people couldn't shake hands with a knife in your right hand unless they happened to be left-handed.

The gray-haired man asked, "Would you care to join me for a cup of coffee?"

I couldn't remember his first name and was too embarrassed to ask him to repeat it. I glanced at my watch, and it was nearly four p.m. I was thirsty and hungry, but I didn't want to be obligated to sit there with him, not after last night's fiasco.

Echoes from what so many friends kept telling me came to mind. "Open up, Kat. Be willing to meet people anywhere and anytime, and not at the usual spots like work or bars." I was given specifics - the gym, grocery store, hair salon, even the subway. No one mentioned art museums, but at least it had class.

"Okay. I suppose so."

He looked at his watch. "We may be able to make afternoon tea. Ready to run?" He glanced down at my feet probably checking to see if I was wearing high heels, but he didn't need to worry about that.

"Sure. Lead the way." Afternoon tea with a fellow British Turner *aficionado* should be harmless and maybe enjoyable.

My new acquaintance took my hand, and we snaked our way through the crowds. He led me to the top of the grand staircase and let go of my hand so we could make our way down the stairs as if performing a special tap dance. We entered the great hall and impressive main entrance, and Greg grabbed my hand again to pull me to the right, down a long hall filled with sculptures lit by skylights even on this dreary day.

My adrenaline flowed. He was intent on the crowd and weaving us through it - a man on a mission. He let go of my hand, and we separated to maneuver around some families with kids and strollers among the Arts of Africa, Oceania, and the Americas.

I started to pant. Even though I worked out at the gym, I didn't jog, and this obstacle course required intense concentration and agility. He looked back at me, and I skipped to catch up with him. For an older guy, he must work out. He sailed smoothly around families and couples dawdling in the aisles.

He grabbed my hand again, as we swung through another group of sculptures with a glass paneled roof overhead and floor to ceiling glass walls at the end facing Central Park.

We arrived at the café's check-in desk out of breath after crossing half the Met in about ten minutes. A family in front of us was being seated for tea.

"Just in the nick of time, Kathryn." He remembered my name, and all I could remember was Mr. Overton. I didn't want to address him like that and was embarrassed to ask again.

The waitress ushered us to a small French bistro table for two and handed us some menus. I couldn't remember the last time I'd had afternoon tea and was glad he suggested this. He was trim, not an ounce of fat, so he might skip the sweets. I sure wouldn't.

My stomach growled. I was about to ask what we should order when a woman said, "Greg, darling."

She stood next to us beaming down with a massive plastic smile on her face. He stood and gave her a quick Euro style air kiss on each cheek while asking how she was. From the looks of her pretty good. She was about his age but petite, glossy looking, and well maintained in expensive clothes with heavy gold jewelry dripping off her.

"Fabulous, Greg. I returned last week from three months in Cannes. Everything was *tres chic*. Oozes out of their pores, you know, but after a while, I missed Manhattan."

She paused and peered at me, but said to Greg. "Is this Françoise? It's been so many years since I've seen her."

I shook my head wondering who Françoise was, but now I knew his name, repeating Greg in my head to remember it.

Greg said, "No, she lives in Greenwich, married with two kids. This is my friend, Kathryn Jensen. Kathryn, this is an old friend of mine, Connie Bradshaw."

Greg sat down and didn't pursue the conversation further and stole a glance at his menu. Tea would end soon, and I didn't think he ran all the way here to miss it. High tea included two options – the type of tea and if you wanted champagne. I'd let him decide since I could go either way. The memories of my hangover and last night were far behind on the other side of the park.

I leaned against our marble-topped table and looked out the windows into the park and saw the tall Egyptian monolith, the oldest object in New York City.

Connie must have gotten the message. "Goodbye Greg, Kathryn. Enjoy your tea. And, Greg, promise me you won't be a stranger."

She lifted her overstuffed Chanel bag with its signature chain strap on her shoulder. "Greg, I'd love to have you over for dinner. Something special catered by Jean-Paul. We Francophiles have to stick together."

Connie winked at him and to my relief walked off. I watched as she left the café and entered the sculpture gallery. She didn't simply walk. No, this was more of a sashay with her jangling bag and the distinct click of her heels against the polished marble floors.

Greg was polite and said, "Sorry about the interruption, Kathryn."

"No problem. I was admiring the view. The oldest thing in New York City."

"I hope you aren't referring to me," he teased and turned around to look.

"Ah, Cleopatra's Needle."

"Pity the Egyptian hieroglyphs are so hard to read. They should bring it inside like they did with the Greek Temple of Dendur or put a glass dome over it."

I couldn't help but come up with an internal audit style recommendation since I'd been trained to evaluate everything despite often annoying Axel and some of my friends.

Before Greg could comment or shoot down my suggestion, the waitress nearly pounced on us to get our order before we were interrupted again.

"Well, I feel like a celebration today. Do you, Kathryn?"

"Sure."

He ordered champagne and an Indian Assam tea after I assured him I liked them all. There should be plenty of food with the sandwiches, scones, and pastries, and was grateful he had rescued me from a lonely dinner at home tonight.

"But isn't this risky? I could see from his face he had no clue what I meant.

I tried to imitate Connie's voice. "You know, treason to have high tea? A British tradition if you are a Francophile."

Greg laughed. "I think I'm safe. But if you see someone come up behind me with a knife or portable guillotine, let me know."

I grinned, but my jaw clenched remembering my antics last night with the knife captured on video for the world to see. I was glad he hadn't seen it since I wouldn't be here now.

"Why so glum? Did you lose a family member to the – ". He made a cutting motion across his throat.

"Oh no. Reminded me of something. Miserable date last night."

"Ah, one of those. Well, let me introduce myself, so this goes better. I'm divorced, two grown children with Françoise, as mentioned earlier, being one. Four grandchildren with another one on the way. My girlfriend moved out a few months ago, so I'm single again. I'm an architect, but most importantly, a huge fan of Mr. J.M.W. Turner."

Greg had a lighthearted way of speaking, so I gave him my standard update. What you must do when you meet someone you know nothing about. "I'm single too. Officially a widow, but I hate that word. My husband died from cancer over a year ago. No kids, grandkids, or current boyfriend. I'm an internal auditor but looking for a new job. And I love Turner's paintings."

The waitress brought our champagne. "To the master artist, Mr. Turner," Greg said, while he lifted his glass. Our glasses clinked, and I sipped the pink bubbly nectar.

"Kathryn, sorry about your husband but I'm glad Turner died back in 1851. Less competition."

I smiled, but he was teasing me since I'd never be the right match for him. Not just from the look of his expensive watch and clothing but the way he handled himself with the waitress and Connie. He was out of my league. He and his friends were in a whole different stratosphere. The chef Jean-Paul was probably the famous multi-starred Michelin chef with a restaurant nearby with his name on it. I'd dined at one of his other less pricey restaurants in my neighborhood, the more Bohemian Upper West Side. And Connie talked about catering a meal. That wasn't even a consideration in my world.

5 ~ *Dreams Aground*

Our waitress returned with a teapot and food artistically placed on a three-tiered metal serving dish separating the savory from the sweet. Bite-sized sandwiches were on the bottom level, then bite-sized pastries on the middle shelf, with small current studded scones on top. Not as much food as I expected, but something. Maybe he was dieting, and I'd get some of his.

"Kat, please. I prefer Kat with my friends."

He looked at me again, reminding me of Charlie last night, as if puzzled and trying to figure me out. Doesn't anyone use a nickname anymore?

Our conversation disappeared and turned into an uncomfortable silence. I focused on eating my share and savored the mini cucumber and smoked salmon sandwich.

Greg asked, "Did you know Turner wanted his legacy of paintings to be displayed as a group in London? But as you can see, they were scattered. He would be happy to see them gathered at the Met."

"He became too successful. His works got snapped up, and museums can't afford them."

"Some can, like the Met, but they have so much art they can't display it all. They exhibit a small portion at a time or lend pieces to other museums. But it's expensive for transportation, insurance, and so on.

"Are you sure you don't work here?" I teased.

"No, I'm an architect, but I'm on the board."

"The board here?" I blurted out. "I'm impressed." I regretted sounding like a silly school girl. Of course, they would want someone like him - wealthy, smart, and most of all, an art lover.

I decided to confide in him. "I have another reason I came today to see the art show. Besides my secret crush on J.M.W.'s art."

He leaned in, exactly what I wanted, to build suspense.

"I'm planning a trip. A cruise and sea journey on an old sailing ship like the ones in his paintings. But without the storms."

He looked at me and sat back in his chair taking a sip of tea. "I see. A unique plan indeed. But where did you find this old sailing ship?"

"Well, I haven't found it yet. But I will, and it must be a clipper ship. They're beautiful and sleek and can move through the water without the noisy, messy engines. The ships move so fast they were named clippers for moving at a clip. I haven't started looking yet, but I'm sure it's – "

The words tumbled out. The more I explained, the more I knew this was exactly what I wanted to do. My dream was now a real plan after telling someone besides Mel.

Greg laughed and tried to say, "Excuse me."

The concerned look on my face must have made things worse since he started to choke. I handed him his glass of water for him to drink and help him, but he put his hand up as if to say, "No, thank you."

I put his water glass back on the table and waited, but he couldn't stop laughing. A few people sitting at tables near us looked over at him and then me to see what happened. I shrugged my shoulders unsure how to react.

When he finally stopped laughing and composed himself, he said, "Oh, that felt good. I haven't had such a good laugh in a long time."

"What was so funny?"

"The ships you referred to, clipper ships, don't exist anymore. Well, there is one that I know of – the Cutty Sark docked in Greenwich, near London. But it's not in the water anymore. Hoisted in the air so tourists can walk under her to see the copper hull. You can even have afternoon tea underneath her."

With his napkin, he dabbed tears from his eyes brought on from laughing. "But it's a lovely dream and sad what happened. All those beautiful ships destroyed, shipwrecked, or rebuilt into steamships. By the 1900's, it was over. Turner painted the sad demise of an old gunship towed for scrap, the

Fighting Temeraire. You can view it in the permanent gallery."

"But there must be some left somewhere. Cruises on big yachts are so popular."

I wasn't willing to give up my search before I'd even started. Annoyed, I focused on savoring each fruity tart dessert and the flavors of raspberry, lemon, chocolate, and vanilla, while I waited for Greg to catch up.

"But those sailing ships would be new or rebuilt with all the modern conveniences and engines. None would risk relying on sails, not today."

"Well, you may be right, but I am still going to try to find my clipper. I don't give up easily." He didn't know one of my internal audit managers used to say I was like a pit bull sinking my teeth in and not letting go until I was ready.

"Kat, I wish you the best in your search for a clipper ship. And bon voyage, as it were. Your face, though. My dear, you were so determined." He started chuckling again.

I slumped in my seat deflated. My journey was already sunk as I watched Greg eat every crumb. Now I regretted telling Greg about my dream cruise.

The waitress brought our bill, and I pulled out my credit card to split the bill, but Greg waved it away and gave her his AMEX Platinum card. I wasn't going to argue since Greg could afford it and insulted me when my dream turned into cheap entertainment.

"I'm sorry I laughed, but you have to admit it's funny. As if you could climb into one of J.M.W.'s paintings and sail away."

We both got up to leave, and he looked at his watch. "Oh, I'm sorry. It's late. I've got to go. I have to walk my dog and prepare for dinner." He took his phone out of his pocket and turned it on. "I had an excellent time today, Kat. We should do this again sometime."

He reached into his pocket and handed me a card. "Here's my card. Call me."

I took it and nodded. But I knew I would never call or see Greg again. I hesitated, standing still, not ready to leave the museum yet. I wanted to see the Turner exhibit one last time and wander around. Nothing was waiting for me at home. And I was so discouraged that I didn't feel like searching the internet for my non-existent clipper ship.

Greg strode off looking at his phone, but when he noticed I wasn't following him, he stopped and turned back. I was still standing there, and he rushed back.

"I'm sorry. Are you upset? I'm sure you will find a beautifully rebuilt clipper for the best cruise ever. I wish I knew more about it, but I get seasick just thinking about it."

"No, it's all right, just disappointing. I haven't been on a vacation since my husband died, and I wanted a magical ship. But like mermaids and unicorns, it isn't real. Not anymore."

I stuck out my hand to shake hands, thank him for tea, and say goodbye. But Greg took my hand and drew me into a hug with the customary Euro style air kiss on both cheeks.

"Oh Kat," he said while he held my hand and leaned towards me breathing my name into my ear. I touched my ticklish ear and giggled.

He stood back but didn't let go of my hand. His hand was soft and warm, so I held on.

"Kat, I have an idea. I have some friends coming over for dinner tonight. Another reason why I must hurry. My son-in-law will be there, and he knows a lot about sailing. He sailed in college and met with the America's Cup crew who raced on the Hudson back in May. If anyone can help you find a clipper, it's him. Why don't you come for dinner and discuss it with him?"

"Dinner tonight? No, I don't think so. I was going to stay here a bit longer and go home. I live on the Upper West Side."

"So, you don't have plans tonight. Even more of a reason to come. I live five minutes from here."

"But I don't have anything nice to wear," I had on a casual Saturday outfit - a cheetah animal print knit top with black jeans and boots.

"You look fine, refreshing. I like your Bohemian look."

"See, Bohemian. I won't fit in. Another time." And if it was going to happen, he could call me. But he still hadn't asked for my phone number or email.

"Accompany me now or take your time and arrive in an hour."

Greg was so enthusiastic. I liked the idea of talking to his son-in-law. Like a job search, finding people in-the-know to ask always worked better.

He took his business card and wrote down his home address and handed it back. He lived on East 88th Street only a few blocks away.

"Please come at seven, and I can show you around. Since you admire old ships, you will enjoy seeing my home. I wanted to modernize it, but my broker talked me out of it."

Greg's address didn't include an apartment number, and doormen could be rude, particularly in his neighborhood. "You didn't write the apartment number down."

"It's a brownstone, so there isn't one. Kat, I must leave. Please promise me you'll come."

"Okay. I'll come. But I was out late last night, so I can't stay long."

"Fine. Drop by for a quick cocktail or hors d'oeuvres. You don't know how happy this makes me." He kissed me on the cheek and disappeared into the crowd.

I checked my watch instead of turning on my phone to see how much time was left. My watch wasn't wildly expensive like Greg's. But I loved my Swiss watch with a band called the wave. Another irritating reminder to find my nonexistent ship.

I trudged up the steps we'd flown down earlier for one last look at the Turner exhibit, and what may be the closest I'd come to a real clipper ship. Just an hour ago I was overflowing with optimism about my voyage. Despite the sliver of hope from his son-in-law, I should face reality and the fact that Greg was probably right. My legs ached as if I was wearing cement boots growing heavier with each step. My plans had been tossed and smashed like one of Turner's shipwrecks.

6 ~ *Dressing The Part*

After glancing both directions on 88th Street, I pushed the doorbell even though I was tempted to sneak off and head home. Greg lived in an impressive four-story brownstone, called a townhouse in other parts of the country, and not far from former Mayor Michael Bloomberg's similar residence. Greg's house was across from a modern school, but his side of the block was historic and from the 1800's.

Greg must have the entire building since there was only one buzzer. Now that I was here, I was curious to see the inside. I'd look around, talk to his son-in-law, have a quick drink, and leave.

A dark-haired woman about my age opened the door holding a big, gray-haired dog around its collar.

"Kat?" She pulled back on the collar as the dog tried to nose his way out the front door to where I stood.

"Useless, sit, stay, something." She smiled while rolling her eyes because the dog was still trying to escape.

I nodded and stuck out my hand to shake hands, while the dog gave up and sat on her foot.

"Not there, Useless. Nice to meet you. I'm Desiree Overton Smith but call me Desi. Please come in. Papa said you were coming."

She said Papa in a different, French sort of way. My Papa was called Dad, so I was already out of my comfort zone. She ushered me into the entryway, and as expected from the outside, it was ornate and filled with antiques. I could have blinked and time traveled back to the 1800's.

I petted the dog with short gray fur. The curious dog sniffed around to get to know me with his nose aimed directly at my crotch.

"Is he a Weimaraner?" I asked while I petted him not minding his curious nose so much. He looked a lot like those dogs in the famous photographs by William Wegman.

"He might have some, but mainly he's a mutt. Useless, stop

it," Desi commanded while pulling his powerful nose away from its target. "Sorry, poor manners, this dog."

"Is his name Useless?"

"No, Ulysses, a fancy name for a rescue. It got switched to Useless by my sister and the name stuck. He's so friendly the only danger to a burglar would be getting licked to death."

I giggled imagining it. A burglar would have a field day here too, with the art, vases, and other collectibles in the entryway.

"Do you want to change?" she asked. Desi was wearing a stylish cocktail dress. I glanced down self-consciously at my jeans, even if they were nice black ones.

"Yeah, but I don't have dressy clothes with me. He invited me an hour ago. I told him I shouldn't come."

"Oh, I know, Papa hasn't spoken of anything else. You know, men, they don't think about how women want to fit in. By the way, it's my husband you need to talk to about your dream ship. Don't worry. We'll find it. If he can't, no one can."

She took my jacket from me and looked me over from head to toe. "You look to be about a size four, or maybe a two. I'm a size eight and so jealous. I don't know if I'll ever get back down there. Not after two kids."

"This will be fun. Come with me."

Desi took my hand reminding me of her Dad today at the museum. She coaxed me up an ornate, wooden staircase to the second floor, and opened one of the doors to a frilly Victorian bedroom.

After we were safely inside with the door shut, she explained, "His ex, Patricia, her only hobby was shopping and spending all his money. Don't remind him though. He gets sad."

She flung open a fancy wooden armoire and pulled some clothes out tossing them on the bed. "See almost all of them still have tags. They were never worn. I wish they were four sizes larger. She probably didn't take them with her since she couldn't squeeze her fat ass into them."

A knock sounded at the door and Greg's voice called out, "Desi, Kat, is everything all right?"

Desi opened the door, and we peeked out.

"Fine, Papa. Kat is going to borrow one of Patricia's outfits if you don't mind. She left all this behind, and someone should enjoy it. Françoise and I aren't skinny enough."

He eyed us both as if we were up to devious tricks. "Thank you for coming, Kat. You look splendid as you are. Desi, don't pressure Kat. But if you want any of Patricia's belongings, take them. Saves me from having to send them to a charity."

He shut the door, and his footsteps echoed as he headed downstairs. I eyed Desi smiling at me, game for whatever I wanted to do. "Well, if that's the case, I should help him out."

We both laughed excited about finding the perfect outfit. "We should box up whatever you think you want. Put a pile over here and take it home to try on later. But for tonight. Hmm. How about this?"

She took out a black cocktail dress with some sparkle, but sleek and not too flashy.

"Pretty." The dress was unbelievably beautiful, and something I would never buy. I could afford it, but I'd rather save my blood, sweat, and tears paychecks for retirement.

"It should be, it's Armani," as Desi checked the label with a price tag still attached.

"Patricia got a good deal on it. I've got to hand it to her. She found tremendous bargains. Kat, try it on. I'd love to see it on you."

The dress was beautiful, no question, and it fit. But to be sure, Desi insisted I try on a few more. My boots weren't going to work with a dress like this and going barefoot wasn't an option. Desi found some dressy black shoes. Not new, but they looked almost new to me. They were tight, but I could handle it for one evening.

Desi glammed up my hair while I agreed to put on more makeup. With the new clothes courtesy of Giorgio Armani via Patricia, I was ready to join the party fifteen minutes before the eight o'clock dinner bell. We went downstairs and joked about my successful makeover.

Greg did a double-take when he saw me. I almost thought he wasn't happy with my new look. But he smiled and said,

"What did Desi do to you? You look even more beautiful."

I smiled at the rare compliment. A waiter circulated the room with a tray of welcome drinks, and I took a glass and made the toast this time.

"To your daughter's magic, and now her husband will find my ship."

Greg introduced me to his guests and called me his friend, not a girlfriend. Desi was just five years younger, and it would be strange to date someone with children so close to my age. Desi and Steve, her all-American husband, were the only people at the party close to my age.

As soon as I was introduced to Steve, he told me flat out. "Hate to burst your bubble, Kat, but clipper ships without engines don't exist anymore. Some new or rebuilt clipper style ships sail around in the Caribbean right now. But they all have engines. Friends of mine take passengers on a small clipper for a few hours around the southern tip of Manhattan, but not in the winter. A beautiful ride so I can see why so many people dream about clipper ships."

Steve didn't waste any time destroying my dreams. I forced a smile and nodded acknowledging the bad news. My plan was foolish from the beginning, and now a slow, dull ache slowly surfaced from deep within my stomach.

Steve continued, "All the damn safety requirements required lots of tweaking to those ships. The time of the real clipper came and went over a hundred years ago."

I thanked him, but I knew I wasn't giving up. Desi listened to him too. From the worried look on her face, I could tell she was disappointed by the abrupt way Steve broke the bad news.

"Kat, you should consider one of those Crystal cruise ships. We went on one for our honeymoon. Years ago, but I'll never forget it. I loved every minute. Steve, remember?"

Steve nodded, but he was busy talking with another of Greg's friends about finance and deals on Wall Street. In New York, you never avoided it.

Greg announced, "Dinner will be served shortly. Shall we transition to the dining room?"

On the way into the dining room, Steve put his hand on my

back and asked, "How much sailing experience do you have? Can you navigate, read charts, hoist sails, stuff like that?"

"Umm. No." My experience sailing and flipping over a small fiberglass sailboat at a lake in Texas wouldn't count one iota.

"You've got to be shitting me," Steve said stopping to look at me. He noticed one of the genteel female dinner guests staring in our direction and added, "Pardon my French."

Steve winked at me. "In that case Kat, do yourself and all the sailors out there a favor. Stick with a large commercial ship with lots of engines. Be a passenger along for the ride. It'll be safer for everyone."

Noticing my unhappiness, Steve patted my shoulder to reassure me and teased, "Forget about it, Kat. I'm sure you'll find something. Now, how about we go splice the mainbrace?"

"What?"

"That's sailor lingo to celebrate and have a drink."

"Yeah, I'm ready." After the wealth of advice and bad news, I was ready to drown in it.

I separated from Steve in the dining room and glanced around impressed. All the rooms in Greg's house were decorated in what I guessed was the Victorian style. The dining room had a large table prepared as if from a scene out of an Edith Wharton novel. We were an even dozen. A large dinner party and not something I'd want to oversee.

Place cards indicated where we should sit. I sat between Greg and Steve with Desi across from me. Menu cards, all in French, listed a long series of courses. Despite a few trips to France, I wasn't familiar with half of them.

After the appetizers and a few drinks, I looked around at his friends. Even in my designer dress, I felt out of place and didn't know what to say. What in the hell was I doing here? It wasn't just my age, but their conversations revolved around an alien lifestyle. I'd never fit in unless I transformed my entire personality and way of life. And I wasn't sure I'd want to live like that.

Steve asked, "Kat, I know I've seen you before or maybe heard about you. You say you have an audit consulting firm.

Have you done any work at Levittman?"

"No, I haven't." I didn't want to explain that even if I'd been offered a job, I would have declined it. No one would believe this since Levittman was the most prestigious and powerful investment bank on Wall Street, if not the world.

I might be the only job applicant in the history of Levittman who sent a thank you note to an interviewer that said, "Thanks, but no thanks."

As intended, this action severed the possibility of any future interviews and employment. The place was cut throat with its annual ten percent deadwood removal but this only applied to staff, not senior management or the board of directors. The people I interviewed with were pompous and condescending and asked ridiculous and insulting questions. I'd never work there.

"Do you have a blog or something?"

"No," I shook my head. "Never had one of those, and I don't blog on anyone's site either. I have a twitter account, but have only put out a tweet a couple of times."

Steve took his phone out of his pocket. "I'm great at faces. I know I've seen you before."

I should have realized he might find the video, but I was drinking a delectable dry glass of white riesling. And after several glasses of champagne earlier, this was slow to sink in.

Steve was persistent. "Maybe we met at a business event somewhere?"

We might have since I'd had lots of employers in New York City before starting my consulting business. I'd had positions at several banks, a hedge fund, broker-dealers, and a big four accounting-consulting firm. But I didn't encourage him or want to remember. I preferred to forget my miserable past employers whenever possible.

Greg left the dining room to talk to the chef, so he had missed our earlier conversation, but returned and was attentive.

"Naw, I've got it."

Steve held his smartphone to show me. Even from a distance, I knew he'd found the infamous video from last night.

What I'd tried so hard to forget. Was he friends with Krista from Levittman?

Steve, proud of his detective skills, showed Desi and Greg his phone with the video on constant replay, and then his phone went from person to person around the dining table. I wanted to hide under the table and would have disappeared down a rabbit hole if I'd found one.

I reiterated to Greg and Desi what happened, what you don't see, and my posted response. But if a picture is worth a thousand words and a video ten times more, my fifteen-word explanation didn't come close.

7 ~ *The Getaway*

Tired and having had more than enough to eat and drink, I excused myself to go to the bathroom. I snuck upstairs and changed back into my clothes. I hung up the dress I borrowed and put away the clothes we left strewn over the bed. I sat on the bed debating how best to leave.

Greg said earlier, "You can come and go whenever you want."

But it would be rude to disappear without telling him goodbye and thank you. My mind skipped back to the Met. After Greg had left, I found another gallery with Scandinavian artists including a moonlight harbor scene by a Norwegian artist. The painting was as crisp as a digital photo of Copenhagen's harbor in the 1800's filled with about a dozen ships, including some clippers. I ached when I saw those ships and the feeling that they were calling me. I didn't want a fancy ship, but with Denmark surrounded by water and harbors and ships plentiful, there must be at least one small clipper ship planning to set sail.

My head throbbed. I opened the bathroom's medicine cabinet and took a couple of aspirin. My tired eyes stared back at me in the mirror. I dabbed my pinky into Patricia's *La Mer* pinkish eye balm and put some under my sad eyes.

La Mer, 'the sea' in English, was an expensive treat, and the label promised this miracle broth would work wonders. As if my ship was sending me a message not to give up. But slathering *La Mer* from head to foot wasn't going to solve my problems, so I slammed shut the cabinet door.

An inviting overstuffed chair in the corner welcomed me, and I sat down to plan my escape. How to politely leave without anyone noticing to avoid further embarrassment? I put my feet up on the matching footstool and shut my eyes. In a few minutes, I'll get up, find some notepaper, and write a thank you note for Greg and Desi. Then I will head to the door and get a taxi back to my cozy, Bohemian abode.

Something wet touched my hand, and a noise woke me. Greg stood over me, and Useless sniffed my hand with his wet, black nose. Both looked concerned.

I mumbled out some apologies while I sat up from my warm chair and put my feet on the floor.

Greg took my hand. "Kathryn, are you ill?"

"No, I'm sorry. I came upstairs to the bathroom, but I must have fallen asleep."

"I'm sorry about all this. Steve should never have embarrassed you like that."

"Oh, well. What's done is done. I should have told you about the video, but I wanted to forget the whole thing."

Greg sat on the footstool and waited. Useless placed his head on my leg, perhaps in sympathy, but probably for attention and another head scratch. I gave him a nice head rub and wished for a moment I had a dog too. But a cat was more suitable for my lifestyle. Besides, I was going to find my ship and leave town for at least a month.

"You shouldn't let that video bother you. Your date, whoever that man was, deserves a severe reprimand. And the person who made the video and posted it does too."

"I don't think they meant for this to happen, so I'd rather forget about it. I didn't even know there was a video until my assistant showed me this morning."

"You are much too kind."

Greg leaned over and kissed me gently at first. I lifted my head kissing him back. I hadn't felt the ping of romance, or whatever you are supposed to feel, but I liked being comforted and having a connection to someone. His romantic kiss was my first since Axel, and my body reacted, even if my mind wasn't quite there.

He looked at me. "Oh, Kat. We should stop."

I didn't agree, but I didn't want to come across as lovesick or desperate.

Greg stood and leaned against the window sill. "There's a story about Turner and how he handled adversity. The first American to purchase one of his ship seascapes for next to nothing was disappointed and said his painting had indistinctness. Turner responded that indistinctness was his forte. Kat, you can take criticism and negative situations and turn it around to work for your benefit, like Turner. And, as we agree, he was a genius."

"Yeah, well, I'm glad for him, and I wish I could. But my dream, the trip on a clipper ship, isn't going to happen."

"Don't say that Kat. Never give up on your dreams."

I wondered if this was where his girlfriend slept or if it was an extra room to store her things. I wasn't about to spend the night here and should find a taxi to get home.

"Is the dinner party still going on?"

"Yes, it is." But he didn't seem to care.

I stood and rubbed my hands through my hair to put it back in place. "Thank you for inviting me, Greg. I better go. See you around again."

He pulled me close and gave me a hug. "I'm going with you."

"What? No. You must go back to your party. You can't leave."

"Why can't I? I can do whatever I want. Desi can handle things."

"But I'm going home, and I don't … I'm not –"

"Kat, I'm not asking you to invite me over. Let's go somewhere."

He looked at his watch. "It's not that late. I'm going to tell Desi and change out of this suit so wait here. I have an idea. It isn't your clipper ship, but the next best thing. You will see the stars like being at sea."

What did he have in mind? Whatever it was I hoped to be home by midnight, and it was already ten. I went to the bathroom and washed my face not caring if he saw me makeup-free.

Greg returned wearing jeans and a casual sweater. He took my hand, and we hurried down the stairs, ignoring his guests in the dining room, and out the front door into his black chauffeur-driven Lincoln Town car.

The driver sped across Central Park to the West Side Highway, along the Hudson River, and headed downtown. I was so close to home for a few minutes that I regretted agreeing to this. The night was cold and rainy, and I didn't want to tramp around in the mud by the Hudson River if that was his plan.

The car was inviting - warm and dark. My head dropped and then jerked back to stay awake.

"Can I please be home by midnight? Last night, at that bar and having to threaten him was extremely tiring." I didn't want to mention my post-date solo party with the aquavit brothers.

He chuckled. "I'd imagine so. This won't be a late night. Sleep, if you want."

He put his arm around me, and I nestled up against his shoulder and closed my eyes, but my body was tense, and I couldn't relax. Here I was cozied up with a guy I'd met less than twelve hours ago and in his car going who knows where. Abby and I will have a good laugh about this tomorrow at brunch. If I'm still alive to tell the story.

~ ~ ~

"Didn't I promise you? *C'est magnifique.*" Greg boasted and stood next to me as we gazed at the nighttime view from his office window. But he didn't have an office. He had an entire suite on the 81st floor of the World Trade Center nicknamed the Freedom Tower. I didn't know anyone with this kind of view. Freedom and priceless views were too expensive, even for most of Wall Street.

We sipped our coffees courtesy of his architectural firm, and the caffeine woke me up. The view extended from Manhattan towards New Jersey, including the Statue of Liberty and Ellis Island. But I couldn't work here, remembering all the lives lost and devastation. On 9-11, I was flying home from a vacation in South Africa. My flight was one of the last flights to land that morning at JFK airport.

If I'd been home, I would've been a few blocks away for a breakfast meeting. To this day, I wondered what would I have done? Most likely I'd have returned to work at my mid-town office. But I might have stayed to watch or even help when the towers collapsed. I had no clue, but perhaps it's better that way.

New Yorkers often traded stories of where they were that

day. A unique survivor's camaraderie that others didn't grasp. But being here on the site, I wasn't bringing it up unless he did.

"Must be hard to work here with this view."

"You get used to it. Kat, look up at the stars."

But it was hard to see the stars. The bright lights from Manhattan blind them, so they can't shine back as they would outside the city.

"Nice. Did you need to pick anything up while we're here?" I avoided my office on weekends and holidays like the plague. And now, you could never unplug with the internet and email.

"No. Only to show you the view. Feel free to look around my office if you want."

I was curious about him. After admiring the view, I wandered along the walls and inspected the framed pictures. They included photos of buildings, groups of other architects, and even some magazine covers. He'd won numerous awards, including something called the Pritzker Prize for Architecture. His Master's in Architecture with a distinction as 'magna cum laude' from Yale was framed. I'd heard architecture was so competitive that a master's degree was mandatory.

I had a master's too but in business from the University of Texas and loads of work-related licenses to build my expertise. I had the requisite Certified Public Accountant license in New York State and was a Certified Internal Auditor, Fraud Examiner, Anti-Money Laundering Specialist. I even went to the trouble of taking exams to get three brokerage licenses. But I didn't plaster it all over my office walls and kept the paperwork in a drawer.

Perhaps it would have helped my business if I flaunted them more. But I liked having artsy prints and colorful photographs, not boring documents, covering the walls. Besides, they were all on my resume. Sometimes having so many, which I had acquired gradually each year or two, overwhelmed prospective employers. I had more credentials than most of the senior employees.

Greg put his arm around my shoulder. "If it wasn't for Yale, I may never have known about Turner. I liked to unwind by looking at art. They had the largest collection outside the

United Kingdom. I got to know all the paintings, but Turner was my favorite."

I nodded wanting to hear more.

"Years later when I started to become successful and had a bit of money in the bank, a Turner was on auction. I got caught up in the bidding and spent all my savings on it. But I never regretted it no matter what the cost."

"Did you have to sell it?"

"No, I still own it. My ex-wife and I argued about it from the day I bought it. She tried to force me to sell it in our divorce settlement, but I gave her other assets to hang on to it."

"Where is it?"

"Oh, it's at the Met, part of the exhibition. The painting you admired so much from the private collection. The one we speculated about who owned it. Mystery solved. A he, not a she, and only a he."

Greg owned the Turner painting? His confession was hard to fathom.

"I went to the Met today to see it, and one of the reasons I tried to find you after you left. We had a special connection via my painting. I'm glad others enjoy seeing it, but I miss it. I know it's a bit perverse, but it hangs in my bedroom so I can see it when I go to sleep and when I wake up. I guess I dream of ships too."

"Yes, I guess you do."

I smiled at him enjoying the moment. He took me to see the stars and told me about his own Turner, the painting I loved the most. Despite what his son-in-law said, I wasn't giving up on my clipper ship.

My entire career focused on identifying problems and figuring out recommendations to fix them, even long-term issues that baffled senior managers for years. That's what internal auditors were trained to do, and the good ones did this all the time. Finding a cruise on a ship, even a clipper, will be child's play.

8 ~ *Brunch In A Barn*

"Right – left – right, left – right – left, slip, hook, jab, cross," Adriana, my kickboxing instructor, commanded. She used a microphone headset so we could hear her above the blaring, rhythmic music. Our warm-up punches hit air against an imaginary attacker, not a training bag.

Sunday morning's class was mobbed as usual and filled with 20 to 30-year old women with a few token males and older ladies like me. They were a tough bunch used to fighting their way for service in stores and restaurants and onto subways, trains, and taxi cabs. This class made them stronger, and I tried to keep up.

My mind jumped back to last night and the passionate kisses in Greg's car on the way home. But he pulled away when things heated up in the back seat and said we should stop. Maybe he was worried I was too young. But then why did he invite me to a party celebrating the close of the Turner art exhibit? Surely, he's realized his mistake by now, and I'll never hear from him. And I was about to invite him upstairs to my apartment last night before he changed his mind.

Focus. You can do this but only if you pay attention. Adriana watched us as if we were training for an Olympic competition scheduled next month. The beat of the music helped me stay in sync and motivated. After fifteen minutes of punches with our arms, we switched to fifteen minutes of leg work that consisted of front, side, and back kicks. My legs followed along to the routine, but when it became second nature, my mind wandered to last week's conversation with Mel.

"Kat, don't sublimate yourself. You have to stop it." Mel said in a helpful tone not wanting to hurt my feelings.

"Sublimate?" What did she mean by this?

"Don't give up on sex and become celibate for some idealized higher calling. It doesn't suit you, or anyone for that matter."

"What higher calling?"

"Don't tell me you don't realize what you are doing. You've been focused on the injustices of the world - fighting corruption and helping underdogs. Thriving on it but it comes at a cost, ignoring your sexual nature."

"Damn, pay attention," I yelled at myself silently. I missed my jump to the left and got out of sync again. Forget about Greg, sex, and everything for that matter. For the next half-hour, I lost myself in physical exertion and mental concentration. Satisfied with my effort, I waved goodbye to Adriana and hurried home to meet Abby for Sunday brunch.

~ ~ ~

Showered and dressed, I raced down the hall to Abby's apartment only a few minutes late. She knew I was religious about Adriana's Sunday gym classes. While we waited for our slow but reliable elevator to appear, I brought her up-to-date on the Friday night date with Charlie and meeting Greg at the museum.

We strolled through the lobby busy chatting. A delivery boy with an enormous bouquet of roses was scanning the buzzers to find the right apartment.

Abby said, "Can we help you with that?"

I stood by waiting as she looked at the delivery instructions the Hispanic guy handed her.

"Kat, they're for you," Abby said in her high-pitched squeal when excited.

"Me? For me?" I was amazed anyone would send me flowers. They must be from Greg.

I signed the form, handed the guy a tip, and told Abby, "I'll put them in my apartment and be right back."

"But who are they from?" She asked as the elevator doors closed.

A note was attached, but I couldn't hold the roses and open it so it would have to wait. When the flowers, a dozen of red, white, and yellow roses, were safely in vases filled with water, I ripped open the envelope.

The card said, "Kat, I trust you understand what the roses represent. Again, my sincere apologies. Please call me.

Charlie."

I left the note on the counter and stormed downstairs not waiting for the slow-moving elevator now on the 11th floor. The nerve of that guy. Why can't he leave me alone? I'd considered emailing him since his texts and emails weren't letting up, and now I couldn't ignore him.

When I got back to the lobby, Abby was chatting with two men I didn't recognize.

"Kat, who were the flowers from?" She asked.

"Oh, the guy I was talking about, Charlie."

"The good or bad date?"

She could tell the answer by the sour look on my face and shrugged her shoulders not wanting to dwell on it.

"Kat, this is Matteo and Alberto. They're from Italy, and here for a while. Matteo is living in 6D, Jim's apartment, two floors about you. Alberto is his good friend."

We introduced ourselves and shook hands, and I noticed their alluring accents.

"Where are you from in Italy?" I asked.

"Milano," Alberto answered.

I smiled. "Nice city." Axel went to a week-long convention there. While he worked, I wandered around the city and took the train to neighboring towns. We added another week to see the picturesque coastal city Portofino and other parts of Northern Italy.

"Have you been there?" Matteo asked.

"Yes, much nicer than I expected. I enjoyed my visit to the beautiful old cathedral and parks. And best of all, the excellent food."

They both smiled. Milan didn't get the attention like the big three: Rome, Florence, and Venice. The city had a bad rap as being too industrial, but it was hidden from view in the city I toured.

"What are you ladies doing today?" Alberto asked.

"Going to brunch. What about you two?" Abby said.

"We are too. Why don't you join us? We have reservations at the Central Park Tavern. We can add two more - two beautiful ladies."

I smiled weakly. I preferred a girls' brunch with Abby and a break from men. I also didn't like the forced compliment and getting a table for four wouldn't be easy. I had to find my clipper ship cruise, so I didn't have time to wait hours for a table. Abby and I usually found a casual place that didn't take reservations and wasn't crazy busy for Sunday brunch, a popular past-time for New Yorkers. But Abby was thrilled with Alberto's suggestion, so I gave in.

Abby walked down 68th Street leading the way with Alberto, and I walked next to Matteo for the short five-minute stroll to the restaurant just inside Central Park. The restaurant was as busy as I feared, but we got a table after a short wait. Perhaps it helped to have two attractive men with us, and the misguided opinion that men were better tippers.

Abby asked how they knew each other. Alberto explained they were both doctors, and reached out his hand to indicate someone who stood up to the table top showing how young they were when they first met in grade school. Alberto had been in New York City for several years, but Matteo arrived only a few weeks ago with plans to be here for about a year to do research.

The waitress came over to our table and took our order. The guys said they loved the big breakfasts in America. In Italy, it's an espresso and maybe a piece of bread while standing at a counter.

"Really?" Abby asked not able to comprehend this, in her distinct New Yorker accent.

I knew what they meant having endured the Italian breakfast with Axel. But I only liked coffee for breakfast, unless it was brunch. And it was nearly two now, so this was a late brunch.

"What kind of research are you doing?" I asked Matteo.

"Addiction. How it affects people differently even within the same family."

"Tell me about it." Thinking back to my brother, the heroin addict, who overdosed about ten years ago. I was surprised when I realized how long he'd been gone.

"Have you experienced this?" Matteo asked.

"Yes, unfortunately," I explained how my brother fought it for years but lost the battle when he was 35. A silence went over the table.

"Not pleasant dinner table conversation," I said. "But what's interesting is that, even though I've never used heroin or illegal drugs, I took Vicodin once. Tons of it and later I learned it's made from opium and highly addictive. But it never bothered me, and I gave it up instantly."

They all stared at me, so I explained further. "I had a bad case of sciatica from aggravated nerves. Herniated discs in my lower back."

"I took the pain killer daily. Don't know how many, and didn't notice much of a difference when I did. I was in tremendous pain dragging my right leg around," patting it for emphasis. "I had to lay down on the floor even at work when it got intense. I never asked my doctors for the prescriptions. They just gave them to me. Luckily, I found a cure. A new treatment called laser disc decompression that vaporized the swelling in my discs and my sciatica disappeared immediately. I stopped using it that same day. No addiction or withdrawal symptoms at all."

No one said anything, so I added, "I guess I was lucky."

Our food arrived as a welcome diversion from my tale of woe. Abby chatted with Alberto about New York brunch and restaurants in our Upper West Side enclave.

I was sorry to have said anything about my brother and my back problems since both topics were real downers.

Matteo turned to me. "I'm glad you told us. Fascinating how brothers and sisters can be so different."

I didn't say anything, but he put his silverware down and patted my arm and said, "It must be hard to lose a brother."

"Yes, it was hard, but we weren't that close. My brother lived in Los Angeles. I was here, and our parents in Texas."

Wanting to change the subject, I searched around as if a new topic might appear out of thin air. I was glad to see this restaurant was open and busy again after the bankruptcy forced it to close years ago.

"Did you know this was a barn for sheep? They used to

graze in the meadow across the road."

"Sheep?" Matteo looked around the restaurant. "Even sheep live well in Manhattan."

"Yeah, until 1930. Now they end up on the menu."

Abby asked, "Kat, are we still on for Halloween? Tomorrow at six?"

I was grateful to have the topic changed from dead sheep. I wasn't a vegetarian, but I hated thinking about dead animals. "Yep, I sure am. Hope to be home early. Shutting the office down you know. The lease is up on the last day of October."

Alberto and Matteo asked us about Halloween. Next thing I knew, Abby invited them along to that too. I tried to motion to her to not do this, but they were sitting right there. I couldn't speak Hebrew and wished she could speak Danish, a lesser known language. Axel and I did that when we didn't want to be understood.

She explained Halloween night and how everyone dresses up while I ignored them and checked my phone for messages.

"Costumes? What do you wear?" Alberto asked.

"I usually go as your standard, ugly, scary, powerful witch," I grumbled.

Abby made up for my lack of excitement by telling not just us but the tables nearby in her loud voice. "I switch around. This year, I'm not sure. Maybe a zombie again."

I added, "You can't go unless you wear a costume. That's the whole point of it. Sorry." This should talk them out of it.

"We can get some costumes, can't we Alberto?" Matteo asked.

"Sure, we can. At Roxie's. We'll get them after brunch," Abby said. Seeing my gloomy face, she added, "It'll be fun, Kat."

9 ~ *Into Costume Again*

Roxie's on 72nd Street and Columbus, an edgy beauty shop turned Halloween superstore, was only a ten-minute walk from the restaurant. But it was mobbed since not much more than 24 hours remained before the big event. Halloween rivaled New Year's Eve in New York City, and to me, it was the only big event to attend. By now, the best costumes were long gone.

Inside Alberto picked up a Zorro costume. He and Matteo spoke Italian together about it with Matteo hanging on to it. I found a wolf costume and held it up to show them. Alberto took it from me to see it up close while Matteo tried on the Zorro mask.

Abby said, "Oh, that wolf is perfect. Here is a little red riding hood costume to go with it." She waved it around.

"Are you nuts?" I would never go as someone weak and sappy. Even though the original Grimm Brothers' *Little Red-Cap* fairy tale was darker than the Hollywood remake. I never wore red, maroon maybe, but never bright red. It would be like wearing a red spotlight. But then I realized Abby was considering the costume for herself.

Since they all had a costume picked out, I wanted to get out of the crowded store. The queue to get in the dressing rooms would take hours. "Great, are we done now? Why don't you buy them and return them if they don't fit?"

"Kat, you need a new costume. I'm tired of that nasty, old witch. You wear it every year."

"I know, but I like it, except for the itchy wig. And I want to be scary. It's Halloween, not a kiddo's birthday party."

She wouldn't give up and pulled out another costume. "This is perfect. In honor of Xena."

I wasn't planning to look at it until she mentioned Xena, my soulmate. I grabbed the package from her. Of course, a Catwoman costume. "But it's a size small. I need a medium."

"Medium? But you're a size two."

"More like a six, and I don't want it too tight." A stretchy black pantsuit was inside the plastic bag.

She squatted down and told Alberto to look through one pile and Matteo another. All three dug through the pile of costumes, while I stood by watching since this was my way out. I loved being a nasty old witch.

Matteo jumped up as if he won the lottery and held up another Catwoman costume. I snatched it from him irritated, but it was marked XL, an extra-large.

"Too big, sorry."

Abby refused to let me off the hook. "Kat, small will be perfectly fine. I'm buying this for you. I'll ask about trying them on at home so we can get out of here."

The cashiers were frantic with the crowds. The clerk told us, "This isn't allowed, but if you return them within the next hour, it's okay."

As we strolled down Columbus Avenue towards our apartments, Matteo suggested, "Let's try them on in my apartment. See them all together."

"Bad idea." But I was outnumbered and overruled again. The next thing I knew, Abby and I were in his guest room changing clothes. I shimmied into my catsuit and hid behind the black cat mask.

Abby looked like a silly combination of a school girl and French maid with the red skirt, cape, and white apron. When we entered the living room, the guys were in costume. The wolf, Alberto, chased and tormented poor little red riding hood. Matteo, an irresistible guy beforehand, made a striking Zorro and could give the actor Antonio Banderas competition for any remake.

Zorro and Catwoman, covered in black from head to toe, looked like typical, black-clothed New Yorkers. We circled each other, and I felt shy and uncomfortable under his gaze in my skin-tight suit.

Alberto and Abby were goofing around, and they looked good together. As if they fell out of a Grimm's fairy tale. Abby shortened her skirt and made it a bit sexier. I hoped our Italians didn't back out tomorrow since she would be so disappointed without her sidekick wolf.

"We're good?" Abby verified that we didn't need to return anything.

"Well, I would still like a medium." I squatted and pulled at my second skin of black latex squeezing me. The actress Michelle Pfeiffer complained about wearing this costume for the film role. Now I understood why. I took some deep breaths. I could still breathe so I'd manage tomorrow night.

"You look perfectly catty, Kat. Xena would be so proud. You are one of her own."

I smiled but ached at the thought of little Xena. Abby was fond of cats and missed her too. But Xena would have freaked if she saw me dressed like this. She didn't like anything strange.

"We have to get some pictures tomorrow before we go with our makeup and everything," Abby said.

"Makeup?" Alberto asked.

"Well, we do, and most people do. Makes it more dramatic, like an actor, you know."

I felt sorry for our Italian friends. Didn't they know what Halloween is all about?

~ ~ ~

Back in my apartment, I had phone messages from Greg and Charlie. I texted Charlie back to thank him for the flowers but didn't answer his question. How was I supposed to know what they represent? Does white mean surrender, yellow cowardice, and red blood from the potential damage from my knife? Not pleasant symbols or a night I wanted to remember.

Greg answered the phone when I called him back. He was in Greenwich, Connecticut at his daughter Françoise's house.

He moaned. "I'm stuck here attending another insufferable birthday party for my grandson. How I get persuaded to come to these things I'll never know."

I could have warned him. Any birthday party that didn't involve someone old enough to drink alcohol was bound to end up being dull.

"Kat, I wish you were here to lighten things up. We could run off into the wilds of Connecticut."

"Yeah, and get shot when we trespass on someone's

property."

"You do have an imagination."

"What's there to imagine? That happens up there."

Spending another minute in Connecticut was one too many. I commuted there frequently when I worked for a Swiss bank based in Stamford. Being away from Manhattan was physically and mentally painful.

"I might prefer dodging bullets than being surrounded by eight screaming six-year-olds with parents that don't tell them to shut up."

Sounded like torture to me, but I didn't want to tell him how lousy I was with young kids.

"How did it go last night after we disappeared? Did Desi manage okay?"

"They thought it was odd, but to hell with them. I haven't felt so alive in months. Desi said, 'So romantic like the final scene in the movie *The Graduate*.' She likes you."

Leaving a fiancé behind at the altar would be life-shattering compared to our escapade last night, but I loved that movie. "Yeah, I like her too." I hoped she and I would stay friends when Greg found someone more his type.

A woman yelled what sounded like Kat in the background.

Greg said, "Did you hear that? Desi said hello. She's busy staging a musical, theatrical performance with the kiddos. A little mermaid show inspired by your dreams of the sea. I'll see if Steve can videotape it for you."

"Thanks, that would be fun to see."

"Now, about Tuesday evening. You will attend with me, won't you? Please."

I didn't know what to say. I didn't want to feel out of place after last night's dinner.

After a moment of silence, Greg continued trying to convince me. "It's a special dinner party. One of a kind to celebrate Turner. And we owe it to our favorite artist to attend. He died in 1861, so we are commemorating with clothing from that period, fine food, and a live band too."

My mind zeroed in on another clothing problem. "Clothing from 1861? I don't have any clothes like that. I don't even know what they wore then, or where I would find any. I'm sorry Greg. I can't go."

"Because of the clothes? I have that covered. An excellent designer and dressmaker made my suit, and she makes my daughters' special event clothes."

"But it's on Tuesday. How will she have enough time?"

"Not to worry. I've talked to Madame Gris. She said to drop by Monday morning. She has dresses in stock. You pick one, and she'll tailor it to fit you."

"But isn't this a bit much?" Not sure how to bring up the cost to someone who doesn't think about money. "You know, expensive for clothes like this?"

"Kat, don't worry about the cost. My treat. I want you to come and be my date. Please say yes." Greg chuckled and added, "And if you find that old clipper ship, you'll have a beautiful dress to wear."

"Well, all right." I tried to ignore my gut and better judgment. "But only if I have the right dress, and it can be ready in time. I don't want to look out of place like last night."

"But you ended up looking beautiful. And when can I send you that dress and the other leftovers? Give them to your friends, charity, or sell on e-bay. I don't care."

I gave him my address for his driver to drop them off. We agreed to meet his dressmaker or magician, as he described her, on Monday.

I wasn't sure this would work and couldn't match his enthusiasm. But my friends will be thrilled about the free designer wardrobe party I'd organize with Patricia's leftovers.

~ ~ ~

I fired up my laptop to find my dream cruise. I checked cruise websites and travel agencies, even shipping lines. I knew what I wanted - a clipper ship leaving from Copenhagen in November and returning home in December.

But why not do something spectacular while I'm at it? Return home next year and avoid all the sad, strained holidays. Last year was painful, even with my friends. If I'm in New York City again, I'd already decided to stay home alone and watch TV.

My first search came through with three modernized clipper ships with details explaining how they were rebuilt to cross the Atlantic as they did over a hundred years ago. But the last extended voyage, a thirty-day repositioning cruise, left Europe for the Caribbean last week. And, now they were puddling around in the Caribbean all winter. I didn't want to be surrounded with couples and honeymooners.

I switched to a mega cruise consolidator we'd used many times before. It didn't include all the cruise lines, but most of them. But the result flashed angrily: "There are no cruises that match your selections. Please change one or more selections and try again."

I started to worry since all the cruise lines disappeared from Northern Europe in the wintertime. Maybe I needed another helpful drink of Aquavit?

Instead, I made my weekly call to my parents. I told Mom briefly about the date and the video. She hadn't looked at Facebook lately. "Well, I wouldn't worry about it. Things like that blow over."

I expected that. Nothing ruffled my Mom. She updated me on what was happening in San Antonio but was anxious to get off the phone. "I'm busy packing for our trip next week to New Zealand, so I'm going to let you go. Your father would like to speak with you."

I was glad to switch over to Dad. I wanted to get his advice on my search for a clipper ship cruise. He was an unstoppable travel fiend and knew about nearly every cruise line and related website. He even taught a travel course for fellow retirees at the local community center. Dad rattled off a list of cruise lines and websites, but those were ones I'd already checked.

"Kat, I'll go through my emails. I get so many and if I find a good one I'll forward it to you. You know, you can come on the trip to New Zealand with us. A cabin might be available."

"Thanks, Dad, but I want to go to Denmark first to scatter ashes with Axel's brother. And then go on a real adventure. I have this rare opportunity between jobs. And Axel always set up our vacation trips so for once I get to pick my own. I've never gone anywhere alone without friends or family. Even on business trips, I've been surrounded by work colleagues."

"Well, Kat, you have lots of good reasons to do this. You are young to have a bucket list. But I know that travel craving. The right ship and cruise will show up. We'll meet after our travels are over."

"Thanks, Dad. Enjoy New Zealand. I'll send you an email if I end up going somewhere."

I couldn't tell my Dad or Mom how down I'd been feeling. How this trip wasn't just a vacation, but a way to save my life and start over again. I couldn't put them through that worry again. Not after seeing what they went through when my brother died, and the pain we still felt.

I went back to my computer search, but I'd lost my optimism. If this was August, not November, there were multiple cruises from Copenhagen. But in August next year, I'd be chained to a desk working again. I logged off frustrated and decided to clear my head with a swim. I grabbed my suit and hurried to the gym.

The pool was nearly empty with only a few swimmers. I jumped into my lane, bracing myself against the shock of cold water, and swam fast down the lane. At the end of the pool, I rolled face first into a somersault, and when my feet felt the wall, I pushed off to swim back.

I was quickly warm and at peace. Swimming was second nature, so I switched into autopilot. My mind wandered to everything and anything, but never nothing. Every moment, even my dreams, were filled with thoughts. I couldn't make my mind go blank, not even during yoga. But for me, swimming was the perfect way to think, and the stress of the last few days dissipated.

The pool was closing, so the lifeguard waved for us to finish.

"One more lap, please," I begged.

She nodded, maybe sensing how much I needed this.

I swam a 'no breather.' Inhaling hard to trap every drop of air, I swam furiously to the other end. Slowly I let out my valuable air supply without taking another breath until reaching the wall. For my return trip, I forced myself to do the same thing.

My sides were heaving from the effort, but I smiled up at the lifeguard. I pulled off my swim cap and dipped my hair warm from sweat under the water and climbed out of the pool. Toweling off, I glanced at the now empty pool. I was breathless but so alive.

10 ~ Finding Max

"What's the damn holdup?" I complained while I stood behind several people at Antonio's, my neighborhood pizza spot. They weren't closing, but I was annoyed. I should have been home by now with the pre-made salad from their fridge, and after my hard swim, I deserved a nice slice or two. But here I was stuck waiting in line forever.

"Impossible," I said under my breath fuming.

The pool closed early, but there was time for a quick hot tub, steam room, sauna, and shower, so I was starved. Like everyone else in New York City, I was always in a hurry, and the entire line was angry.

At the gym, I'd switched out of my wet swimsuit into my hoody and sweat pants but left my hair wet. I didn't bother putting on my underwear since I was going to switch to my nightgown when I got home. Finally, the bozo at the counter finished his order and moved aside, and the line moved.

"Kat, is that you?"

I was pointing out my favorite, a mushroom, onion, and cheese slice, to the clerk, so he heated up the right thing. I didn't want to respond to whoever it was since I resembled a wet rat. Besides, I was socialized out from this weekend.

I glanced over after ordering and saw Matteo. "Hi there. What's up?"

"Getting some pizza. It's not like in Italy. I had questions. But I guess I slowed people down -"

I interrupted his lame excuse. "Yeah, New Yorkers are always in a hurry. Big city and too much going on." I didn't let him off the hook completely. He needs to realize this. You must move along or get out of the way.

The guy behind the counter handed him a large pizza box, and Matteo took it but didn't leave and waited with me.

I was all wet, no makeup, nothing. "I went swimming."

"So that's why. I thought it started raining."

The clerk handed over my warm pizza box.

As Matteo and I walked across the street into our building, he asked, "Will you join me for dinner? I have a nice bottle of Chianti waiting."

Dinner out was the absolute last thing I wanted to do. "No thanks. I'm all wet and everything."

"Please, Kat. I hate to eat alone."

He looked sad and almost childlike without that hard New York City exterior. Was Alberto his only real friend in town? Soon there will be a line of women, even men, outside his door wanting to spend time with him. They just hadn't discovered him yet.

"All right. But I have work to do tonight, so it must be quick. Okay?"

"*Perfetto.*" I wasn't sure what he meant, but from the way he said it, it must be 'perfect.'

Inside his apartment, he offered to take my jacket, but I declined not wanting to explain I was naked underneath. He set the table and opened the bottle of red wine. I took out my salad and offered to share it along with my slice.

He put some music on, something Italian I didn't recognize, and lit some candles. I hoped he wasn't in a romantic mood since that wasn't happening. He was attractive, but not my type. Too gorgeous and with his accent, I had to concentrate whenever he said anything. But his English was good and in the 'great' category. Switching to Italian wasn't an option. Apart from ordering food from a menu, I only knew some tourist basics.

"*Saluti.*" We clinked our wine glasses together.

"To Italy, the birthplace of pizza," I said unsure what we should be toasting. He'd put our slices on a round plate, and together they created an eclectic pizza. Life was a lot like pizza: ooey-gooey but often delicious.

"I couldn't decide, so I got four. People were upset."

Yeah, including me. "Oh well, let them." I tried to cheer him up. After a few weeks, he'd adapt.

He asked me about our annual Halloween celebration. I explained the parade through the West Village, and if you are in costume, you can join in. And how it's shown on a local TV station.

"On TV?" He was shocked it would merit such important treatment.

"You can record it and watch it later. If you have cable, I can help you."

"That would be nice. If you could show me how."

We chatted about what it was like to live in New York City, and I explained I'd lived here for fifteen years. But I grew up in Texas and lived in San Francisco, so it was different for me too. I answered his questions about living here. He was easy-going, and our conversation flowed, so I relaxed forgetting about my cruise ship worries. We finished eating, and I thanked him and got up to leave.

"The TV," he said, reminding me.

"Yes, of course." I picked up the remote to turn on the TV. As soon as I pressed the power button, the screen filled with what looked like a threesome having sex. He quickly took the remote from me and switched it off.

"Kat, I'm sorry." Matteo looked at me strangely and watched my reaction. He must know this was embarrassing, but I tried to ignore it. I'd seen all sorts of antics up close and personal, even on the trading floors at work.

"Some research into sex addiction," he added and pointed at a DVD cover on the coffee table.

The Marquis de Sade and 120 Days of Sodom. I shivered uncomfortably. I'd seen a movie about de Sade before but not X-rated.

While Matteo removed the video, I browsed his bookshelves. Jim, the owner of the apartment, had a series of books on ships called the Seafarers. I bent down to look closer. Gold lettering shined out at me, 'The Clipper Ships.'

"Could I borrow this book from you? From Jim? I'm trying to find a ship like this for a cruise. I'll bring it back in a couple of days."

Matteo nodded. The TV was on, and he handed me the remote.

I found the local TV channel and scrolled over to Monday night and the Halloween parade on the local channel and showed him how to record and cancel a recording. I set the show to tape and handed him back his remote. He could go back to his 'de Sade research' or whatever. I had my own research to do - cruise research. And the book on clipper ships was coming with me. Another message to not give up.

"See you tomorrow for the parade Matteo. A unique New York City experience and lots of fun."

He walked me to the door, but instead of reaching to open it, his arm was around my waist, and he kissed me. And this wasn't the fatherly peck on the cheek I'd received from Greg last night. This was a full-blown French kiss, but spicier since it was Italian.

I pulled away surprised, but reluctantly since I enjoyed it. Matteo's kiss was warm and friendly, not too aggressive or passive, but as he was, sexy and curious. He put his hands lightly on my shoulder. I hesitated not moving so he leaned down to kiss me again. His hands moved down my back pulling me closer.

He said, *"Bellissimo,"* while he pulled at the zipper on my jacket still kissing me. I looked down at his thick, wavy dark hair. But this was moving too fast, and I wasn't ready. Still clutching my book on clipper ships, I held the book up in front of my chest and put my hand on his shoulder pushing him away.

"No, Matteo. Not tonight. I'm sorry."

"Perchè no?" I knew that meant 'why' since it was almost the same in Spanish.

"I'm tired and have things to do. And this is moving way too fast for me. Goodnight, Matteo."

He opened the door kissing me Euro-style on the cheeks one last time. I was proud of being able to resist him since not many women would do that. They weren't so stupid, but I was scared. If his bedside manner was anything like the way he kissed, I was missing out on an experience of a lifetime.

He smiled not giving up. "I want to swim with you. Inside you. I will dream about it."

I was tempted to stay, but I couldn't change my mind now. With my clipper book protecting me, I hurried down the hall to the stairway and safety.

Back in my apartment, I dressed for bed. I debated turning on my laptop again. I was exhausted from my hectic weekend. But after Matteo's passionate kisses and his romantic parting words, I couldn't fall asleep. I climbed into bed with the book on clippers and browsed through it, devouring each page, particularly the colorful photos. The book's cover was embossed with the image of the perfect clipper at sea with full sails. The book included quotes from sea captains and how they loved these ships. They could do anything, but speak and were magical like a mermaid.

The book explained how perfect these ships were for the China opium-tea trade since they were so fast and flew at a 'clip.' I studied the map of the world and a route I would most want to take. Leaving Denmark, sailing past Spain, around South Africa, to Asia and ending in India. I'd always wanted to go to India, but I never could convince Axel.

It was midnight, the bewitching hour, when I usually shut everything down, including my overactive brain. But I still couldn't sleep. Matteo had seen to that. I stared at the ceiling knowing there were just two floors between us.

I checked my email, and dear old Dad came through and forwarded information on three travel agent and cruise-related companies.

One firm advertised 'build your unique dream trip.' The email teased, "Get transported and experience a different cruise custom-tailored for your lifestyle. We will meet and exceed your inner needs and desires."

"Sounds promising." Worth a try but making dreams come true wasn't cheap. I patted the clipper ship book reassuringly.

The travel agency was named 'MAX - Maximum Adventure to the Extreme.' Their website said, "We can plan your ultimate vacation with our advanced computer system, but only if you provide enough data points." A warning added, "Our questions are lengthy and take time. But the more you answer, the better your odds we can scour the globe and find for the right trip for you."

One hundred questions? Hard for me? Not hardly. If they

can find my ship, I'd answer a thousand. But luckily, it wasn't that many since their hundred questions were time-consuming. A set of ten appeared, and then when completed, another ten. Each set probed deeper. I was often tempted to stop, but they continued encouraging me, almost goading me, so I kept going.

By two a.m., I was finally done. I rolled over onto the clipper ship book. I pushed it to Axel's side of the bed. Maybe sleeping with a clipper would bring me luck. I placed my hand on the book feeling the smooth outlines of the sails and drifted off.

11 ~ *Monday Misery*

My alarm blared from out of nowhere with one of my favorite bands and their song; *It's My Life*. I replied back to Jon Bon Jovi, "All right, already. I know, but that's the whole problem. What should I do with it?"

I was grumpy from staying up so late the night before, but I dragged myself out of bed. Monday's were always the worst day of the week. One positive with closing down - I won't have to get up so early until I start my next lousy job.

My Catwoman outfit hanging on my bedroom door caught my eye reminding me that tonight's Halloween parade should be fun. Now just to get through this miserable day.

"And no crying. Do not, whatever you do, get emotional about it," I stared at myself in the mirror and wagged my finger for more staying power.

It's just a job and even though I enjoyed having a consulting company, as they say, 'all good things come to an end.' Besides, I'm ready for a break from all the stress and responsibilities. I slid into some old jeans and a casual blue sweater since moving was a dirty job. We had to box up the last bits and clean the office for the next tenant.

~ ~ ~

I pushed open the unlocked office door and called out a greeting to Mel. She had already started boxing up her personal stuff. We began our day as usual with cups of coffee. Our desks were in the same room, and the extra room was a conference room for rare client visits. We weren't secretive and preferred working close by.

"So how was the rest of your weekend?" Mel asked tentatively as if she didn't want to hear the answer.

"Not too bad. I met another guy." She looked at me in alarm as if this was the worst news possible.

"This one was different, polite. Maybe too polite. We met at the Met." I smiled at the play on words. "We had afternoon tea, and then I had dinner at his place with some friends."

I didn't tell her about being surrounded by Greg's one-percenter friends since I knew she'd hate that or bring up Matteo. He was like a fantasy guy on the cover of a Harlequin romance novel and a 'what if' boyfriend.

I wanted to tell her more about Greg since he was so different from everyone we knew.

"He's an architect, but a bit older. He invited me to a costume party on Tuesday."

"A post-Halloween party?"

"No, a celebration for the artist J.M.W. Turner. Closing party for the special exhibit I went to on Saturday. He's a big fan of that artist too."

I checked my email, and Greg sent an update.

"He's coming at ten, in about half an hour, so I can go get this dress from someone he knows. You'll get to meet him." I hoped she liked him, or I'd never hear the end of it.

We worked silently, and I cleared out my desk drawers. Mel started taking down the framed pictures and art from the wall. All our mementos, news articles, and photos from our infamous Hong Kong trip and opium investigation were packed away.

Yelling and the sound of commotion filtered in from the hallway. We peeked out to see what was happening. The other office tenants, all creative and artistic types, swarmed into our small office to say goodbye. Crowding them in was a giant cluster of balloons with "Goodbye" and "Miss You" signs. We thanked them all, and lots of hugs and sad looks followed. But I reminded them I'd return for mosaic classes and say hello.

About ten minutes later, Greg arrived and looked around our empty office filled with colorful balloons. He gave me a hug and kissed me on the cheek, and I introduced him to an amazed Mel.

"So this is where you work? Artsy for a business person." Greg looked around, but there wasn't much to see.

"We're closing today, so it's ugly and bare bones now. I've been coming here for years for mosaic classes. Mel and I liked the building and location." The barely affordable Manhattan rent was a huge plus. He probably knew this, but I added, "I'm not your typical business person."

I'm glad, Kat. We need more free thinkers and artists. And this is a convenient place to meet with Madame Gris. We can walk over there."

"Not run?" Teasing him about our crazy trip through the museum's obstacle course on Saturday.

He grinned and looked at his watch. "Well if we don't get started soon, we may need to, but that's part of the fun. Are you game?" He laughed and grabbed my hand pulling me to the elevator.

Escaping from the office, even if it was my last day, was pleasant on this sunny day in October. Perfect weather for the Halloween parade, without a cloud in the sky to threaten rain and not too cold. We stopped at his car, and Greg told his driver he'd return soon.

We hustled over to a nondescript warehouse building a few blocks past the massive Fashion Institute of Technology that towered above my daily subway station on Seventh Avenue. I glanced at Greg wondering if this was the wrong address.

"Appearances can be deceptive. Madame Gris is the best costume designer in town."

Greg pressed the buzzer, and we were let in. We rode up to the fifth floor in what might be the building's original freight elevator. The doors opened into a huge loft taking over the entire floor with a small reception area on the side. Clothes were everywhere - on tables, hangers, racks, and even the floor. Clients were standing on pedestals in all forms of dress and undress being fitted and in some cases, sewn into their clothes. Halloween must be her busiest time of year.

An older woman came up to Greg, and they exchanged a warm hello with air kisses on both cheeks. Then she turned to look at me.

"So, Gregory, is this is the young lady you mentioned?"

I stretched out my hand, but she grabbed it and gave me a quick hug instead. Up close I realized she wasn't a woman. Either a man who was now a woman or a man who liked to dress as a woman. I should have realized this when Greg explained Madame Gris was a bit different. But I wasn't repelled, merely fascinated.

She looked me up and down and asked me to take off my sweater so she could see my size.

"But I'm not wearing anything under it, besides my bra," I argued and looked at Greg embarrassed, not wanting to undress in front of him.

"Oh, a shy girl," she said and looked over at Greg.

Greg got the message and grinned. "Madame, I'll leave you to work your magic. I'll call you later, Kat."

When he was out of earshot, I explained, "I don't need anything special. Whatever you have will work."

She studied me. "Nonsense. Everything I create must be special. Today is crazy with tonight's festivities, but we can have it ready tomorrow. Those society ladies at your event don't understand this Halloween crowd."

She motioned for an assistant to take my measurements and asked me again to take my bulky sweater off so she could judge more quickly what dress will work. I slipped it over my head not wanting to cause a delay.

"Good, you are thin under all that. Plenty of dresses for you to choose from in your size. Easier to take in than let out."

My measurements were taken and written down by a young assistant. I slipped back into my sweater grateful that was over.

Madame Gris instructed the young assistant. "Take Kat to the back wall over there. The rack with long dresses that need hoops."

And then she gave me my instructions. "Pick what you like. You'll try them on and pick one. We will take measurements again and tailor it. Come back for a second fitting tomorrow at two, and you can take it home by four. Does that work?"

"Sounds fine." I doubted the ball started before six.

Her assistant escorted me to the far wall past row upon row of rolling garment racks. We walked down the aisles hidden behind the rows of clothing until we came to the section with lots of long puffy skirts nearly blocking the narrow aisle. She took one down and held it up for me to see.

I hadn't fully realized what 1860 meant, but now I knew. These were *Gone with the Wind* Civil War style dresses. Big full skirts with hoops like Scarlett O'Hara wore in the film. I had imagined the long straight hoop-less dresses from Jane Austen's time.

The assistant gave me an empty rolling rack.

She said, "Select at least three to try on so we can choose one."

I apologized about the timing with Halloween, but she said, "It's always crazy in the fashion biz. No worries."

Many dresses were fancy with ruffles and lace, even embroidery, but I found a few less opulent choices. A deep burgundy velvet dress, a purple dress made of taffeta, and another brownish one with glints of gold. Not my favorite blue-green shades, but all three would suffice. It wasn't like I would wear this ever again anyway. I put all three on the empty rack and rolled it to the fitting area.

Madame Gris looked at my selections. "Nothing a tad more decorative or colorful?"

"No, I like them plain." I envisioned the green curtains Scarlett recycled to make her beautiful dress, but I didn't want to mention this and upset her.

I stripped down to my underwear and stood on a two-foot high pedestal for the fitting. My body automatically slumped down trying to disappear.

"A corset," Madame Gris yelled. "Can someone bring me one in small?"

"Oh no, not a corset." I shook my head trying to dissuade her.

"But the fit, the dress, it will never work without one. Even if no one knows, you will. And it will make you stand and sit taller. You could use that."

I could tell I wasn't going to win this battle, so I didn't argue further. Another assistant, breathing heavy, ran over with one, and she helped me put it on. But I was still unhappy. This wasn't part of my plan. At least I didn't have to take off my bra. The corset was laced up behind me while I cautioned, "Not too tight."

The dress was two separate pieces - a fitted sleeveless blouse and a skirt. I stepped into the burgundy skirt and pulled the ties at the waist relieved I could do this myself. The corset would require some assistance. If Abby couldn't help me tomorrow, I'd skip it.

After trying on the burgundy dress, I slipped on the next one, and then the last. The trio circled me assessing each one while dealing with other clients and questions.

"Any dress works. Which do you prefer, Kat?" Madame Gris said.

I could tell she was in a rush, while I tried to figure out how to say this. "I like the burgundy one, but whichever is cheapest and easiest for you."

"Cheapest? Don't worry about the cost. Gregory is one of my favorite customers. Now that's settled. The burgundy one it is. That color looks good on everyone."

"Thank you, Madame Gris." I stepped off the podium and slipped back into my clothes in about two seconds. I was uncomfortable with all this fuss, but I was glad Madame Gris liked my first choice. The vibrant color of pinot noir. And convenient, if I happened to spill any red wine on it tomorrow night.

Madame Gris eyed me carefully. "You aren't used to this, are you?"

I shook my head. "No. I've never had a dress tailor-made. Even my wedding dress was off the rack."

"Think of this like going to your senior prom with an exceptional date."

"I didn't go to my senior prom."

Madame Gris raised her painted eyebrows and started to say something else, perhaps sympathetic. But two assistants ran up asking her multiple questions at once. I left without saying goodbye to not take up more of her time. But I smiled at everyone and everything all the way back to my office overjoyed about honoring Mr. Turner in such a beautiful dress.

12 ~ Expect The Unexpected

When I got back to the office, Mel left a note saying she'd gone out for lunch and errands. We rarely had lunch together, and today wouldn't be any different. I wanted one last Korean rice bowl called a *bibimbap* from the hidden away deli downstairs.

I checked my emails and had a message from MAX, the travel agency. I held my breath in anticipation and opened it while praying for good news. They acknowledged the receipt of my questionnaire and thanked me for answering all their questions.

"Yeah, they sure better appreciate it, all hundred." I stifled a yawn remembering how long it took.

Their email suggested a November two-week cruise on a clipper from Panama to the Caribbean and said I just missed a four-week repositioning cruise from Europe to the Caribbean. But I'd read about those cruises last night, so this was disappointing.

The travel agency's email continued, "If you wait until April, there would be plenty of cruises that meet your criteria."

But no, I wanted to go now. I had to go now. Next year I'd be trapped at work and may not even get a vacation. The end of the year was dead. The worst time to hunt for a job.

In closing, the email said, "We are investigating other possibilities on private, smaller ships not available through standard web searches and will be in touch when we have other leads."

At least they were still looking, and I wasn't giving up either.

The balloon bouquet strings dangled right over my desk distracting me, so I pulled them over to the corner of our office out of the way. But the big red 'Miss You' balloon broke loose from its string and floated up to the ceiling out of reach.

"Great, now what?" I said. I couldn't leave it there since the office had to be left empty.

I moved my chair under the balloon and stood on it, but I still couldn't reach it. It was closer to Mel's desk, so I took my shoes off and climbed on top. I stretched my arms as far as possible and could almost touch it. But I was in a precarious position angled over the edge of her desk.

A man called out, "Careful," breaking my concentration.

I ignored whoever it was since I was so close. His hands grabbed right above my knees holding my legs stable. With his support, I leaned further and grabbed hold of the end of the runaway balloon.

The man's hands were still touching my jeans. He wore an expensive business suit, so he wasn't someone that worked in this building or neighborhood. His hair was light brown, not gray, so it wasn't Greg. He looked up at me smiling, and then I knew.

"You! What are you doing here?" I almost let loose of the balloon when I realized it was Charlie. But I held on and climbed down from the desk keeping my distance.

"I came to see you. You never called me back, and I only got that one text. I've been worried about you."

Charlie picked the broken string off the floor and reached out for the balloon. Still in shock, I handed it to him. He tied it back together and guided it over to the others. Then he ambled towards me.

"Well, I'm fine. Thanks for your help with the balloon. And for the flowers." I moved to stand behind my desk for safety.

But learning from my mistakes and what happened before I asked, "You didn't make a videotape, did you?"

"No, Kat, please, I wouldn't do that to you. I spoke with Kristin, and she deleted it. She is sorry and sends her apologies too. I want to explain. I was an awful date Friday, and you were fully justified in being angry and doing what you did."

I glared at him not willing to believe a word of it.

He smiled and lifted his hands up as if showing me he had no weapon, was surrendering, and meant me no harm. "Kat, can I please buy you lunch and explain?"

"I have lunch plans already." It was a half lie, but I didn't want to be trapped in a restaurant again after Friday's fiasco.

And I did have plans - take out from the Korean deli.

"Okay. But can I please have five minutes of your time to explain?"

Charlie looked sincere but Friday night started out okay too. Against my better judgment, I motioned for him to sit. I sat behind my desk and opened the drawer to look for my letter opener, the only weapon at my disposal. But it was packed in a box on the floor and out of reach. He sat on a chair sideways as if he didn't feel comfortable on that side of the desk. I was curious to hear what lame excuse he dreamed up for his miserable behavior.

He cleared his throat. "Friday morning, I lost a major deal with a client. It would have been a huge win, not just for my team, but the entire company. Deals have been slow all year and were coming back in the fourth quarter. On top of that, I spent the afternoon at my attorney's office and blew up over my divorce. We had a conference call with my ex and her lawyer. They keep demanding, not just every cent I have, but everything I ever made. She's already spent most of it, and she was the one that had an affair and left me."

I listened to his rant and let him blow off steam. He was livid while retelling it. But he shouldn't have bothered coming over to tell me this. We were incompatible. After meeting Greg and Matteo, two easy-going men, I'd come to a decision. I should avoid all Wall Street guys.

Charlie shifted in his chair as if he was in some discomfort. "I planned to power through our date. I didn't want to reschedule a third time for God knows when. Next year sometime? To unwind, I had a few drinks. I was nervous about meeting the infamous Kathryn Jensen. At the restaurant, you looked so self-assured and beautiful. And, with the culmination of everything that day, I turned into a jerk, a real asshole. So, I sincerely apologize. I deserved much worse than the water you threw at me."

I was still mulling over what he said earlier. "You're still married?" Shocked that I dated someone still legally committed to someone else.

"Technically yes, but we've been separated for over a year.

Our divorce attorneys keep getting richer, so they are in no hurry to end this. That's her game. Wear me down and get everything."

Well, this was a surprise. My girlfriend assured me he was single and not in a relationship. I'd been propositioned by married men, even when they knew I was married. But that was a line I'd never cross.

My stomach started to growl since I hadn't eaten anything today, and it was almost one. Where was Mel when you need her? When she figured out who Charlie was, he would be tossed out on his rear. I smiled thinking about it, but the timing was terrible.

"Is that a smile I see? Have you forgiven me?"

"Nope, not exactly. But I did want to know what you meant by the colors of the roses."

"Well, the white roses are for peace. I'm sorry about how our date turned out. The yellow roses are for you, for Texas. Linked-In said you are a University of Texas grad, one of the reasons I wanted to meet you. And the third, red, is from the bottom of my heart."

He touched his chest or where most people have a heart. But his must be black, and I nearly told him so.

"Why did you want to go out with someone from Texas?" I tried to remember what his on-line bio said, but I'd skimmed it months ago. I had the impression he was an East Coast Ivy League guy and not from Texas.

"I'm from Wyoming. I got my MBA from Harvard but grew up fifty miles west of Cheyenne on a cattle ranch. So, I'm an outsider too. And my real name isn't Charles Richmond."

I looked at him in surprise. He reached out to shake hands, and I instinctively took his hand to shake it.

"I'm Travis Rich, Kat. Pleased to meet you." He stood and bowed as if taking off an imaginary cowboy hat. His voice changed to what must be his real accent from Wyoming. Different from a Texan accent. Soft with a smooth, slight twang.

He added, "No one at work knows this. I'd like to keep it that way, Kat. Charles Richmond is my legal name now." He smiled and added, "I'd like to try again, Kat, if you will. And you can call me Charlie, or Trav, like my friends' back home."

"But why?"

"Because I like you. You are so much like me. I know you don't think so. But despite our bad start, I believe we have a chance."

"No, I meant why did you change your name?" Shaking my head not wanting to consider the possibility that he was anything like me. I'd never been to Wyoming and grew up in the suburbs of San Antonio, not on a cattle ranch.

"When I applied for Harvard, my friend's father was an alum, and he helped me with my paperwork. He said my name would make me stick out. To be 'in the game,' he said it'd be better to have a less country sounding name. So, I took Charles from the Prince of Wales and switched 'Rich' to 'Richmond,' the original spelling of our name before it was shortened."

My cell phone buzzed breaking my trance. The caller was Amber with the travel agency, so I answered immediately.

She got right to the point. "We found a cruise that might interest you. But there is only one cabin left, so we need to know soon. It's significantly discounted and could disappear at any minute." She gave me more details, and I jotted them down.

While I did this, I looked over at Charlie, or Travis, whoever he was. He was checking his phone for messages. Then he walked into our conference room. I told Amber I'd get back to her soon and hung up radiating with hope. So much so, I might glow in the dark.

I went to see what Charlie was up to in the conference room and found him looking at our collection of eclectic art prints that used to be up on the walls. I'd considered giving them away after Mel picked out her favorites. But at my next job, I'll need something pleasant to look at instead of ugly walls. We'd selected a weird mix of modern and impressionist art to cover the boring off-white walls.

"Is that a Frida Kahlo, the wife of Diego Rivera?" Charlie asked. I nodded.

Charlie lifted the reproduction print to look more closely at

Frida's self-portrait. She wore a necklace of thorns with a black monkey and cat on each shoulder. When discouraged, I only had to look at Frida and remember all she went through - polio, a trolley accident, medical issues, a philandering husband, and even having her leg amputated. Nothing I went through came anywhere close. All her suffering somehow gave me the strength to continue.

"I work in Rockefeller Center. They removed his mural since it was too leftist with Lenin in it."

"Yeah, the idiots. They destroyed it. A real shame."

He wanted to see the other prints laying underneath, so I flipped through the others to show him. Andy Warhol's *Green Cat*, Picasso's *Woman by the Window*, Danish impressionist P.S. Krøyer's *Summer Evening on Skagen's Beach*, and a few others.

"I'm hungry," I said. Charlie wasn't so threatening anymore so what the hell I'd invite him. "I'm going to get take-out *bibimbap* from a deli downstairs. If you want to join me, you can, but it's not for everyone." I wanted to stress that also applied to me.

"Sure. I'm game. Haven't had that before."

He followed me to the elevator. I whispered Trav, his name, to hear it out loud as the elevator doors closed.

I was quiet, but he heard me. "I knew you'd like my real name."

"And you made it all up too, didn't you?" His story was some joke to insult or get back at me.

"Would I do that? I couldn't even if I wanted to. Not that much imagination, I'm afraid."

"I'd rather call you Charlie."

He nodded and waited for me to say something.

"Why did you leave Wyoming?"

"It wasn't easy. My family is still there. But I didn't want to be a rancher like my father and his father generations back. I liked the cowboy part, riding horses, and managing the ranch, but not the slaughter. I'm not a vegetarian, but I couldn't deal with all the killing."

We entered the deli, and I explained what *bibimbap* was

showing him the photos on the wall and describing how good they taste. He said he would have whatever I was having. I ordered two standard beef *bibimbap* bowls of white rice topped with cooked veggies, peppers, seasonings, and a fried egg.

Charlie insisted on paying and gave my Korean friend, the cashier, a very generous tip so at least someone was won over and fond of him.

While we were waiting for our take-out, Charlie asked, "Do you remember Peter Demler or Thomas Harrington? They're pals of mine. You audited their group at Barnaby Bank years ago."

"Nope, sorry. Don't remember them."

"Oh, it's just as well. They said your audit report was accurate and all. But it cost their manager his job. With so many issues, he looked incompetent to senior management."

"I'm sorry. Most of the time some training will solve the problems if it's staff-related issue. And the real culprits typically have someone else take the fall. Why did you ask?"

"Oh, nothing. Another reason I was apprehensive about meeting you last Friday. I usually don't drink so much. The hangover was extreme. One of the worst."

I hadn't considered my internal audit work was scaring off potential dates. Were other men afraid of me too? Greg and Matteo weren't, but I wouldn't audit their firms either. And they'd probably never met an internal auditor before.

Our *bibimbap* was ready, and we headed back to the elevator. I was sad knowing how much would change after today. I'd miss all the friendly people like the staff at the Korean deli and the guys in the lobby.

Charlie must have noticed. "So Kat, what are you planning to do next? I know a lot of people and can make some calls if it would help. Just not to Pete or Tom."

"No, thanks. I'm going to look for another job in January. I'm taking the rest of the year off. That call was about a cruise I might go on."

The door to my office was slightly open, so Mel was back. I dreaded their meeting and what she would say to him. Her tongue had hidden barbs that could lash out and cause deep wounds. I'd seen it before, and it wasn't pretty. I was tempted to suggest eating outside, but it wasn't that warm, and there weren't any parks in the vicinity. I inhaled deep for bravery and pushed open the door. Mel stood next to Greg, and they both stared back at us.

13 ~ Service With A Smile

Back in my office, Greg looked at Charlie, and Mel went back to her desk and ignored us. Charlie and Greg looked out of place in their formal business suits and appraised each other.

"We wondered where you went," Mel said.

"Down to get some lunch." I lifted my take-out as evidence.

Greg gave me a quick peck on the cheek as if establishing I was his property. I felt strangely uncomfortable by his sudden show of affection in front of Charlie.

I introduced Greg and Mel to Charles, not Charlie. I wasn't sure if his nickname was only for my benefit. I could tell Mel was trying to place him, and I estimated about three minutes before she figured it out and exploded. This would be so embarrassing. But with Greg here, she might stay under control.

Charlie said, "You're the architect, right? Your buildings are beautiful. Real works of art."

Greg smiled and thanked him, but promptly ignored him and said to me, "I was on my way uptown so stopped by to see if you found a dress and the fitting went well."

"Yes, I did. A nice one, thank you. I have another fitting tomorrow, and it should be ready by four. What time is the ball?"

Mel sat behind her desk packing. Charlie sat in the chair he vacated when we went downstairs but was watching us and could hear every word.

"Cocktails are at seven, so we have plenty of time. I'll pick you up a half hour before."

I didn't want to say goodbye in front of everyone, so I escorted Greg to the elevator. He kissed me goodbye but this time on the lips. "Tomorrow will be special. A once in a lifetime evening. I promise you'll enjoy it."

I doubted I would fit in with his crowd. But I didn't have other plans that night, and I'd do this for Mr. Turner.

I went back to our office hoping a catfight wasn't in

progress. Mel glared at Charlie, but he was oblivious and eating his lunch.

"This is delicious, Kat. I had no idea it would be this tasty."

"Yeah, I love it too. Oh, stop. You didn't mix it up." I took his chopsticks from him to blend it all up. "You have to do this. It's the Korean way to eat it."

He leaned back looking up at me, and our eyes locked for a second. I moved back to sit behind my desk and mixed up my dish before getting a bite. The blend of spices, meat, and vegetables with the rice was perfect. The flavor was unique, unlike other Asian dishes, and hard to describe. I savored each bite reminding myself this won't end.

To get Mel to take her invisible daggers out of Charlie, I said, "The travel company I told you about this morning called. They suggested a cruise from Dubai to Cape Town. It lasts a month and starts in late November."

I glanced at my notes from the call. "The ship goes to places like India, Maldives, Seychelles, Kenya, Tanzania and even Madagascar. All new places I've never visited."

Mel looked horrified. "Dubai? Why would you ever want to step foot there? They treat unmarried women awful, like second or third class citizens. Those poor women are repressed, covered in burkas and headscarves, and forced to follow all those stupid, idiotic rules. You would never stand for that nor should you. It would drive any sane woman over the edge. Almost as bad as dealing with all the arrogant men on Wall Street."

With her last complaint directed against Wall Street, effectively him, Charlie looked at Mel trying to peer into her brain. I tried to deflect the situation before he said anything and caused a fight.

"Well, I've heard Dubai isn't so restrictive anymore. But you're probably right."

Dubai wasn't on my wish list, and I'd heard the warnings for women traveling there alone. Axel had told me I'd hate it. A hot desert with modern high rises and shopping malls wasn't that appealing.

"I've heard Dubai is pretty nice, especially the golf,"

Charlie added trying to be helpful.

"Your kind would," Mel spat back. She apparently couldn't bear being there any longer, and announced, "I have errands to run, but I will be back soon," stressing soon. As expected, she didn't say goodbye to Charlie.

After she had left, Charlie asked, "What's eating her?"

"Well for one, the video, and I told her about our conversation that night."

"Oh, I see," and he added, "Should I send her flowers too?"

"No, it's okay. I'll explain, but you know, Charlie … can I call you Charlie? The thing is, I don't think you're our type."

"But I don't want to date her, just you." His voice changed and was soft with hints of Wyoming.

I hesitated not wanting to be cruel. Maybe Charlie was right, and we might get along, but it was a long shot. At least, he was closer in age to me.

"I'm leaving on a trip soon, and I don't date married men, even separated men. When I get back, let's meet for coffee or a movie. I must finish all this packing and get these boxes home so you should go now. I'm sure you have client deals to work on."

"When are you leaving?"

"On my trip? Hopefully in the next few weeks."

"No, I mean today. You live up the street from me. I'd like to help you with the boxes."

"By four," as I glanced at my watch. In two short hours, I needed to clear everything out and clean up.

"I'll be back at four with a car and help move the boxes. Thanks for lunch and listening to me, Kat. See you later."

I didn't know what to say and stared at the carpet. Charlie took my silence as agreement, and his lips brushed my cheek. My hand waved goodbye instead of pushing him away. After he had left, I touched my cheek worried it might be contaminated and slimy. But it felt fine.

I called Amber to tell her that cruise wasn't for me, but to please keep looking. I buttered her up by adding, "I have total faith in you."

Mel stomped her feet notifying me of her return. I started

to explain what happened, but she put her fingers in her ears forcing me to stop. In silence, we finished clearing out our desks and stacked up all the boxes in the hall. Again, I tried to explain. She didn't accept the excuse that Charlie saved me from falling off her desk and busting my head open.

Some artist friends in the building picked up our unwanted furniture and large pieces we had no room in either of our apartments. Mel tackled the vacuuming while I cleaned the windows. My can-do, invincible attitude was back pushing me along. While I worked in a tense truce with Mel, I knew I should be optimistic. My cruise on a real clipper is out there somewhere, and Amber's company will find it.

Charlie, true to his word, arrived on time and helped me move the boxes down to the sports utility vehicle 'SUV' parked conveniently right in front. I'd convinced Mel to leave a half hour before so they wouldn't cross paths again. I couldn't tell her he was returning since she wouldn't have left.

I argued with Charlie that he shouldn't move anything. I didn't want to mess up his expensive suit or get saddled with his dry-cleaning bill. But he wouldn't listen to me.

In the SUV on the way north to the Upper West Side, I confessed, "I'm strangely relieved now. Turning in the keys and locking the door today for the last time lifted twenty pounds off my shoulders."

But the stress of another job search would soon replace it and might even be worse. But this time, I'd try to enjoy the time lapse 'between opportunities' as a former colleague put it, not stress so much, and be more selective. Find a job I'd enjoy and an employer to be proud of for once. Besides, I could afford to take my time. With no debt and no mortgage, I wasn't strapped for cash forced to live from paycheck to paycheck. But to stay in New York City and cover my expenses, I needed a higher than average base salary. Starting something new with a fluctuating income wouldn't guarantee that level.

"Glad to hear it. You seem to adapt well. I'm sure you'll find another position you'll enjoy. Be a consultant again. If that's what you like doing."

"Maybe." How had Charlie changed so much since

Friday? He seemed pleased to be here and help me move, but I didn't understand why. In the bright sunlight, he looked older but had boyish brown hair. His green eyes glittered and reminded me of my departed cat, Xena.

We reached my apartment building, and I waited to hear what he would say. My building wasn't a fancy 'white glove' building with doormen like his upscale complex. But if he was thinking it, he politely didn't say anything. At his level at Levittman and being on the income generating side, he probably made more than my annual salary in a month. If he closed deals and hit his numbers, his annual bonus would be up in the stratosphere.

I told him he could help put the boxes inside the front door, and I'd get them upstairs. But he shook his head, signed off for the car service, and said, "I want to see this through."

Did he think he was running the gauntlet? We stacked the boxes in the freight elevator. I thanked him again outside my apartment door, but he asked if he could use the bathroom, so I let him in. If he wanted to see his flowers, at least they were still there, alive and well. I showed him the guest bathroom while I checked the time. I had less than an hour to change into my catsuit and meet Abby and the others for our Halloween adventure.

Charlie joined me in the living room. "Do you have plans tonight?"

"Yep, I'm meeting some friends in about an hour for the parade. I have to shower and change first."

"Don't let me stop you." Charlie didn't make a move to leave, crossed his arms, and waited.

"But I can't do this with you here." I had no intention of letting him wait or see me in my Catwoman costume.

Charlie winked and chuckled. "I'm teasing."

He had a pleasant laugh. Our date on Friday was so tense we hadn't laughed about anything.

Charlie glanced at his watch. "I have to get back to the office and make some money. But can we go out again, please? I promise to behave."

I didn't want to, and he was still married. "After my trip

and your divorce."

"Now Kat, I'm as good as divorced. And I promise you'll enjoy it." He stood waiting for a yes.

"How about a movie this weekend?" Something that wouldn't require much discussion. And if I didn't enjoy the date, I might like the film.

"Done. I'm going to London tomorrow, but I'm back Friday. How's Saturday night?"

"Okay, but if a cruise comes up, I may be leaving this weekend."

"As soon as all that?"

"Maybe. I already missed one. I'll email you if something happens."

"I hope you won't go that soon. But if I ever get two months off, I'd do the same thing."

He hesitated not willing to leave, so I walked over to the front door signaling that he should go. He strolled from the living room while looking around. "You have a cozy place here. Much nicer than I expected. And my roses look beautiful."

I thanked him for his back-handed compliment. He lingered, so I opened the door to steer him out. Did I need a Wyoming sheepdog to herd him out? Charlie wrapped his arms around me in a sudden bear hug embrace. I stood stiffly unsure how to react to this affectionate hug.

I was about to say something, but he kissed me. His lips opened, and his tongue searched for mine. I wanted to say stop, but I couldn't. Then he released me and smirked having stolen a kiss. "A short reminder of what you're missing and can look forward to Saturday."

Oh, the nerve and attitude he had. I was tempted to take back the offer of the Saturday night date, but I liked his daring sense of adventure. He reminded me of Rhett Butler's pursuit of Scarlett O'Hara. Besides, I may be traveling this weekend so our date won't happen.

He swaggered over to the elevator and called back chuckling again before getting in the elevator. "And Kat, take it easy on Grandpa at the ball Tuesday night."

AQUAVIT

I closed the door and shook my head. But he was right. Poor Greg was a Grandpa.

14 ~ Tricked

Fifteen minutes late, I ran down the hall to Abby's apartment. The catsuit was hard to pull on my wet skin from the shower and creating a cat's eye with eyeliner took extra time. Witchy makeup was messy and easier. I apologized on the way in, but with the two Italians in her apartment, I knew she hadn't missed me. Her little red riding hood costume looked perfect on her.

Alberto and Matteo, or Zorro and a wolf, sat on her sofa. I couldn't resist laughing. Alberto took his mask off briefly to drink, but he enjoyed being a bad boy wolf. Matteo looked like the same as yesterday, a lady killer. They laughed amused and excited about this weird American tradition tonight.

Abby gave me a glass of red wine which was critical to relax in this costume. I kept a safe distance and sat on a nearby chair. All three checked out my catsuit and meowed.

Alberto warned me while he licked his lips. "You know wolves like cats. They taste so good."

"This isn't any old cat. Catwoman has super powers." I lifted my arms up as if I could fly. "An old wolf doesn't have a chance."

None of us knew much about Zorro, but Matteo said, "I've got special powers too." He imitated me by waving his arms around like he could fly.

We finished our drinks and left to see the local block party on 69th Street before heading to the parade in the village.

Alberto suggested, "Let's take a taxi the thirty blocks south."

But I argued, "No, the subway is better. We can see the other costumes, and it's faster since we're running late."

Alberto and Abby started across Columbus Avenue, and Matteo and I followed them. Out of the corner of my eye, a bicycle delivery guy was headed northbound against the traffic on the one-way street. Matteo must not have noticed since he started across the street. I stuck my arm out and slapped him in the stomach, so suddenly he stopped. We stood there together as the bicyclist whizzed by us.

Matteo looked at the bicyclist now long gone and said something in Italian. From how he said it, I didn't need or want a translation.

"What a daredevil idiot. I'm tempted to knock them down to teach them a lesson."

He nodded and grabbed my upper arm while thanking me. Abby and Alberto didn't see what occurred but waited while we caught up. After my close call with the taxicab on Friday, I vowed to be more careful, but my impatient habits would return soon enough.

We got off at a subway station in the West Village and walked towards the middle of the parade route. Costumed spectators packed the sidewalks, but people moved around letting us in. We found a good spot to observe the annual spectacle.

This parade must be experienced in person - not as a voyeur on TV from the comfort of a living room's overstuffed sofa. The parade was mainly the domain of the lesbian-gay-bi-transgender-queer LGBTQ community. But they didn't mind straight people joining in, if in costume. We were all disguised, but they could tell we were outsiders.

My catsuit was tight, and I had boots on with three-inch heels, so it was hard to walk at my usual fast pace. I missed hiding behind the long flowing robes of my witch outfit. We'd decided against walking in the parade. If you did, you didn't get to see the all the floats, and it was a long walk in heels.

Matteo said, "Lots of women, aren't there?"

"Yeah, colossal, busty women." I teased wondering when he would catch on. "You know they weren't born that way. Or maybe they were, but they weren't …."

I stopped not knowing how to explain most of these women either were born with or still had penises. Some would never have a sex change. Understandable since the surgery must be incredibly painful. I was thankful I'd didn't have to go through that. Matteo finally laughed when he understood what I meant.

We bought some beers from one of the small bodegas. I had

a small black leather bag slung over my neck and shoulder with the minimum - some cash, a credit card, keys, and lip gloss. I traveled light without a bulky purse in crowds. Abby had a straw basket that wasn't easy to carry, but she insisted since she bought it especially for her costume.

A huge float with lots of singing and dancing went by, and Abby fell against me. I struggled to stay on my feet.

"What happened?" I called out to her.

"My bag! Someone took my basket with all my stuff."

"Oh no, Abby." Matteo and Alberto ran off. They must have seen who did it and went after them.

"I'll be back. Stay here." I hurried after them, but it was hard to run in my boots. I wished I'd worn my black tennis shoes. But I couldn't see Alberto or Matteo so after several blocks I headed back.

I hated thieves. I'd been burglarized before but never robbed. If someone asked for my wallet, there was no way I was giving it to them. Even if they had a weapon, I didn't think I'd give in without a fight.

Abby welcomed me back, but she looked worried. "I lost them, Abby. Maybe the guys will catch him. I hope you didn't lose anything valuable."

"Only my wallet, keys, and phone."

"Oh, no." I didn't remind her that I'd warned her. Crime wasn't that widespread in Manhattan anymore, and it lured you into being less alert. Her bag was too tempting and easy to grab.

The final float at the end of the parade arrived. A giant ship filled with spirits and evil pirates. Some had hooks covering their hands and eye patches. At night, it was surreal and eerie. I shuddered as if a creature ran up and down my spine. I wanted to go on a ship, but not one like that.

Matteo and Alberto returned, but from their expressions, we knew it was bad news. The thief got away. Abby was devastated with her hopes of recovering anything gone.

"Let's take a taxicab home. I have your spare key, and you need to report all your cards and do that 'find my phone' to disable it." She nodded and knew this was for the best.

After we were back home, I gave Abby her spare key and offered to help. But she was upset and preferred to be alone. I gave her a hug goodnight and reminded her it was just stuff. At least she was okay.

Matteo invited us over for drinks, but I declined. I'd been up so late the night before, and the theft put a damper on everything.

At home, I had a voice message from Amber at the travel agency, "We found a cruise that might work for you. On a small charter and nothing fancy. A real clipper sailing ship. Call me tomorrow for the details. But the ship leaves Copenhagen this Sunday. You have to be there Saturday and fly out on Friday."

I kicked off my boots and hugged myself while twirling around the living room and stubbed my big toe against the sofa. The realization that, against all the odds, they'd found a ship gave me so much hope I didn't feel the ache. I wanted to call someone to share my fantastic news, but it was late, and there were too many unanswered questions. Tomorrow I'd find out, not just about the trip, but my voyage to a whole new life.

15 ~ Dishing Men

Despite hating early mornings and relishing my first break from the daily grind, I couldn't sleep late. Amber at the travel agency wasn't available when I called. I paced around my apartment feeling trapped, drinking coffee, and staring at the phone willing it to ring. About an hour later, she finally called back.

Amber said, "MAX found a clipper ship, and it sounds like what you requested. It doesn't usually take passengers, but this time, it's accepting four. It's leaving Denmark for Hong Kong, approximately a two-month journey, on Sunday. Are you interested?"

"A real clipper ship leaving from Denmark?" I was still in a state of shock having heard so often this was a 'mission impossible.'

She put me on hold for a minute to double check. "Yes, it's a real clipper ship. Old and not modernized so this won't meet our luxury standards. More of a freighter ranking since passengers are secondary to the cargo, and the passenger facilities and cabins are rated on the low end."

"How much will it cost?"

"I have a rough quote of around eight thousand dollars including taxes, but airfare is extra. The cost covers the journey, cabin, and meals from Copenhagen to the final port of Hong Kong."

That worked out to about a thousand dollars a week and within my budget, so I immediately agreed. Amber said she'd book the cruise and airfare and email the paperwork.

After we had hung up, I cradled the phone still in awe this was happening. But I shouldn't count on it. Not until I got the paperwork, and I was on the ship.

~ ~ ~

The waiter did a double take when Kathleen, Abby's new friend, cried out, "Listen to that sex columnist. I forgot his name. He knows what the fuck he's saying. Pardon, my

French. My suggestion and you can't go wrong. Always remember three key letters: D-T-A."

What? Did she say 'DNA'? She must be talking about something else since I didn't think DNA had much to do with sex. Unless she's referring to a DNA test to find the parents.

"Sorry, what does that mean?" I asked Kathleen and glanced over at Abby who shrugged her shoulders.

Kathleen leaned in. "Dump the asshole."

Our conversation started when Abby told Kathleen about my miserable Friday night date and the now defunct viral video. And it was further complicated by having lunch yesterday with the villain and agreeing to go to a movie with him on Saturday. With some distance, I realized it was an unbelievably dumb move. Something a weak heroine would do in a silly romantic comedy.

"But Charlie isn't mine to dump." I'd already canceled our movie date on Saturday via email thanks to my upcoming cruise.

"You've got to nip it in the bud," she hissed. "Been there. It gets worse."

"Well, I have since I'm leaving Friday for about two months." Leaving town would end most relationships.

"What? Did you find a cruise?" Abby asked.

I told them the bits I'd heard from Amber. They were impressed that I was so adventurous. They both firmly stated they couldn't do it - leave for two months and not know anyone on board. Especially when it's not a luxury cruise ship. "No way," they both agreed.

"But it's not that challenging. I'm a passenger and not responsible for sailing the ship."

"You better check into that," Abby said.

Kathleen jumped in with advice. "Yeah, you could be stuck having to work in the kitchen, peeling potatoes, and cooking for all those sailors. Remember DTA."

They had it all wrong. This cruise wasn't going to be a survival exercise. And I'm not going with any man, so there isn't anyone to DTA. I tried to explain again. "This is a ship, a cruise, not a guy, and I'm going solo. I've got to give it a chance. That is if all works out, and I get on board."

We ordered lunch, all salads and so typical when I went out with women. Kathleen regaled us with some of her dating adventures. Now I was part of their tribe, single again, and fortyish. Kathleen was divorced, and Abby never married. We griped about the lack of eligible, appropriately aged, decent men.

Kathleen said, "Men have a much wider, socially acceptable dating and mating age range. A huge unfair advantage. Women twenty-one on up are fair game. But women our age can only date someone maybe ten years younger or older."

"Speaking of older men. I met a guy the other day at the Met. We are going to a museum event with a costume ball tonight. Abby, they said I should wear a corset under this fancy dress. If I have trouble can I come by around six tonight for help?"

Abby said, "Of course. I'd love to see you all dressed up even if you don't need my help."

I promised her I would.

Kathleen and Abby pressed hard for the scoop on Greg, so I filled them in. "I'm not exactly sure how much older he is. Maybe ten or fifteen years but it's a big age gap for me. What do you think? Too old?"

Kathleen didn't waste time. "I can answer that in three words: How's the sex?"

Technically, that was four words, not three. But Kathleen wasn't the sort of person to squabble with over minutiae.

"Don't know. We just met." Not wanting to explain how we'd come close Saturday night, but it didn't happen. Would we have sex tonight? And would I want to since this would be a big deal? My first time before I got married twenty years ago.

I wasn't planning to fall in love, and sworn I'd never marry again. Abby knew my feeling on that. Finding a guy like Axel rarely happens. This topic depressed my friends, and I wasn't about to ruin our lunch.

Abby grinned. "Well, girl, I'm surprised but happy for you. Two guys in one weekend. I hoped something might happen with Alberto last night, but with the theft, things were a downer. Matteo sure is attractive."

"Yeah, maybe too much," I said. Abby nodded agreeing with me.

Kathleen joked we should send Matteo her way. She was proud of the fact she used Tinder, the popular dating app, and passed on some tips.

"Don't waste too much time looking at their details since it might be all made up, and even the photos can be fake. Meet at a nearby bar, or in public somewhere with other people around to decide. Never meet at your apartment. You might have ordered sushi and get a hamburger if you know what I mean."

We laughed, but Abby and I had talked about it before and doubted we would ever have the nerve to do this. If blind dates were traumatic, meeting strangers in a bar or even a coffee shop would be much harder. But it was refreshing to hear from a woman our age like Kathleen. She embraced her sexuality, took ownership of her body, and had sex when she felt like it.

I was tempted to ask her what she thought of the term 'tinderellas,' but I didn't want to insult her. I'd heard women using the app were considered easy pickups. But the term should apply to the men too.

Kathleen had plenty of advice on how to snare the perfect mate. "Ladies, don't waste your time or money on personal ads."

She told us how a woman advertised in an upscale magazine's personal classified ads for someone tall and handsome, but not specifying anything else. "She ended up with a skinny, pimple-faced, junior college basketball player. What a waste."

We laughed again, but not as much, and I cringed. That poor woman must have been so lonely to go to that extreme. I hoped I wouldn't end up that desperate.

I said, "In the Sunday wedding announcements, the paper often mention how couples found their mates. Many met through websites like Tinder, OK Cupid, or Match.com. I miss the old days of meeting guys through friends, parties, and even at a bar."

But Kathleen was thoroughly modern. "It's not just dating. It's everything. Who wants to waste time wading through the aisles looking for groceries when you can click and buy on the web and have it delivered the same day for free."

I didn't want to argue with her, but after my blind date fiasco, I was going to be more cautious. Part of the fun was figuring out in person how compatible you were with someone.

"Speaking of groceries, you know, men are like ice cream," Kathleen said. "You have to figure out what flavor you want."

Abby said, "I'm pretty dull. Plain vanilla without bits of bean."

I laughed. "I like to experiment with different types, and I've had lots of that kind of company in bed lately. Luckily, Ben & Jerry's has lots to choose from."

She clapped her hands, to the dismay of a couple sitting nearby in a serious discussion. "That's the way to do it. Try them all!"

Abby asked, "What kind of man are you looking for?"

Our waiter overheard this question when he delivered our salads and lingered, offering us fresh ground pepper, more bread, and whatever else he could suggest.

Kathleen considered this for a moment and said, "I'm like Kat. I like them all - any race, nationality, profession, or whatever. But I require an alpha in bed, and an easy-going beta the rest of the time."

The waiter still hovered about to get as much intel as he could. Too bad he couldn't educate all the men out there to help us find one. Our lunch together, sharing stories, companionship, and bonding was worth a well-deserved toast. I lifted my glass of wine, and our glasses made a sweet clink.

"To women," I said.

Kathleen added, "To men."

And Abby concluded spot on. "To us."

16 ~ Not A Turner-Ella

My rush to Madame Gris' studio was completely unnecessary. They were way behind schedule per the young, fuchsia-haired receptionist. Agitated, I glanced at my phone and read the email from Amber. I skimmed to confirm what she told me by phone, but at the top, in a bold red screaming text it said, "Because of the historic nature of the ship, all passengers are required to wear appropriate period dress for the duration of the journey."

What does she mean by period dress? Clipper ships operated for about a hundred years, and women's styles often changed, as I learned yesterday. I called Amber not wanting to scream at her via email.

"Amber, what are you saying about the dress code? You can't buy these clothes at your local department store. And what time-period is it exactly? Dress styles changed a lot."

Amber apologized and said she'd find out. "This is the clipper ship cruise you requested, and it has re-enactors wearing period clothes. Many cruises mandate evening black tie and theme party outfits so this isn't unusual."

But I wasn't backing down. "Amber, this is not the same. Modern evening gowns aren't even close. Believe me, I know."

I was annoyed having to wait to pick up this period dress for tonight. "But the rest sounds fine. I'll confirm when we get the clothing situation ironed out."

What an idiot, I fumed under my breath. The email didn't mention the airfare. I hoped the last-minute flight didn't cost me a fortune. And now I had to waste money on clothes I'd never wear again.

An assistant said they were ready, and I was ushered to the podium again to strip down. She helped me put on the corset and altered scarlet colored dress. The dress alterations changed the fit to a second skin, tighter than I liked and emphasized cleavage I wasn't comfortable showing. I stared across the studio at the mirrors covering most of the walls unsure who stared back at me. I wouldn't have recognized myself if her assistant hadn't rolled a portable mirror closer.

Madame Gris stopped by and noticed a few areas where the stitching needed to be touched up but nodded an overall agreement to her assistant.

I decided to ask her about some adjustments. "Don't you think it's too low?" I placed my hand near the top of the blouse and covered my skin never shown in public.

"Too much cleavage?" She stared at my breasts up close and reached up to rearrange the shirt and my breasts to verify the dress fit well. Now I wished I hadn't said anything and tried to look away but didn't know where to look.

She dropped her hands, and I took a deep breath not realizing I'd been holding it in while she checked. "Nah, it's fine. The corset gives you better posture. You simply aren't used to it. If you feel modest about it, we have some fans. Help yourself to one." She pointed to some large plastic bins in the back. I nodded uncomfortable with all the fuss over my dress.

"You shall have your senior prom, just a few years late." She beamed putting some stick pins into a pin cushion strapped around her wrist.

"Yeah, what're a few decades. This dress was worth waiting for."

Madame Gris looked pleased, and a smile sneaked across her lips. "Do you have a suitable handbag for tonight?"

"I have a small leather bag."

"Leather? No, no that won't do. You need a cloth handbag, preferably velvet or lace." She shouted to an assistant to bring the black velvet bag with needlework roses. With a flourish, she handed it to me. "Consider it a gift for the girl who missed her prom."

"Thank you, Madame Gris. You are too kind."

I admired the small stitches and elegant design. If handmade, it must have taken weeks to create. Perhaps worth more than the dress. The small delicate purse blended in with the elegant outfit better than anything I owned. After I put my hair up, I'd qualify as an extra on a Civil War film set.

With nothing to lose, I asked her about more clothes like this. "I am planning a trip and heard it requires period clothes. Maybe like this," as I lifted up the skirt. "Could I buy more like this from you? They don't need to be fancy, but I'm leaving on Friday. Another last-minute thing."

She looked at me as if imagining the cruise. "Of course. Come by tomorrow for another fitting."

Well, that worked out after all. I rode the mobbed subway uptown with the massive dress, new evening bag, and the largest fan I could find. I should have taken a taxi, but old habits were hard to break.

~ ~ ~

The ball was not at all like the West Village's Halloween parade. Everyone to my surprise followed through on the request to dress from the mid-19th century. And nothing looked cheaply made. These were all spectacular, couture outfits. Would they wear them again after tonight? But perhaps they do this all the time since they have the money.

Greg wore a large jacket he called a waistcoat with a bow tie. He thanked me again for accompanying him making me wonder how many women, besides his daughters, turned him down. I stopped offering to reimburse him for the dress and accepted it as a gift since it might be perfect for a fancy re-enactment dinner on the clipper ship.

Since the event commemorated his death, I joked to a few women, "If poor Turner saw us from his death bed dressed like this, he might wave us over to chat." But they didn't see the humor in it.

The party took place at the Plaza Hotel on Central Park South, not at the art museum. Greg explained that this happened often, but I was disappointed. I wanted to see the Turner paintings again.

"On Sunday after the exhibit had closed, they were removed. But, Kat, you can make a private appointment anytime to see my Turner."

The way he said it surprised me. Maybe it was the drinks. I laughed but tried to banish the idea that he was referring not just to the painting but his anatomy.

We were in the Plaza's large ballroom that resembled an embellished European castle. Our clothes matched the décor. If I blinked, I would have sworn I time traveled to the 1860's into a wealthy and privileged society.

When the ball ended, it was still early, so I agreed to go to his house to see his Turner. The night was so magical with exceptional food, music, and costumes that I didn't want it to end. All night I knew I should inform him about my upcoming trip, but I kept stalling.

On the way to his house safely hidden in the dark interior of his car, I knew I couldn't delay any longer. "A travel agency that specializes in unique vacations found a clipper ship leaving on Sunday from Denmark. I'm flying there on Friday. I still can't believe it, but my dream is coming true."

Greg was looking out the window but glanced back at me. "I'm surprised they found one. That's excellent news, Kat. I'm leaving tomorrow night for Paris, but I'll be back in about a week. How long is the trip, a couple of weeks?"

"No, about two months."

At first, he didn't react. I wasn't sure if he heard me, or maybe he didn't care. But then he repeated it with his voice escalating as he said it, "Two months? You're going on a two-month trip?"

Before I could answer, he asked, "But why? Why so long?"

"Well this is the only clipper ship they have leaving from Denmark, and it goes to Asia. So it's a long trip since the ship travels only by sail. Besides, I don't need to be back until January. Looking for a new job at the end of the year is a waste of time."

"But what about us? I wanted you to spend Thanksgiving with me at my place on Long Island."

I didn't know what to say. I didn't expect that Greg had made plans.

He didn't pause for a response. "Kat, that's a long time to be on a ship. What if you hate it or get seasick? In December, we could take a cruise together. I did some research on my own and wanted to tell you about a beautiful old sailing ship like a clipper in Havana. We could tour Cuba, something different you said you'd like. And I'll take sea sickness medicine to survive it."

"Oh, Greg that sounds fantastic, but I've already signed up. The time will go fast."

I felt guilty since I hadn't mapped out a future with him. This whole dating routine was all new. And now that I found my dream cruise, I couldn't give that up.

Kathleen's advice still echoed in my head: "How is he in bed?"

17 ~ Back In The Game

Pushing the sheets off my sweltering body, I slipped out of bed to find a glass of water. Greg's bedroom was dark, and I wasn't sure I could locate the bathroom without waking him. I still couldn't believe I was up close and personal with both Turners last night. And while the painting was, as always, breathtaking, the sex wasn't. Not awful, but different, as I guess it should be. At least I wouldn't be grilled by Kathleen anytime soon, and Abby was too polite to pry. His bedroom was large and opulent filled with expensive drapes, fabrics, and carpets.

Despite my efforts, Greg heard me. "Is anything wrong?"

"No, just thirsty and trying to find the bathroom." I was tired and wanted to sleep in or until he decided to get up, but it was strange being in bed with someone.

"On my side," and gestured to a doorway. I tiptoed trying to avoid stepping on my dress and Greg's clothes strewn over the floor.

Inside his Victorian-styled bathroom, matching the rest of his townhouse, I gulped down cold tap water from an ornate silver cup. Surprisingly, I recognized myself in the mirror and said under my breath, "Well, now you've done it."

I hadn't made 'a fine mess of things,' but this was a major turning point. Sex with Axel had ended months before he died. I didn't want to remember so never bothered to commit the exact date to memory.

I returned to bed after washing my face with cold water and self-consciously pulled the sheet over my naked body. I hoped I hadn't smudged Greg's expensive sheets with my makeup and wondered when he went to work. The alarm clock must be over on his nightstand since I couldn't see what time it was. I didn't wear my watch last night or bother bringing my phone to stay true to the 1860 period.

He leaned over on his side propping his head up on with his hand. "Did you enjoy last night?"

I rolled on my side to face him and said, "Yes, very much, thank you."

Was he referring to the ball, dinner, or sex? I'd enjoyed all three - a once in a lifetime, storybook night. And I was glad I broke my unintended celibacy with him, so there were no regrets. He was a gentle lover, but I didn't know if I could fall in love with him. In the darkness, I could only see his outline.

He reached over and kissed me, and I embraced him. He wasn't a stranger anymore, and I was slowly getting used to his touch. He whispered in my ear, "Have I changed your mind?"

He meant my trip. I wanted to pull away and say no, but I kissed him and didn't answer. The coward's way out.

~ ~ ~

Following the sound of a piano, I walked downstairs dressed in a Yale sweatshirt and gym pants Greg had loaned me. I was grateful for something else to wear besides my fancy ball dress. I hadn't thought ahead when I agreed to stay over.

Greg was on his phone and eating breakfast in the formal dining room. I hesitated at the door, but he waved for me to enter. His chef offered me coffee or tea. I thanked her and accepted coffee in a small, delicate cup, a teaser size for me. But to my relief, she placed a fancy coffee pot on the table.

The music flowed from his stereo. I was disappointed he wasn't playing the piano, but that would be odd to do before work. Greg was reading the New York Times and offered me the Wall Street Journal.

"No, thanks. I'm taking a break from all that." I never cared much for the Wall Street Journal even though it was the Bible for financial professionals. Except for some in-depth investigations and scandals, most financial reports were dull.

I sipped my coffee and looked around his ornate dining room listening to the music. I poured another cup of coffee while ignoring the homemade breakfast rolls, fruit, and cereal on the dining table.

Greg noticed. "You aren't eating."

"No, I'm not hungry this early. I prefer brunch." I waited for the typical lecture on how breakfast is the most important meal of the day, but he didn't mention it.

I noticed his dog on a small carpet in the corner of the room and took my coffee with me to pet him. I sat down on the floor next to him and whispered, "You aren't Useless, are you? No, Ulysses, a good boy."

Did he sleep down here last night? Maybe Greg, unlike me, didn't sleep with his pets. "Did you name him Ulysses because of the book?"

Greg lowered the papers to peer over at me. I must look odd sitting on the floor next to his dog wearing his gym clothes. "Yes, James Joyce was the greatest author of the 20th century, possibly ever."

Useless nuzzled my arm and wanted more petting, so I continued. "I'm sorry, Ulysses. I haven't read your book. Not yet, but I'd like to."

"Well, now you will have plenty of time, two months at sea, to read and broaden your education."

Greg tone was harsh and made me sound like I was illiterate. I read everything - books, magazines, and newspapers. My line of work required research and reading almost nonstop. Prepping to audit new business groups and keeping up with rapid changes in the industry kept me on a constant learning curve. Audit's educational requirements were often overwhelming, but I thrived on variety and challenges.

"Ready?" He wouldn't need to ask me twice, and I gave the dog a quick pat goodbye.

"I can take a cab home if it's easier."

"No, it's not. Go get your things." Greg sounded annoyed and started to pack his briefcase.

I ran upstairs to get my dress and handbag from last night and glanced one last time at his beautiful Turner ship painting from the Met now hanging in his bedroom. I'd probably never see it again.

"Please wish me luck, Mr. Turner. I may need it." I walked downstairs balancing my folded bundle - the dress with its petticoats, hoop skirt, and corset.

Greg called to his chef on the way out. "Take the afternoon

off. I have a client dinner tonight."

The sunlight was bright outside, and I blinked and squinted while I greeted his driver Rakesh. I didn't have sunglasses with me not needing them last night.

Rakesh drove skillfully around traffic and headed south on Fifth Avenue along Central Park and cut over to the Upper West Side. I thanked Greg again for a 'remarkable evening' trying to use the types of words he used. Awesome and fantastic weren't part of his vocabulary.

Greg stopped me, as I slid towards the door. Rakesh double parked and got out to open the door for me. "I wish you would reconsider, Kat. What if you took a series of shorter trips over a two-month period? At least I could see you."

"I'm already signed up, and it will go fast. But who knows? It may not work out after all, and I'll be back earlier."

"Kat, I understand the desire for wanderlust and adventure. Once I went to Singapore for a project, and two months turned into six. I came home when I could, but my wife was livid. I was so far away for too long. It was the beginning of the end of our marriage. My girls were young and forgot who I was."

His experience wasn't relevant to our situation. I hadn't even known him a week and based on his bad mood this morning; I wasn't sure I wanted to continue seeing him. His efforts to change my mind were having the opposite effect and made me more determined to see this through to the end.

A taxi's horn blared from behind us since the narrow one-way street was blocked by Greg's car. The timing of the yellow cab was perfect.

"Got to run." I kissed Greg quickly on the cheek and jumped out. "Thanks, Rakesh."

Right before the car door shut, he said, "Think about it, Kat. I don't want this to happen again, not to us."

~ ~ ~

Relieved to be home and in my own clothes again, I read an urgent email from Amber and called her back. She emailed me a ten-page attachment including sketches of 'acceptable' clothing. The dresses had big full skirts and looked like my dress last night. So at least I had one dress. But just in case, I printed the information to show Madame Gris.

Amber answered the phone on the first ring. "We booked a flight from JFK to Copenhagen via Heathrow on Friday night, but a new rule came into effect. Since this cruise is over sixty days and the ship is so old, MAX requires you get medical clearance. We just need a copy of your most recent physical from within the last year."

"But I haven't had one lately. And now with only 48 hours left there's not enough time!"

"Sorry, this rule is mandatory. This voyage is strenuous so you can't have any serious health issues. Some older clients got sick and had to be evacuated recently."

"But I'm not old. I'm only 47 and in excellent health. I work-out at the gym all the time."

"Sorry, Kat. Fine for me, but not the company."

But I can't get an appointment with my doctor in two days. I'd have to book it weeks ago. Do you have a suggested doctor I can use?"

Amber put me on hold again while I fumed. This problem was the glitch Greg counted on. He must have jinxed me. Ridiculous, but how else could things get so screwed up?

Amber said, "No, we don't have a suggested doctor. I emailed you the complete list of test results we need."

"Well, if this is required, I may not be able to do it in time." I played hardball, but she wasn't receptive. I would have to talk to her manager if this didn't work.

"Sorry. Let me know later today if you can't. I have to cancel the booking."

The familiar click and hum followed. Amber hadn't even waited for me to say goodbye. She was so smug and uncaring. Didn't she realize this trip meant everything to me? I might as well die if I don't go. If I could have reached out through the phone and grabbed her by the neck to shake some sense into her pea-sized brain, I would have.

Immediately I called my doctor's office getting the answer I feared. Unless I was critically ill, they couldn't see me. A physical for a trip overseas would have to wait until next week. I gave them my number begging to be notified if there was a cancellation. But they were overbooked today and the rest of the week so I shouldn't expect it.

I flung myself head-first on my bed and struggled to figure out what to do. My shoulder banged up against the clipper ship book left behind. I traced the clipper ship drawing on the cover with my finger outlining the beautiful ship with its white sails furled to catch the wind.

"Wait for me. I'm coming. I'm not giving up."

The ship was my white knight, and it would rescue me from all this. If Don Quixote can mistake windmills for giants, my ships can be men. And my ships were graceful, powerful, accommodating, and magical.

I got up determined again and googled some walk-in health clinics that had recently sprouted up around the city. One was just a few blocks away on Broadway, and the website said they handle routine physicals. I printed the email from Amber detailing the medical tests needed and ran over there.

The clinic was open, and I handed the list of tests I needed to the receptionist. She handed it over to the doctor who came out of the back office. The young physician, who looked like he was still a college student, took the list and said, "I can do most of the tests but not all. We don't have the right equipment for some. When do you need the results?"

"Today or as soon as possible. Which ones are problems?"

"We can do the STD, HIV, cholesterol, diabetes, and thyroid screening with a simple blood test and give you a tetanus and diphtheria booster shot and the flu and yellow fever vaccines. But we don't do pap smears or pregnancy tests."

"They need that too?" I hadn't bothered to look at the details in my rush to get this done. I'd need a gynecologist too.

"The T/D booster is suggested every ten years. When did you last have one?"

"I can't remember. Go ahead just in case."

My arms ached from giving blood for the tests and the shots. I started towards the subway and Madame Gris for more period clothes. But I shouldn't bother if this was all going to fall through. And I'd forgotten the period clothing email printout.

On my way home, I stopped by to see Abby who usually worked from home. She asked about the cruise, and I explained my medical predicament.

"Can it be any doctor?" she asked.

"Yeah, the travel agency doesn't care."

"How about asking Alberto or Matteo? They are doctors and might know someone who could squeeze you in."

"Perfect idea." I hugged her overcome with emotion.

She dialed Alberto's number and handed me the phone. But it went to voicemail, so I left a quick message.

"Try Matteo." She suggested and gave me his number.

This time, he answered, and I explained the two medical tests I need. He agreed to call me back. I tried to stay optimistic. Damn tests wouldn't destroy my plans.

~ ~ ~

When I arrived at Madame Gris's studio, it was still in a flurry of activity, and I dreaded a long wait. I explained to the receptionist I was here yesterday and knew where the racks and dresses were and what to get, so I didn't need help. But she was reluctant, so I had to wait.

My phone beeped. Matteo said he could get the two tests done for me later this afternoon.

One of the assistants I worked with yesterday heard me begging the receptionist a second time and said, "Come with me," and led me to the racks. "This isn't permitted, but I'm going to help you out." Then she disappeared.

I sped through the clothing racks, row upon row, to where the dresses were two days ago. But the rows were a maze, and I was lost searching for an exit.

Heat radiated from within. I fought it off but became engulfed. My head spun, and pale yellowish spots appeared out of nowhere and danced around. My legs softened, and I sank down on my knees to the hard, wooden floor.

A wet, squishy towel covered my eyes and forehead and then rubbed my cheeks.

Someone said, "Can you open your eyes?"

I opened my eyes but didn't recognize this voice or the woman either. "Miss, are you all right?"

"Of course, she isn't all right. She fainted."

That voice I recognized - Madame Gris herself. She sat on the floor, and her face was inches from mine. She scrutinized my face as if it might need some tailoring.

To prevent her from smoothing any wrinkles with a needle and thread, I propped myself on my elbows and said, "I'm all right. I had a blood test today and haven't eaten yet. I'll be fine."

Madame Gris said, "Glad that's all it is. Stay right where you are." She used a softer tone I didn't know she possessed. Two assistants hovered over me, and she barked some instructions.

"Bring the poor girl some water, juice, and whatever's left in the break room. A bagel or muffin."

They both scurried away to do her bidding while she yelled after them. "And if nothing's left, go buy something."

"I'm sorry, Madame Gris. You're so busy. I'm trying to find some more dresses like the one I wore last night. It was the most beautiful dress at the ball, so I had my prom."

"Ah, yes. Gregory's lovely young friend who missed her prom."

"Not missed. I was never invited."

She frowned when she heard that. "I trust last night made up for it."

I nodded. "Oh yes, very special."

One of her assistants returned with some water and said, "Mona's gone for a muffin. She'll be back soon."

I thanked her and gulped down the water. Madame Gris squatted next to me. I told her my predicament about the ship, the clothing from 1860, and how I must leave on Friday. I reached for my purse lying on the floor nearby and pulled out the paperwork to show her.

Madame Gris flipped through the pages and asked an assistant to check for hoop skirt dresses. But while she was looking, she said, "I fear we don't have any dresses like that left in stock. They were all bought for another ball. For some strange reason, they're insanely popular right now. And handmade so they take a week, and you don't have a week."

I stared at her trying to swallow more bad news.

"Go to the New Imperial Tailors on Mott Street. They use machines, but the Singers were mass produced back in 1850. They're incredibly fast with custom orders and inexpensive too. Ask Reception for the address."

Mona handed me a blueberry muffin and a plastic bottle of orange juice.

Madame Gris smiled and patted my arm. "Good luck, prom girlfriend," and disappeared.

I scarfed down the muffin and drank the OJ to rejoin the living.

18 ~ China Here I Come

Chinatown, my next destination on what felt like a never-ending scavenger hunt, wasn't far from Chelsea but not easy via subway, so I splurged on a taxi. The address on Mott Street for the New Imperial Tailors was anything but new in an old, rundown tenement building. The shop was on the fourth floor, and the elevator had an old sign stating it was 'out of service.' Probably permanently but I wasn't concerned and hurried up the stairs. A good sign since maybe they weren't overly busy and could handle my order.

A young Asian woman greeted me inside the open doorway. I looked around for racks filled with dresses. But I only saw a few clothes hanging with papers attached pending pick-up. Rows of large sewing machines hummed with seamstresses busy making clothes. I showed the smiling clerk the sketches of the dresses I needed by Friday. This didn't alarm her, or if it did, she didn't show it.

She quoted a reasonable price, much less than what I paid for an off-the-rack business suit, and asked how many. To pick fabrics, she took me to another room filled with ten-foot-long bolts arranged in rows and stacked from floor to ceiling.

These fabrics weren't luxurious but perfectly fine. The clerk suggested stronger cotton for daytime and silk for evenings. I selected some of my favorite colors: blue turquoise and greenish teal, the aquamarine colors of the ocean. I ordered additional blouses so now I had plenty to wear and will fit right in. Scarlett would be green with envy matching her infamous dress.

~ ~ ~

Like old times, Robert, Chee, and I were surrounded by our favorite Szechuan dishes on 39th Street, not from the bank where we met over four years ago. I worked with Robert in Internal Audit, and he introduced me to Chee to help with our infamous account investigation. Chee was from Hong Kong and still a citizen of China but worked as a quant under a special visa. Robert was second generation Chinese but one hundred percent Americanized.

Maneuvering my chopsticks, I grabbed a pot sticker and dipped it into the dish of spiced soy sauce and my mouth. I savored the flavors of pork wrapped in the delicate noodle. A plump little pillow of food, crispy on the outside, and soft and soothing inside.

"So, tell us more about your cruise," Robert said while he reached across to finish our appetizers.

"Yeah, we heard some from Mel but not much," Chee added.

The waiter brought our spicy dishes: shredded pork in garlic sauce, kung pao chicken with rice, and dan dan noodles. He placed them on the lazy Susan in the center of our table, so we could rotate them around and serve ourselves.

"I'm going on a beautiful old sailing ship called a clipper for about two months and back in January. The ship leaves from Copenhagen, Denmark, and arrives in Hong Kong where I'll get off and fly back home again."

I was busy spooning some of the food onto my plate. When I glanced up, Chee and Robert looked horrified.

I turned to look behind me worried something awful must have happened, but it looked ordinarily busy.

"Hong Kong? Are you nuts?" Robert said. And Chee looked at me and shook his head as if I had lost it.

"Oh, come on. Those guys, the drug dealers, are in prison. And this isn't like before. I'm not working or searching for them. I'll be okay. Not even noticed."

Chee shook his head. "No, it's not safe. You shouldn't go there. Maybe not ever again."

Robert started to eat again but stared at me as if this was hopeless.

"But why isn't it safe? I'm arriving on a ship, staying maybe a night or two in a nice hotel." At least I hoped it was a nice hotel. "And I'll leave the next day or so. No investigation or snooping around. I don't even have a job anymore."

Starved, I scooped up more food for my plate. I wasn't going to let these worry mongers scare me. I'd been through enough crap to get this far for my cruise, and I'm going. I'm not a wuss hiding behind my shadow. Even if they're out of prison, why would they bother monitoring old clipper ships for my arrival?

Robert stopped eating and said, "Big mistake. I sure wouldn't go back."

"Well, it's not like I said I wanted to go to Hong Kong. The ship's itinerary goes there, and I guess it's the closest major airport. Maybe I can get off at an earlier port and fly home from Bangkok or Manila. I'll ask. Would you be happy then?"

Chee started eating again apparently relieved I would avoid Hong Kong altogether.

Robert said, "Did you clear this with Jackson Chow? He'd give you sound advice."

Jackson was the FBI guy we dealt with on the drug dealing and money laundering investigation.

"No, I haven't talked to him in months. I think he left the agency."

"Yeah, he did, but I have his private number," Chee said. "You should call him." Chee pulled out one of his business cards, looked up Jackson's number on his smartphone, and wrote it on the back.

"But this isn't official business. Jackson won't want to get involved."

"He will. He's a friend. We stuck our necks out and helped him catch those guys. He owes us."

"You know, I'm not naive. They have drug buddies all over the globe, and when some go to prison, others pop up instantly to take their place."

The drug war was a no-win situation particularly against these powerful drug cartels, all depressingly apparent to me. The profits were too high to eliminate the illegal drug trade. If the demand continued from addicts like my brother, it would exist forever.

"Besides, if they wanted to kill me, I'd be dead already. The drug dealers could easily find me here. Right now, if they tried."

Chee said, "But the difference is you are going to their

home territory." He pointed his chopsticks at me with some bits of food still attached for emphasis. "You are tempting them and reminding them."

"Okay. Okay. I will try to change my destination port from Hong Kong. And I will call Jackson."

They both smiled now that I agreed to avoid Hong Kong.

We waited for the bill after cleaning the platters of every morsel. I told them more about the ship. How it's an old sailing ship called a clipper since it moves fast, 'at a clip' and the clothing from 1860's they wanted everyone to wear.

Chee said, "It sounds like those old ships the British used to bring opium in from India. The Chinese drug lords used small, nimble ships hidden along the coast, bought the opium from the British, and then sold it to Chinese locals."

"Well, I'm sure this isn't the case with my ship. Not in today's world. This ship would be subject to all sorts of inspections and rules."

"I hope so." Chee continued enlightening us. "They were beautiful ships, but it wasn't a glamorous time in our history. Over twenty-five percent of the Chinese population was addicted. Even the Emperor of China wrote letters complaining to the Queen of England. But nothing happened. The opium trade was too profitable. Fighting back just led to two Opium Wars which Britain won, further bankrupting my country."

Chee looked as if he was going to be sick. Was it the food? But then I realized it's only natural. His country and his ancestors, who he's still close to, must have suffered through this.

"I know. That was an awful time. But you know me. I would never step foot on a ship involved in drug laundering. That was the wild east over 150 years ago." I tried to reassure them that my ship and its cargo were law abiding. But how would I know until I got onboard?

"Well, I hope so. Or those guys will be there at the dock waiting, not for you but their shipment." Robert looked at his hands deep in thought.

Chee might understand with his more mystical side. "I have

to get away from my life here while I can. It's a perfect trip right now with a few months off. And Chee, the ship keeps sending me messages as if it's trying to find me too."

But Chee shook his head unconvinced. Behind them, a picture of a sailing ship was on the wall, not a majestic clipper, but a ship with sails.

"See, another sign," and I pointed behind them.

They both turned to stare.

Chee said, "That's a Chinese junk, not a British opium clipper."

"Still, it's a ship with a sail." And I laughed.

Out on the street, I gave them both hugs goodbye. "Please don't worry. I'll get in touch with Jackson, and let you know what happens."

19 ~ Up Close & Personal

I hurried north to the medical offices on West 57th Street in Midtown for my last two tests - the pregnancy test and dreaded pap smear. The receptionist gave me new patient paperwork to fill out. I quickly completed it but skipped some details that didn't seem relevant for a one-time exam.

While I waited, I called Amber. "You will be happy to hear I'm getting all the tests done today. The results should be ready today or tomorrow." But I was still annoyed and hoped it came through. "Is it possible to switch my last port from Hong Kong? Or get off at a port before Hong Kong?"

"You can ask the captain when you board. But your return flight will be booked via Hong Kong. You'll have to get there eventually."

I sighed and hung up. At least I could tell Robert and Chee I tried.

I was about to call Jackson when my phone rang. Charlie called from London to confirm our plans for Saturday.

"Sorry. I can't go. The travel agency found a cruise. I'm leaving on Friday."

"Already on Friday? How long will you be gone?"

"About two months. I'll be back after New Year's."

"What? You've got to be shitting me."

"No, I'm serious." I grinned. Serves Charlie right. "It's on an old sailing ship, so it takes a while for to get to Asia from Denmark."

"I'd say. Excuse me a sec, Kat."

He was talking to someone and shouted. "This is an important call. That can wait a sec."

"Sorry, Kat. One of our deals got snagged up. Things are crazy here."

He cleared his throat. "But I won't get to see you for two long months."

"I know, but this is a great opportunity and perfect timing for me. I can't pass it up. We'll go out when I get back." While

I'm gone, he could finalize his divorce and possibly learn how to be a nicer person.

"Yeah. Well, I've got to go. Sorry. I'll call you later."

Charlie hung up not waiting for me to say goodbye. What is it with people not exchanging a polite goodbye before hanging up? But I was relieved. He wasn't the right guy, so better to end it now.

"Nip it in the bud," as Kathleen would say. I wasn't a client or a deal Charlie needed to chase and close.

Matteo poked his head into the waiting room and gave me a quick air kiss on both cheeks. "Not much longer."

I dialed Jackson's phone number when a nurse asked me to follow her, so I hung up. She escorted me to a bathroom and handed me a small test tube with my name on it. Plastic cups were available for the fun task of pouring my urine sample into a test tube. I'd done this before but not for a pregnancy test. Such a waste of time but at least painless.

When I left the bathroom, she showed me the examination room across the hall and handed me a paper gown to put on. "Everything off, opening to the front, and the doctor should be with you in a moment."

I was in the typical exam room with the chair-bed and stirrups and wondered if she would do the examination. I preferred a female gynecologist but wasn't going to quibble. This exam had to be done today.

I undressed and put on the flimsy paper gown. But I knew about those 'moments' in a doctor's office. Nothing ever was a moment except for undressing and re-dressing. Last time, I waited about an hour in a room like this, so I might as well be productive.

I took out my phone again and called Jackson. We exchanged pleasantries for about five seconds. He was busy but said he was glad to hear from me. When I mentioned being in Hong Kong in January for few days, his tone changed from friendly to guarded.

"Kat, I'm not comfortable talking over a phone. Can we meet at the usual place? And if I'm not carrying my usual, stay away. Say around 10:30 tomorrow morning?"

Matteo knocked and opened the door. I felt odd being naked under the paper gown but raised my index finger, the universal sign to wait a second.

I told Jackson I'd be there, disconnected, and wrote a reminder: "10:30, Union Square, pizza box." Jackson wouldn't want me to write this down, but with all the stuff going on, I was afraid I'd forget it.

I apologized to Matteo. "Sorry. More logistics. This trip better be worth it."

"No problem Kat. Going away for two months. Better to be sure."

He must think it's all about the medical stuff. He had no idea. He wore a white doctor jacket and held a clipboard. Not at all like Zorro, this was a serious, official-looking Matteo. He surprised me by shutting the door and sitting down.

"When's the doctor coming? The gynecologist."

"That's me."

"You? But you aren't a GYN. You're doing research into addiction."

"I'm a trained doctor. All the other doctors are busy. If you want this done today, I need to do it."

This was so unexpected. I took a deep breath and couldn't help exhaling loudly in surprise.

"Kat, is this a problem?"

"Well, it's a bit weird. Don't you think?" Not wanting to admit it, but I kissed him romantically Sunday night. And here he was about to do a very personal exam. About as personal as it gets for a woman.

"No, it's the human body, and I've examined hundreds."

"I guess you're right. Okay, I'm ready." I wasn't going to let this test snag my trip.

Matteo had my paperwork and went over a series of questions. He asked about things I'd not bothered to fill out. If he continued being so thorough, he'd never finish this exam or for that matter his research.

He reminded me of how sometimes internal auditors got overwhelmed planning an audit. They spent days, sometimes weeks, doing research. Then the time budget was used on planning, so the actual audit testing and fieldwork were rushed. Problems weren't found, and the review was shoddy.

Matteo asked me about my last period, and I tried to remember approximately when that was. "About a month ago, I think. I'm 47. Starting menopause."

He stopped to look at me. "That would be early. Typically, at fifty menstruation ends, and then a year later it's official."

"Yeah, I know. But it's fine with me." Not having children was deliberate. Being pregnant would hurt my back and create serious issues with sciatica. Axel and I agreed on no kids from the beginning. I still didn't regret it, even with him gone. I would be an awful mother since I just wasn't interested and didn't have the time.

"Did you stop using birth control? You didn't mention anything here."

How much does he need to know? But I should appease him. "I stopped about ten years ago when my husband had a vasectomy. We'd heard about the side effects from the pill, and we didn't want kids."

"Oh, I see."

But he didn't. He wore an impassive doctor mask. He was the macho type who would never have a vasectomy. He probably wants a big family or has some kids. I knew so little about him, and his life back in Italy.

I'd had unprotected sex with Greg last night. He didn't have a condom or couldn't find one. I hadn't worried about it, and he didn't climax so I couldn't get pregnant. Since Dr. Matteo wasn't shy about asking me all these personal questions, why not ask the professional?

"Do you think I need to take birth control?" I hadn't needed it before. I was a wife who never strayed, despite having some uncomfortable offers from men at work. At work, women were outnumbered, and some of the men wanted to prove themselves. But after last night and if I started dating more, maybe I should.

"At your age, the odds you could get pregnant are slight. You have fewer eggs now, and they often contain chromosomal abnormalities."

Abnormalities? As in *Abby Normal* in the film *Young Frankenstein*? I grinned remembering one of Axel's favorites movies. "But what about the women you hear about in their fifties, even sixties, who are pregnant?"

"Are you worried about getting pregnant?"

"Not really, but you hear about it."

"Like I said, your chances are insignificant and less than one percent. Pregnancies over forty were from donor eggs, either their own or from someone else. The best time for a pregnancy is in your twenties or early thirties."

So that explains it. And now, the inevitable, not-so-fun part, was beginning. Matteo lay a sheet over my waist and legs and asked me to slide down on my back to the edge and put my feet in the stirrups. Exactly what all my gynecologists told me to do over the past twenty years. But this was unnerving.

"What happened here?" He traced with his finger a small area near my right hip. I had a four-inch scar on my lower right side that the surgeon placed below my bikini line. Not that it mattered, I was in so much pain I wasn't debating where he made an incision.

"I had an appendectomy about twenty years ago."

"You didn't mention it on your form under surgeries."

"Oh, I forgot." To be more transparent and honest, I added, "They thought I had appendicitis. But it wasn't. It might have been a kidney stone."

"Poor Kat, that's painful. I've heard it's like being in labor non-stop."

"Yeah. Nothing I'd want to go through again."

Matteo warned me about the cold metal speculum to collect skin cells or whatever for the test. "I'll follow it with my finger." At least it was quick and painless.

He asked if he should do a rectal exam.

In a full state of panic, I answered quickly, "No, thank you."

"Fine. It's part of the examination, but not necessary for this request."

I peered up at him, and he referred to his notebook perhaps following a list of what to do.

"I assume you don't want a breast exam to screen for

cancer."

"Nope, thanks. Good there too."

He smiled, and our eyes met. "You are taking some of the fun out of this, Kat."

If he expected me to laugh, I couldn't. Being in this position was the worst. The exam must be over. I pushed back with my feet and sat up trying not to rip the paper gown covering the last bit of dignity I had left.

"All done?"

"Yes, unless you have any other requests?"

Was he dense or something? I didn't need or want anything else except to get dressed and home. Even if he was the most attractive gynecologist on the planet. "I'm good. When should the results be ready?"

I slid off the examination table and reached down to pick up my clothes while holding my paper gown together.

"Either later today or tomorrow morning. Do you want to wait until they are ready?"

"No, tomorrow works fine. I'll get dressed now."

He stood there waiting as if I would do this in front of him. I may be quick but not that fast, and I needed my privacy after that exam. "Dr. Matteo, how much do I owe you for this?"

"Nothing. How do you say, it's 'on the house'? But I have a request. Have dinner with me tonight."

"Tonight?" But it was Wednesday and my three-hour workout marathon. I checked my watch. If I got out in the next fifteen minutes, I might make my kick-boxing and sword fighting classes. The third class was weights but that I could skip.

He waited, and I knew it was lame, even rude, to say I had a date with my Romanian gym instructor to push me past my limit for three hours.

"Can we meet later? Around nine p.m.? I have some gym classes tonight. My last chance for a while."

"Nine is perfect Italian time. Ciao."

As soon as he left, I scrambled into my clothes and out the door in about two seconds.

~ ~ ~

Matteo's choice for dinner was a combination upscale Italian delicatessen and restaurant nearby on Amsterdam Avenue. The waiter greeted us speaking Italian with Matteo. We were seating in a secluded and romantic nook with the deli counter only a few feet away.

I'd been here before, but tonight with an attractive Italian was different. I didn't want to think about it being another date and swigged down my first glass of red wine to calm my nerves.

We looked at our menus, and Matteo asked, "What would you like?"

I would usually study the line-up, and make my decision. But after rushing around all day and my two-hour gym workout, I was worn out. It was nearly ten p.m., and I'd be in bed watching TV exhausted and eating dinner. "Why don't you order? I'm sure I'll like it all."

I leaned back against the padded bench and let the ambiance of the darkened restaurant cover me anticipating the culinary surprises. I wanted to imagine being on vacation in Italy.

This restaurant didn't serve typical bowls of pasta but individual small plates of Italian delicacies, like Spanish tapas. We feasted on never ending dishes of feather light carpaccio, fritto misto, grilled radicchio, cheeses, seafood, and meats. I sampled everything placed before us, and it slid down my throat with the gentle push of a red Chianti.

We finished with a cupful of blood orange panna cotta accompanied by an Italian dessert wine called Vin Santo, the Saint's wine in English. Matteo, the good Catholic, made the sign of the cross before drinking it, and I did too. If Matteo had asked me to convert then and there, I probably would have after this heavenly meal.

20 ~ *La Dolce Notte*

Staring at the ceiling Thursday morning, I was hungover and annoyed since this wasn't my ceiling. I must stop letting myself getting talked into things. Not that it wasn't enjoyable, but I didn't have the time or energy right now.

Last night was a fantasy. I was briefly an Italian with an attractive man and lucky to be noticed. Like eating the most mouth-watering, flavor-packed slice of tiramisu dessert, you could imagine. But something you have once in a blue moon. And not something I'd ever attempt to make at home, or believe I could since it would never measure up. That summed up Matteo.

Matteo was lying on his side with his back towards me. His back was beautiful matching the rest of him. He reminded me of the Roman statues I'd rushed by at the museum on Saturday. But he wasn't missing his penis or anything else. I could confirm everything was there. I'd become familiar with every inch of his body. Matteo was built like a Roman god without any fat or loose skin. He must have superior Italian genes.

Last night after dinner, we returned to my apartment. I wanted to return the book I'd borrowed about clipper ships and show him why I was so excited about my trip. Showing him the clipper ship illustrations and trying to explain how it all works wasn't easy after sharing a bottle of wine and drinks. When he saw the pictures, he wasn't excited but warned me about the dangers at sea. How far I'd be from medical facilities or doctors on such a small ship and long journey. But I shrugged them off.

And then it happened. We kissed. Axel smiled down at us from his perch on the shelf, and I froze. Matteo convinced me to come upstairs to his place. He probably wasn't comfortable under Axel's watchful eye either.

When we got to his apartment, we were laughing, and I bet the Roman god of wine named Bacchus was too. Matteo picked me up and carried me over the threshold into his apartment. Like newlyweds, which we weren't and I had no intention of ever being again, but I didn't care. I was floating on air after being charmed all night, and what must be a primal desire pulled me to him. I was intoxicated, not only from the wine but now that my cruise was a reality.

The only disturbing part of the night was when he pulled a small case from under the bed and asked if I was interested in any of his toys. He had an array of colorful dildos, vibrators, and all sorts of sex toys. But when I glimpsed a pair of silver handcuffs, I shivered. Handcuffs weren't toys, not after what I'd been through, and I started to leave. He sensed my fear and put them away while whispering reassurances and kissed me to convince me to stay.

My five minutes were up. I couldn't lay here and re-live the entire night again, even if it was special. I'd do that later if, or more likely when, I was bored at sea. Matteo noticed I sat up and reached out to hold me in his arms wanting to cuddle again. I forced myself to ignore him.

"Morning, sleepyhead. I've got to get going. Go back to sleep."

"Kat, don't leave yet. What time is it?"

"About eight. I must go. Too much to do for my trip. I'm sorry."

"One quick hug goodbye, please Kat."

I wanted to, but he may not limit it to a hug.

"And you're leaving me. I may never see you again."

"I'll be back in January." I slipped on my underwear.

Matteo's eyes looked sad, and he was right. I may never see him again. He explained last night his work might last about a year. He was on a special visa with grants supporting him, and when the money ran out, he'd have to return to Milan.

I leaned over to hug him and touched his skin. He was still naked under the sheet. His skin was soft but firm. He kissed me still tasting of red wine and garlic.

"Bad breath, I know. I'm sorry." But he ignored my apologies, and his tongue searched and found mine.

"Mine's the same." He kissed me more passionately, this time, moving down uncovering my breasts. "Was it as good as you remember?"

"What do you mean?" I was annoyed that his implication that I'd stayed chaste for him.

"Well, I heard you hadn't had sex for a while, and I'm glad to be the one."

"What? Who told you that? And whoever did is wrong, I've had sex."

I couldn't believe he'd said something so personal and rude. He lifted his head up, and I quickly put my legs together blocking access.

"Ah, I know, you have with me." He rested his chin on my stomach and looked me with sleepy but kind eyes.

"No, someone else, before." I didn't want to argue or explain I'd had sex the night before with Greg. My dry spell was a long time, and I didn't want him to think I was desperate and sleeping with anyone.

"Oh, good. How was it?" He asked reminding me of how he asked his doctor-patient questions yesterday.

"Fine, but it's none of your business." I pushed his head to the side and looked around for my underwear again. Finding them under the sheets, I slipped them back on and stepped into my jeans before he got any more ideas.

He rolled over on his stomach propping himself up on a pillow watching me.

"Touchy. Doesn't sound like it was that good. No *fuochi d'artificio*?"

I wasn't sure what he meant by this. I pulled my knit top over my head. He rolled over onto his back and was opening and closing his fists and making popping noises like a game of charades.

"Do you mean fireworks?"

"Yes, fireworks. Exactly."

"Well, no fireworks," as I sat on the bed to pull on my boots. I could tell Matteo was dying to hear more. What the hell, I can be honest.

"He didn't come."

"Didn't ejaculate? Oh no. How disappointing," he said chuckling.

"Not for me. But he wasn't happy about it."

Greg was frustrated and apologized even though I said it didn't matter. The alcohol from the ball didn't help, and we were both tired. He's old and probably in his sixties. But at least, he didn't need Viagra.

"Oh. I can only imagine. I've never had that happen. At least not yet." He looked down at his penis as he lay there in the full Monty pose. "Poor man, but at least there are medical treatments to help."

I didn't want to tell him more personal details about Greg or my limited sex life.

"Is he your boyfriend? I didn't know you had one."

"No. A close friend." Greg's style included nothing oral but kisses in expected places without any supplemental toys or games. Plain, straight, simple, vanilla sex. Matteo would call it boring. He probably found sex with me dull after I refused to play with his toys. I wouldn't be here right now if Greg were my boyfriend. Didn't he realize I couldn't be unfaithful?

"Kat, please, come back here. I want to give you some more ... what did you call it?"

He motioned by closing and opening his fists in the air again.

"Fireworks?" Even though he was the best lover I'd ever had, I didn't have the time.

I leaned down to give Matteo a quick goodbye kiss, and he said something in Italian in my ear. I had no clue what he said. It should be 'to get my fat ass out of here.' But whatever he said, it was a devilish trick, and I was under his spell again.

21 ~ *Action À La Jackson*

I wandered through Union Square looking for a man with a pizza box - special agent and former FBI guy Jackson Chung. Through the grapevine, I'd heard he broke some unwritten rules to help us out when we were in a bind, especially me. Now I was here to find him and make Robert and Chee happy. But a big part of me was curious to see Jackson again after so many years.

The rain let up, but it was chilly typical November weather. This square was a major shopping venue, and I planned to do just that afterward. I scanned the area hoping Jackson saw me and would signal it was safe to meet. A major subway hub was underneath the park, so it was always crowded here around this square. I circled around the park to see if he was outside on a bench.

Someone said, "Psst."

"Jackson?" The man didn't look like him, but it was about two years since I last saw him.

"Yeah," he said so low I could almost not hear him. I forced my tired brain to concentrate and remember his instructions. I learned the hard way not to write down what he told me.

"Meet me at the Coffee Cafe on the west side."

"Sure." I walked across the park eager to meet him there. My stomach growled thinking about their yummy banana pancakes. After my unexpected exercise with Matteo this morning, I was ravenous.

I arrived before Jackson and told the waitress a friend was joining me, or at least I hoped so. On a weekday, the restaurant wasn't crowded, and she led me to a booth. I was enjoying my new freedom from work with lunch whenever and wherever. I hoped he would sit with me, but from the strange way he was acting, he might sit at another booth with his back to me like we did once.

Don't be silly. This time, it won't be cloak and dagger. Not today at a restaurant in New York City on a quiet Thursday.

I begged the waitress for coffee and studied the menu. Those pancakes were gone, but I found something better: Eggs Norway in a benedict-style with smoked salmon. My all-time favorite Mexican breakfast, huevos rancheros, tempted me, but Scandinavia won. I'll be sick of smoked salmon a week after I arrived there, but I doubted they'd have eggs benedict. Danish breakfasts were usually cold - granola, yogurt, and bread with cheese.

Startled by some sudden movement, Jackson now sat across from me. I hadn't heard a thing.

"Oh, you surprised me." But I smiled since dramatic entrances were embedded in his nature.

"Yeah, comes with the territory." He grinned with a sly look on his face.

With Jackson, everything was super secretive, even how he talked. He looked about the same, maybe a few more gray hairs, but still had intense dark eyes.

He checked around. "Let's trade places."

We switched sides, and now he had a better view of the front door and entrance.

Since I knew what to order, I watched him. He looked at his menu briefly and returned to maintaining a vigil not just on the front door but all around. Was this necessary or a bad habit?

"Heard about Axel. Sorry, seemed like a good guy. I would have been at the funeral, but duty called." He lifted his hands as if everything was out of his control. "Lung cancer, right? Sucks big time."

"Yeah, lung cancer. Ironic since we didn't smoke, but Axel's Dad and his old girlfriend were smokers. There wasn't a funeral. He didn't want one."

Jackson stared into my eyes, and I detected a hint of sympathy. His compassion surprised me since he was such a matter of fact guy, dealing with murder and mayhem all the time. What was his average week like, and who did he work for now? But if it's like what I went through with the bank and Hong Kong, forget it. I wouldn't want to read a book about it much less re-live it.

"What's this I hear about you going to Hong Kong? Why would you want to do something so stupid?"

I frowned not liking the way this conversation started or his tone. "I'm going on a cruise on a beautiful clipper ship leaving Denmark for Asia. It stops in various ports in route, and Hong Kong happens to be the last one. But the itinerary is not fixed, and the travel agency said I could get off at any time."

I omitted that my flight was out of Hong Kong, so I'd still need to get there.

"Sounds fishy." He cracked a smile at his lame joke.

"Ha, ha. But the fish are under the ship, and I'm on it. And I must do this. Go on this trip. A well-deserved break from all this." I waved my hands in the air as if I was trying to escape.

The waitress must have noticed my arm waving and came to take our order. Jackson put a finger to his mouth to remind me not to discuss anything while she was near us. He ordered an omelet with cheese. I hesitated until he prompted me that it was safe to speak and ordered my Norwegian eggs.

"This trip isn't related to work. I know the drug dealers are still out there. They'll never disappear. Do you really think they'd have a problem with my brief visit?"

"Yeah, I do. If those guys knew, they definitely would."

"But Jackson, why? I don't even have a job anymore. My only dealings with banks the past two years has been sucking money out to pay expenses. I'm not there to do anything."

"It's simple. You embarrassed them."

The waitress dropped off our order, and when she left, I was ready to argue. "But it wasn't just me. There were others. You, Robert, Chee, even Mel."

Jackson had a big mouthful of omelet but waved his fork to emphasize whatever he was about to say. "Yeah, but you were their de-facto leader. They'll remember you. You, a ghost woman, humiliated them. You and Mel aren't Asian, and you in particular stick out with your blonde hair and blue eyes."

I knew what he meant. A foreigner was called a ghost, and I was a woman who fought back. Both didn't go over well.

"But Jackson, I don't think there is anything I can do. It's too late to change my trip, and I can't miss this. It's something

I must do. I have to find my mojo again." I didn't want to tell him how ready I'd been to give it all up. "And this trip is for Axel too. I'm meeting his brother in Copenhagen to scatter some of his ashes."

"Copenhagen isn't the problem. Skip Hong Kong." We stared at each other for about a minute. Neither of us was backing down. "Oh, Kat. Stubborn as always. I knew it."

Jackson reached into his pocket and took out a tiny one-inch metal cylinder that looked like a dime. He put his hand over it and slid it across the table to me.

"Don't open it. In fact, don't open it unless you get to Hong Kong and something happens, and you need help. Inside you will find some names and numbers but no email. And again, don't call them unless you are in a bind. This isn't for I need help with a dinner reservation."

I took it from him as discretely as I could and stuck it my wallet's change purse.

"Sure. Thanks, Jackson." I knew what he meant. Only use the information if I'm being followed, threatened, or in danger of being kidnapped. I swallowed hard. I'd learned the hard way.

To change the subject, I told him more about the magical cruise. "I'm bringing some period clothes from 1860 to re-enact when the clipper ships used to sail to Asia."

Jackson cased the restaurant again. "This square has a history dating back to the 1860's too. I know, a strange bit of trivia. I was a history major."

"Was Union Square related to the Civil War?" I was curious about the time-period I was going to re-enact.

"Yep. One of the largest public gatherings with over 250,000 people demonstrating the fall of Fort Sumter captured by the Confederates. That led to the start of the Civil War."

I didn't know this about New York. But I'd visited some Civil War sites and battlefields in other parts of the country.

"You know Kat, the 1860's weren't pleasant. Sea battles even took place in Europe. We lost more Americans in that war than all the others. Why anyone would want to imagine going back there. Well, it blows my mind."

My second great-grandfather died during the Civil War. He was too old to serve but went to see his oldest son in the Louisiana Calvary. The family story was he fell ill and died, but no one knew how or where he died or if he was ever buried.

"I know, but the Civil War isn't associated with this trip. I'd prefer to stay dressed in jeans. But if I must wear long dresses a few times to go on one of these beautiful sailing ships, I'm doing it."

"Aren't there other beautiful sailing ships around?"

"Not like this. And, it's all set up. It's not a luxury cruise. But I'm up for an adventure while I'm relatively young and still can."

He shook his head, and his eyes disarmed me. "I'd swear you'd had enough adventure in Hong Kong to last a lifetime."

I switched topics while he finished his omelet. Other things were more worrisome than my little cruise and a brief stay in Hong Kong. "I've heard how widespread fentanyl use is now. It's making heroin and cocaine look like child's play."

Matteo explained last night more about his addiction studies into illegal drug use, specifically fentanyl. He said it was scary epidemic no one wanted to discuss. But he was optimistic and said, "If we can break the addiction, the game is over. That's why I have grants to study this."

Jackson was to the point, not so optimistic, but real. "Yeah, it's a fucking madhouse out there." He wiped his mouth with his napkin as if this would wipe off his disgust.

He was done eating and flagged down the waitress while pushing my cash back at me.

"Keep it. You may need it for your trip. Chee told me your consulting biz closed. When you're back, let's meet again. I want you to consider working with my team."

"Your team? But I don't have training using guns and all that." I could feel my voice tighten just by the idea.

"We need fraud and forensic investigators to help us sort through the paper trails. Banks aren't the only ones under attack. Now they're targeting Swift."

Swift was a group that oversaw cross-border payments for the banks. If terrorists infiltrated it undetected, we were all in trouble. Jackson knew what was happening. Some stories never hit the press as part of so-called national security to prevent widespread panic. Publicizing the details hampered finding and stopping the criminals.

"You're a CPA, right?" He asked.

"Yeah, but I never practiced. I don't like doing the boring accounting side of internal audit."

"This isn't accounting; it's forensic science. And it's anything but boring."

"Well, if it doesn't involve guns and shooting people, I'll talk to you about it in January."

"Good. Glad to hear it. I'm leaving now. Wait ten minutes before you leave. I'm in between secure workplaces, so we had to meet here. No hugs or displays. It's safer for you that way."

"Okay, Jackson. And thanks again. Please be careful. I'd hate to lose you too."

"Back at you, babe." And with that he didn't just leave, he vanished. Typical Jackson.

I tried to sit still for ten minutes. The café wasn't busy so I could wait at our booth.

Jackson was right. I stood out in Asia. I racked my brain for a solution. I needed a disguise. I'd packed away my new Catwoman outfit but remembered seeing my Japanese kimono robe for a geisha costume with an Asian style wig. It made my head itch, but that was nothing like the pain of a bullet.

22 ~ The Lake House

As I cut across Union Square to shop, my phone rang. I was surprised to hear Greg's voice when he should be in Paris or on his way.

"My flight leaves tonight. Have lunch with me, Kat. Please. I have a goodbye gift for you too. I'll swing by in the car and get you."

"But I'm in Union Square doing some shopping." I still wasn't certain I wanted to see him.

"Perfect. That's on the way, and a late lunch works best for me. We'll pick you up on the southwest corner at one."

I hurried to see what deals I could find in an hour. At least, I wouldn't have to lug my purchases home on the subway. Greg's black Lincoln was waiting at the corner when I descended from the store carrying two large shopping bags. I was ten minutes late with the slow check-out line.

Rakesh, his driver, said hello and opened the trunk to store my bags. Rakesh was a great guy and always upbeat.

Greg was on the phone when I climbed into the car, but when he hung up, he gave me a friendly kiss on the lips.

"You've been busy shopping."

"All for less than a hundred dollars. I save lots of money there." I beamed with pride at my scavenging skills.

He looked amused but was probably wondering how he ended up with someone like me. I bet his ex-girlfriend, Patricia, never stepped foot in my favorite discount shops. Or if she did, only after spending thousands on one dress, and for her, one that didn't fit.

"I'm glad you could join me for lunch. Here's your gift."

He handed me a package wrapped with fancy ribbons and paper. Almost too pretty to unwrap, but I ripped it open. I uncovered three reproduction prints of J.M.W. Turner seascapes, including one of his painting.

"I wanted to have them framed, but I ran out of time. But you could take the prints on your trip. Turner might brighten up your cabin and remind you of me."

"An excellent idea, but I hope they won't get damaged." I gave him a quick thank you hug and kiss.

He whispered, "I haven't given up hope you'll return after a week or two."

"I know, and maybe I will." But I wasn't the type to give up without a fight. The cruise would have to be terrible for me to get off at the next port and find my way home. But anything was possible, and it could happen. Sometimes I regretted being so stubborn and not cutting my losses.

"Once I was on a week-long cruise in Brazil during *Carnaval,* the annual celebration before Lent, for my fortieth birthday with my husband and some friends. The entire ship was overrun with young, wealthy and loud Brazilians partying all night. We couldn't sleep with all the noise, and after a few nights, we wanted to get off the ship."

"Did you?" He looked curious and eager to hear more.

"No, but we tried. We wanted to get off at Salvador, the next port, about halfway through the cruise. But we couldn't get back to São Paulo for our return flight. Because of the holidays, everything was either shut down or fully booked – trains, cars, hotels. We were stuck on the ship. When we returned to São Paulo, I must have slept twenty hours non-stop."

"Well, I'd like you to come back early, but because you wanted to, not because you're miserable."

But I didn't think that would happen again. I didn't want to be home and forced to make plans for Thanksgiving and Christmas. Greg or Matteo may be dating other people. I'd rather stick it out on the ship unless it became unbearable.

"Are we going to your house for lunch?" I asked looking out the window as we headed north. Midtown's rain clogged streets were filled, not just with the city's residents, but the millions of bridge and tunnel commuters.

"No, another surprise." His phone rang, and he apologized, but he had to take it. I checked my phone, and I had a text from Charlie. He was coming home from London today and wanted to see me before I left.

I debated for a few minutes and looked out at soggy umbrella-filled Manhattan. Having a private car was convenient even if it was over the top. I didn't have any plans tonight. Everyone I asked said they were busy tonight. Charlie was well-behaved on Monday and thought my trip was a good idea too. Why the hell not?

"Okay," I texted back hoping I wouldn't regret it.

Rakesh parked on a side street adjoining Central Park on the Upper East Side and opened the door for us. I wanted to open the door myself but waited since Greg didn't like that.

"Let him do his job," Greg said. But it was silly. I could easily open a car door. Why bother the poor man? Driving in all this traffic was enough stress.

The rain stopped, and the sky started to lighten up. Greg noticed and said, "The gods are thoughtful today." If he considered it kind to not have to use an umbrella, I'd agree, but not in general. Most gods played mean tricks on us, so I wasn't fond of them.

Greg took my hand, and we crossed Fifth Avenue into the park. I buttoned my jacket and tightened Axel's cashmere scarf to stay warm. We wound our way along the wet walking path and past the pond used for model boats in good weather.

We passed the statue of the Danish fairy tale author Hans Christian Andersen, reminding me of some trivia. "When the architects built this park, they didn't want it to be littered with statues."

"That was their intention, but it now has about thirty. Even the best-laid plans can go awry."

He was probably referring to my plans for my trip, and I clenched my jaw preparing for more complaints.

"Kat, I need to explain. I wasn't in a good mood yesterday morning, and I want to apologize."

Greg stopped walking, and I stood next to him. He put his hand on my elbow. I nodded but didn't respond. He was in a lousy mood yesterday, and if he hadn't begged, I wouldn't have met him for lunch today.

"I know this isn't a polite question, but how old are you, Kat?"

"Forty-seven."

"You're older than you look. I'm 66. I've never dated someone so much younger."

I shivered chilled to my core. I didn't see the need to discuss our ages. I stamped my feet and flexed my fingers to get the blood flowing again.

"You're cold. Let's continue walking, and I'll tell you on the way. We're almost there."

He put his arm around me, and we walked side by side towards the restaurant. His warm wool coat and moving again made a huge difference. We were nearing the Lakehouse restaurant near the center of the park, but I wasn't going to ruin his surprise by telling him.

Greg continued, "I spoke with my therapist yesterday about our relationship. I've stopped myself several times, but I'm attracted to you. I was anxious when you stayed the night."

Why did he talk to a therapist about us? I didn't want to know the details and debated walking straight home. I'd seen a therapist once. Mel dragged me from my bed when I refused to leave home a week after Axel died. But it didn't do me any good. A waste of my time and money.

I stopped, and he did too and glanced around. Greg put his hands on my shoulders and stared into my eyes. "You've said being a widow is hard. I don't want to put you through that again. I'm in good health, so I should live to be at least eighty. Maybe another twenty years. My therapist said the average marriage only lasts about eight years."

We started towards the restaurant, but his comments were confusing.

"Kat, what I am trying to convey is that I care deeply for you. If you give me a chance, I can make you happy."

"Thanks for your honesty. The age gap doesn't bother me, but my life is so different from yours. You are so wealthy, accomplished, and I'm -"

He tapped my nose and interrupted me politely. "You have no idea how perfect you are."

I was far from perfect, more imperfect than perfect. But I didn't want to argue or explain. I wanted a boyfriend but nothing serious. One husband was it for me. When I'm back, I'll explain if he wasn't already started dating someone else.

"*Voilà*," he said when we arrived. If I did continue seeing him, I'd need to learn French.

"An old boat house was the appropriate send off when I couldn't arrange a ship. Boating activity on the lake started in the 1850's, the heyday of the Clippers. But I'm afraid, this building only dates from the 1920's and was re-built in the 1950's."

He could probably tell me exactly how it was built and re-done. An architect would enjoy all those details.

"Yes, it's a great surprise, perfect for my trip." I pulled him towards me to kiss him, but he turned his face, and I only grazed his cheek. Was someone nearby he didn't want to see? He only kissed me on the lips when we were alone.

I ordered their braised tuna salad, their take on a French *Salade Niçoise* for lunch. He surprised me by ordering the twin burgers, upscale sliders, and so American. We shared a bottle of pinot noir from California.

I teased him he was eating and drinking American, not French since the gourmet dishes were waiting for him in Paris. I stole some of his fries like I did with Axel's. But Greg didn't mind and teased me that he liked a girl with an appetite. But could he satisfy mine?

The lunch was a delicious treat, and our conversation, more Greg's than mine, covered fascinating topics - art, architecture, and New York. We avoided talking about my trip. The wine loosened me up, and I didn't want our meal to end. I rarely drank at lunch but I was in a vacation mindset, and we didn't have to go back to work.

Outside the restaurant, he showed me a bronze statue. I'd walked by it hundreds of times but never noticed it. The sculpture was of a man and a woman in a row boat from the 1960's.

"I hope you will think of me while you're gone. And when you return, and we have the weather for boating, I want to take you out on the lake. Like the couple in this sculpture."

I smiled. "I'd love that."

23 ~ *Service Without The Smile*

Greg's driver, Rakesh, maneuvered Greg's car through the traffic and the jumbled roadways like an expert. We drove over the busy Triborough Bridge across the East River leaving Manhattan behind to cut through Queens County. JFK airport was only twenty miles away but took over an hour with all the traffic.

After the wine and perfect meal, I'd agreed to accompany him to the airport. The car inched along in the brutal afternoon traffic. Being tipsy from too much wine was the only rationale excuse I could find for my stupidity. And it was annoying since I had to make this same long drive for my flight tomorrow. Greg must have sensed my irritation. He squeezed my hand and thanked me for coming along.

Frank Sinatra's greatest hits were playing on the car's stereo and the bittersweet lyrics from the song's *Somewhere Beyond the Sea*. I'd heard the song many times but never realized Sinatra was singing about being unhappy at sea, separated from his lover, vowing to return and never go to sea again.

"You see, even Sinatra doesn't think your cruise is a good idea."

I wasn't regretting my voyage, but this ride to JFK with so many things to do.

Greg put his hand on my leg and kissed me. "If you don't enjoy the cruise, fly back from whatever port. I'll arrange it. We could spend the holidays at my weekend house."

"Another house?"

"I spend my weekends in Sands Point. I was only in town last weekend for the Turner exhibit and decided to host the dinner party."

"Where's Sands Point?" I'd never heard of this place.

"On the North Shore."

"On Long Island?"

The North Shore of Long Island was the infamous Gold

Coast where the top of the pyramid lived. Not the one percent but a tiny sliver of one percent - hard to imagine, much less calculate. Compared to the Gold Coast, the Hamptons were filled with nouveau-riche beach bums. Gauche Hamptonites like Charlie amused by how outclassed he'd become. I'd been there before to visit a friend with a modest, but pricey cottage-style home.

"Yes, that fictionalized area where Gatsby lived. But I can assure you, the parties are not that glamorous." He put his arm around me and pulled me closer. "So many things I'd like to show you, Kat. Places we must go when you return. I know it won't be easy for us, but I'm genuinely fond of you."

He leaned forward and said something to the Rakesh and closed the tinted privacy window that separated the front seat from the back.

Frankie was belting out his song *Come Fly with Me* while Greg whispered, "I wish you were flying with me to Paris." He kissed my neck. "I suppose you don't have your passport with you?"

I shook my head. "No, I have to go on my trip."

I squirmed when I realized this wasn't going to be an ordinary trip to the airport. Not that I objected to trying again, but it was the strange surroundings. I tried to remember when I last had sex in an automobile. Some heavy petting in college, but that car was parked in a secluded area. And in New York, I didn't own a car or want one.

"Kat, it's all right," Greg whispered tickling the inside of my ear. "He can't see or hear us."

I tried to relax and enjoy his kisses. Closing my eyes, I leaned back against the plush leather seat using my purse as a pillow. I wasn't sure I wanted to see this.

He pulled off my wet boots and jeans and wasn't as prudish as I'd classified him. I tried to enjoy his attention down below as the car crawled along in heavy traffic. I hoped he wasn't going to ask for reciprocal treatment and was relieved to hear plastic ripping. He asked if I was ready, and I nodded. As ready as I ever would be in a car.

I was tempted to sing along with Frankie and urge him to

'*Fly Me to the Moon.*' I was serenaded on both sides with Greg and the music. I was tipsy, but not inebriated like Tuesday night and hoped he wouldn't have performance issues.

Our coupling or his earlier therapeutic confession must have worked since he moaned and stopped moving. I opened my eyes relieved this was done without having a car accident. He propped himself on his arms smiling at me, and I could feel some wetness around my stomach.

"Was it good for you? I know it was rushed."

Sinatra was serenading us now with *I've Got You Under My Skin*. Somehow the song lyrics were synchronized to the right moment as if he was watching us with some minor tweaks.

"Yes, lovely." Pleased he was concerned. Would I ever relax enough to enjoy it again? It takes time. But with Matteo, it didn't take long. "I have a lot on my mind. You know with the trip and every – "

A loud pop rang out, and the car dipped to my side. Greg sat up and slid open the back window. While he zipped up his pants, he asked Rakesh, "What happened?"

"I believe we have a flat, Sir."

Rakesh steered the car from the far left fast lane to the right side of the road and the shoulder. I pulled my underwear on and grabbed my jeans from the floorboard to get dressed and hoped we wouldn't be rear ended.

Greg watched Rakesh and the highway as we came to a stop. What perfect, ironic timing. At least Greg was fast, or he would have been really upset. The whole situation was one of those too funny to believe moments, but no one was laughing.

Greg looked at his watch, and I asked him when his flight was leaving.

"Not until five thirty," But it was already after four.

"Don't you need to be there two hours before?" Now I was worried he wasn't going to make it.

"No, an hour is fine."

Rakesh and Greg got out to assess the damage. They went around to the trunk, and I climbed out too. The car was parked on the shoulder next to a grassy area between the highway and the access road

Rakesh lifted the spare tire out of the trunk. He searched around and said, "Last time I had the car serviced they didn't put the tools back."

"What tools?" I asked hoping it wasn't going to be bad news.

"Tools to change the damn tire," Greg said. He marched off to the back seat and took his phone out of his briefcase and returned to glare at both us.

Rakesh and I stood there, and I scrunched up my shoulders as if to say "So what. Things happen." Rakesh looked nervous, but I think he appreciated the gesture.

Greg called someone. "Miriam, we had a situation here on the way to the airport. We have a flat tire, but we appear to not have the proper equipment to change the damn tire. Can you arrange for a car or taxi, or I'll miss my plane." He specified the closest freeway exits and hung up.

"I'm sorry Greg." And put my hand on his shoulder, but he jerked away as if my touch stung. I didn't know what to do or where to go, so I got back into the car. I left the door open a crack and checked my phone for updates. Greg approached, and I started to say something to console him.

"Kat, don't. You're raising my blood pressure. If we hadn't had lunch."

I didn't like his reaction one bit. "This isn't my fault. I didn't cause the flat or forget the tools."

"You're right. It's been a hectic week."

I was about to suggest he try my week, we could even trade, but didn't want him to snap again and bite my entire head off.

I had an email from Amber at the travel company. The email was welcome news and stated all my medical tests came through, and I was cleared to go. She reminded me about the deposit due with the rest payable in Copenhagen on Saturday.

I called her and gave her my credit card information. She said a local representative would meet me on Saturday at my hotel to go over the final updates, documents for signing, and specifics for boarding the ship on Sunday.

After I had hung up, Greg told Rakesh a taxi was on its way and that she ordered a second car from town to help him with the flat.

Greg turned back to his phone and said, "Can you check on flights too. I'm on Air France flight 23, my usual, but I may not make it. Can you see what their status is and if there is space on the next flight? There used to be a few more going nonstop. I'll hold."

He looked stressed. "I must get to Paris tonight. I have a full schedule tomorrow with appointments that took months to set up."

Whatever. Keep it in perspective. I want to board my clipper ship this weekend, but the world won't end if I don't make it to Copenhagen. It's not like his livelihood depended on getting to Paris. He wouldn't lose his job or go down one iota in his standard of living. He lived vastly superior to almost everyone else on the planet.

He was still on the phone. "Great news. Thanks, Miriam. But this has convinced me, can you put through the order on the Esplanade? I want to switch to the SUV."

He sighed and added, "Yes, I know, I prefer the town cars, but adapting to the times. And, Miriam, let me know via email what you want from Paris this time."

As he hung up, a taxi pulled up and stopped in front of us.

Greg reached into the car to take his briefcase and said to me, "Aren't you coming?"

"Okay. Or I can wait here with Rakesh. I have to get my shopping bags." They were in the trunk, and I wasn't leaving without them. I wasn't sure I wanted to be around him in his foul mood, but it would be faster to get a cab from JFK than wait here with Rakesh.

"Right," he said and marched to the trunk. He took one shopping bag while Rakesh took the other, and they loaded them into the cab's open trunk.

"Madame," Greg said and waited by the cab's open door. I climbed in and slid over to the other side so he could join me in the back seat. He could have gotten in first, but it wasn't his modus operandi. Make the woman go first and struggle over to the other side. I regretted this whole trip, even the sex. Greg had again morphed into someone I didn't want to be around.

We were speeding along the highway to the airport, and I hoped his plane was still there.

"Oh, your luggage." I hated to remind him, but we must have left it behind and going back would cause even more unwanted delays.

"This is it," he said indicating his large briefcase still looking ahead.

"But aren't you going for a week?" This would barely hold one clean shirt.

"I am. I have an apartment in Saint-Germain-des-Prés. I don't need to bring anything but my laptop and some paperwork."

"How convenient," I said relieved. Naturally, Greg would have an apartment in one of the best, historic neighborhoods in Paris. I envied him. That was the way to travel. No packing necessary. Buy what you need. One of these days I would make a trip just like that.

He looked at his watch. "It will be tight, but I think I can make it."

It was almost five, and I didn't know why he was optimistic. Even with no luggage to check, he still had to get through security and to the gate. And for an international flight, they had to check his passport. I was glad I wasn't accompanying him. Running through the Met once was fun, but this was too stressful.

I glanced over at him and wondered if he thrived on this last minute crazy stuff. I sure didn't when it meant missing a flight or something important.

He tapped his leg with his fingers, and I was impatient too. I couldn't wait to get back to Manhattan and hoped rush hour wouldn't take too long.

We turned off at the airport exit, and he leaned forward giving the driver his credit card. "She's returning to the city. Put both fares on my card with a twenty percent tip. She'll sign for it."

He turned to me, "Kat send me the receipt. Do you still have my card?"

"I think so," and I took my wallet out to check. "Yes, I

have it," waving the proof at Greg to avoid being scolded like a school girl.

"I'm sorry Kat. I didn't expect such a stressful conclusion today." He patted my leg. "It's usually boring and routine. You made today very special for me."

I didn't say anything and didn't plan to when the cab stopped at the Air France terminal. I stared straight ahead so he could only kiss my cheek goodbye. But he put his hand under my chin and coaxed my face towards him. Our eyes met for a second, but I refused to smile and looked away.

"You're upset, aren't you? I'm sorry, Kat. I must run. I'll call you." And with that, he kissed me and disappeared flying in his special way through the airport.

24 ~ Bon Voyage

Goosebumps formed on my arms, so I grabbed a towel and glanced down at the blue-green water swirling down the drain. I hadn't bothered to wash off since I liked leaving the salty layer on as a form of protection. Soon, I will smell like this daily.

On my taxi ride home, I pushed the memory of Greg away and made a to-do list but decided to leave it for tomorrow. After all, I went through today, I deserved a break. I debated putting on my pajamas after showering, but Charlie was coming over. While wrapped in my towel, I decided to be proactive and sent Charlie a blunt email. "If you can't make it by nine, let's meet when I'm back."

Within seconds he responded, "There soon, Kat. Looking forward to it."

Kathleen would not approve. My 'nip it in the bud' skills needed improvement. But how without being rude? Politeness was ingrained and hard to shake.

I dressed and called my parents to update them on my trip and say goodbye. We agreed on a January Christmas when we're all back. They weren't concerned about my two-month trip and went "off the grid" whenever they traveled not bothering to check email or phone messages.

I had their itinerary for New Zealand, but they liked to wing it. Mom was telling me about one of the highlights, staying at a chateau in the North Canterbury wine region, when my doorbell rang.

On my way to the door, I said goodbye to my parents and glanced at my watch. It was too early for Charlie, and I was surprised to see Abby since she said she was busy tonight.

"Hey, Kat, there you are. Come on over for a drink."

"Oh, Abby, thanks but I'm worn out. I'll stop by tomorrow."

She frowned. "But Kat, I need to talk to you, please."

I stood back from the door. "Come on in."

"No, I have food in the oven. Can't you come to my place for a few minutes?"

"Oh, all right," with a sigh. I grabbed my keys and locked the door behind me. I didn't need to since I'd be right down the hall, but strangers and delivery men came in all the time. My apartment had too many hiding places.

She opened her unlocked door which was strange since she was diligent, even paranoid, about locking it all the time. She stood aside and gestured with her arm. "After you."

I ambled down her long, narrow entryway and heard a loud chorus of surprise. I put my hand on my chest in shock at seeing so many friends and could only manage to utter, "Wow."

"Bon voyage, Kat," Abby said in her high-pitched, excited voice.

I was stunned and couldn't move. Matteo walked up, handed me a glass of red wine, kissed me on the cheek, and whispered, "*Buon viaggio, cara.*"

I took the wine glass and thanked him still so surprised. My friends were focused on this gorgeous mystery man taking some of the pressure off. Everyone was used to Axel, and Matteo was almost his opposite with his Latin look and dark hair.

Mel and Jen gave me a quick hug. "So, it's finally happening, I guess?" Mel asked.

"Yeah, I got the okay this afternoon from the travel agency. Thanks to my friends and my last-minute gynecologist," nodding towards Matteo now chatting with some friends. Mel appraised him again in different eyes.

"He's your GYN?" another girlfriend said. "Sign me up. Please." I knew she was searching for a new boyfriend.

"Well, I don't think he does it that often. This was an emergency for my trip, but he is a doctor. So embarrassing when you've met before."

"But the perfect ice breaker for … you know. Gets things out in the open so to speak."

"Yeah, I know." We laughed enjoying her joke.

Mel told me I should cut the official first slice of my cake decorated with what else, a sailing ship. I hated to destroy it, but Mel urged me on. "Come on Kat; it's now or never. Don't let life pass you by."

I wouldn't let that happen. My knife made a brutal cut to the bow, and after that, I kept cutting. Mel put the slices on paper plates to hand out.

"You know, Mel, I'm going to be braver, and stop being so damn accommodating. Not to you, but people trying to manipulate me." I was annoyed remembering the disastrous trip to the airport with Greg. "I must stand up for myself even if -"

"Glad to hear it. You deserve all the happiness out there. Don't let anyone take that from you. I'm looking forward to this trip too. Like it's my own. Going to live vicariously through you."

The crowd was an eclectic mix of work friends and neighbors, even my book club, and the ages of the group ranged from eight to 80.

A male friend asked, "Hey, Kat, how's your sailing skills? Didn't know you were remotely interested."

"This came up pretty quick. The urge to go on a ship like this. And as for sailing, it's been a while." I'd tried to sail, but figuring out the wind's direction, how to position the sails, or use the rudder confused me. My friends waited to hear more.

"Back in high school, I did some sailing at Canyon Lake in Texas. On a little sunfish sailboat with a girlfriend. We used to tip it over. Fun and crazy hot summer days."

I smiled at the memory. "Once we had a hell of time flipping it back upright. We'd coated ourselves with baby oil to get a better tan, so we slid all over it."

"Sounds like you're well prepared." A friend teased.

"Hey, I'm not part of the crew. I'm a paying passenger. There to enjoy it." But maybe I should have taken a refresher sailing course. I was a strong swimmer, but you could only survive a few minutes in the North Sea and cold water around Europe. And Greg's son-in-law warned me against this. Nonsense, I told myself. I'm sure they will have lifeboats and emergency equipment if they run into trouble.

Abby dragged me over to the dining table piled with gifts. I started unwrapping thcm amazed my friends were so thoughtful.

The first few were gag gifts, including a life vest and some floaties, the inflatable arm bands kids wear. I tried them on for laughs. "I feel much better now with my limited sailing skills."

Abby cackled. "No more worries. Put them on in case you drink too much and fall overboard."

"Yeah," I teased back, "they'll look perfect at dinner with my fancy outfits."

Robert gave me some dark chocolate since he knew I loved it. "Emergency provisions," he said. Chee gave me some cash in an envelope, so typical Chinese, with a note suggesting a recommended e-book on China at the time of the clipper ships.

Mel gave me a book celebrating the Bard's 450 years and collection of his plays. I'd complained after seeing a Shakespeare play recently how I hated missing out on most of the jokes.

Jen said, "We thought you'd like a real book to give your e-readers and eyes a break."

Matteo gave me a small cloth pouch. I started to look inside, but he said, "Open it later. Keep it safe. It's an emergency medical kit with prescription medicine. All legal and in your name." He squeezed my arm affectionately. "Come back to me healthy. As you are right now."

"Thanks. That's my plan."

Another friend gave me a bottle of spiced rum cautioning me, "Beware of the Kraken."

I laughed. Sailors are known for being superstitious and fear giant squid creatures that could capsize a ship. I opened the ornate bottle and passed it around for tasting.

After I had opened all my gifts, there was a debate about whether my trip was the best one to take. So, I turned the whole thing around. "Where would you go if you could travel in November and December and not want to spend a fortune?"

The answers were predictable: Hawaii, Australia, the Caribbean, and California.

"My clipper ship voyage is perfect for me." There was

nowhere else I'd rather go. Warmer weather would await me once we reached South Africa and Asia.

I wandered into the kitchen and poured a glass of viognier chilling in an ice bucket. Abby remembered my favorite white wine. A hardy little grape that almost went extinct but now is grown all over the world, even in India. A bit like me - rugged but slightly hidden. "We like it that way, don't we? So what if talking to bottles is a sign of insanity?"

I tried to mix and talk to everyone since some people started leaving. Lots of my friends were worried about the trip. Many said, "Be careful" and "Stay in touch, so we know you're okay."

Robert and Chee were chatting, and I told them about meeting with Jackson today and the emergency contacts he gave me.

Robert nodded. "I talked to him too. He said you shouldn't spend one minute longer than necessary in Hong Kong. Kat, please don't. For us."

They were overly cautious, but I agreed. I asked whether Jackson was invited or would come tonight.

Chee shook his head. "He never does parties. Crowded, small spaces make him nervous."

"If he were here, he'd be crawling the walls." I teased.

Robert speculated. "Already out on the roof, rappelling off the side of the building to the street, not trusting the elevator or the stairs."

"Yeah, after he crawled sideways on the walls to the front door." And I pointed to the walls behind us that led to the long, narrow hallway to Abby's front door.

We laughed visualizing this, but with Jackson, it wasn't a stretch. We'd seen him in action.

~ ~ ~

I exited the bathroom when I overheard a conversation in Abby's bedroom. A woman's voice said, "She doesn't know and never suspected. Why tell her now and break her heart?"

I was about to knock on the bedroom door when Mel pushed past me into the bedroom shutting the door behind her. I headed back to the living room but kept an eye on the door to see who was in there. When the bedroom door opened, Abby and Matteo exited and later, Mel and Jen.

Who were they were talking about? Maybe I could help her. But I was surrounded by friends and didn't have a chance to ask.

Mel and Jen came up and hugged me goodbye. Mel said, "I'm going to miss you. You're going to have a phenomenal time, you know. Forget all about this crap and come back refreshed. Ready to start something new and incredible."

"Yep, that's the plan." I beamed at her and knew I was going to miss seeing her every day. This trip would be a welcome distraction from our forced separation.

"Kat, we have to head back to Brooklyn. Starting my new job tomorrow."

"All ready? On a Friday?" That sounded odd.

"It's a paycheck. I'm counting on you, Kat. When you find a new job, I'm there."

"Deal." Would Mel want to work with Jackson if I decided to do that? I was intrigued by the idea, but it was premature to bring it up.

Kathleen tapped me on the shoulder apologizing for arriving late. She gave me a big hug and slipped a wrapped package in my hand. "Open it later, in private," she whispered. "Didn't want you to worry about this when you are onboard, or if you run out. Dangerous with all those seamen's semen." Kathleen threw her head back and roared at her play on words.

Kathleen asked me to point out Matteo and clutched her chest as if having a heart attack. "Too bad he won't fit in your suitcase. But Kat, you said you preferred American ice cream to Italian gelato."

We laughed remembering the jokes about men at lunch.

"Well, a girl has to be open and try different things. Isn't that what you suggested?"

"Sure do. But if you decide to switch back to Ben & Jerry's, let me know. My souvenir spoon from Florence is ready and willing."

Kathleen was more Matteo's type. She'd be game to play with those toys hidden under his bed. I was about to suggest she should go out with him, but then Charlie strolled in.

My jaw dropped, and I swayed unsteady and afraid I'd lose something else. Charlie swaggered down the hallway and right up to me still wearing an expensive business suit with his tie slack, hanging like a decorative silk noose. A Cheshire-style grin was plastered on his face as if he had something devious planned. I was tempted to back up and hide, like a cornered mouse, but I froze.

Charlie didn't hesitate one iota. He pulled me close and gave me an affectionate hug and kiss like we were long, lost lovers. I didn't know how to react and was off balance when he released me.

After I had recovered my senses, I glanced around. To my relief, most people were distracted and chatting, but I noticed a few sly glances. I was glad Mel had left, or she might have slugged him. I was still their Kat, the grieving widow, and now I had not one, but two new affectionate male friends. Three, if Greg was here, imagining how complicated that would be.

"Didn't know you were having a party tonight. Ran into Mel by the elevator. At least her friend fessed up and told me where you were. She let the cat out of the bag." He smiled pleased with his play on my name.

"I'm sorry Charlie. This was a surprise party, and I forgot to leave you a note," Abby's large wall clock said it was only eight thirty. He was early if his flight arrived at eight.

He leaned over whispering, "No problem. I just got here, but I deserve another half hour."

"All right, sure." With all my friends surrounding me, I was energized and could stay up all night. But I knew I shouldn't. Not if I wanted to be on my flight tomorrow.

25 ~ *The Interloper*

Matteo came over to me and stared at Charlie, so I introduced them. They were polite but eyed each other, and Charlie excused himself to get a glass of wine.

Matteo asked me, "Is that the guy?"

"What guy?" I whispered back not thinking straight.

"The guy you told me about yesterday. You know, the one who couldn't."

"Oh, him. No, I haven't had sex with Charlie," or anyone else in the room I was about to say. Usually, I was well behaved and not a promiscuous tramp. "He's the bad blind date, the one with the video." I started to giggle but tried to get past it.

"The guy you pulled the knife on?"

"Yeah, strange, I know. Charlie apologized, but I still haven't forgiven him, not one hundred percent."

"What's not one hundred percent?" Charlie asked, now standing between us.

Matteo looked at him and then me not wanting to interfere. I tried to think of what to say, but my brain drew a big fat blank.

To help, Matteo said, "Kat isn't one hundred percent. She doesn't have her appendix anymore."

"Oh, no? Sorry to hear that. Should you sit down?" Charlie looked concerned as if I'd just had surgery.

I laughed and threw my head back at how preposterous this was. Technically, Matteo was correct, I didn't have all my pieces anymore. Matteo smiled and chuckled sharing our secret.

"Oh Charlie, that was years ago. I'm fine. Too funny." I leaned on Matteo's shoulder and laughed some more.

"And how do you happen to know that?" Charlie asked Matteo as if on a client-related due diligence assignment. Charlie didn't sound amused at being left out on our private joke and one so personal.

Matteo was comfy to lean on. Is this a fuck buddy? Friends

in bed but not much else. No strings and no commitments. But I didn't want that. I would worry about who he was with. Some things, like boyfriends, shouldn't be shared.

"She has a small four-inch scar right here. The surgeon did an excellent job, so it's almost unnoticeable." Matteo showed him the size of the scar measuring between his thumb and index finger and pointed to my lower right abdomen.

Charlie smiled, but he didn't look pleased that Matteo knew this. I explained, "I needed some medical tests for my cruise. Matteo is a doctor and helped me out yesterday."

"And she came through with … what do you say? 'Flying Colors,' a strong, healthy woman." He winked at me.

"I see," Charlie said, gulping down his red wine and emptying his glass.

Matteo wandered away and before a few more friends approached I told Charlie. "Matteo is a good friend." Probably all every would be. I had enjoyed last night, my night of *la dolce vita* with a charming Italian. The sex was great - even better than the meal. But Matteo would never be interested in someone ordinary like me. So did I regret last night? Hell no.

"Whatever." Charlie sounded annoyed. "Kat, I came here direct from the airport, so my suitcase is right outside your door. I could bring it here, but your friend's apartment is packed."

"Sure, let's go lock it up in my apartment."

I explained to Abby her guest of honor would be right back.

Charlie followed me down the hallway with his briefcase. Luckily his suitcase was still there. I started to open the door but dropped my keys and fumbled around trying to open it. Once the door was opened, he rolled his bag inside my apartment. He shut the door behind him and put his arms around me and kissed me again. "I've missed you, Kat."

I pulled away. "I have to return to the party. My friends are starting to leave, and some I haven't seen for a really long time."

"Of course, don't let me keep you." He didn't sound upset, and if he was, too bad. No more Ms. Nice Girl, as I promised Mel earlier. "Can I take a quick shower and join you later? I feel grimy. Last night was a late client dinner, and this morning, I didn't get a chance before my flight."

I knew that feeling all too well. A shower was the first thing I craved after a long trip. I showed Charlie my guest bathroom and gave him some clean towels and handed him my keys to lock up.

When I returned, a group of us huddled around the bottle of black spiced rum with warnings of bizarre and fierce sea creatures and bravely downed a round of shots. I couldn't believe how good it was. As good as aquavit. But I knew I should watch it with Charlie still hanging around, and if I wanted to get through my to-do list tomorrow.

"Kat, what are you going to do when the Kraken shows up?" one of my friends asked.

"Push it back into the water, so it doesn't die. And if it won't leave, practice my kickboxing skills."

Some friends joked, "I'd cut it up for a barbecue. Like giant calamari."

And another said, "Tastes like chicken."

We joked about all sorts of dangerous marine sea creatures, but I wasn't worried. I'd handled small live octopus and seen giant clams and sharks when scuba diving with Axel all over the world. They didn't scare me. I was fascinated, but the ones I observed weren't aggressive and didn't try to attack. Giant squids were rare and lived deep down in the ocean. Even the bottle said a Kraken was imaginary. I'd be more likely to see a mermaid.

Charlie joined us after he showered, wearing jeans and an old Harvard T-shirt from his alma mater. He was game for a drink of spiced rum, so I poured him a generous half-cup. He held it up to the light, sniffed it, and swirled it before swallowing it all. After his showmanship, we watched him wondering what came next.

Charlie smacked his lips. "Fine. A strong taste of vanilla, raspberries and hmm, yes, I do believe, the belladonna."

"What's belladonna?" I sipped some more and smelled vanilla and maybe raspberries. He must be making the rest up.

Charlie bent over laughing. "Belladonna is the devil berry

or death cherry, take your pick. Extremely lethal."

Did Charlie like being a jokester or was he compelled to do this to fit in?

Matteo joined the crowd, and Charlie spoke to him in Italian. I was surprised how fluent he was and couldn't follow the discussion.

Charlie stopped to apologize. "I spent a semester in Rome, but I don't get a chance to speak Italian much."

Feeling excluded, but wanting to let him practice, I sat next to Alberto on the sofa with one of my 80-year old neighbors. She said goodnight, and we were alone. The party had dwindled down to a handful of guests. Abby was chatting with Kathleen punctuated with periodic screams and yells from their direction. Abby was lonely and wanted a guy in her life, so I was glad Kathleen could keep her company while I was gone.

I asked Alberto, "What are your plans for the weekend?' A safe topic to bring up with anyone. I hoped his plans included Abby.

"My sister, Valentina, is coming for a visit. She's Matteo's girlfriend."

I swallowed hard not expecting to hear this. Of course, Matteo would have a girlfriend, at least one, with others waiting in line. But it hurt to hear this so soon and not from him.

Alberto continued while I tried to hide how upsetting this was for me to hear. "We will show her around the city. She is here a month, so we won't have to rush. And they haven't seen each other for a while so who knows with Matteo."

Yeah, she may never get out of his bed, our bed. But Matteo and his bed were never mine. Just thinking about it made me angry. The fiasco date this afternoon with Greg, and now with Matteo. I'll never fall in love again. Now, I just need to get rid of Charlie. He was still chatting with Matteo. At least I wasn't going to miss any of them while I'm away.

I gave Alberto a hug goodnight and made my usual excuses which tonight were real. I was tired and did have a million things to do. I told Abby and Kathleen goodbye. I still wanted to ask Abby about the mystery woman in trouble, but when she was alone.

I braced myself to say goodnight to Matteo since I didn't want any hugs or to be touched. It felt wrong and dirty now. I didn't want to come between him and his girlfriend or be a plaything. I wanted to get rid of Charlie too, but his suitcase was in my apartment.

After saying goodbye and thanking Matteo for the gift, he gave me a big hug and kissed me on both cheeks. Charlie looked uncomfortable even though they bonded over Italy and went to thank Abby for letting him crash the party.

Now that we were alone, Matteo suggested, "Come by later tonight."

I shook my head. That was the last place I would ever go. "No, you should be thinking about Valentina." When I met Axel, he was in a relationship, and I swore I'd never get in the middle again.

"It's not what you think. I can explain."

But before Matteo could say more, Charlie was at my side. I told Charlie, "You can stay if you want, but I'm leaving."

Charlie looked offended. "I've been ready to go. I'm only here for you."

I gave the others a quick hug and thanked them before I headed towards the door. I knew Abby was tired and wanted to toss out the stragglers.

Matteo looked wistful, if not disappointed. To him, where else would we end up, but in bed? But I was tired of trying to please two guys in a row and feeling used afterward. I wasn't going to take a chance on a third strike out. A dull ache rose from my gut as if an angry Kraken was stirred up at the bottom of the ocean.

26 ~ *Rocking & Rolling*

Back inside my apartment, Charlie didn't get the hint to gather his stuff from my guest room and leave. He had checked into the Kat Jensen Hotel with his belongings spread out and hanging from his open suitcase after using my guest shower.

Charlie ignored my unspoken wish and followed me into the living room. I must do what I promised Mel. Be more assertive. "You must be exhausted after your trip, Charlie. Thanks for coming by."

"Kat, I'm not that tired. Are you?"

Yes, but my immediate problem was dying of thirst after all the booze. I offered Charlie some water, and he accepted. I poured two large glasses of sparkling water with a raspberry-lime flavor and gulped mine down in a hurry.

He laughed when he saw the bottle. "Even your water is weird."

Revived, I ignored his comment and poured myself another glass. At least he didn't say I was boring or ordinary since that would bother me more.

"Nice party, Kat. You have some great friends. People care about you."

"Yeah, it was a pleasant surprise."

He sat on the bar stool in the kitchen and stared at the coffee can with Axel's smiling face.

"Are those photos of your ex?" Charlie pointed at Axel's can.

"You mean my husband? Yes."

"What's with the decorated can?"

"Those are his ashes. Part of the reason I'm going to Denmark. To see his brother and scatter some near his home and other places."

"You have an ex-husband like I have an ex-wife. We've both been through it."

"No, it's not the same thing at all. For one thing, your wife's still alive, and things didn't work out. My husband and I were happily married until cancer stole him from me."

We sat in the kitchen under Axel's watchful eye. I wished Axel would send him a subliminal message to leave.

"Do you have the specs on that ship you're going on? I'd love to see it."

"No, but I can show you this." I had returned the clipper ship book to Matteo, so I retrieved from the freezer my bottle of aquavit with the sailing ship label.

"Beautiful. Tell me again, where does the ship go?"

I opened my Atlas eager to show him my journey and the general direction from Copenhagen to Hong Kong with possible stops along the way in Europe, Africa, and Asia. We would cross parts of the Atlantic and Indian Oceans with many seas and bays along the way. I had studied the maps and wind currents for late fall and winter to prepare.

"Nothing in writing on which ports?" He probably didn't believe me, and it was kind of crazy to get on a ship without these critical details. So many friends were surprised and concerned about the trip tonight, so I was more apprehensive.

"No, it depends on the ship's cargo. When I get to Denmark, I'm meeting with the local agent to go over the specifics. And Sunday, I'm on the ship, and we set sail."

"Well, you are brave. I'll give you that. I didn't realize what an adventure this is. I visualized a big cruise line, like Norwegian, but this is entirely different."

If I were a man, no one would have worried. Guys run off for months without anyone stressing. But a woman can barely leave for more than a week.

"But you know, I'd love to do that. If I had the time, it makes perfect sense." He retraced the route on the Atlas with his finger.

"It does? You're one of the few."

"Others aren't like us, Kat. We're tough. We aren't New Yorkers, but we've adapted. I know you aren't happy about your company closing. But it's an opportunity for you to do something new and different."

"I know. Find the damn cheese. But I'm tired of chasing it."

"No, nothing like that. When you return something new

will come along. And you'll love it more than ever. And I'll be here waiting for you."

I didn't say anything surprised at his supportive comments.

"Shall I watch your cat some while you're gone? Come by to keep it company?"

"Cat?"

"You have cat beds around. There must be a fur ball hiding somewhere."

"My cat Xena died last month. She's up there." I pointed to the bronze cat food container holding her ashes on the shelf near Axel's coffee can. I didn't think there was a heaven, and even if there was, how in the world would a cat find its owner? "She was my soulmate. I'm saving her ashes. We will be mixed together."

"I'm so sorry, Kat. Must be hard to have lost them both."

Tears welled up in my eyes, but I hoped it would pass. Since Xena died so recently, I ached, particularly at home with her memories everywhere. She was the perfect little four-legged companion. Charlie took me in his arms and gave me an affectionate hug while stroking my hair murmuring soothing sounds.

I wiped my eyes with the side of my index finger discretely. "I'm going to adopt another cat, maybe two, from a rescue group when I'm back and have a job again."

"Perfect idea." Charlie let me go. "Can we put some music on?"

"Sure." I turned on the radio connected to the big stereo in the living room. My favorite jazz station came on, and we caught the end of one of my favorites, *Naima* by John Coltrane.

"Nice, but now I will fall asleep. May I?"

I nodded, and he switched to a classic rock station. The same station I listened to in the shower.

Bon Jovi's *Living on a Prayer* filled the room, Charlie swayed and danced around caught up in the music and played imaginary drums. I couldn't resist and joined him moving around the floor dancing and played some air guitar to support his drumming.

Next, Boston's *More than a Feeling* began. We continued

our dance playing imaginary instruments, and Charlie joined me on his air guitar. With the song *Seeing My Marianne Walk Away,* Charlie switched the lyrics and sang, "My Kathryn." He went down on his knees and clutched his chest as if in pain.

I grinned and pulled him back up, and he rested his hands on my hips, but I pushed him away. "Watch my fancy footwork." While I did some fast sliding, hopping, and jumping.

He clapped amused. "Excellent."

After my fast-paced dance, I wanted to sit down on the sofa to rest, but I didn't want him to join me afraid of what might happen next.

The House of the Rising Sun began, and Charlie said, "My turn." He pulled out a dining chair for me to sit on next to our makeshift dance floor and got down on one knee to serenade me. Charlie knew all the words and had a powerful voice. I wondered if he wanted to be a musician and got sidetracked to Wall Street.

A slow song, Pink Floyd's *Dark Side of the Moon*, started. Charlie bowed and held out his hands without saying a word. I curtsied and let him embrace me for a slow dance. His cologne was a mix of musk and lemons. I closed my eyes enjoying his scent and warm embrace with the music swirling around us. I forgot all about our awful blind date and his rudeness. Even the disasters with Greg and Matteo faded away. I was connected to someone and safe here at home listening to some of the best music ever made.

Another classic from the 1960's, *A Whiter Shade of Pale*, began its familiar notes. I nestled in closer, and his hands moved down to my waist. We pressed up against each other with only a thin layer of our clothes between us. The song ended, and we were barely moving. My head rested against his chest, and I heard his heartbeat.

Charlie put his hand under my chin and lifted my head back. He leaned down and kissed me while weaving and swaying. He clicked off the radio and led me to the guest room where he'd unpacked his suitcase. I knew I shouldn't, but I was captivated and didn't want him to go. No wonder he closed so many deals and made so much money. He charmed and captivated me like a python mesmerizes his prey.

27 ~ *Sharing Scars*

Friday morning, I woke up in my guest room, not pleased, but at least I was home. My last day here for a long while, and my to-do list before my flight tonight weighed on me. Charlie lay flat on his back snoring softly, reminding me of Axel. Charlie must be exhausted from the jet lag, but his passion last night didn't stop.

I picked up my clothes holding them in front of me like a shield and scurried through the living room back to my bedroom and adjoining bathroom. I contemplated how this all happened. Three men in less than 24 hours. Not that I had regrets, but it was so unexpected and unbelievable. Even to me, and I was there. I slipped on my nightgown, climbed into my bed, and shut my eyes trying to fall back asleep.

My hair was being pressed down and petted.

"Kat, oh my Kat."

I opened my eyes and saw Charlie leaning over me, naked and looking concerned.

"Kat, you left me." He sounded like a lost child.

"I came back here so you ... we could sleep better."

"But I can't. I missed you."

Oh, brother, what a load of crap I was tempted to say. I rolled over to Axel's side of the bed and patted my side of the bed inviting him in.

Just like my first impression as Gotham's Batman, Charlie flew under the covers. But he was wide awake and pushed off the comforter, so we were under the thin sheet. My bedroom was warm, and he heated things up, so I didn't object.

"I'll show you mine if you show me yours."

"Afraid we've been there, done that. Nothing left to show." I mumbled and rolled over trying to ignore him and go back to sleep.

"I mean your appendix scar." He pulled the sheet back moving down to see below my bikini line or where it would be if I wore one. Not that I was concerned about the thin line. I hadn't worn a bikini for over ten years. From my intense workout routine, I was more toned and leaner than I'd ever been, but when you are pushing fifty, it's time to give them up.

"Hmm." He said tracing it softly with his finger. "He's right. You can barely see it." He rolled on his back and said, "Your turn."

"What? Were you hurt?" Although, I wasn't that concerned after his energetic dancing last night.

"A bit. Laid up for about six months when I was fourteen." He took my hand and rubbed it against his knee. I could feel his knee cap, and what felt like scar tissue, but I didn't want to see it.

"Oh, must have hurt." I was awake now but didn't want to pry. He was probably one of those annoying early birds. Something else we didn't have in common.

"I was working at home at the ranch. Moving some cows from one pasture to another. One was injured and went a little crazy. My horse reared, and I went down hard with my knee stepped on."

"Sounds painful."

"Yeah, well, at least I have a full range of motion. Even played football in high school." He rolled on his side to look at me. "And, I know you'd be concerned about the animals. They were unhurt from the ordeal."

"Glad to hear it."

"In the end, Kat, it worked out. I started reading the Wall Street Journal while recovering and discovered a whole new world of finance. Maybe it was fate."

Charlie lay next to me and traced soft circles on my skin with his index finger. "Do you believe in soulmates?"

"Aside from my cat?" I teased back, but I knew what he meant. "You mean finding one perfect person out of seven billion people alive right now?"

"Doesn't sound very likely, does it?"

"Nope. I think most people find someone to love and adjust as best they can to the problems or differences, whatever you want to call it. Like finding a job."

"Is that what you plan to do?"

"Find a soulmate or the perfect job?"

He didn't respond, but I knew he meant the former. He didn't care about my job.

His hair hung down over his forehead, and I combed it back with my fingers. I knew he wanted a positive response, but I was a realist. Even if the truth hurt, I couldn't sugarcoat it.

"I'd like to say yes, but I really don't know. Part of the reason I need to get away."

~ ~ ~

Charlie was talking to someone in the living room by the front door, and I wondered who came by this early. I grabbed my robe, but when I got to the living room, Charlie walked towards me buck naked. He had already made coffee, and hazelnut was in the air. When he saw me, he pranced around bringing back memories from last night, but this time, he was dancing in the full Monty. I blushed and looked away.

"People can see you. There are offices over there." I pointed towards the living room windows facing where employees work across the courtyard.

"Shoot. This is Manhattan. They're used to it." He stood facing the windows so they could appreciate him in all his glory. He reminded me of a guy at a rodeo waiting for applause after lassoing a defenseless cow.

"Well, I hope you don't end up on YouTube like me. Those offices are used by ABC TV."

Now that he was naked in the daylight, I couldn't help but compare him to the others. He wasn't fat, but not as trim and fit like Greg or the perfect model for a Roman god statue like Matteo. Over the years, he'd probably gained a few pounds, maybe ten, around his waist. Not quite love handles, and it suited him.

"I'll chance it. You know Kat, I deal with risk all day, all the time." He looked around the apartment. "This apartment suits you. Bohemian, edgy, and filled with small treasures. Great and unexpected like your heart."

I wasn't sure what to say to his series of compliments, but I liked my apartment. If I didn't, I could redecorate. After watching hundreds of home renovation shows on HGTV, I knew what to do. My apartment was a little dark since it was on the fourth floor and nearby buildings towered above it. But while I didn't have a view or tons of light, I liked it here and had no plans of ever moving.

Bread was burning, and he ran back to the kitchen pulling them out of the toaster oven and onto the counter. "Not to worry. They're salvageable."

"Fine," I said, not concerned. Kitchen accidents happened often. I frequently put things in the toaster or stove and got sidetracked, so they ended up burning or boiling over.

Maybe breakfast or brunch gods did exist. Twice in one week, someone made me breakfast in my own kitchen.

"Who were you talking to before I came out?"

"Oh yeah. Matteo came by to talk to you. But I told him you were plumb worn out on account of this old cowboy." He spoke with an exaggerated Wyoming accent and beamed with pride.

"No," I said horrified. "You didn't say that." And even worse, Charlie had nothing on.

"Just kidding. Oh, the expression on your face. Priceless. I would almost think you had a thing going with that Italian."

I took the cup of coffee he offered me and added some milk. Sitting on my kitchen bar stool, I drummed my fingers on the counter impatient for him to tell me the truth about what actually happened.

"I told him you'd call him later. Don't worry. He didn't see the goods," looking down at his crotch. "I stood behind the door. He only saw my head and maybe my shoulders."

I slumped down on my bar stool relieved he hadn't paraded around in front of Matteo. "Maybe you should wear something. Isn't it dangerous cooking in the kitchen like that?"

"You mean with knives around? Are you planning something?"

"No," not wanting to be reminded of our first date. "I mean it doesn't seem sanitary, and you could end up with a sautéed sausage."

He grinned. "We wouldn't want that."

I opened the door to the kitchen pantry and pulled out an

apron hanging behind the door. Axel bought it on a trip to New Orleans a long time ago but never used it. Then again, he never cooked in the buff.

Charlie slipped it over his head tying it in the back. "Perfect fit," he added sarcastically since it would fit anyone.

My doorbell rang again, and I stood quickly not wanting a half-naked dancing man as my doorman. "Let me. You stay here."

Abby stood in the hall, and her arms were overloaded with my gifts from last night. "Thought you might want these before you finish your packing."

"Thanks. I'll be over soon to help clean-up."

"No need. All done. I knew you'd be busy today."

I tried to take the gifts from her, but she didn't want to hand them over. She let me take the half-full bottle of spiced rum from last night precariously held by her thumb through one of its glass loops.

She said, "Allow me," and pushed past me into the living room that was open to the kitchen.

Before I could stop her, she froze in her tracks nearly dropping my gifts. I started to explain but how do I explain a half-naked man making breakfast? At least she'd met him last night.

"I'm sorry, Kat. I didn't know you had company." She said in shock.

I was about to say, "I didn't either," but I didn't want to offend Charlie who was working hard on breakfast. I was hungry and looking forward to whatever he was creating.

Charlie, the consummate host, smiled and offered Abby some coffee and thanked her again for the party last night. At least he was partially covered by the apron.

"Thank you, Charlie. Great to see you again, but I better be going. I'm telecommuting today so back to work." She looked mesmerized seeing him in my kitchen only partly covered with the black apron that said, 'Louisiana Yard Dog' with a green alligator sprawled across it.

"Suit yourself," Charlie said while he turned around to look in the fridge.

Not only did he turn around, but he leaned over to find something giving us a clear view of his naked rear. Abby and I couldn't help but giggle.

"Looks like a Cajun coonass." I joked with Abby to hide my embarrassment.

"I heard that," Charlie said good-naturedly. He probably did that on purpose to shock us. "I do believe Texas is a hell of a lot closer to those Cajuns than Wyoming."

Abby grinned and shook her head still in shock. "I'm leaving you two to enjoy your breakfast. See you later."

I walked her to the door still not knowing what to say about Charlie. We agreed that I should come by later this morning. She was going to pay any unexpected bills for me while I was gone.

Returning to the kitchen, I asked Charlie if I could shower and change first.

"Only if you want a cold cheese omelet."

I stayed in my seat and watched the showman as he made do with an old chunk of cheese abandoned in the fridge and Mel's remaining eggs. I was starving since I'd missed dinner last night.

He said, "You like it spicy from what I can recall."

I nodded and pointed to the spices in the cabinet. At least, Charlie paid attention to something on our ill-fated first date.

"Not much to work with, but I know you're leaving town." I didn't have the heart to tell him the fridge stayed bare all the time. Axel was the grocery shopper and cook, but it was the basics and not something he enjoyed.

"Do you like cooking?" He looked genuinely happy working in the kitchen.

"Yeah, but I rarely get a chance. I work late all the time, but I grill a mean sirloin steak."

"I'm not much of a cook, but I make a pretty good lasagna and Mexican food. And deviled eggs."

He grinned. "I'd expect no less."

Charlie divided up the omelet adding the partially burnt toast and sat down next to me. I didn't want to visualize his naked rear on my bar stool. Not that it was unattractive, just unusual.

Between bites, he said, "You know Kat, I had a perfect night. The best time ever, even if I was beyond tired. I've been dating around, mainly younger woman. They don't click with me like you."

I didn't say anything savoring my side of the cheese omelet he'd made extra spicy for me. Not quite as delicious as Mel's cooking, but better than mine.

"I could have sworn you purred last night."

"Oh, you. Well, you were howling at the moon, like a dog or gator, whatever you are." I jabbed him in the stomach with my index finger where the alligator was covering him.

But he was right. Sex with him was almost perfect. So good it was scary. Greg was tentative and gentlemanly while Matteo was the extreme opposite, a professional who could bill me for services rendered. Charlie was more the American boy-next-door enjoying it, but not taking it too seriously. Maybe our mutual girlfriend Susan who cajoled me into this blind date after months of arm twisting was right. We were well suited for each other.

He laughed and looked up at Axel's face peering down at us. Axel's everyday 'I can't be bothered' smile wasn't a full grin like Charlie's.

Charlie glanced at Axel and me. "Cool to be in a coffee can. His idea, I guess? Loved that movie. Jeff Bridges and the Dude. My idol too."

I wasn't sure what to say and what Axel must be thinking. Here I was in my kitchen with the first new man I'd slept with in our apartment. He'd even stayed the night and was wearing his apron. I knew Axel wouldn't like him. Charlie was too American, over-confident, and driven, not to mention super-rich. All things Axel would want nothing to do with.

"You know, in a way, you are luckier than I am." Charlie started up at Axel and his photos.

"What do you mean?"

"Sometimes I wish my wife had died instead. Not in a painful way or anything but the ten years we were together was destroyed and replaced with pain. I played by the rules, but she broke them all. I can't look back on anything in our past without anger after all the fighting through our attorneys."

I didn't say anything. I couldn't imagine something so awful.

"At least when he left, you still loved each other. You have all those happy memories together. I have nothing, and it's not even over. It's worse than death, all this hate and disgust."

I considered the pain he'd gone through while I put our dishes in the dishwasher. But I wasn't lucky and would have preferred a divorce not death for Axel. "I'm going to shower. Feel free to use the shower again, if you want."

"Thank you, Kat," and he went off to the guest room on the opposite side of mine. He'd be dressed and gone soon. And if he didn't leave, I'd kiss him goodbye and push him out the door to get things done.

With my radio blaring, I climbed into my steamy shower. I knew I wasted water by letting it heat up first, but I couldn't bear a cold shower, not even for a minute. Despite all the fun last night, I didn't feel tired. Maybe Charlie cleared some clogs out of my system.

I started shampooing my hair and heard Charlie say, "May I?"

Before I could answer, he climbed into the shower. I leaned my head onto his chest.

"You said to feel free to use the shower."

He knew I meant the guest shower, but it was nice being scrubbed and bathed. Not only was he an excellent shampoo boy, but he also added in a nice head and neck massage. If I could have purred like he said I did, I would have. I offered to wash his hair, and he accepted.

"Now I know why you tasted a little salty like the ocean last night." He held up my jar of coconut salt scrub. We took turns with the scrubs and bath gels which led to other fun and games. At the rate this was going, I was never going to make my flight.

28 ~ Too Many To-Do's

Holding my printed boarding passes for my flight tonight made it feel real. Charlie was still hanging around not taking any hints to leave and asked to see them.

"I'd like to take you to the airport, Kat."

I shook my head no. After yesterday's miserable trip with Greg, I'd rather go alone. The sex was the only good thing, albeit nerve-racking, and I'd had enough sex now to last me at least two months.

He tried to grab my boarding passes from me, but I held them out of reach. "It's on the way, Kat if you are going out of JFK. I'm going to my house in the Hamptons to put the place on the market. Going to finalize my divorce per your instructions."

"Don't do it for me. Do it for yourself or your ex-wife."

"Sure Kat, this is for me. Please let me see them." He reached around my back to steal them, so I surrendered.

He checked them and said, "Great. JFK. I'll arrange a car at five, so you have two hours at JFK before departure. Shame you aren't going non-stop."

"Yeah. Well, it was a last-minute flight to Copenhagen. And London isn't the worst place for a stopover."

"What are you doing today?"

"Washing clothes, packing, and picking up some clothes in Chinatown. And, since I'm gone for two months, some financial stuff."

"Is that all?" He asked with a smile.

I frowned not amused. Charlie was a distraction.

"Let me help you, Kat. I'd love to wash and pack your undies, please."

"Oh, you pervert." I teased while I avoided his kisses.

"Maybe I am, but I'm all yours."

"I'm sure you tell all the ladies this. Of course, there aren't that many at Levittman."

Charlie frowned as if I struck a nerve and jolted the memory of a bad relationship. "I never date anyone at work. Don't even joke about it."

"Good. I'm glad at least one Wall Street guy can keep his thingy in his pants."

"Yeah, and aren't you lucky you found me? A diamond in the rough." He started to kiss me again.

"Speaking of work," pushing him off, "don't you have mega deals to do on a workday? Won't your clients shrivel up and die without you?"

"Oh, you. My accounts can manage a day without me. I took the day off to have one last day with you before you run off to the high seas. My little sailor boy."

"You won't say that when you see what I have to wear?"

"Wear?" I didn't answer but must have had looked sly since he looked worried. "Don't tell me this is a clothing-optional cruise."

"Not hardly." I laughed. "I'll look like a proper lady from the Civil War."

"What Civil War?" He was confused, and his eyes begged for an answer.

"The American Civil War. The 1860's."

"Well, that's sure different. Gone with the Wind style, huh?"

"Yeah, but this is the part of the cruise I'm not looking forward to."

Charlie picked up his phone to check email and said he needed to make a few calls and sat at the dining table. I knew his clients and his team were probably lost, unable to manage without him. I rarely saw Axel work from home so hearing Charlie on the phone working was strange. Axel kept strict barriers, rarely worked on weekends, and never on his days off. Axel's kept the work-life scale weighed towards life. Axel often lectured, "We don't need the money. You keep working because you enjoy it."

A part of me did, but if I wanted to stay in Manhattan in my big apartment, I needed money and a decent nest egg to relax. I wasn't relying on social security, and now, without a job lined up, it was going to take even longer to save enough to retire.

In my small home office, I calculated monthly expenses for the next two months and added a cushion if the trip took longer, or unexpected bills came in. I logged into my brokerage account, sold some stocks, and set up some transfers to my main bank account. Then I signed a handful of blank checks for Abby and any unexpected bills and printed Mel's and my parent's emergency contact information for her.

I gathered the paperwork and checks to take to Abby's and walked into the living room.

Charlie was on the phone. "Now listen, once more I am again going to make this crystal clear." After a short pause, he yelled, "You've got to be kidding me. Don't be so asinine."

I didn't want to continue eavesdropping. Charlie didn't notice me and stood to look out the windows with his back to me. He screamed into the phone. "What an idiotic screw-up! No, whatever you do, don't tell the client that."

I sympathized for whoever was on the other end of the phone. Charlie sat and jotted some notes down. "You have to fix this, or it's your head. Here's how you have to …"

He glanced up and saw me. I didn't want to what to what sounded like a long series of steps, so I waved to indicate I was leaving.

Charlie barked into the phone, "Hold it." He put his hand over the receiver and glared at me with eyes that could inflict real pain. I was taken aback at his sudden transformation from a fun-loving gator to a growling attack dog.

"Kat?" Before I could form the words, he urged, "Yes?"

Wary of having my head bit off, I found my voice. "Going down the hall to see Abby."

As I escaped to her apartment, I contemplated why he turned on me like this. The Charlie on the phone was the same Charlie from the bar on our first date. His true nature reappeared. Everything else is fake. I never barked at my colleagues like that. I had a collaborative management style with my staff to build loyalty, and I believed I got better results than by being an obnoxious dictator. But my way wasn't the norm on Wall Street.

Abby greeted me at the door apparently recovered from the shock of seeing Charlie's backside, 'his morning glory' as she called it. I didn't have the heart to tell her he was completely naked a few minutes before.

She pointed out a cardboard box containing a case of wine. "Charles is a real gentleman. I'm happy for you, Kat. I just wrote him a thank you note."

"He sent that to you?" He must have called the wine store around the corner since he hadn't left my apartment.

"Yes, as a thank you for letting him crash the party last night. And an apology for not bringing the hostess a gift."

I was speechless.

"Kat, you must tell me how you found him. Did you try Tinder?"

I decided to confess. "Nope. A mutual girlfriend suggested we meet."

She smiled, but I couldn't keep the rest of it secret. "Charlie is the bad blind date video guy. The one that sent the roses on Sunday. He stopped by my office on Monday and helped me take my boxes home. And last night he came back from Europe early to say goodbye before I left."

She did a double take. "Seriously? Wow!"

"Yeah, last night was great. Figured it would be a short visit, but we danced and had fun together, and, well, you saw him this morning. But just minutes ago, he was scary angry on the phone with someone at work. Now I'm afraid he is the same guy from Friday. I can't date someone like that."

"Don't worry, Kat. He seems perfect for you. More your type than Matteo or that old rich guy you mentioned. He's probably dealing with a problem at work, and it sounds worse than it is to you. Maybe the other guy was yelling back, or his boss did. Talk to him. Tell him."

"Yeah, you might be right."

"Can you give him this thank you note for the wine? By the way, I'm happy to keep an eye on him while you're gone. Guys like that don't stay on the shelf long." She snapped her fingers emphasizing how quick someone could snatch him up.

I took her card for Charlie and started to leave, but

remembered the discussion I overheard last night. "Abby, who was that woman you were talking about last night in your bedroom?"

She looked alarmed, so maybe things had gotten worse. "No, it's nothing. Focus on your trip and have a fantastic time. We'll catch up on everything when you're back."

I didn't like being brushed off since maybe I could help her. But she stood and said, "Sorry Kat. I've got to get back to work and set up some showings."

She gave me a hug and kiss on the cheek goodbye, and a tear slid down her cheek.

"Oh Abby, don't worry. I'll be back in a few months. Thanks again for watching over my apartment and bills. Email me if you need something. I got a good price for this cruise. When I'm back, we're going to celebrate and do whatever you want. A Broadway show and dinner. Pick out something special."

"Yeah, that'll be fun. Don't rush back, Kat. If you are having a good time, go with it. No worries. A new job and this place," as she waved her arms around her apartment, "will be here waiting for you."

When I returned home, Charlie sat at my desk with his laptop using my printer cable. My laptop was still open to my brokerage account, and the screen with my investments and account balances was showing.

"Pretty penny you have there, Kat. And this place, I heard you say last night you don't have a mortgage. Must be worth close to two million."

I snatched my laptop from him. "That's private. And this apartment is only worth it if I sell it, and I'm not selling ever."

"Whoa, sorry Kat. I didn't mean to snoop. Just using your printer. The wireless setting didn't work, and your account info was right there. You should log off when you aren't using it. What if someone broke in?"

"Right, like you?" I shut down my laptop and stormed out to my bedroom to pack. I should book my car service in case they get busy. Charlie had worn out his welcome.

My clothes were clean and ready to pack, and I had to be

prepared for all types of weather. The ship probably doesn't have washer-dryers, so I threw in extras. I was packing too much, but I didn't want to run out of clean clothes.

I glanced up and saw Charlie hovering in the doorway as if he wanted to test the water in my bedroom. He should put a stick in so I could chew it up and scare him away.

He left finally but came back with a cup of ice coffee. "I'm sorry, Kat. You're right. I should not have looked at your account. I'll show you my brokerage account, but yours is a lot healthier."

I glared at him. He should have millions more. Charlie and his wife were idiots and probably spent it as fast as it came in. He put his hand down on my dresser close to the door as if to prop himself up and glanced down at the washed and folded sweatshirt and gym pants I had borrowed from Greg.

"I didn't know you were Ivy League," he said, noticing the word 'YALE' in big letters on the navy sweatshirt.

I ignored him. Charlie grabbed it and observed, "A bit too large for you."

"I'm not Ivy League, and they aren't mine." Would I ever see Greg again?

"Good, I'll get you a crimson from my alma mater, the winning team and a much better school."

I assumed he was referring to Harvard since he had that sweatshirt on last night.

"Whatever," Annoyed with this stupid rivalry, I picked up Greg's clothes up to find an empty box to mail them. Another chore I'd nearly forgotten.

"Who owns them?" He blocked me from passing through the doorway with his arm.

I ducked under his arm. "Greg's. I'm sending them back." I left not caring how he reacted.

I shut the door to my office for privacy and ordered online the DVD for the 2014 film *Mr. Turner* as a thank you for Greg since he hadn't seen it. Charlie was pushing me right back to Greg when he acted so possessive.

I returned to the living room with Greg's clothes and taxi receipt ready to mail. Charlie was working on his laptop like he owned the place. He must need to go home, at least for a few hours, but he didn't seem to have any intention of doing this. I stared at him wondering how to get rid of him.

"You have lots of mosaics around. I especially like Bacchus, the god of wine, in the kitchen, the mermaid in the guest bathroom, and the seahorse in yours. They're all so unique. Where did you buy them?"

"You can't buy them." He looked surprised. Some things aren't for sale, but a deal guy like Charlie thought so. "I made them."

"You did? What a talented girl even if she's only 99 percent there. Come here for a second. Please." He begged and made some funny cat chirping noises. I ignored him and put my coffee cup in the kitchen.

He pranced over and put his arms around me while he nuzzled my neck and kissed me. "I'm sorry if I upset you with your account and on the phone. I have some new imbeciles working for me, and I get angry when we piss off clients. We can't lose more over stupid shit. You know, Kat, it's business, not personal." I squirmed and extracted myself from his arms.

"You remind me so much of back home in Wyoming. The wet untamable always surprising Laramie River."

"Well, that may be," not wanting to be under his spell again. "But I've got to go to the post office and then to Chinatown to pick up some dresses for my trip. Can we meet here later to go to the airport?"

He didn't answer either way. Impatient, I picked up Greg's package and grabbed my coat from the closet. I didn't want him to stay. But if he wouldn't leave, he'd have to wait here. Nothing was that valuable. What would he steal? A mosaic? Not likely, and if he did, I'd track him down.

29 ~ Views To A Park

Somehow Charlie weaseled his way into coming with me to Chinatown. "Kat, let's stop at my apartment. It's on the way, and I need to pick something up. The 59th Street subway is just as easy as the 66th Street station. We could skip the post office too since my doorman can mail your package."

I agreed, but only if we were quick. I couldn't leave town without my dresses. We walked down 68th Street to Central Park West, the street filled with ultra-expensive apartment buildings facing the park. I was curious about how he lived and his bat-cave. I often walked this way since the sidewalks were less crowded than on Broadway and to see a glimpse of Central Park.

Charlie let go of my hand outside his building, Nine Central Park West, known as Nine CPW. One of the newest, most upscale addresses in the city.

We entered Charlie's lobby, and a doorman greeted Charlie as 'Mr. Richmond.' Charlie was brisk, but pleasant, greeting him by his first name. I was relieved to see this friendly exchange since I couldn't tolerate blatant rudeness to receptionists, waiters, or doormen. A receptionist once told me the way to identify if a person was genuinely kind was how they treated the little people. By little, she meant the less wealthy, or at a business, the less senior people.

Charlie handed him my package with a twenty-dollar bill which more than covered the postage. Charlie glanced down at the mailing address on East 88th Street.

"Is this his home or office?"

"Home. He works at the Freedom Tower."

"At least I'm closer and Central Park's between you two."

A park was nothing. Soon a massive ocean, if not several, will be between me and everyone and everything I've ever known.

The gleaming bank of modern elevators made the one in my building look like a lonely, old man. I reminded myself there wasn't anything wrong with vintage, and it was reliable too. We stepped into a white marble elevator that was bigger and cleaner than my bathroom.

Charlie asked, "Do you like to swim?"

"I do. I swim at my gym every week."

"We have a private pool downstairs. When you're back, we should go for a dip."

"Love to." A New York City apartment with a pool was rare, and he wouldn't need to ask twice.

We reached the 18th floor and entered his apartment and admired Charlie's fantastic view of Central Park. His apartment was small, and boxes were scattered around adding clutter. I was disappointed it didn't look more like where Bruce Wayne would live, but the view made up for it. The only gadgets visible included the usual - a stereo, big screen TV, and an espresso maker.

Even though his apartment was about half the square footage of mine with only one bedroom, it was probably worth three or four times more. Location and a swanky lobby, besides other amenities such as meeting other residents who head major companies, drove the price higher.

His apartment reminded me of something out of trendy furniture store catalog. He tossed his coat on one of his black leather club chairs. I left mine on not planning to stay long.

"Sorry about the boxes. I still haven't unpacked."

"How long have you been living here?" His home was sleek with almost nothing on display or on the walls. So bright I almost needed sunglasses.

My apartment's walls were painted different colors in each room with lots of pictures, statues, paintings, and mosaics scattered around. I didn't like knick-knacks or clutter, but Axel convinced me they gave a home some personality.

"A year, maybe a bit more. My ex has our place in SoHo. A friend was moving to Chicago, so I bought his small one bedroom. Home sweet home until the divorce is signed."

He went into his kitchen and picked up a stack of envelopes and flipped through them and opened one. I glanced at my watch and waited ready to go.

"The bedroom is through there." He pointed to the entrance. "If you want to see the rest of the place. But it's a mess. The maid cleans up, but I didn't call her since I've been away."

I peeked in from the doorway. Charlie's king bed was unmade, but the rest of the room was neat and clean. His large walk-in closet was open, and I glimpsed a large selection of clothes and expensive suits ready to go like soldiers standing at attention.

"Ready?" he said standing behind me and startling me from my snooping. "Unless you'd like to spend more time in here?"

"No, not now." I shook my head shyly at the vision of being entwined with him in those sheets. When I returned, I'd be busy working so having a weekday like this one would be rare. I enjoyed this brief freedom and life of leisure away from the daily slog of working in an office on client audits and investigations.

The only thing on the wall was a huge tapestry recreation of the famous medieval Italian painting, *The Birth of Venus,* above his bed. I walked over to see it up close.

"I couldn't resist buying that on my honeymoon to Florence. Same size as the original and as intended, hanging about the marital bed. That is if I was still married."

"She looks like she's popping out of a sea shell."

Charlie put his hands on my waist. "That's Venus, the beautiful goddess of love, emerging from the sea. You two look a lot alike."

"Me? Thanks, but I don't have long red hair like that, and she's a bit hefty in the hips."

"Not the hair color so much, but the rest of her. She has a perfect body." He moved behind me, but I pulled away.

"You don't like compliments, do you?"

"No, not really. We should go." Before he convinced me to test his messy marital bed.

"Sure. I have what I needed to pick up."

While we walked to the elevator, he suggested having lunch in the private dining room in his building or Chinatown, my pick. I wondered if this was a joke and shook my head. A culinary adventure in Chinatown versus a dull private dining room? Anyone who knew me wouldn't bother asking.

The elevator was empty, and I stood on the far side across from him. He crooked his finger as if trying to hook a fish and pull me over. I ignored him and stood my ground.

"Oh you," he said. He walked over and stood behind me putting his hands on my shoulders and leaned around. "I can tell I may have to do some of that -"

"What?" I interrupted. After last night and this morning, there wasn't much else a man and woman did together.

"Horse whispering."

My ear tickled from the air mixed with his words. "Oh, don't whisper me. I know all about horses. I had two back home in Texas. I was in some rodeos and did pretty good at barrel racing and pole bending."

He didn't ask so he must know about those contests. Both were timed competitions on horseback popular with women and kids and didn't injure the animals like so many of the men's rodeo competitions. I hated the cruel side of rodeos. Seeing young calves roped that were scared to death refusing to give up without a fight, and the tight straps that made animals buck.

Barrel racing followed a cloverleaf pattern around three barrels, and pole bending was a race around six upright poles. Both races were timed, and points deducted if you knocked anything over.

"Great. Maybe you can keep up with me when we ride back home."

The elevator opened, and he put his hand on my lower back as if to guide me out or maybe he was trying to hold onto me. Did he think I was a city slicker? I couldn't resist giving him a hard time, and it wasn't that difficult to do since Texas was the bigger, more well-known state.

"Yeah, well, if Wyoming has any decent horses, it shouldn't be a problem at all." But it was a long time since I had ridden, and he was probably much better at it.

After crossing his modern lobby, we were back on Central Park West. Outside again, Charlie grabbed my hand. I was tempted to pull away, but he smiled sweetly, and it reminded me of the couples, usually tourists, you see holding hands, so I relented. We passed the huge silver world globe above the station and weeded our way through the crowd. I let go of his hand and hurried down the stairs into the Columbus Circle subway station glancing back hoping he was still following me.

30 ~ *Hong Kong NYC*

Thanks to the fast-moving subway, we were soon seated inside a hole-in-the-wall Cantonese café. The place was vaguely familiar when we passed by, and now I remembered eating here with Jackson. This café was the extreme opposite of the dining room at his apartment building and had the ominous name 'Hong Kong.' But the food was delicious, and only a few blocks from our destination to pick up my dresses.

We got a couple of lunch specials and Chinese Tsingtao beers. I rarely drank at lunch, but I'd officially started my vacation, and Charlie had the day off too. If I drank like this on the cruise, I better not come back an alcoholic.

Charlie looked around and didn't seem comfortable, but didn't comment on the décor. He had a tough time using chopsticks and used a fork with the Korean *bibimbap* on Monday, so I asked the waiter for a fork when he delivered our lunch. While he was waiting, he told me, "Go ahead. I like to watch you eat. You enjoy it so much."

"When the food is good, I sure do." Not wanting to wait for my eggplant and garlic sauce to cool off, I dove in. The dish was a perfect blend of soft eggplant and spiced with more than a hint of garlic.

"You have to have some of this when you get your fork. Otherwise, my garlic breath will kill you."

"We wouldn't want that now, would we?" He teased back. The waiter found him a fork, and he started in on his General Tso's chicken.

"You sure like ethnic food."

Mexican wasn't ethnic to me since I grew up in San Antonio where it's a staple. "Yeah, I like variety."

Part of the whole reason to live here was to take advantage of all the different cuisines, cultural events, and neighborhoods. New York City was an adult Disneyland, and I had a permanent admission ticket by living in the middle of it.

"You'd find my eating habits dull. Egg sandwiches or bagels for breakfast, roast beef or turkey sandwiches for lunch, and burgers or steak for dinner. Unless I'm out with clients, but I usually order the same thing. I'm a basic meat and potatoes kind of guy. Most of my meals are behind my desk between calls or meetings."

"That sounds dreary." I hated eating the same thing even in the same week.

"I look forward to traveling the world and eating all sorts of different things with you right here in our city."

At least he was willing to try something new, but if we dated I'd never see him with his demanding work schedule. I put some of my eggplant on his plate and stole a taste of his.

"Hey, I like that. Keep your sticks over there." He said teasing me.

"But food is better when it's shared. And eat your veggies. Good for you."

"Yes, Mama." He hesitated, but ate some and must have liked it since he stole some more.

"I like American food too. Burgers and steaks. My Dad used to grill steak for supper every Friday night."

"I like him already. I don't hear 'supper' often. You are a southern girl."

"Nope. I'm a Yankee. I was born in Ohio when my Dad was in the Air Force. But my parents are from Texas, and we moved back to San Antonio when I was young."

"And they still live there?"

"Yeah, but they're always traveling."

"Where do they go?"

"All over. My Dad's retired, and my Mom wants to go to every country in the world she can legally get into without getting shot. They're going to New Zealand this weekend."

"Wow. My parents don't travel much. The ranch ties them down. Must be where you get your wanderlust."

"Yeah, maybe." I smiled back. But it was more from Axel's love of traveling, and I didn't want to bring him up.

"Are you dating that Italian guy, Matteo?" Charlie scanned my face for an answer. We had finished lunch, but he was waiting for a second beer.

"Who wants to know?" I was taken aback at his sudden question.

"I do. Come on, Kat. Do I have a reason to worry?" His beer appeared, and he took a sip and put the bottle down keeping eye contact with me the whole time.

"No. We're just friends." All we will ever be. I must have said this with a hint of frustration. He looked as if he didn't believe me, so he may as well hear the truth. "His Italian girlfriend is coming to visit tomorrow."

"Oh, I see. And what about the architect?"

"Greg?"

"Yeah, the world-famous Gregory Overton."

He remembered his full name. "I've gone out with him a few times, but …" I drifted off not finishing my sentence. A mistake, I knew, leaving it open for him to push me for more.

"But what? I didn't see him at your party last night."

"He's in Paris." I couldn't imagine him being there. He would have hated it. "I don't think he's the right guy for me."

"And why not?" He leaned in to hear every word.

I wasn't sure how to answer and didn't want to make a verbal snafu. Yesterday may have been a bad day, as Friday was for Charlie, so I hadn't completely given up on him.

"His life is so different from mine. I'm probably too independent for him."

"I would say so. I learned that the hard way on our first date." Charlie leaned back and looked more relaxed since Matteo and Greg weren't real obstacles, and started to chuckle.

"Yeah, well that was a bit extreme. You were incredibly rude. I like my freedom and not being lectured. I get enough of that at work." I hoped this warning would sink in.

Charlie finished his beer and excused himself to the bathroom in the back. I signaled for the waiter to bring the bill and got some cash ready to cover our lunch.

"Kat, what brings you here?" Jackson slid into the vacant seat where Charlie sat a moment before.

"Oh, you surprised me." I clutched my neck with my left hand. Jackson wore a baseball cap slung low over his eyes, and his hoodie was stained and torn. If this was a disguise, he was doing a pretty good job of looking like a teenage bum.

"This is my turf. I hope it's as close to Hong Kong as you plan to get."

"I'm sorry Jackson. I've got to go there for the flight home. But I promise it'll be brief. I'll be careful. I'm taking my Asian black haired wig."

He shook his head while he glanced around. "Not a smart move, Kat. You shouldn't tempt them, even with a disguise. Take the wig and wear it."

"I will, and if I can, I'll skip Hong Kong."

"Take the info I gave you. Get in touch with them as soon as you get off the damn ship, and before you check into a hotel. They will loan you a local passport and set something up."

He pulled out his wallet and took out some Hong Kong currency, and folded them into a tight wad. Jackson cupped his hand to hide it and slid the wad across the table to me.

This happened so fast as if he was a magician. I would have missed it if I'd blinked. I hesitated in surprise.

"Take it, Kat. Consider it an advance for when you work for me or a loan, your choice. Don't use your credit cards or ATM over there."

"Okay. Thanks. I'll pay you back." I didn't want to owe him anything. "I'll buy some local currency before I get there too."

"Good idea. And, no unnecessary moves, snooping around, or anything. Stay around tourists and in public spaces. Wear the wig and buy some clothes there, used from a flea market if you can. Try to dress like them, but a poorer version to blend in."

"Sure, will do. Thanks again."

"I've got to run before your Prince Charming returns." He stood in one swift move. His timing was uncanny as Charlie was on his way back.

"And Kat, just an FYI. He doesn't seem like your type interrogating you like that. You shouldn't let him push you around."

"Yeah, I know." But he didn't hear me since he was

already out the door, and probably halfway down the street.

"Who was that?" Charlie asked as I stood ready to go after leaving cash to cover the bill.

"Who was what?" I quipped back and headed out the door. I knew Jackson didn't want people knowing who he was, and I couldn't jeopardize our relationship. Charlie didn't need to know everything.

We were on Bayard Street filled with the old tenement style four-story buildings dating back to old New York. The area was still filled with immigrants but in a different way.

Charlie came up from behind me and grabbed my arm. "Kat, I asked you something."

I jerked my arm back. "No one. Someone. It's not important. Okay?"

I kept walking, not caring if he followed me. I was tired of being grilled, not just about Matteo and Greg, but now with Jackson too. All this endless questioning grated on me.

Charlie caught up and said, "Fine. Forget it. Chill."

I knew Charlie was annoyed. Axel never complained or asked about my male friends or colleagues, so this was new to me. On Wall Street, especially at the senior levels, women were vastly outnumbered by men, so being around men all the time was normal for me.

"Kat, are you still angry?" He yelled from behind me since I wasn't stopping. The sidewalk was narrow and crowded, so there wasn't room for him to walk next to me.

A woman crossed in front of me to enter a store. I had to stop to let her pass and turned back to look at Charlie. "Damn straight."

He stood with his hands on his hips, and I did the same. We were in a Mexican standoff out of place here in Chinatown.

"Okay. I apologize. What do you want me to do?"

"Leave. Go." I pointed behind him, and away from the tailoring shop. "I don't have time for this."

He put his hands up surrendering, and then slowly walked a few steps, smiled, and put one hand cautiously on my shoulder. "Kat, I'm sorry. I promise to shut up, but I'm not leaving. Not yet. You are disappearing soon enough."

I twisted out from under his hand and glared at him. I was more concerned about picking up my dresses and being ready to go. "Whatever."

I jaywalked across the street and hurried into the old, decrepit building and up the stairs eager to see if the New Imperial Tailors had created anything magical.

31 ~ Dressed To Go

Charlie followed me up the narrow stairs refusing to give up. The entire building was so old and worn down that it may be one of the originals from the 1800's. I'd toured the Tenement Museum not far from here and while fascinating, I would have hated to live back then.

I loved a big pillow-top bed and a hot shower, not to mention my smartphone, TV, movies, and especially music. Back then it would be a rare treat to hear music since it would all have to be live. Jazz, blues, and rock n' roll didn't even exist.

My dresses in shades of blue and green with a few more neutral-colored tops hung on a rack ready to try on. I waved off the salesclerk's suggestion and wrote a check for the balance, arguing I had to get home.

Charlie disagreed. "You should at least try on one. We've got plenty of time. We're taking a cab back," and glanced at his Rolex.

Charlie didn't like taking the subway, and Chinatown was on the east side of Manhattan and a long subway ride requiring transfers to get back to the Upper West Side.

"All right," I said, resigned. "Only one to make sure." Not that there was time to change anything if they didn't fit. But I might get a discount and have fewer things to pack.

"I want to see you in one too," he said with a devious look.

To console them both, I went into the dressing room and tried on a cotton sky blue dress. To my surprise, it fit nicely and wasn't too tight. These dresses weren't fancy like the velvet ball gown, but I needed daytime outfits if I had to dress like this. The skirt flared out, and one of the seamstresses poked her head in and asked if I had a hoop to wear with it. I explained it was at home already packed for my trip.

Charlie called out. "Are you decent?"

I walked out in my fancy dress to the mirror, and Charlie did a double take when he saw me. "Wow. Are you supposed to dress like that all the time?"

"No, just for special occasions." I planned to wear jeans most of the time. "The ship is old, so they want to commemorate it. Re-enactors get into this."

"That's a shame. You looked beautiful in that dress. I'd want you to wear one every night if I was there. Maybe when you get back, Miss Scarlett?"

"Does this mean, Rhett, you are inviting me to a fancy ball too?" I could play this game too.

He didn't respond at first since he was out of his league. A pauper compared to Greg.

But Charlie bowed down with a flourish and wave of his hand. "If you will honor me with your presence, I will create a special evening for the two of us when you return. An unbelievable date. You'll never forget it, and never look at another Ashley."

"We'll see. I haven't met Ashley yet."

He frowned, but I didn't want to be manhandled. Scarlet was feisty, and Ashley was her big love even if he wasn't right for her.

The clerk packed the dresses between layers of tissue paper and into some large shopping bags so taking a cab was a necessity now.

Charlie reminded me of a love-starved puppy dog. Luckily, cats weren't that dumb.

~ ~ ~

Back home, I ran up two flights of stairs to see Matteo after dropping off the dresses in my apartment. He left a few voice messages to come by before I left. While Charlie was at the nearby Apple Store, I decided to see what he wanted.

Matteo opened the door and slumped up against the doorframe as if it would hold him up. He smiled but his eyes were bloodshot, and he looked awful. Nothing like the Roman god I once admired.

"I hoped you might stop by." He motioned for me to come in.

"Only for a few minutes. I'm still not packed and have only a few hours left."

We walked into the living room, and he sat on the sofa. I wanted some distance, so I sat in the chair across from him.

"I should have told you about Valentina. I didn't want you to hear like that. She is my girlfriend, but we've grown apart over the past few years."

I didn't say anything but snuck a glance at my watch.

Matteo continued. "Last night I was up late with Alberto. Paying for it today." He shook his head probably still hung over. "I told Alberto things weren't working out with Valentina. He hoped we'd stay together, get married, and be one big family."

I stood and put my hand on his shoulder to soothe him. "Matteo, I'm sorry, but I have to go. I wish you the best. Do whatever you think best but …"

I was tempted to say, 'not on my account,' but I couldn't be so presumptuous. His breakup had nothing to do with me which was a relief. Getting between Axel and his old girlfriend was bad enough.

"Do you like that guy, Charlie? He's very American - goal oriented."

"Yeah, I guess he is." Goals were a good thing, and I wasn't ready to discuss how I how felt about Charlie particularly not with Matteo.

"I hope he doesn't disappoint you again, Kat."

Matteo walked me to the door, and I gave him a quick hug goodbye. I didn't want to leave on bad terms.

"Are you sure you want to go on such a faraway journey? Your ship is so small, and the oceans are vast. Those countries are full of dangers. Deadly viruses and diseases exist especially in Africa and Asia."

"I've got to go, or I'll always regret it. And don't worry, I'm stronger than I look. Besides, helicopters do emergency airlifts. I've seen it happen before on a cruise ship."

"Please stay healthy, and don't forget the emergency medical kit. All legal in your name with instructions in English. Be sure to follow the directions, and only take it if necessary."

"Thanks, Dr. Matteo. I hope to bring it all back unopened."

"And Kat, send me an email or call me. Let me know how you are doing. I will worry about you. When you return, we'll go to dinner again."

"We'll see." Just looking at him I knew I might want to but only if we were both single. But that wasn't likely. Not for him.

He kissed me on the lips, but I pulled away not wanting to kiss him like that again. And I couldn't help thinking about Charlie.

He whispered, "You aren't living if you aren't loving."

I pulled away from his embrace but stared at him wondering how he could be so cruel. Does he mean if I'm not in love I might as well be dead?

"Kat, we aren't all evil, just human." I wasn't about to debate this, and I was in a hurry.

"Ciao. See you." I ran to the stairwell to be back in my apartment before Charlie returned. I missed his mischievous green eyes, familiar kisses, and even all those infuriating questions. Was I falling for him and all the aggravation?

32 ~ *Jam Packed Fun*

Sitting on the leopard rug in my bedroom, I was surrounded by overloaded suitcases and the unpacked new dresses. I was stumped. How would I fit everything? These dresses had so much material and traveling with three bags was out of the question.

I must leave some behind. But I'd gone to so much trouble to get these outfits specifically for this trip, and I'd never wear them again. And if I had to wear a dress for dinner for two months, I'd need more than one.

Charlie called from downstairs, and I buzzed him in.

My cell phone rang, and I answered automatically. "Okay, I'll come downstairs." I assumed Charlie couldn't get in. My building didn't have a doorman, and the buzzers were tricky.

"Shall I call you later?" I recognized Greg's voice.

"Oh, no. I'm sorry. I thought you were someone else. I'm in the middle of packing. How's Paris?"

"It's lonely here without you."

I was surprised to hear that since he was so irate yesterday.

"Maybe another time. Paris is a beautiful city." I shut the door to my bedroom for some privacy and sat on the carpet. Charlie would be back any moment. I'd left the front door ajar, and Charlie wouldn't be happy to know I was talking to Greg. I didn't have the energy or time to argue.

"Yes, it usually is, but not today. Rainy and cold but I'm working all weekend. Are you proceeding with your two-month trip?"

"Yes, that's still the plan."

"Kat, I wish you'd reconsider. Why not two or three weeks instead? Plenty of time for an adventure."

"It's too late to change."

"It's never too late. Tell the travel agent you changed your mind. End of story."

I didn't respond. I didn't want my story to end before it even started.

"Desi wanted to do something like this once. Back when she was in the theater. After years of struggle and auditions, she was selected to go on a Broadway touring show."

"She did? What happened?"

"She was dating Steve. Her mother and I knew she faced insurmountable odds to succeed. We withdrew our financial support. Desi came to her senses and gave up the tour."

How awful. I tasted the bitterness of Desi's lost dreams. "But why? You said before, like Turner, we should follow our dreams."

"That was different. Turner was a man with talent, and this trip you've planned is foolish and irresponsible. Desi came to her senses and made the right decision. She's happily married to Steve. He's a good provider. They have beautiful kids and a lovely home in Westchester. She has no regrets."

"But why couldn't she have both – a career and a family?" My chest tightened, and breathing hurt.

"Now Kat, you know it doesn't work that way. Something has to give."

Yeah, and it's always the woman who does the giving. Charlie called my name from the living room.

"Greg, I've got to go. I'm leaving for the airport in a few hours, and I'm still not packed."

I hung up and knew I couldn't contact Greg when I returned home. The memory of how Desi was forced to give up her dreams was too painful. I wouldn't let him destroy mine.

Charlie knocked and opened my bedroom door. I clutched my phone and stared out into space thinking of poor Desi. Now I knew why she was so excited to dress me up last Saturday. I was a character in a dinner party scene and part of her old acting life.

"Everything okay, Kat? Who was that?"

"A friend saying goodbye." I wanted to forget Greg.

"That Italian guy?"

"Nope." I didn't like being grilled, so I wasn't going to tell him. I was angry at men that pressured women to follow these pre-ordained old-fashioned rules.

Even though I knew I should ignore Charlie, I turned the

tables on him. "How many girlfriends do you have Charlie? What's her name, Krista? The one from the bar who likes to make videos?"

"Nice that you should care. It's simple. Zero. Krista is a friend. She was part of my deal team at work. Nothing more."

I sat on the floor moving stuff around in my suitcases, and the dresses that needed packing but would never fit.

"I have to focus on this." I waved my arms in frustration.

Charlie kneeled behind me and rubbed my back and shoulders, but was unable to loosen what felt like a boulder attached to the back of my neck.

"Kat, I don't mean to badger you. I know you are leaving, but before you leave, I want to know if we have a chance. I've only met Matteo and Greg, and perhaps there are others too." His tone was kind but firm.

"No, no one else." How had things gotten so complicated from zero men in my life to juggling three? But I still didn't know if any were right for me.

"Glad to hear it, Kat. I don't want to share you with anyone."

"Charlie, I got massive problems right here. I can't think about two months from now. I have to figure this out."

I stood to survey the piles from a distance and come up with a game plan. No wonder the women back then traveled with massive trunks and dozens of pieces of luggage. And with servants and staff to lug them around too.

His phone rang, and he glanced at it. "Sorry, I have to take this. I'll be right back. I'm a pretty good packer."

Charlie answered the phone but didn't yell or snap like before. "Yeah Pete, what's up? I've got to apologize about earlier. I was out of line and shouldn't have yelled at you like that …"

I shut the door not wanting to listen. At least, he apologized to the poor guy. Maybe I'd convinced him to be a smidgen nicer.

I dumped everything out of my suitcases. Men had it so much easier. They just had to pack a few shirts and pants. Women needed that and more with shoes to match. I removed all the tissue paper and rolled the dresses up tight and stuck them in one suitcase. They still took up a lot of space, but I could use the other bag for my toiletries and modern clothes.

Charlie sat on the floor next to me to help, and I told him what I had to take with me. I removed a few casual tops and an extra pair of jeans. For two months, it would have to do. I'd buy whatever else I need in the ports of call. Charlie helped stuff socks and small bits into my shoes and other hiding spots. He even zipped up my bags and rolled them into the living room.

"I'm all done for the day, and you are all packed. And, I do believe, we have about two hours before our car service shows up." He sat on the carpet next to me, nuzzled my neck and pulled me onto his lap. He leaned in and sniffed my neck. "You sure smell good. You better not fall overboard."

"Yeah, it's an Italian, a new guy in my life," I teased starting to feel better now that the packing was done.

"F for Fascinating by Salvatore Fierro," I whispered.

"Yes, definitely F. Those sneaky Italians." He kissed me lightly on my neck. "I know another better F word," he teased, his voice low and husky.

"Fabulous, fantastic, freedom?" I said playing along and trying to guess.

He pulled me around to face him, and I sat eye to eye with him. "Close. Rhymes with luck."

Oh, of course, he had his mind on that. He held me tight and took my hair clip off and let my hair fall on my shoulders. His nose caressed my neck, and his breath tickled.

He inhaled deeply and whispered, "I'm going to miss you, my little Miss 99 percent. Nothing's dull when I'm around you. But what a wild ride you have ahead of you."

"I hate to tell you this, but besides losing my appendix, I don't have my wisdom teeth either."

"Well, then it's down another notch to 98 percent. Don't let anyone take any more body parts until they check with me first. Promise?"

Charlie started to tickle me, and I giggled but managed to say, "Yes, I promise."

He stopped, and I didn't move still comfortable on the carpet in his arms.

"I'm serious, when you're back, I want to take you to Wyoming, Kat. You'd like it there."

"Sure. And we've got to visit Richmond in the Spring. It's only right since you adopted that name."

"Anywhere you'd like to go, but right now there's no place I'd rather be."

His hands reached down into my jeans. And at this moment, I didn't want to be anywhere else either. The barriers I erected were collapsing as if he had a magic key card to open any door.

The timid and nervous part of me wanted to forget about this trip and stay. Even a once a week Charlie-fix would be enough. But I knew I had to go since I'm not a quitter. Besides if I stayed behind like a love-sick fool and lost him, I'd regret this forever.

~ ~ ~

"Kat, so about Hong Kong. When you get off the ship, I want to meet you there."

Oh, shoot. I almost forgot to pack the wig. I jumped up, stepped into my jeans and zipped them up on the way to my closet. I dragged my bag filled with costumes from the top shelf.

"Is everything okay, Kat?"

"Yeah. You reminded me that I forgot to pack something."

I dumped the contents of the bag on my bed and rummaged around looking for it. The wig must be here somewhere.

Charlie stood next to me. He picked up my Catwoman outfit. "This?"

"No, a wig."

"Good. I'd hate to imagine you running around on the ship in that."

"I already wore it. Monday night at the parade."

"You did? Oh, you are brazen. You know, I have a Batman costume."

I stopped, and my heart skipped a beat or two when he mentioned Batman. "You do? You've got to be kidding me."

"No, I do. It's my favorite, standby costume. Why?"

"Oh, nothing. I just thought … never mind." How could I explain he'd reminded me of Batman on our first date and not favorably?

"Next year we should dress up and go to a party or the parade together. Here in the real Gotham."

"Maybe." I couldn't think about this while searching for the elusive wig.

"I think Batman and Catwoman were attracted to each other. They even got married."

"Yeah, well, that's Hollywood." I resumed my search for the wig. "Finally. What a relief." The hair was a crumpled mess. I shook it and found my wide-toothed comb.

"Are you going to Japan too? Do you need this?" He picked up my kimono, a gift from a Japanese friend.

I shook my head no. "What did we agree about unnecessary questions?"

"Come on, Kat. Fine, I guess it's for a bad hair day. December, Hong Kong. Just give me a week or two notice."

"No, sorry. As soon as I get off the ship, I'm flying back."

"Come on, Kat. It'll be fun for Christmas shopping."

"I won't arrive until January."

"January? I guess it would be if it's two months. Okay, post-holiday shopping."

"No shopping. You have to do that on your own."

"What's the deal? Don't you like Hong Kong? You were there before, and got all that press."

I stared at him wishing he would shut up. I wasn't going to tell him about the dangers.

"Oh, I know. It's the drug dealers, isn't it? You shouldn't go there, so that's a disguise."

I didn't say anything. I hated to admit Charlie was smart. I wouldn't have put it together this quick. The wig combing was done, and it looked slightly better. I left the bedroom to stuff it into my suitcase.

Charlie followed me. "Kat, you can't go there. It's way too dangerous."

I ignored him and stowed the wig carefully between some dresses. "No, it's not. I'll be careful."

I took out the small metal disc and Hong Kong cash from my wallet and stuck it in the pouch with medical stuff from Matteo. They were all emergency related and safer together in my carry-on bag.

Charlie scrutinized my every move and looked so worried.

"Take the ship anywhere, but not Hong Kong." He stomped his foot, and the sound reverberated on the wooden floor.

I stood up after kneeling beside my suitcase, and he put his arms around me. I expected an apology, but he whispered, "I forbid it."

"You what? You can't forbid anything." I wasn't about to be bossed around by anyone.

"You have to leave now, Charlie. I'm going to the airport alone." It was too early to head for the airport, but I was ready to go and could shop in duty-free.

"Kat, no." He slumped down as if all the air was sucked out of him while he watched me. I saw the pain in his eyes as if I was a 'dead woman walking.' His concern unnerved me.

I lifted the handles on my suitcases and balanced my carry-on bag and purse on top. I had a lot to lug, but taxis were plentiful at the corner of Columbus Avenue, so I didn't have to go far. I rolled my luggage towards the door, but he had to leave first so I could lock the door. I wasn't about to loan him a set of house keys.

He sat at the dining table and put his elbows on the table. His hands were together as if in prayer shielding his nose and mouth. This whole situation was getting ridiculous. I tapped the wall near the door impatient.

He stood with a grimace. "Okay, Kat, you win. Do what you want. I won't bring it up again. Please let me take you to the airport."

My heart pounded from a toxic mix of nerves and stress. Maybe I had lost my mind to consider returning to Hong Kong.

"I need a drink," I said not caring what he thought.

I left my luggage by the front door ready to go and marched back to the kitchen. I plopped my shot glass on the counter and opened the freezer. Charlie came into the kitchen and sat on a bar stool watching me.

"Extra shot glass, Kat?"

I motioned to the wall unit with the shot glasses next to my non-existent liquor collection. Inside the freezer, I found my two Scandinavian buddies waiting. I pulled them both out, but I only wanted one small shot from the bottle with my ship for courage.

I filled my faithful shot glass, a souvenir from Sweden, and admired the little red horse called a *Dala* horse. The wooden horse carvings, dating from the 16th century, were from the Dalarna region, near my Swedish grandfather's birthplace.

Charlie returned with his selection. "You have an unusual assortment of shot glasses."

Most were souvenirs from trips with Axel, and it was hard not to reminisce when my life was happier and easier. Charlie picked the one from Iceland with an Icelandic pony. Of course, we both selected glasses with horses. Axel never wanted to go horse riding, so that was something only Charlie and I shared.

I offered him both aquavits, and he selected the Norwegian one with the ship on it.

I filled up his glass. After we said, "Cheers," we both drank it down. The cold tickled my throat, and I stared at the ship logo feeling better.

"That's good. What's it made of?" Charlie asked.

"Like vodka, it's distilled from potatoes, and they add spices."

"Are you going to be drinking it on the ship?"

"Probably. Scandinavians drink this all the time. If it hadn't been for you and this guy here," as I pointed to the Norwegian aquavit bottle, "I wouldn't be doing this."

He waited, and I sensed he was eager to hear more. "After our date, I had a close call with a taxi, so I needed a drink when I got home. I forgot about these bottles and then …" I drifted off.

"What happened?" He asked urging me to continue.

"That night you said I should do something more productive. I'd been trying to plan a trip for weeks. With help from this guy," as I pointed at the Norwegian bottle, "I decided to do what he did."

I pointed to the back of the bottle that explained the journey.

"Get away from people like you and my failed business on a unique trip. And for at least a little while, forget about all these sad memories here." I glanced up at Axel and Xena sitting on the shelf.

Charlie read the label on the back of the bottle and scrutinized me but was silent for once.

"This is something I have to do. If I don't do it now, I never will. And the ship is somehow encouraging and pulling me. I know it sounds crazy, but I can't explain it." I looked at the ship to avoid seeing a dreaded smirk on Charlie's face.

"Now, Kat. You aren't losing it. Sometimes people get messages like this. I grew up in Wyoming with Native Americans. I've been to tribal spirit ceremonies and heard the stories. I'll tell you more about it when we have some time. It's a gift, not a curse."

I searched his face for a sign he was lying. He, of all people, shouldn't understand this. I sniffed with relief since he looked genuine. "Well, life would be easier if these guys had behaved more like bottles."

He took me in his arms, a warm, bear hug, and whispered sweet reassurances in my ear. Maybe he's right about Hong Kong, not to mention the warnings from Jackson, Chee, and Robert. Why not deal with some minor inconvenience to reduce my risk?

"Oh, all right. I'll get off the ship at the port before, fly to Hong Kong, and change planes there. Hong Kong's International Airport should be safe enough for a few hours. Happy now?"

Charlie smiled and kissed me. "Oh, yes. Thank you, Kat. More than you'll ever know."

I knew he was relieved, and I hated to admit it, but I felt the same way.

33 ~ *First Leg*

When our car service loaded with my suitcases and Charlie's bag from his London trip, pulled away from the curve, I exhaled with relief.

Charlie hadn't bothered to go home to pack for the weekend. He explained, "I don't need to. I have everything I need at my beach house. I'll be back Sunday night."

As we went down 68th Street towards Central Park and the airport, I wanted to scream, "Goodbye. I'm free," out the window. But I'd forgotten the most important item besides my passport and wallet.

"Stop, please," I called out to the driver. Charlie looked at me. "I forgot Axel. I can't leave without him. He's the reason I'm starting my trip in Denmark."

"No problem. We have time," Charlie said. The driver circled the block back to my apartment building.

I ran into Abby on my way inside and yelled hello not stopping. "I forgot Axel, and Charlie's outside in the car."

I ran up the stairwell not waiting for the slow elevator. Out of breath, I got the coffee can and stuffed it into a zip-lock plastic bag on my way downstairs. I didn't want his ashes spilling in my bag.

I tripped on the stairs and slammed down on my left foot but grabbed the railing and didn't stop. I was unbalanced without the second shot of aquavit, but it was too late now. That'll have to wait for Denmark. Traffic on a Friday afternoon could be brutal with commuters heading home and weekenders, and Charlie hadn't left any wiggle room for delays.

As I ran through the lobby, Charlie stood outside and leaned against the car chatting with Abby.

"Ready? Anyone else you want to bring along?" He asked teasing me while he held the door open.

"We're ready." I slid across the back not wanting to waste a second. I looked back to see what was the holdup. He gave

Abby a hug and a kiss on the cheek.

She peeked in the car's window. "Thanks again for the wine, Charlie. Have a fun trip, Kat."

"Bye, Abby. Thanks for watching over my apartment." Was she going to watch over Charlie too? I was surprised how much this bothered me. He wasn't mine, and even if he was, I was leaving for two months. And Charlie wasn't the type of guy who would wait around, regardless of what he said.

Back in the car, we sped off, and this time, I would live without or buy whatever I forgot. I leaned back against the plush leather seat and looked over at Charlie. "That was a close call. I'm not sure I could get his ashes sent to Denmark, and once I'm at sea, it would be a logistical mess."

He patted my leg and said, "Not to worry. I'm glad you can say goodbye with this memorable send-off. But shouldn't your husband be your soulmate, not your cat? Any issues?"

I wasn't surprised since others had asked me the same thing. "Axel wasn't the soulmate type. If you'd met Xena, you'd understand. She followed me around, slept right next to me, and even groomed me sometimes."

"Well my next wife, not a pet, will be my soulmate."

I was tempted to remind him he hadn't planned it well with wife number one but didn't want to be rude. "Good luck with that."

"Oh, yes, I'm having lots of luck," while he smiled.

Our car headed west, not towards the east side of Manhattan. "Excuse me," I said to the driver. "We are going to JFK, not Newark airport." It was easy to go to the wrong one since there were three airports regularly used by New Yorkers.

Charlie broke in. "We are going to the west side first. Relax, Kat."

"West side? But why? There isn't time. I'm going to miss my flight and my cruise too."

He didn't answer me. "Chaaarrrrliiiieee." I wailed his name as if it had five syllables.

"Kat, calm down." He put his arm around me for reassurance. After kissing me on the cheek, he whispered, "It's a surprise. You'll like it. I promise." Then he laughed and said, "But that was good. You sounded just like one of my sisters back home."

I was fuming and ready to scream at him if I missed my flight. I extracted myself from his arm and sat back against the leather seat by the window with a thud. I crossed my arms ignoring him and stared out at the busy streets as we headed the wrong direction. If I missed my flight, he'd have to buy me another ticket for Copenhagen. I had to get to my ship on time.

We pulled into the Chelsea pier area along the Hudson River. The driver went through a security gate. A couple of helicopters were parked nearby. "Are we going by helicopter? He nodded. "Oh, how amazing." I reached over and kissed him in anticipation of the ride.

"Only takes about six minutes. Plenty of time for a drink at the airport before you go."

We climbed out, and a uniformed man introduced himself as the pilot and said he was ready. He said to Charlie, "You've used the service before. I brought you in yesterday, didn't I?"

"Yeah, more times than I can count. Good ride Thursday night too. I made it in time for her goodbye party," motioning at me. So that explained how he arrived at my apartment so quickly last night.

Our luggage was removed from the car. I tried, but I couldn't fit Axel's can inside my carry-on bag. I unzipped a suitcase but debated what to remove. Tennis shoes or boots? It'll be easier to buy new tennis shoes in Europe so out they went replaced by Axel's tin can.

Charlie watched my struggle. "I'll keep your shoes for you," he said, while he zipped then inside his bag.

I'd never bothered to confirm if I was permitted to take cremains on a plane. But I was doing this and would play dumb if it wasn't. Some rules were stupid. One reason I wasn't always the best internal auditor. My common sense couldn't abide ridiculous rules.

I followed Charlie to the helicopter. He pointed to the front seat next to the pilot and said, "You should sit there, if you want. You can see more, and I'll be right here behind you."

"You don't mind? Ah, this is great. Once I did a test flight in a small Cessna in Marin County, California." I wanted to learn to fly and get my pilot's license. I would have if it weren't so expensive. Axel and I were on a tight budget when we first got married.

"Somehow, I'm not surprised," Charlie said and smiled.

Seated in front, the pilot asked, "Have you been up before?

"Yes, once on Maui." About twenty years ago on my honeymoon, but I didn't share that detail.

The pilot checked my seat belt to make sure it was locked and secure, and we put on headphones. Cleared for takeoff and within seconds, the pilot guided the helicopter with ease into the sky. The view was fantastic. Not only of Manhattan, but we could see New Jersey across the Hudson River, reminding me of the sights from Greg's office.

The Freedom Tower gleamed, and I swelled with pride knowing it would take a hell of a lot more than a plane to bring that building down. We'd never stop fighting back no matter what terrorists tried to do.

Looking across the vast city, I whispered, "See you later."

My island of Manhattan was blanketed with buildings and pointed, gleaming skyscrapers, filled with opportunity. I knew Americans committed plenty of offensive and misguided actions. The CIA and the FBI certainly had, but I chose to believe that most of us kept trying to get it right.

Axel never became an American citizen since there wasn't any real advantage to it, and he said our political system was a sham. But I never wanted to live anywhere else or give up being an American.

The pilot asked if we wanted music, and we both said "yes" in unison. He gave us some options, and Tom Petty's song *Free Fallin'* filled our ears. Charlie tapped me on the shoulder and wagged his finger at me, and when I glanced back, he was singing as if performing on a stage.

I wanted to pinch myself still shocked that I was in the sky and on my way. If I wasn't strapped in and could stretch out my arms, I knew I could fly. The trip I've dreamed of was finally happening.

34 ~ *Down But Not Out*

The helicopter veered downward for our descent into JFK. Phil Collins with Genesis and the song, *Follow You, Follow Me,* was blaring through my headphones. Charlie tapped on my shoulder. He was singing his heart out and gesturing to me. But with my headphones and the helicopter's noise, I couldn't hear him. I turned back not wanting to miss my last bird eye's view from the air before landing.

As promised about six minutes later, we landed on the tarmac at JFK. This ride beat the hour plus trip in a car. Greg should travel by helicopter to reduce his stress level. Hell, he could afford to buy his own.

The pilot said goodbye and wished us a pleasant journey and weekend. Charlie thanked him.

"I'm just seeing her off. Going to the Hamptons tonight."

After confirming our luggage was headed to the terminal, I gave Charlie a thank you kiss. "Fantastic, best-ever surprise. Thanks so much."

As we walked across the tarmac into the nearby terminal, Charlie took my hand and beamed with pride. "Great ride and an excellent soundtrack. Brings back memories of the old days playing all those weddings."

"Weddings?"

"Yeah, I was in a band in high school. Played guitar and all those classic songs."

No wonder he was so accomplished at singing and dancing. He must have thought my air guitar was lame. I'd had piano lessons, but they didn't last long. I couldn't endure practicing and stuck inside while my friends were out having fun. But maybe being in a band would've motivated me to play more.

We entered the terminal and picked up our luggage. Charlie motioned to the check-in desk for my flight. His helpfulness bordered on annoying. As if I couldn't figure this out and hadn't traveled all over the world before. I ignored him and got in line.

"Wait a sec." Charlie fished out a sheet of paper from his briefcase slung over his shoulder and handed it to me. "Not that line. You've been bumped up to first." He pointed to the first-class check-in counter.

"How?" I always flew coach. Business class was rarely offered to internal auditors since they didn't generate revenue.

"I upgraded you when you were with Abby today. But only on this flight. First to Copenhagen wasn't available. But at least you're in for the long transatlantic piece."

I thanked him and wheeled my bags over to the first-class counter. Charlie's phone buzzed, and he glanced down at the caller and walked away to answer it. He motioned he would stand next to an unused counter.

The airline attendant was efficient as they should be for first class, and I headed over to where Charlie stood. He had his back to me with his briefcase on the check-in counter.

He was on the phone, and I didn't want to eavesdrop or interrupt him since this could be an important business call. But from what he said and how he was laughing, it didn't sound like it. I moved a bit closer and heard snippets.

"Yeah, Krista, the cat's in the bag. You owe my big time."

Krista was the video-making culprit, so that sparked my attention.

Charlie continued, "I should say so. She's declawed and even purrs."

Dread washed over me and flowed from my nostrils and down my throat threatening to choke me. Was Charlie talking with Krista about me? I clutched my stomach feeling my shoulder bag land with a thud on the floor.

Before I could retrieve my bag and leave, he added, "Videos? Naw didn't do that, but I have photos. That'll be proof enough. See you later. Yeah, Krista, our usual spot ..."

What photos? He took some with his phone a few hours ago when I sat on the floor surrounded by my suitcases. He'd said he wanted some memories before I leave. And we'd both used our phones to take photos from the helicopter. I'd even taken a few of him.

I couldn't listen anymore. A roar of sound, like waves at a

beach, echoed in my ears blocking out everything around me. I strained to reach my heavy carry-on bag desperate to get away. He saw me, and from the expression on his face, he must have realized I'd overheard some of his conversation.

He pocketed his phone, and his smile disappeared as I turned to escape.

"Kat, don't go. I don't know what you heard or thought you heard, but I can explain."

"Don't bother." My voice sounded odd, and it hurt to speak. I hurried towards the security checkpoint and my gate.

"No, Kat, please." He sprang towards me and grabbed my arm.

"Stop it," I cried out. I tried to pull away with all my strength, but Charlie held on tighter.

Memories of the bar, our first date, flashed before me. I glanced around to see if anyone was videotaping me again. But that was silly. I don't care. I must get away from him. He was a liar using me in some evil scheme with Krista.

I pushed back against him hard with a jab from my elbow. This was a practiced move from my kickboxing classes that happened without thinking. All the training at the gym was finally paying off. This move surprised him, and he let go of me but clutched my bag.

I kicked behind me to keep him away. I didn't know if I would even reach him and was worried he would grab my foot like Axel sometimes did when we were playing around. But he didn't expect it, and I hit what must be his prized possessions since he went down on his knees clutching his groin.

"Oh, you're a fighter," Charlie hissed. I stared at him astonished. My kick must have hurt, but he deserved it. The past twenty-four hours was a sick game. The pain he felt was nothing compared to mine.

Some people in the airport were looking at us, and I didn't want to be surrounded by a crowd or in another video. I shifted my bag on my shoulder to leave, but Charlie grabbed my leg and wrapped his hands around my ankle.

"Calm down," he commanded, but this stressed me out more.

"Let me go," I yelled and kicked my trapped leg again to loosen his grip. But he didn't let go and pulled my leg towards him.

I lost my balance and fell forward at an angle. I reached out my hands to brace myself, but my left knee hit the floor and sent a shooting pain through my body. My left foot was still sore from the incident in the stairwell when I retrieved Axel.

Charlie sat on the floor, and now I was there too. We stared at each other for a few seconds, but I scrambled to reach my purse and carry-on bag to get away. A crowd stood around us watching.

Charlie, the consummate entertainer, addressed them. "Nothing serious. Just a minor spat."

Minor? Maybe to him. This was major in my book.

A security officer came up and asked, "Everything okay, folks?" eyeing me.

We both got off the floor and stood, but I ignored Charlie and faced the guard.

"He's bothering me. I'm trying to get to my flight." I was about to cry and clenched my fists to prevent it.

Of course, Charlie contradicted me. "No officer, we're doing okay. A minor misunderstanding. That's all."

Charlie turned to face me. "Kat, you have plenty of time before boarding. Let's get that drink and chat. I don't want you to leave like this, all emotional and upset."

"No. I'm going to my gate."

He couldn't follow me through security since he didn't have a ticket. Before he could catch me, I was in line with my boarding pass, passport, and TSA card being checked by Security. I was in the fast-moving, expedited line, and I sighed with relief. The extra cost for my pre-check card was so worth it.

My carry-on bag and purse went through the x-ray machine behind me. I didn't see Charlie, but my phone buzzed. It was Charlie so I turned my phone off while wishing I could turn off my memory of him.

35 ~ *A Magic Mushroom*

After I had passed through Security, I glanced around to make sure Charlie hadn't sweet talked his way into the airport's inner sanctum. The coast was clear, but there was over an hour before I could board my flight. I searched for somewhere to wait convinced I wasn't safe here in the open or at the gate.

A few bars and fast food joints were ahead but not great options. Signs listing a slew of airlines' private lounges beckoned. With my first-class ticket in hand, I might be able to get in. My hand shook as I gave the employee sitting behind the counter my boarding pass. She glanced at it and welcomed me to the club. I wanted to hug her for admitting into this sanctuary.

The club was like entering another world. This lounge was the largest, most over-the-top resort-like airport club I'd ever seen. A sign even advertised a hair salon and spa. A perfect place to hide and unwind.

After everything I went through, Charlie owed me this first-class upgrade. My sore knee throbbed from my fall. He and Krista probably planned this from the beginning. My face got hot, burning from pure anger. Krista was probably his girlfriend. He lied about that too, and they had fun playing their cruel joke on me. But at least I was safe, and on my way, so I tried to stop thinking about the jerk.

The bar beaconed to my right, and I made a beeline in that direction. A massage or facial would be healthier, but I would never be able to relax especially if the masseuse was a man. The bar wasn't full, and I sat on a stool and leaned against the counter.

The bar menu offered all sorts of bite-size dishes, but I couldn't decide and didn't have an appetite. First things first - order a drink. Champagne bottles chilling in ice buckets were on the bar waiting, so I ordered a glass from the friendly bartender. I had several reasons to celebrate and thought about having a series of toasts. First, I escaped from Charlie, and second, I was on my way.

The waiter brought my champagne in a fancy flute, and I took a big sip letting the cold liquid numb my throat. I would love to get drunk, but too many alcoholic drinks and jet lag were a recipe for disaster. I swiveled around on the stool and leaned my back against the bar to see who was here in the bar. The crowd was a mix of business travelers and older vacationers either chatting or glued to their phones or laptops.

I should call Mel to say goodbye like I promised. I asked the bartender if he minded since I always thought it was rude. He smiled and said, "Be my guest. Nice of you to ask."

I ordered a glass of rosé wine and hit my speed dial for Mel's cell phone. Mel's familiar voice made tears roll down my face. I pulled out a tissue to dab them. I didn't plan to tell her what happened since she'd warned me, but she could tell something bad happened. The trick Charlie played on me with Krista and the fight in the airport spilled out.

After I had stopped for breath, she asked in her steely, calm voice, "Where are you? Right now?"

"In the airline lounge past security. Charlie's probably on his way to the Hamptons now."

"Kat, he may show up. Promise me this. Tell an employee. If a man starts to bother you, they should get Security. Do it now. Don't wait. Then board that plane, and enjoy yourself."

"Okay. I'll ask the bartender, but he's going to think I'm nuts. Charlie needs a boarding pass for first-class."

"Those aren't hard to get. Charlie might be a member of the airline club. Promise me. Do it now and have a drink. I can tell you need it. You have two beautiful months ahead of you on a dream ship where no one can bother or hurt you, least of all him."

I sniffed and wiped my nose with my tissue.

"Oh, and Kat, you probably don't want to hear this. I asked a friend of mine who works at Levittman about him. She thought she'd heard of him, but he's not in the employee directory. The jerk lied about that too."

I was speechless and wondered why he lied. He must work

for someone. He was in London on business unless that was a lie too.

Mel continued lecturing. "I know this is harsh, but this should be a wake-up call. Stop letting people take advantage of you, Kat. You've got to stand up for yourself. There are way too many Charlies out there. They're everywhere. I know you want to think the best of people and help the underdogs. But there is nothing 'under' about these guys."

"You're right. Thanks, Mel. I'll tell the bartender to be ready to call Security just in case. No more soft, furry Kat. I'm building a hard, protective shell." I visualized those huge old turtles in the Galapagos.

After we had said goodbye, I focused on my rosé wine, savoring the taste as it flickered lightly on my tongue. At least my rosé wouldn't lie to me and try to be a riesling or viognier.

Mel's advice wasn't anything new. I'd heard it before but can you change your fundamental nature? At least I hadn't been duped into giving him money or something stupid like some of those sad sack women.

I was trained to be polite, and it came naturally. Those ingrained habits were hard, almost impossible, to change. When on occasion I'd been the stereotypical, brusque New Yorker and didn't hold a door for someone or ignored a greeting, I'd regretted it.

My mind darted back to Charlie. Why would he lie about Levittman? Was he a con man? At least I had my laptop with me, and he didn't know my bank or brokerage account passwords or have a key to my apartment. But could he have made a copy of my key or hack into my accounts? I was getting paranoid and motioned for the bartender to return.

"This will sound weird, but a guy was bothering me out in the terminal. If he shows up will you call Security? But not until I ask you to." I didn't want Security arriving in the unlikely event I ran into a real friend.

The young bartender smiled and nodded. "Sure thing."

Like psychiatrists, they must hear all sorts of bizarre stories. I picked up the menu again and contemplated my options. I hadn't eaten since lunch, and dinner on the plane was several hours away.

The bartender was busy with other customers but returned and placed a large brownish speckled mushroom wrapped in plastic on the counter in front of me. I wasn't sure what to say.

"Do you like dark chocolate?" The bartender asked and grinned mischievously.

I nodded and stopped myself from quipping back with a smart-ass response since I couldn't imagine anyone not liking chocolate.

"Good. You looked like you could use it. From my personal stash, and it's perfectly natural." Before I could ask him about his gift, he was at the other end of the bar busy washing out glasses.

Unwrapping my treat, I sniffed it carefully. The smell of sugar and dark chocolate greeted me. I took a bold bite into the crisp meringue and crunch of chocolate. A few quick bites more, and sadly, it was all gone.

When the bartender came back, I had to know more. "Thanks. That was delicious. Where did you get it?"

"My kid sis is interning with them. Magic mushrooms from the Brooklyn Cookie Company."

"Wow. Delicious." I smiled and pulled out my cell phone and added it to my electronic to-do list. "When I get back from my trip, I'm buying some."

The bar was filling up now that the flight to London was only an hour away, and my mushroom supplier was busy attending to his thirsty crowd. I scanned the menu now having more of an appetite thanks to the magic mushroom's great beginning to my dining adventures ahead. What would the food be like on the clipper ship? I dreaded the traditional boring boiled potatoes with brown gravy.

A familiar voice boomed, "Kat, thank God. I knew I'd find you here."

I dropped the menu so fast my wine glass teetered about to fall, but I grabbed it in time.

Charlie approached and stood about a foot from me but didn't try to touch me.

"What are you doing here?" I knew I should move, but I

AQUAVIT

was so surprised and didn't want to leave my comfortable perch.

"Kat, I know you're upset, but please hear me out." Charlie looked calm but tired with his briefcase balanced on his carry-on wheel bag behind him. He sat on the bar stool next to me, and I strained under the pressure of his closeness.

The bartender ambled back from the other end of the bar, and I hoped he remembered what I said. But instead of saying to me that Security personnel were on their way, he said to Charlie, "What can I get you?"

Charlie didn't take his eyes off me while he ordered. "Beer, a bottle of pilsner, whatever you have."

I recovered from my shock and decided the best option was to let him drink his beer in peace. I stood and started to pick up my bag.

"Kat, please. I bought an expensive ticket I'm throwing away to talk to you. May I have five minutes of your precious time? Please?"

He looked pained, and with some wine and distance, I felt oddly safer. His green eyes and brown hair now matted and messy and wondered what sort of bogus excuse he was going to come up with to explain the phone call. After all, it was a game, and I didn't mean anything to him. Part of me wanted to hear him say it so I could move on.

He rested his hands on the bar, and I stared at them. Those hands and his fingers had touched me, made me feel close to whatever you are supposed to feel when you almost think second chances and magic are real. That state when you've tapped deep into your soul and felt the warmth flow down to your toes. That feeling someone cared for you and might worship you slightly. But now I knew it was all a mistake and a lie. Those hands and that person hurt me. And he lied from our first miserable date to today, our last.

"I know that call and what you heard sounded devastating. It would seem like that to me too. I should never have spoken to Krista about us. That was wrong."

The bartender put his beer and an empty glass down in front of him. Charlie turned down the glass preferring to drink from the bottle. He glanced at it before sipping and made a sad sounding chuckle. "Perfect, it looks like you." He showed me the bottle of pilsner with a blonde-haired mermaid logo.

Another sign I'm doing the right thing, but I wouldn't see any mermaids. Not unless I went to see the Little Mermaid statue in Copenhagen, and there wouldn't be extra time for that. I waited for his explanation, but I would never forgive him. Not again.

"After our first date on Friday when you left, Krista and the other two guys you met that night joined me. We used to work together and got drunk. She bet I couldn't win you over. Like the ass that I can be, I agreed to the challenge. When she called, I couldn't resist boasting. Not that I won but happy and thrilled to have this second chance with you. I hated it when you left Friday so angry and can't bear it again tonight."

I was a cruel joke and bet. The deal maker couldn't resist playing a game of Russian roulette with my heart. I wasn't amused and said cruelly, "Yeah, well enjoy it. You won. I lost."

"No, Kat, that's not it. I'm crazy about you. I don't want us to end. The bet was stupid and idiotic. I could have left this morning or even last night if that's all it was. In fact, I won the bet back on Monday when we had lunch. It was never about sleeping with you. I enjoy being with you, dancing, making breakfast, shampooing your hair, even helping you pack. I want us to have a future together. I've never said that to anyone but my ex-wife. Kat, I'm going to wait for you. Two months or however long you are gone."

After his speech, he put his beer down and with his elbows on the bar massaged his forehead with his fingertips. I wanted to believe him, but I couldn't.

"You lied to me. I can't believe anything you say. You don't even work at Levittman."

He stopped rubbing his forehead and rested his chin on his hand and turned to looked at me. "Levittman? I didn't say I worked there. I left months ago for E.J. Stephenson, the hedge fund."

I'd heard of Stephenson. One of those ultra-secretive hedge

funds and a much smaller company. But one of the most profitable firms that could afford to reward their employees significantly better than public corporations like Levittman.

"I needed more money to pay off my ex. After my bonus, I joined Stephenson in March. I spent over twenty years at Levittman. Right after graduating from Harvard. Never got around to updating that business site LinkedIn. But if it makes you happy, I'll do it right now." He pulled out his phone to access it.

"Don't bother. Not for my sake."

He sighed deeply and took a business card out of his wallet and held it out, but I refused to take it not wanting to touch him again. He put it on the bar and slid it my direction. I glanced down and saw his name, Senior Managing Director and the Stephenson name and logo.

"Kat, please, I care for you. I'm serious. I couldn't bear it if you left tonight hating me for two long months."

I was unconvinced he wasn't still lying and determined to leave. "No, not two months."

He seemed to brighten up with a slight up-tick to the corner of his mouth just before a smile. I got up slowly not wanting to put extra pressure on my sore left knee and foot and slung my carry-on bag over my shoulder. I wanted him to hurt and feel as betrayed as I did. Like taking a knife and turning it slowly and painfully in his gut, I said, "Forever."

I glanced at him trying to keep my face impassive, but I could feel tears gathering. I focused on taking some cash out of my wallet to tip my friendly bartender, even if he wasn't much of a bodyguard.

Charlie stared at me as in disbelief as if his blood was flowing from a stomach wound to the floor. If he felt like he was slowly dying from the inside out, then he knew how I felt until I spoke to Mel.

"Goodbye, Charlie."

"Kat, no, please. Not like this."

I ignored Charlie, waved goodbye to the bartender, and turned to leave. This time, Charlie didn't make a move to stop me. All the fight must have left him. He was visible in the reflection of the bar's mirror, and he stared straight ahead focused on the rows of liquor bottles.

As I shuffled away trying to ignore my aching knee, Charlie asked the bartender. "Double Jack on the rocks please, and keep the bottle handy."

In a daze, I stood behind the front desk and asked the attendant for my boarding pass. Overwhelmed with what Charlie and Mel said, I watched myself go through motions but couldn't feel it. Even with all the ups and downs today with Charlie, I hadn't had such a good time or spent 24 hours with another man since Axel. And now it was all a cruel trick and bad memory.

I felt like the mermaid on his beer bottle, washed up on the rocks looking for a prince but never finding one. Like her, I nearly traded my tail for legs and my free will for a liar.

36 ~ *Leaving On A Jet Plane*

Nestled into my first-class seat with my seat belt snapped, I waited for takeoff. If the pilots asked for assistance to taxi to the runway, I would have volunteered. I monitored the entryway worried that Charlie would somehow reappear.

After the door was closed and we finally took off, I relaxed and stared out at the clouds and white fluffy masses filled with endless combinations and possibilities. Just like clouds, millions of guys are out there, so there was no need to rush or worry.

The only positive thing, when looking back at my sudden trio of boyfriends and romantic liaisons, was ending my unintentional sexual hiatus. And I'd had a fun filled week, even if it was stressful.

I searched around in my purse for a pre-packaged face wipe to prepare for a long night aboard the plane. I touched some folded paper in my purse and pulled out an envelope addressed to Charlie, but his name was crossed off with mine scribbled instead.

I ripped it open tearing the letter inside. The envelope contained British pound notes along with a VISA credit card. I unfolded the handwritten letter and saw 'Charles Richmond, Senior Managing Director, E.J. Stephenson & Company' printed at the top with the firm's address in midtown.

> *Kat,*
> *By now you are somewhere over the Atlantic, and I'm missing you already as I write this. If you need anything during your adventure, let me know. Please be safe and avoid Hong Kong. You are my one in a seven billion.*
> *Love,*
> *Charlie*
> *P.S. Here's some UK cash from my last trip and a prepaid VISA card for $1000. Mad money for*

whatever you want. I'm counting down the 60 odd
days until we are together again.

I stuffed his note with the cash and VISA card back in the envelope and blinked back tears. These gifts didn't change anything. A pittance compared to the money he probably won from his stupid bet. And money means nothing to people like that.

I was tempted to throw it away or mail it back to him. But it was a waste to throw it away, and it might get stolen in the mail. Instead, I'll do something good with it. Give it to a charity and help some homeless and sick animals. I'm bound to see them in ports along the way. Something good can come from this nastiness.

I opened the emergency medical pouch from Matteo and jammed the envelope inside. I struggled with the zipper but forced it to close and stashed it back in my carry-on bag. The pouch was now 'stuffed to the gills' as we say in Texas for some odd reason. The thought of fish gills made me squeamish. Would I have to help in the ship's kitchen and learn to filet a fish?

I moved around trying to settle into my seat that reclined into a flat bed and wrapped myself in a cocoon with the blanket covering my head. I tried to sleep comforted that I was 30,000 feet above the earth flying over 600 miles an hour to a place where I wouldn't have to worry about Charlie or anyone else.

Hours later, I woke in a new time zone ready to start Saturday and the weekend. I was eager for some conversation, and the person sitting closest to me looked like she wanted to chat. She looked about my Mom's age with dark hair and smiled when our eyes met briefly.

We introduced ourselves and chatted about the flight and New York while we ate breakfast. Vicky was a friendly American but lived in Britain and was on her way home to London. She was the first in a long series of strangers I'd meet over the next few months. I hoped to find friends on my journey and wondered if the sailors would be as 'salty' as I'd been warned.

Vicky asked about my destination, so I explained about

Denmark and the clipper ship voyage. She was impressed by my bravery, so I told her about Axel and my company closing. How it was all perfectly timed. "I'm sorry. I must be boring you with too much information." Remembering how Axel used to complain when I carried on like this.

But Vicky shook her head. "Quite an experience you've had and a most exciting trip. Like a fairy tale."

"Yes, but no Prince Charming. I've given up."

"Oh, my dear. Never give up. You are too young to throw in the sponge, as we say in the UK."

"I may try again, but I'm taking a well-deserved break."

We didn't say anything while the flight attendant refilled my coffee and her tea.

Vicky said, "I gave up on men after my husband died. You see, I married well the first time and marrying an ordinary commoner wasn't viewed as proper. There was a man, but my friends convinced me it would never work. To this day, I regret it. Life isn't always easy but taking chances is part of it."

I half-listened while I stared at my nails in dire need of a manicure. I couldn't remember if I packed any nail polish and should have avoided Charlie and gone to the airport's spa yesterday.

"Oh, I've taken chances all right. With three different men in the past week and each ended terribly." The three unwanted stooges all came to mind.

"But my dear, trying to find the ideal mate to fall head over heels with is nearly impossible. I may sound jaded, but that attitude will break your heart more than any man will. Find someone you love to be with at least most of the time."

Before I could come up with a decent counterpoint, she continued. "You know, romance novels like these." Vicky waved her book in my face with a half-naked hunk on the cover. "They've ruined us. We think there is this perfect person out there who will send us flying over the moon in ecstasy," and whispered as if she dared to continue, "both in and out of bed."

"I know. The perfect guy doesn't exist. No wonder we can't find them."

"Exactly. All men have an Achilles' heel, but some are better at hiding it." Vicky patted my hand. "My dear, I have a confession to make. I saw you in the lounge before the flight and in the terminal."

"Oh. That was so embarrassing. Not one of my finer moments." I was surprised this refined woman wanted to talk to me after such unladylike behavior.

"I felt sorry for you, both of you. A soap opera unfolded before my eyes."

"Yeah, well I wished it hadn't. He was a liar, and I was a plaything. A bet, if you can believe it. I wish I could forget I'd ever met him."

"But, my dear, Charles is sorry about everything."

"Charles? How do you know his name?"

"When you left the bar, I spoke with him. He was distraught, and it brought back sad memories. My husband would often bury his sadness in whiskey after a disagreement. I wished someone had intervened and talked to him."

This was unbelievable. Charlie wasn't here but sent an ally to badger me. The flight map on my personal screen estimated at least an hour before our arrival. Airlines don't want anyone standing around in the galleys, so I excused myself to go to the only place where I could be alone - the bathroom. On my return to my assigned seat, I lectured myself. Be polite, but avoid discussing men and specifically Charlie.

When I got back to my seat, Vicky apologized for interfering and handed me an envelope. "Charles asked me to give you this."

The envelope bulged at one end, and I debated opening it, but I was curious. Vicky was polite but leaned forward eager as well. I ripped it open, and an Apple shuffle in bright red with earphones attached spilled out. A handwritten note said, "*Play List for Kat. A few favorite songs from my days in the band to keep you company. Love, Charlie.*"

Vicky glanced at the shuffle with fascination, and I wasn't sure what to do.

"Would you like it?"

"Oh no, I couldn't. But If I were twenty years younger, you

might have some competition." Vicky grinned making the wrinkles around her eyes more noticeable.

Why was she so enamored with Charlie? To tune her out, I stuck in the earphones and turned on the shuffle. At least I wouldn't have to hear her fawn over him. Who knows what lies he told her.

The first song was REO Speedwagon's *Take It on the Run* which struck me as perfect since it was about a woman leaving. I skipped to the next song, and Meghan Trainor and John Legend were belting out the love ballad *Like I'm Gonna Lose You*. He had great taste in music, and I'd left my shuffle behind so it would be a treat to have some decent music on the trip.

I clicked to the next song and heard the classic *Leaving on a Jet Plane*, but Charlie was singing this one. The song was sad, and I didn't want to hear his voice again. I jerked the earphones out, switched it off, and found a tissue to blow my nose.

Now I missed Axel more than ever. He would never have done something so devious and cruel. Did Axel have an Achilles' heel like Vicky said? I couldn't think of one. He was kind if sometimes distracted. Axel never fawned over me like Charlie, but that was all fake.

Vicky must have noticed I was upset since she patted my arm. She was busy writing letters on some pink stationery. "Old-fashioned. I use email, but like to send real letters. I even get some back."

I was eager to see England from my window, but it was still a broad expanse of ocean. The water below was a perfect shade of aquamarine, and I couldn't wait to be riding those waves from aboard my ship. Now I wished my trip was longer. Two months was too short. I rummaged through my seat pocket and flipped through the airline magazine. But nothing caught my eye, so I stuck it back in frustration.

"Would you like to write him a short note? A thank you or something to console him."

"Console him? He hurt me. Everything was a lie." Vicky's suggestion was annoying, but I didn't want to argue with her.

"I don't know all the details, but Charles said the only thing he won from the bet was a lousy chopped salad. I can assure you he regretted making that bet and gambling with your feelings. He was completely devastated, my dear. I could tell."

I knew what he meant by a chopped salad. The best salads in New York, if not the world, were from a local chain with incredibly long lines. For a while, I refused to wait not understanding how a salad could be worth it. But once I did, I was hooked like the rest of their fans.

Vicky handed me a few pages of pink paper and an envelope. "I'd be happy to post it for you."

"Damn," I muttered under my breath. Maybe Charlie will choke over his hard-won salad. Vicky was the persistent type, so to placate her since there was no real escape for another hour, I wrote a quick note thanking Charlie for the gifts. But I was still beyond angry and warned Charlie he shouldn't count on hearing from me ever again. I signed it and fished out the envelope with his address. I sealed the letter and handed it to her since I wasn't going to bother sending it. Hopefully, she'd forget or lose it.

Vicky smiled and said she'd post it soon. "Don't you feel better?"

"No, but I will."

This fiasco, like everything else, would roll off me. The flight attendant announced we should prepare for landing. I smiled, more than ready. I'd be willing to parachute if need be.

37 ~ *Another Danish Please*

Waiting to check in at my hotel, I glanced around. The hotel hadn't changed since my last trip to Denmark about two years ago. Axel didn't like staying with his brother, and now with two kids, they didn't have the room. The lobby was bright and white, a modern Danish style, tempting me to put on my sunglasses. The hotel's attendant handed me my key and a large envelope from the travel agency.

In my small, cozy hotel room, I tore open the envelope and glanced over the paperwork that needed my signature. The local agent, Annette Nielsen, included a note to get in touch so we could meet to go over the details. The paperwork said the ship was scheduled to depart tomorrow at 1600 or four p.m. in bright red underlined letters. They apparently didn't realize how much this meant to me. A date and time I would never forget.

After emailing Annette to tell her to come by whenever I showered to get rid of any traces left of Charlie. I sat on my bed and skimmed the paperwork. I'd swear it minutes later when there was a knock at the door, but I'd slept a few hours without realizing it. Losing a decent night's sleep on the way to Europe was always exhausting.

Annette was a tall, thin blonde woman and the stereotypical Scandinavian. I pronounced her name incorrectly, but she set me straight. Danish names with an 'e' at the end sounded like an 'a.' Annette was pronounced Annetta in Denmark.

After apologizing and stumbling along verbally in my rusty Danish, she smiled but spoke almost perfect English and got right to the point. "Sorry to wake you. I must go over some updates on your cruise that may not have been communicated via New York."

I frowned worried about more tests or hoops to jump through with only about 24 hours left.

"Because the cruise will recapture life at sea in 1860, I want to make sure you understand and agree to all the requirements.

The crew and passengers cannot bring anything modern onboard the ship. Any electronic devices, books written after 1860, modern clothing, etcetera are prohibited."

I rubbed my eyes trying to wake up and process what Annette said. "But I have a laptop, cell phone, and clothes. Jeans and normal things like that. What am I supposed to do with all my stuff?"

"No problem. We do this all the time. You leave your modern belongings in your suitcases for shipment to our Hong Kong office. They will be at your hotel in Hong Kong when you arrive. I brought some carpetbags for you to use on the ship."

"What?" I stared at her old carpet covered suitcases not comprehending this and sat down on the bed.

Annette repeated it all again. These new rules must be a joke, but she wasn't laughing or smiling.

"Okay?" she asked when I didn't respond still contemplating the drastic change of plans.

"No, not okay. I'd rather take everything with me."

"If you do, it will ruin the cruise for everyone. The whole idea of being on the old clipper ship is to experience something authentic to the period. Modern equipment will destroy the ambiance on board."

"But what about the ports? Everything will be modern there. They can't escape civilization."

"Naturally, the ports are excluded. If you miss the internet, you'll have access then. These rules only apply when you're on the ship."

I considered the pros and cons of what Annette said. I didn't often use my cell phone or computer on a ship with the extra fees and slow service. And I liked reading real books and the classics. At least in the ports, there are internet cafes. But those trips were one or two weeks, not two months.

"What if something goes wrong, and I need a phone?"

"The captain and crew will take care of it."

"All right. If I must." But I was unconvinced and unhappy about all these dumb rules.

"Great. I would almost pay to get rid of my damn phone for

a while."

I skimmed over the details and the standard disclaimer. The ship's itinerary was subject to change. But another part was underlined in red. The cruise may extend past sixty days.

"How much longer? Does it cost more?" I worried about going over my budget.

"Oh, it may stretch another two or three weeks. The two months didn't factor in the port stops. But it's all included in the cost. To make it easier, there are some clothes in your cabin for you to wear at no charge. And they have a library on board too."

But I didn't want to wear someone else's clothes. "I brought my own clothes." I unzipped my suitcase and unrolled one of my dresses, proud of my ingenuity.

She looked impressed. "Nice but make sure there aren't any synthetic fabrics. Also, you can't bring toiletries or cosmetics in plastic either."

"What? That's taking it way too far. How do I bring sunscreen and lotions?"

"Just transfer them to glass containers. Easy to get cheap ones over at the Lion discount store near City Hall Square. Also, there is a bookstore over there. You can bring books written before 1860. Just mark out any recent publication date."

I knew those shops and had planned to do some shopping this afternoon. "This is too weird." The elimination of anything modern was crazy and expensive if I had to buy new replacements in ports along the way. Reluctantly, I signed the documents.

We agreed to meet at the hotel tomorrow afternoon at two p.m. to sort out what's impermissible and pack the carpetbags. This gave us plenty of time for the ship's departure from a nearby harbor.

After she'd left, I lay on the bed and thought over these new developments. Taking nothing after 1860? Well, I must bring my sunscreen, deodorant, creams, and lotions. All part of my daily routine. I wasn't leaving without them, not even for three days.

Stores closed early on Saturday and might not be open on Sunday, so I forced myself to get going.

~ ~ ~

Listening to the multi-talented piano guy belt out old 1970's Danish hit songs from the local bands named *Shu-bi-dua* and *Gasolin* brought back fond memories. The catchy tunes with Danish lyrics were a mix of The Beach Boys meets Huey Lewis & the News.

In the bar, I was surrounded by smiling, happy Danes. Or as Axel argued when all the reports came out, "Happy, as in content, but not jumping up and down ecstatic."

My Danish friend, Lena, sat across from me singing Danish songs along with our musician. I did my best to sing along what I could remember. Lena and I met when I was in Denmark for a year as a foreign exchange student, and we'd stayed in touch. Everyone thought I met Axel when I lived in Denmark, but I'd met him later in California.

We were in one of my favorite pubs called The Leather Pants in English. The name referred to what the establishment's patrons and carriage drivers wore back in the 1700's when it was established. The place sounded like a dark S&M hangout, but if the name kept the tourists away, that was even better. Compared to back then, my soon to be re-enacted 1860 time-period was downright modern.

We both ordered my favorite dish, a *Stjerneskud,* or a Shooting Star in English. The plate was covered with a huge, open faced sandwich piled high with fish and toppings over a hidden slice of bread. A fork and knife were mandatory. I popped a mouthful of the fried and poached white fish coupled with some shrimp, asparagus, and a sprinkling of caviar into my mouth. None of the Danes I'd asked knew why it had such an odd name.

Lena said, "Your cruise sounds fantastic. If I had the time, I'd go with you. Kind of cool to give up your modern gadgets and really unwind."

At least it was a notch or two above camping. We drank a toast to my upcoming self-deprivation and survival.

"I have a gift for you," she said, while we finished our beer.

I turned down a shot of aquavit, even though Lena had one. I knew it wouldn't blend well with my jet lag, and I didn't want anything to go wrong tomorrow.

"Oh, Lena. Just being here with you is a great gift."

"This is better." She smiled but wouldn't tell me more and checked the time on her phone. "We've got to go now."

Out in the cold air, we walked past *Magasin du Nord*, the Saks Fifth Avenue of Copenhagen, facing the city's opulent Royal Theatre and around the massive Kings New Square. But not new anymore since it dated from the 1600's. We headed towards *Nyhavn*, New Harbor, also not new, and a picturesque street lined with small boats where the fairy tale writer, Han Christian Andersen, once lived.

"Does this have to do with the little mermaid?"

"Maybe. You'll see."

We went down a small side street filled with shops. But late at night, the streets were quiet with only bars and restaurants lively now.

Lena buzzed one of the apartments and giggled, while she hid the sign next to it to keep it a secret. At the top of the stairs, a young man greeted us, and we went into his apartment. He hugged Lena like an old friend.

"Hi, Kat. I'm Steen. Heard you have an exciting trip coming up. Lena wanted to surprise you with a reading."

Lena sat in a chair, and I sat on the sofa next to Steen. "A reading?"

"Yes. Whatever you want," Steen said. "Lena, did you have a preference?"

Lena scratched her head gently. "I liked the crystal more than tarot cards. I think Kat would too." She smiled at both of us.

"You mean fortune telling? I'm sorry. I don't believe in that."

"No one does in the beginning." Steen took my hand and glanced at my palm. "I have a better idea. I'll be right back."

Lena moved to sit next to me on the sofa. "Come on Kat, if nothing else, just for the fun of it. Steen is awesome. All my friends have been here and tried it."

"All right. For you, I will." But I was tired and would have preferred listening to music at the bar or sleeping in my hotel room.

Steen returned with a large bowl of water and placed it in the center of his round dining table. He scurried around and set other objects on the table, lit some candles, and dimmed the lights.

When he was ready, he motioned for us to sit around the table.

"This is called hydromancy with salt water instead of a crystal ball. More appropriate for your sea journey."

We stared in a trance at the large bowl of water in the center of the table.

"Kat, you'll drop these small stones into the water, and I'll read the waves and tell you what I see."

Steen handed me five pebbles. This was a silly waste of time but I decided to go along with it and humor them. At least, I didn't have to dunk my head and leave with wet hair.

I threw the first stone into the water and watched the ripples. Steen looked at the water and then stood up to look at the water from another position. Why was there such a delay?

But once it was still again, he said, "You have a well-balanced life. Lovely home and friends but you are bored and searching for an adventure."

I glanced at him and nodded since this was accurate. But maybe Lena had told him this when she booked my reading. These predictions would apply to most people.

After the second pebble, he cautioned, "The man you mourn and miss should be forgotten. Left in the past. He doesn't warrant this adoration."

If he meant Charlie, I couldn't agree more.

And then after the third. "I see other men, two, no three. All care for you, but you have dismissed them. Many would say unjustly."

"Unjustly? That's ridiculous. You haven't heard what happened."

Lena looked at me but didn't say anything. I hadn't mentioned Greg, Matteo, or Charlie to her. I didn't want to be reminded, and she wouldn't ever meet them.

Steen explained that the following two stones covered my upcoming journey. I leaned forward interested in what Steen had to say about this. Steen didn't speak after the fourth pebble but waited until I tossed the final stone. He waited so long, and Lena frowned ready for this to end too.

"Kat, this journey you are going on will be difficult. No secret there, but it's not what you had in mind. It's dangerous. Your voyage is on a real, working ship filled with hardships and many dark moments. But you will return. Your determination and optimism will see you through."

We stared at Steen, shocked after his bleak report. But it's all made up. It must be. How can someone look at rippling water in a bowl to see the future?

Lena broke the silence. "Kat, you don't have to go on this trip. Another cruise will come along. Stay here in Denmark. We can take a week charter to Mallorca together."

But Steen shook his head. "That's not possible, Lena. Kat must go to sea on that ship. It's her destiny."

I was numb from such a bleak forecast. Lena and I thanked him for the reading, but we couldn't recapture our happy, carefree mood. Outside Lena insisted we get a shot of *Gammel Dansk* or 'Old Danish' as a cure. Some Danes drink this for breakfast, convinced it has medicinal value.

We went into a bar in nearby *Nyhavn* in search of the special bitter made from Danish herbs, spices, and flowers. I was unnerved, not just from what Steen said but the way he said it. How this trip was my destiny and free will had nothing to do with it. Ironic, since I'd chosen this journey and fought every step of the way to get here.

This bar was another old one. From a time before and not modernized with the stylish glossy white look. The bar was lit mainly with candles and had that authentic, cozy feeling. Hans Christian Andersen, who died in 1875, would feel right at home here and probably had. We tossed back our shot of the comforting, room temperature *Gammel Dansk*.

"Kat, I'm so sorry. I never expected this type of reading. All the others were happy and upbeat with lots of sunshine and blue skies."

"Don't worry. I'm used to it. This week has been one of the craziest times of my life."

She frowned, and I could tell she was still worried. Her nervousness compounded my own, so I changed the subject.

"Love this place. It's pure *hygge* and so cozy. A huge trend in the U.S. now."

"What? *Hygge* is popular in the United States?"

"Yeah, they've analyzed and dissected it. How the Danes create a *hygge* cozy atmosphere with candles and blankets. Some friends asked me if this was part of Danish foreplay."

"Foreplay?"

"Yeah, you know. Setting the stage and getting romantic before sex."

Lena laughed, slapped the bar, and leaned back. "How funny. Americans have sex on the brain."

I smiled and tried to laugh with her, but it was hard. The forecast of hardships ahead was still dragging me down.

In the cab on the way back to my hotel, I promised Lena I'd stay in touch while at sea so she wouldn't worry. She hugged me goodbye so hard my body ached. But not from the hug, from real, visceral fear. As I rode up in the elevator, I couldn't stop worrying about what I'd done and what Steen saw ahead.

38 ~ *Retail Therapy*

Gasping for air, I rolled on my side while still in bed struggling to breathe and put my hands on my aching stomach. I vividly remembered tribal people kneeling and standing around and staring at me. My stomach ached from cramps, and a thick liquid flowed from between my legs.

"Oh, no. What in the hell happened?"

I touched my crotch to stop the flow of blood. I was warm but dry as a bone. Unconvinced, I reached for the nightstand light and fumbled around to find the switch. The lamp's light was faint and didn't illuminate the entire bed. I threw off the comforter convinced I must be swimming in blood. But the bed sheets glowed a pale off-white.

"This can't be."

The nightmare was so real. I still felt the hard ground through the thin mat against my back and legs. I'd begged, "Please let me return to the ship. I must get to Hong Kong to get home."

But they didn't understand, and I was afraid of dying. I wasn't worried about the immediate problem, but the aftermath and creating a mystery. No one would know what happened to me just like when my second great-grandfather disappeared during the Civil War.

I drank some bottled water and turned off the light to sleep again. This time I woke with a searing pain encircling my upper left arm. I turned the light back on and looked at my arm. It looked fine, not even pink, but it throbbed, so I rubbed my bicep and around my arm.

I tried to remember what happened this time. It was the same tribal group from my first nightmare. My left arm was extended and held down by several women, and I struggled to break free. An old man bent over my arm dabbing it with a splotchy red rag. When he finally stopped, he smiled and let me see his handiwork. He'd made a series of black marks about an inch wide circled my upper arm with blood still seeping out.

He must be a tattoo artist, and this is a tribal tattoo.

I shivered but was relieved it wasn't something worse like an amputation. A tattoo you can deal with if you don't get a severe infection, and I could get it removed later.

I closed my eyes but heard a loud bang. I sat up dizzy with the hotel room spinning. On the floor, I found an explanation for the noise. I reached down and picked up Axel's can that had fallen out of bed, relieved his lid was still firmly attached. I kissed Axel's face in each photograph while tears streamed down my face.

"Oh, Axel, what should I do?"

~ ~ ~

Denmark in November was dark. Only lighting up mid-day if you were lucky. I'd left my stifling hotel room to escape the nightmares and see the city. Despite how safe Denmark was, for protection and company, I took Axel along. One last tour of the city he loved before we headed north to his hometown to meet his brother.

I cut through the ornate train station and exited facing the lights for Tivoli, the amusement park created in the 1800's. Many said Tivoli gave Walt Disney the idea for his theme parks. I pulled Axel's cashmere scarf tight and wandered up one of Europe's longest pedestrian walking streets nearby called *Strøget*. Tightly-packed shops and cafes lined each side, but at this early hour on a Sunday morning, everything was closed.

I wandered down a quaint side street and passed the famous bakery, more of an upscale teahouse from 1890, called *Conditori La Glace*. Despite being closed, I gazed hungrily at the photos in the window of their fancy layer cakes with unique names.

The bakery was a meeting place for resistance fighters when Denmark was held captive by the Nazi's during World War II. They ordered a pastry called the radio horn to signal other resistance fighters. I shuddered remembering the memorial park north of town with what looked like the original wooden posts where people were tortured and executed.

I couldn't imagine facing a firing squad and knowing your

death was imminent. Here I am worried about going on an old ship from 1860. Those resistance fighters knew real fear and would gladly exchange places with me.

I sat on a bench and took Axel out of my bag and put his can next to me. "So Axel here we are. Back on *Strøget* and how you like it. Quiet and empty. "

I turned Axel in his can above my head, so he had a 360-degree look around. This was Axel's first real excursion in his current state. Even though no one was around, I felt silly and put him back on the bench.

"What do you think I should do Axel? I know you would just do it. Like the resistance fighters, it would be nothing to you. I need some of that bravery."

I didn't feel any braver. The cold metal of the bench penetrated my jeans and long underwear. I had to move to warm up and put him back in my bag. I wandered around purposeless in the picturesque narrow streets.

A Danish bakery appeared with the help of a giveaway clue - the smell of yeasty, freshly baked bread. I bought a Danish roll called a round piece. True to its name, the rolls were perfectly round. I also purchased one of the world's renown sweet Danish pastries called *wienerbrød*, which translates to bread from Vienna. Danes were brutally honest and wouldn't steal the honors for the Austrian recipes even if the whole world gave Denmark credit. But I didn't care who came up the recipes, they were delicious.

I would have stayed inside the warm bakery, but like most Danish bakeries, it was small and didn't offer seating. I ambled along nibbling my roll and saving the sweet pastry for dessert. Doubts started to creep in attacking my normally pragmatic self.

Could I give up all modern conveniences for two months, maybe three? Leave everyone and everything I knew and be cut off from the grid?

And would it be as dangerous as Steen predicted? Even if I survived like he said, I didn't want to end up in pain in some strange place and not have happy memories of the trip. Worries kept crisscrossing my brain like impossibly knotted ropes. As soon as I unraveled one, another grew tighter.

I had scarfed down the roll and starting to devour the sweet pastry while slowly window shopping. The Danish pastry was topped with sliced almonds and filled with ground almonds, known as marzipan. I sat to drink my coffee and glanced at the windows across from me.

The mannequins wore thick cream-colored knitwear with a Scandinavian design. They wore modern clothing and looked so lifelike. What would they say if I told them, "I'm leaving on an old ship without any modern clothes, cosmetics, or electronics for three months."

I knew what some friends in New York would say. "Only if you can pry them out of my cold, dead hands first."

I stood next to the store's window admiring a mannequin's sleek black pants suit. Something I'd wear but now off limits. I was freezing and turned to leave.

From behind me someone said, "Don't be a fool. Don't get trapped into something you won't like."

The streets were empty. I didn't want to hear more and hurried to get away. But I could still hear the mannequin's voice echoing against the store windows. "You'll regret it. Mark my words."

I ran down *Strøget* for the safety of my hotel. This cruise wasn't right for me. I was a fool to do this all alone without anyone I knew. And they keep changing all the damn rules and making it harder. I'm not a huge risk taker, not like Axel or Charlie.

I put my cold hands in my pockets to get warm and entered the train station. In my pockets, I felt some loose coins, and pulled out a handful of Danish coins, called *kroner* or crowns, and studied the odd assortment. The one, five and ten crown coins all had holes punched in the middle. A gold-colored coin worth twenty kroner had the current Queen of Denmark, Margarethe II, on one side, and a large crown with three lions leaping through the air on the other.

The Queen wouldn't be afraid of a trip like this. She was often at sea on her royal yacht. This must be a sign. "Queens, I go as planned, and Lions, I cancel."

I kissed the golden coin on both sides for luck and threw it in the air and almost tripped trying to catch it. I flipped the coin from my fist to the top of my left hand and looked down expecting to see the Queen's profile smiling sideways up at me. But the Lions stared back at me.

"Fair and square, it's been decided." I won't antagonize over the decision. All these warning signs forced my hand, and the brave Queen lost.

Back inside my warm hotel room, I considered my options. It was too early to call Annette on a Sunday morning. But if I wait, I'd lose my courage.

I wrote her a brief cancellation email. The coward's way out, but I couldn't tell her a fortune teller, some bad dreams, a talkative mannequin, and a coin toss won by Lions convinced me not to go. My finger hovered over the send button, and I hesitated for what felt like forever. But then I pushed send and painfully let the email go.

I climbed back into bed and tried to get a few more hours of sleep. I lay still and relieved Friday morning. Charlie ran around my apartment, full of energy and charm. I wanted to email or call him so badly it hurt. He would understand these mystical visions and know what I should do. But then I'd be admitting I was desperate, lovesick, and under his control.

"No, I must rely on myself."

Better to be like a cat. Brave, adventurous, and independent with plenty of 'my time.'

39 ~ Up In Ashes

I grabbed a handful of ashes and flung them into the water below. "Goodbye, Axel. I will always love you."

I handed the can to Axel's older brother Carsten, and he did the same. "Goodbye, Bro. Have an aquavit and a beer waiting for me. Or what the hell, have two or three ready."

I smiled remembering how often they had shared Danish beers together.

Before Carsten handed the can to his wife, Elsebet, he looked at me first to see if he should. I was tempted to say no. Elsebet wasn't just missing the final 'h' but a sympathy chip as well. She wasn't blood-family or fond of him, but I didn't want to ruin our quiet family ceremony, so I nodded okay.

Elsebet took a handful of ashes and threw it into the water but didn't say anything. Carsten elbowed her in the side urging her to say something.

"Yo, Axel. Hope you found whatever you were looking for." But I froze when she added quietly, "Piece of shit, asshole."

Carsten handed me Axel's can. It was lighter but still probably half-full. Lots of ashes left to scatter somewhere else. But where now that I'd backed out of the cruise?

We looked out at the water, and I wanted to stay nearby to reflect. But the grass was wet, and the benches were further away.

Elsebet said, "We need to get back to the kids."

Magnus and Lucas, their sons and my nephews, were in their car seats up the hill in the parking lot. They fell asleep in the car after brunch, and Elsebet didn't want to wake them to participate in the ceremony. I preferred not having them involved since it would be distracting to keep an eye on them and away from the water.

Axel and I weren't fond of them at this young age. Axel used to say, "Maybe when they are older, ready to share a pizza and beer."

Carsten convinced Elsebet to wait a minute and reminded her that Axel was his only sibling. We gazed at the water until the whitish gray layer of ashes disappeared. I turned and headed back up the slope, and they followed.

Behind me, Elsebet said to Carsten quickly in Danish. "You need to tell her now or I will."

"Not, today. Please." He argued back.

"Yes, today. Kat has a right to know to put all this behind her."

We stood in the parking lot next to their car with the kids sound asleep in their car seats. The day was cold and overcast, but the window was open slightly for some fresh air.

I told her, "Don't wake them to say goodbye." I envied them at this age without a care in the world. We hugged goodbye, but it felt strange and forced, not quite right.

Elsebet said, "Goodbye Kat. If you decide to stay in Copenhagen longer, get in touch."

But I knew she didn't mean it. We had nothing in common and were never close. And now there wasn't a reason to meet. Our future contact would be rare, a Christmas email and posts or messages through Facebook. I'd see my nephews grow up if they posted photos online or sent an annual holiday photo card.

Carsten took the coffee can from me and stared at Axel's face plastered all over. "Kat, I should tell you something. Elsebet asked me to do this for a while, but I couldn't over the phone."

He motioned to a nearby bench. I wiped off some water drops with my hand and sat down. I dreaded hearing he had cancer or some other fatal, incurable illness too.

"Kat, you know Axel. He was impetuous, even mischievous. I wanted to let this die with him, but we've seen how you're having such a difficult time getting past this. Elsebet insisted you know the truth." He sighed and added, "I've stopped her from emailing or calling you several times."

Now, I knew this bad news had to do with Axel. I put my hands under my thighs pinching my legs to prepare for the worst.

Carsten held Axel's can in his hands and looked down not making eye contact with me. "I don't know how to say it, so I'm just going to say it. Before your big Hong Kong ordeal and he got sick, Axel started planning to move back home. Back to Denmark."

"But how? Why? He never told me this." Tears gathered in my eyes.

"He said you didn't need him anymore. And he was tired of New York and knew you'd never leave. On a trip to see Mother, he met up with Pia again. You met her once I think. They were together a long time. He asked some friends about moving back, and they told me. I confronted him about it later."

He patted my knee and gave me a hug. I tried not to cry, but I could feel a flood of tears roll down my cheeks.

I'm so sorry, Kat. My brother was an idiot sometimes."

No, I'm the idiot. I've missed Axel for so long - as if he was the only man in the world and the perfect husband. What a fool I've been for months.

I took the handkerchief Carsten offered me and wiped off my cheeks and around my eyes. I didn't trust my voice to say anything resembling human sounds but nodded my thanks.

Carsten put the coffee can on the ground next to me. I tried to ignore my newly renamed 'traitor husband' and zoned out staring at the trees near the water.

"Kat, I better be going. We promised the boys a visit to the aquarium."

Carsten waved over to Elsebet signaling he was on his way. "Axel did love you, you know. In the end, he told me this was all meant to be. Axel was happy he stayed. But Elsebet and I want you to move on. Not think of him so much, and not as this perfect human being."

I forced a smile, but it was a grimace and swallowed hard. My throat ached as if a stone from last night's reading was stuck. Carsten wouldn't leave until I assured him I was okay. But it was like being a target of a drone strike. I'd survived, but everything held dear was obliterated.

I should have noticed the signs and thinking back; there

were plenty. The more I reviewed them, the more I wanted to hit Axel. Make him feel what I felt, but he was dead. I cleared my throat, took a deep breath, and straightened my back to sit taller.

"Elsebet was right. I needed to know. I'll always love him, but he's fallen off the pedestal. And you're right. I should never have put him up there."

"I guess I still can't convince you to come with our two screaming boys to the aquarium."

I shook my head. If I went with them, I'd be drowning in their pity. And the aquarium with the fish and aquatic life would be depressing since it would remind me of the ocean and my canceled cruise.

"Do you want a ride to the station?" He looked back to his car and family waiting.

"No, thanks. I'll walk back. It's not far."

"Well, then, I guess this is it."

"I suppose so. But, Carsten, do I have black under my eyes?" I never asked anyone but Axel this. I must start again with someone else even if this was a baby step.

He smiled. "Yes, a bit."

With my tissue and his guidance, I wiped it away. But on second thought, I should have left it to match my black mood.

"All right, take care of yourself. And, Kat, for what it's worth, the cruise you booked sounded perfect. I'm sorry to hear you canceled but …"

"But what?"

"You aren't that adventurous. Always so busy working. You followed Axel's lead. But I'm sure you will find something more suitable and less exotic."

Carsten said his goodbyes, kissed my cheek and patted my shoulder. I watched through my tears as he hurried back to his car, and they drove off. I sat glued to the bench processing what Carsten said about Axel and my lack of adventure. Courage, I'm sure he meant. I don't have any in his book.

I rubbed my hands and blew on them to warm up. Damn it was cold here. It was early afternoon, but the wind from the water made it worse. Axel's coffee can was on the bench next to me. I couldn't keep lugging it around and didn't owe him anything, not anymore.

I picked it up and marched down to the water. If Axel wanted to live in Denmark, he could stay here. I opened the can without touching the ashes and shook it emptying the rest of his ashes into the water. I watched transfixed as they floated for about a minute and were gone.

Past the shoreline, I observed the busy ship traffic headed north and south on the Øresund, a narrow waterway, and the Danish-Swedish border. Watching them glide by was therapeutic like watching fish in an aquarium. I'd see my clipper ship sail by eventually and could wave goodbye. But that would hurt, and I might freeze in the meantime. Now I regretted canceling the cruise and listening to all those ridiculous bad omens.

"So dumb," I lectured as I trudged back up the slope. I pulled at the photos of Axel trying to strip the can bare, but the glue held them fast. I wanted to hurt him for hurting me. But, how could I? At the parking lot, I tossed the empty can into a blue recycling trash can. The environmentalist in him would like this. I considered fishing him out again for the regular garbage but muttered under my breath, "To hell with it and him."

That familiar tightness in my chest returned, and I held my breath willing it to end. Tears escaped again in a flash flood down my face despite vicious threats to stay away. I reached into my purse and pulled out some tissues. A pink business card fell out, and I scooped it up from the grass. I glanced at it, curious about the unusual color, while I wiped my eyes and blew my nose again.

The card was from Vicky, or per the card 'Lady Victoria Sandford,' the woman from the plane and Charlie's ally. She suggested I visit her the next time I'm in London. And now London would be sooner than I expected since I would probably go home in a few days. But I couldn't see her and admit defeat. Not yet.

Vicky was right about the Achilles heel. Axel's must be the size of his entire foot. I should have noticed something was wrong. He was grumpier than usual after he got sick, but I attributed it to cancer.

I must be the poor mystery woman they talked about at my goodbye party. Jen must have heard this from Mel, and she old Matteo and Abby. That's why Mel looked annoyed with Jen, and Abby wouldn't say anything. Matteo's strange parting words made sense now.

I put my hand on my chest and pressed hard against my heart.

"If only I could reach in and remove that piece that was in love with Axel."

I sighed loudly and told myself to be strong for once and move on. The park at the waterfront was behind me as I walked up the incline towards Charlottenlund's train station. Feeling weightless without Axel, I floated along as if a gust of wind might knock me over.

But as I walked uphill, I warmed up and felt more determined. "Forget about Axel. It doesn't matter. You aren't going to run into him again."

I stopped to let the unyielding bicycle riders cross in front of me, careful not to intrude into a hazardous Danish bike lane a second longer than necessary, and continued my pep talk. "You've managed the past year on your own. Nothing went that wrong. Keep your head up. Things will get better. But you shouldn't have canceled the cruise. That was incredibly stupid."

If I hadn't left my phone in my hotel room during my rush to meet Carsten, I would have called Annette right now and begged forgiveness. Carsten was right. I was a spineless wimp for backing out. But even if I hurried back to contact Annette, it was too late. My proverbial ship had sailed.

I peered up the road towards town, but through my hazy tears, I couldn't see anything. Ahead of me was an endless stretch of days, weeks, and months, possibly fifty years, with nothing special to do. A living hell on earth.

40 ~ New Antiques

The dreary weather was a perfect analogy for how I felt. The sun hadn't come out, and if it didn't break through in the next few hours, it would be dark soon. The darkness was Denmark's curse for being so far north. But in the summer, Scandinavia got its due with sunlight almost around the clock.

As town came into view, I devised a Plan B. When I get back to my hotel and my phone, I'll call Annette and beg her forgiveness. Take her out for drinks or dinner tomorrow. They must have another trip coming up in the next few weeks, and I won't be picky. I can wait around.

Maybe they'll have a Viking ship that needs barnacle removal or something. I grinned imaging their miserable dead animal pelt and bone dress code. But I'd suck it up and do whatever they suggested. I couldn't return home without doing something so extraordinary that no one would believe it and when they did they'd be proud.

I wandered in an out-of-body experience past Charlottenlund's train station to the quaint main street filled with old-timey, but well-maintained buildings, now bustling with upscale shops and eating places. Sandwiched between a bookstore and a secondhand shop, I noticed a small antique hole-in-the-wall shop. The windows were dusty and filled with old nautical equipment, including a ship's anchor and wheel. Another reminder of the trip of a lifetime I was missing.

I pushed the door open and squeezed into the overstuffed rows filled with paintings, furniture, and knick-knacks. The tiny store was empty, except for the clerk, which was a plus since it was jam-packed with items for sale. I crouched down to look at an old framed watercolor of a sailing ship. It resembled the ship I was supposed to be boarding today, and I felt another sharp stab of regret.

"May I help you?" A man said in Danish from behind me.

"No thanks, just looking," I said in my best, but heavily-accented, Danish.

The tall blond Danish man said, "*Svenska*?" which means 'Am I Swedish?'

I was often mistaken for a Swede. The Danes had a centuries old rivalry with the Swedes, their next-door neighbor. My paternal grandparents were Swedish immigrants, and I had some second cousins there, but that was as close as it got. I couldn't speak Swedish. Danish was so hard to pronounce that my accent was hard to determine. Immigrants that lived here over twenty years still had trouble perfecting their accent.

My maternal ancestors weren't liked any better by the Danes. That grandfather was from Bohemia, a German-speaking country, now part of the Czech Republic. Germans brought back memories of the World War II takeover that still goes on, albeit peacefully, with the German tourists' annual summer beach invasion.

"No, American," I said in Danish putting the picture back down. I brushed my dusty hands against my jeans and glanced at him. He was about my age, maybe older, with a friendly smile.

"That painting is one of my favorites," he said in English but with a British accent. "My great-grandfather's ship used to sail to China. He had it painted on one of his journeys."

"Nice. I was going to go on a clipper ship today but …" I trailed off not wanting to explain how I'd chickened out for such stupid reasons.

"A clipper? You should see some of the other things we have from his old ship."

I followed him through a narrow pathway to an area filled with nautical maps, equipment, and tools. He seemed pleased, even eager, to show me around.

"I'm helping out a friend today who owns the shop. He is selling many of the items I've had in storage. My sister and I are cleaning house."

"Hmm," I said, unsure what to make of it all. I couldn't buy much with my overstuffed suitcases. And I wasn't sure I wanted to return with memories of a ship I could have been onboard.

"Fascinating stuff. But I can't buy much. I'm traveling and not sure where I'm going."

"Of course. Glad to have some company, a slow afternoon." He gestured to some clothes worn by a woman back then. I glanced at a rack of dresses that were the same style as what I had taken great pains to buy and bring with me. If I'd known, I could have saved myself a lot of trouble and bought them here. Now I had plenty of these dresses without needing them.

"This was the fashion back in 1860." After so much planning, I was an expert now. "Were they your great grandmothers?"

"No. A woman who went to sea with my great-grandfather owned them. But she left in Asia and was never seen again. He gave up the sea later when he returned to Denmark. But he never forgot her and saved all her belongings. Another reason we have so much to sell."

I wondered what happened to her and hoped she didn't bleed to death, remembering my nightmares.

"Here's a photo of them from the journey when they arrived in Hong Kong. She is standing between the captain, and another ancestor of mine, the ship's doctor. His daughter married a descendant of the captain, so we're all related now."

The black and white photograph was old and fuzzy. The captain was tall and thin with the women short or maybe medium height. The other man was dark haired and medium build. But you couldn't see their faces clearly in such an old photograph.

"Fascinating." I liked watching genealogy TV shows when they found long, lost ancestors and explained how they lived.

He showed me the contents of a glass case, and some of the jewelry she left behind. "I hate to sell it, but my daughters and my sister aren't interested in keeping them."

I stared at the gold ring with a cluster of brilliant blue stones. "Beautiful aquamarine and the color of the ocean."

"Exactly. The magical Seven Seas." He grinned and admired the ring.

I'd broken rule number one when buying something

expensive and open to negotiation. I should pretend I wasn't interested, even walk away, to get a better price. I tried the ring on my left ring finger where I used to wear my wedding ring until about six months ago, and it fit surprisingly well.

"How much do you want for it?" I expected the ring to be over my budget.

He quoted me 250 kroner or about $50 which was next to nothing. I hesitated in surprise.

"I have a matching bracelet and necklace too. It's a set, so it should stay together."

He placed all three on the glass countertop. "How about 500 kroner for all three?"

He was practically giving them away so I couldn't resist. Even if they were gold-plated or gold-colored metal, I wanted them. If real, the gold was worth more than that. But it would be a shame to melt them down with such an attractive setting. I was rescuing them from that terrible fate.

"Are you sure?"

He nodded, so I said "Sold," and pulled out my credit card.

I was thrilled with a nice memento. Not a direct reminder of the clipper ship, but close enough. I put the ring on and admired the bright blue stones accented against the gleaming gold.

"Sorry. Cash only." He pointed to the sign on the counter.

"Oh, sorry. No problem. I have cash." I opened my wallet and counted my Danish kroner, but I was short after shopping yesterday. "I'll find an ATM and come back. When do you close?"

"Soon … now." as he looked at his watch. "I'll close up and go to the ATM with you. I need to stop there too."

"Sounds great. Deal." I backed up to turn around, while he wrapped up my jewelry. My leg brushed up against something, and it fell over with a thud. I crouched down to right it and touched a furry animal that felt like a cat. I panicked and put my hand up to my mouth to stifle a scream.

"Oh, no." The animal, or whatever it was, wasn't moving. I leaned down to help it stand up.

"Oh, that's a stuffed cat. An odd custom back then. The cat

was from the ship and lived with my great-grandfather. He couldn't part with the cat after it died, and had the unfortunate thing stuffed."

I lifted the stuffed cat back up and tried to put it further from the counter and the narrow aisle. The cat was solid black with a trace of white on its stomach, not a tabby like Xena. I could never have done that to Xena even though I missed petting her soft, dense fur.

I clutched the bag of jewelry he handed me and glanced around the shop while he gathered his paperwork. "I'm not sure when I'll be back, but I want to see more. I love all these old nautical things."

He turned off the lights and locked the door behind me. "We'll be waiting."

~ ~ ~

After paying him for my purchase at the ATM, he suggested a drink. I was tempted to say no, but with nothing better to do, I accepted. Over beers at a local pub, I was still amazed the store clerk, Andreas Mikkelsen, was the great-grandson of a real clipper ship captain.

His hair was shaggy and a windblown blonde as if he didn't have time to bother with grooming, and his blue eyes were lively. He was friendly and talkative but didn't mention what he'd done or accomplished. The polar-opposite of Charlie.

Danes usually don't talk about themselves much. It's considered a form of bragging and culturally inappropriate with its own definition, Jante Law. Not a real law but a custom that doesn't exist in the United States since so many couldn't adhere to it. I wasn't aware of this cultural tradition until I was promoted to Managing Director, a big deal for women in Internal Audit. The reception from Axel's family and friends in Denmark about my good news was low-key, almost non-existent, and later he explained why.

We ordered food and waited, so I had time on my hands. I didn't want to monopolize the conversation. I'd have to slowly coax more information out of Andreas so he wouldn't feel like he was bragging.

"Your English is excellent. How'd you manage that?"

"I worked in London for many years. My ex-wife was English."

"Oh, do you live there now?"

"No. I moved back to Denmark after getting divorced about four years ago. I live here in Charlottenlund."

I hated to turn our discussion into an internal audit interrogation when it didn't matter. I blabbed on about myself, New York City and my single status. "Right now, I'm technically unemployed. Trying to view it as being 'between opportunities.' I might make a career change too if I can afford it."

Our food arrived. Small bowls of Danish pickled herring to share and place on our base of rye bread. I couldn't bear to eat herring in the United States since it was often old and mushy. Here it was fresh and prepared in unique ways. We ordered the traditional plate. A trio with plain, red wine, and curry flavored herring. To wash it down, we added the requisite aquavit, called *snaps* in Denmark.

With a shot glass in our hand, Andreas and I said s*kål* meaning cheers in English. Without dropping eye contact with each other and part of the Danish custom, we downed it. I'd heard this tradition dated back to the Vikings so they could monitor their surroundings for any danger. I should tell Jackson this trivia next time we met.

Anders had picked a strong aquavit, and it filled a large shot glass, so my throat was first chilled, then numb, until the warmth kicked in.

He became chatty after the shot of snaps. Encouraged from the liquor or my confessional.

"I'm a dull corporate attorney, but my sister followed in the path of our great-grandfather. She is one of the few women captains on a cruise line. We live in the house my great-grandfather, the sea captain, owned. It's large, and we broke it up into two apartments. I have one, and my sister, the other."

He proceeded to tell me all sorts of stories from his great-grandfather's time at sea. His diary is filled with stories about thieves, storms, and pirates. Even a Kraken.

He didn't know much about the mysterious lady who

disappeared, but Andreas said he was very much in love with her. His sister tried to find more information about her, but she couldn't find any records anywhere in Scandinavia.

"My great-grandfather married again, to my great grandmother, after he returned home. He settled down in the house I live in now. But he never forgot her. She was the great love of his life.

"Sad. Sounds like a great book, even a movie."

"Yeah, it might be. Are you interested in taking on the project?"

I laughed, but he looked sincere. "Turn the diary into a book? Well maybe, I've always wanted to write one. But if his diary is in old Danish, it will be hard to read, much less translate."

"I'll help out. I just don't have the time to do it myself. You could work on it from New York too."

"It's a shame I wouldn't have the experience of being at sea first. I was supposed to go on a cruise to Hong Kong on clipper ship today." I glanced at my watch. "The ship leaves soon."

"What? A cruise on a real clipper?"

"Yeah, I was an idiot this morning. Got nervous and backed out."

I didn't intend to tell him my lame reasons for canceling. But loosened up from the aquavit, I went ahead with the whole tale - the fortune teller, nightmares, and rules prohibiting anything modern.

"Well, Kat sounds like the trip of a lifetime. Damn, I'd go in a second. My great-grandfather would be so proud. And such a nice break from all this."

Andreas sat back and sipped his beer. "You can't miss it because of a bad dream, not having enough sunscreen or not wearing jeans. The ports will have everything you need, and you could discretely and accidentally take a few modern things with you."

"But it's not allowed," I whined, taking a big sip of my beer. "I might get in trouble or thrown overboard and freeze to death."

He grinned. "They'd never do that. I'll be your attorney. If you get in a jam, call me, and we'll dream up some excuse. If it's that old and authentic, they'd never know unless you waive it around in their faces. It's not like they'd have x-ray machines in 1860."

"Yeah, I was stupid to cancel, but it's too late now."

"Maybe not. There could be a delay. Why don't you call and ask?"

"I would, but I left my cell phone in my hotel room. I'm going to call the travel agent when I get back to see if they have another trip I can go on."

He pulled out his phone eager to help. "Do you have a number or a name?"

"No … wait … maybe I do. She gave me her business card, but I may have left it behind." I pulled out my wallet and took out my driver's license, credit cards, notes, insurance and everything putting it all on the table. Annette's card was wedged behind some receipts.

He took her card and said, "We'll have an answer soon." He dialed her number and reminded me of Axel with his 'do it now, why wait' attitude.

I held my breath while he made this all-important call. But even if it doesn't work, I can resolve this all by myself. Tomorrow I'll figure it out. Better not to depend on anyone.

He put his index finger up and spoke to Annette in rapid Danish explaining, "I'm a friend of Kat's, and she changed her mind. … yes … that's right. She wants to go if it's still possible."

He hung up, and I braced myself. "It's too late. Right?"

"Nope. She's checking and will call me back."

Andreas looked optimistic, but I knew it was a long shot. Danes were punctual, like Germans, so the ship was at sea by now.

He picked up his beer again and said, "Cheers."

I responded back in Danish, "*Skål*. If I go, I've got to speak Danish for three months. I better practice."

He laughed and said, "*Snak dansk.*" These two Danish words were the most frequently repeated words to foreigners and meant 'speak Danish.'

While we waited, I twirled a piece of my hair and tried to stay calm no matter what she said. I pulled out my new bracelet and necklace and put them on for good luck.

Andreas said, "Beautiful. I'm glad you bought them."

His phone beeped, and I jumped worried about what Annette will say and more bad news. He listened and smiled at me. "She can be back in Copenhagen at her hotel in about a half hour, maybe less. We're going to the train station now. Thanks, Annette."

He stood and motioned for me to get up and took some bills from his wallet for the waitress. "Kat, you're back on, but we must hurry."

We sprinted down the town's main street to the station. Andreas took my hand but didn't drag me or turn it into a race like Greg.

"We'll see when the next train leaves. I'd drive you, but the train is faster since your hotel is right there."

Inside the station, he glanced at the overhead schedule and figured it out quickly. "Perfect, five minutes."

He purchased a train ticket and validated it for me in the machine and refused reimbursement.

"Kat, promise me you'll call me when you get back. I want to hear all about your voyage and what it was like to be on a real clipper ship. I'm serious about that book too. His story deserves to be told."

Andreas handed me his business card and added his personal contact information. "When you return, let's get together for dinner. You can tell me all about it. I'll show you his diary and house."

"I sure will," I was tipsy from drinks still not believing I was back on again. I even looked forward to meeting Andreas when it was all over.

The train pulled into the station, and I reached up to give him a quick thank you hug goodbye. He pulled me close and kissed my cheek, but promptly let me go so I could board the train.

Before the doors closed, Andreas pushed his hair back and

grinned. "Have a great adventure, Kat. Take care."

The train pulled out of the station, and I looked back to wave goodbye. I expected Andreas to have walked away without looking back like Axel. But Andreas stood there smiling and waving, and I did the same until he disappeared from my sight.

What luck as I anxiously bit my lower lip. Here I am leaving for months, and I find a guy I'd like to date. Was Matteo right? To live is to love, or to love is to live. But a long distance four-thousand mile relationship with six time zones?

To relax, I scanned the paperback book I'd bought yesterday at the Danish bookshop about King Neptune's reluctant wife named Salacia, the goddess of salt water and the sea. She feared him and his marriage proposal, swam away, and hid in the Atlantic Ocean. But a dolphin found her and changed her mind. King Neptune and Salacia were happily married and had three children. Ariel, the little mermaid, was their granddaughter.

But I couldn't focus on my book. Too many worries had taken control. The ship may leave before I could arrive. I needed a Plan B to relax and racked my brain for ideas to fill a few months. I'll leave my extra suitcase and fancy dresses at Lena's house and take the ferry from Denmark to England. Spend some time there, take the Chunnel train to Paris, buy a one-month rail pass, and explore. When I got bored or low on cash, I'll return to Denmark, see Andreas, and head home.

The train pulled into Central Station, and I glanced at the unfinished but intriguing paperback and grinned. My first piece of banned literature to smuggle onboard.

41 ~ Mad At MAX

Back in my hotel room surrounded by suitcases and carpetbags, I scrambled to sort and pack what was permitted and to smuggle some contraband. I was so happy being devious thanks to Andreas, my lawyer and de facto partner in crime.

I'd left my hotel door ajar and heard Annette's footsteps a few minutes later.

"Hey, Kat. I'm glad you changed your mind. We must hurry, so I'll help. The ship stopped to pick up supplies from *Helsingør*. They will dock in a small harbor south of there, but not for long."

"Great, thanks." Barely looking up to acknowledge her. "I'm sorry I canceled. I panicked, but I'm ready and back on board so to speak."

I snuck some modern toiletries and my small makeup bag into a carpetbag. I tossed in the emergency medical bag from Matteo and a plastic jar of ginger, a natural herb for seasickness.

I decided to disconnect fully. I could at least comply with that rule and left my electronics on the bed. Annette packed them away in my suitcase between layers of modern clothes. Such an odd feeling to not take them, but they wouldn't have internet reception at sea and three months of salty air might ruin them.

"By the way," she said while she zipped up one of my suitcases, "we reduced the fee by 30 percent, and we're covering the airfare back from Hong Kong. Amber in our New York office should have explained more what you were getting into."

"Oh well." I was often surrounded by things done incorrectly or inefficiently. As my colleagues joked, this was job security for an internal auditor. "At least I'm going." The discount was nice, but without my modern clothes, I'd be spending that savings and more at our first port.

"What's this?" She asked about the art prints, Greg's Turner gift and my twentieth century Frida Kahlo self-portrait, rolled up but sticking out the side of a carpetbag.

"A Turner painting reprint. Don't worry; it's old. He died in 1861." Luckily, she didn't unroll it to check. I might need Frida and her moral support if things got as tough as Steen warned.

She checked her watch. "You need to change into one of those dresses."

"Now? Before I get onboard?"

"Kat, the whole idea is you look like you belong in 1860. Otherwise, why do this if you are wearing that?" She pointed to my outfit - blue jeans and a sweater.

She fished around inside one of the carpetbags. "How about this dark blue dress?"

I wasn't crazy about this idea since people in the lobby would see me. I'd look silly, but I'll have to get used to it, and I managed at the ball on Tuesday. "Okay. Sure."

I stripped down to my underwear while she pulled the dress out of the carpetbag. I hoped she wasn't going to find my contraband. But if she did, she didn't say anything.

"Don't you need…?" She made a motion around her chest.

"A corset? Nope. This dress doesn't need one."

"Good. That must be uncomfortable."

"Yeah, it is." Remembering how restrictive it felt Tuesday night. But I brought it along for the fancy velvet dress to keep the Madame Gris's of the world happy.

She noticed my bra and panties. "I'm not sure about your underwear. I don't think they looked like that back then."

"What? That doesn't matter. No one will ever know or see me like this. I have a private cabin, right?"

"Yes, you do. You're right. It'll be okay. Extra clothes are onboard for you too. It'll be cold in the North Sea and Atlantic. You may need some extra layers and petticoats."

I slipped on the chemise, a fancy name for the matching top, and the long skirt. She helped me lace them up. The hem nearly touched the ground without the hoop skirt.

"I have the hoop. But if you don't have a large car, I'll put it on when we get there." It wasn't easy to fit into Greg's Lincoln, and most Danish cars were small. I pulled out the hoop with thin metal links folded to fit inside my suitcase to show her.

"Oh, Kat, this keeps getting better. I prefer the flapper style." She waved her hands back and forth with her feet dancing as if back in the 1920's.

"You and me both. But it's not as bad as it looks. I was at a costume ball Tuesday night and wore a fancy dress like this. I brought it along if there's a special dinner with the officers."

I winked at her since she knew I was single. We laughed bonding over this. I felt weird but ready to meet my ship as I lived back then and belonged.

"You should come with me, Annette. I'll need help. You can be, what do they call them? A lady's maid to dress me, and all those other fun chores."

"Well, if you can arrange my time off that would be grand. But, I don't think my boyfriend or kids would let me go away for three months."

When Annette turned her back, I hid my toiletry bag into one of the carpetbags.

She looked at me and said, "One last touch, we should braid your hair." Annette took out my plastic hair clip and braided my hair starting on my right side.

I shook my head. "No way. I'm not going to look like Heidi coming down from the Alps. You can make one long braid in the back."

When she was done, I twisted it up into a bun.

"Ah, sweet. You look like a respectable young lady from 1860."

"Yeah, like a Swedish farm girl."

After checking out of the hotel, we walked out to her small compact car with a hatchback. Danish cars were small with gas prices so expensive. My suitcases and the carpetbags were squeezed in and barely fit.

"See there's no way the hoop skirt would fit inside your car. Unless you want me to sit in the back and stick my legs out the back?"

"No silly," she laughed. "Put it on later. The port is about an hour away. We shouldn't cut it too close."

On our way to the Danish motorway, Annette asked, "Who was that guy? The one who called?"

"Andreas, my lawyer. He's going to help me in case there are any more screw-ups."

She didn't respond probably nervous I might sue her and the company. Danes rarely file lawsuits, and Americans had a sue-happy reputation.

"Just kidding. But Andreas is a lawyer. I met him today in an antique shop and told him about the ship. He offered to help so here I am."

"Well, that worked out nicely."

"Yeah, it did. Andreas is a great guy. I'm planning to get in touch when I'm back. He's the first I've met since…" I was about to say since Axel, but I couldn't say his name. Ironic that I found a guy I liked within hours after finding out Axel didn't love me much after all.

Annette didn't say anything probably waiting for me to continue. But I didn't want to think about Axel or Andreas. The Danish radio was coaxing me on with the song, *Don't Worry Be Happy*, and I smiled wanting to follow this advice.

"I bought some jewelry too. Beautiful, huh?" At a stoplight, I showed her my new vintage bracelet, ring, and necklace.

She turned on the interior light on to see it better. "They're beautiful."

"And don't worry. The jewelry is vintage. At least from 1860 and worn on a real clipper." I wasn't going to let her stop me from taking them along. And for some strange reason, it was soothing to wear my ocean-colored jewels.

The classic *Stairway to Heaven* by Led Zeppelin started playing on the car radio. I loved that song, but I didn't believe in heaven or hell. When you're dead, you're dead, end of story.

"Do you believe in fate, Annette?"

"No, I think we make our own."

"I've always thought so too. But sometimes I wonder when rare events like today happen." I hoped to meet Andreas again, and I keep my promises even if I sometimes regret it.

Annette turned the car abruptly and said, "I'm an atheist like most of the rest of us. I don't believe in that hocus pocus."

"Yeah, I don't much either, but it sure would be nice. Sometimes I can see why so many people do."

As we traversed Copenhagen, her phone chimed, and Annette clicked off the radio and put it on the speaker setting.

Peter, her colleague, was on the phone, and even though he spoke Danish, I could follow along. Danish was like riding a bike and coming back after just a day.

He cleared his throat. "Is our client, Kathryn Jensen, there with you? I need to talk to her. Max got a message from the captain, and gave us some new intel we should relay."

She glanced over at me, so I answered him in Danish, "Yeah, this is Kat Jensen. You're on a speakerphone. What's up?"

"The ship is waiting for you with extra clothes and belongings. You should have everything you need."

"Great. Thanks." I waited for him to continue, but he didn't say anything.

Annette interrupted. "What is it, Peter? We'll be at the harbor in less than thirty minutes. We don't want to hear about any more problems."

"Annette, it's not that serious. Kathryn, about the ship and journey Max found for you."

We waited. I asked Annette, "Did we lose him?"

"No, I'm still here," Peter said, "Max heard from the captain today. His sister isn't going as planned, but another female passenger in England might go."

"All right, no big deal. I didn't know his sister was going."

"Max said it's rare for a woman to travel alone. Usually, the only women on board are accompanied by their husband or family."

"But I never had anyone coming with me."

"Are you saying Kat's not allowed to go on her own?" Annette asked frustrated. We both wanted to get to the bottom of this.

Peter said, "No, Kat can still go. Max said the captain told him it was improper without a companion. But Max vouched for you, and he consented."

I looked at Annette and felt anger bubble up. "Well, that's mighty fine of him. I don't see why I need to bring someone along. I've traveled all the world on my own and live alone, so it's not improper to me."

Peter said, "Hey, I hear you and agree. But Max insisted we tell you."

"Tell Max to tell the captain I still want to go. But I want to confirm I'm not part of the crew. I don't mind helping out, but I'm a paying passenger."

No one said anything. I glanced over at Annette, but she was focused on the traffic ahead.

Peter said, "I don't think you will be doing any crew-type work onboard. We could send in a request to Max to confirm, but it will take a while to hear back. And, you don't have the time."

"Put Max on the phone. I'd like to iron this out before I board the ship." Amber mentioned this mysterious Max a few times to me, but this was also the name of the company.

No one said anything. I was about to repeat my request when Annette said, "But Kat, you can't talk to him. Max isn't human. He's a computer programmed with AI, artificial intelligence, by neuroscientists."

"What? A computer planned my trip? Found this cruise?"

"Exactly. We aren't sure how Max does this, but he finds these unique, off-beat trips. Our clients are thrilled with the results since it's such a unique adventure. We're studying ways to use EEG's, electroencephalograms, and transfer data directly to Max bypassing the lengthy questionnaire. Customers aren't always honest, and this causes problems for Max."

"But I was honest. I wanted a clipper ship. But as a passenger not part of the crew. This cruise is for relaxation. Can't we call the captain? What's his name again?"

Peter said, "Mikkel Kløve Madsen. He's an expert seaman and has done this route many times. I tried to call him myself, but the number Max gave us isn't working."

"So typical." I fumed at how inept this whole operation

worked. They're lucky I'm not doing an internal audit since they wouldn't be happy with the final report.

"Forget it. I'll ask the captain when I board."

But then I reconsidered my options. "What if this trip your computer found isn't so great and I hate it? Can I get off at the next port and fly back home?"

"I don't see why not," Annette said. "Your first port is in England, either Dover or Southampton, after a few days at sea."

The signs for the *Helsingør* exit appeared. We'd be there soon, so I had to decide.

"Okay. I'll handle this myself. I'll confirm with the captain that I'm a passenger. And if I'm part of the crew or don't like it, I may get off in England."

Annette agreed. "I'm going with you. We'll confirm it together."

"Sounds like a perfect plan," Peter said.

"All right, Peter. Thanks for letting us know. Better late than never. But someone needs to screen this stuff from Max better. A topic to discuss at our next Advisory Board meeting. I'll get back to you on what the captain says, and if there's a problem. We're here."

Annette exited the motorway following the signs for *Snekkersten* harbor. She pulled into a parking lot with lights illuminating the path that led to the shore. I took out my wallet to give Annette some cash for gas, which was so expensive in Denmark, but she refused and argued the company would reimburse her.

"The ship should be over there." She pointed through a grove of dense foliage partially lit with streetlamps. "I think I see the masts. Kat, are you ready?"

"Do you think it will be dangerous? Not the crew thing, but being the only woman on the ship? Maybe Max misunderstood the captain's concern."

"I'm sure the entire team will be well-behaved. Back then everyone was ultra-conservative and polite." She glanced at my dress as if this was proof since it was the extreme opposite of a sexy mini-skirt.

"What would you do?"

"I'm in a serious relationship with two kids so I couldn't take off for months and do this. But if I were you - single, unattached, with the time, and looking for an adventure, I'd go in a flash.

She's right. Why the hell not?

Annette added, "Just think, you get to be the only woman onboard with all the attention. Plenty of guys to party with and forget the ones back home."

I'd confided in her my recent dating fiascos. Visions of returning to New York City, and how disappointed my lawyer Andreas would be swirled around in my head. How complicated everything had become and what happened to my determination? Even to the bitter end, with the nasty aftertaste of fish and beer lingering in my mouth from this afternoon.

"Yeah, but this is for three months. Possibly very long months."

"But England is only about three days from here. You are free to get off if you don't like it."

Once I got onboard, I'd hate to quit and would stick it out. I considered the alternatives. Thanksgiving or Christmas with Greg, the control freak; Matteo, the two-timing lover; or Charlie, the master manipulator. Even if I didn't hear from them again, I'd be stressed and my holidays would be ruined.

"I'm going." I got out of the car and squinted to see if I could see the ship. Some noise was coming from the water. I was dying to see my clipper ship, the subject of so many dreams lately. I could easily handle three days.

Annette got out of her car, "I'll help carry your bags. I want to talk to the captain too and straighten all this out. If you decide you don't want to do it, we'll leave. Besides, I'm curious to see this incredible ship too."

"Great." I'll trust my instincts once I'm onboard and not ignore them as I have lately.

"Oh, by the way, your watch, it's too modern and safer in your suitcase. Could get ruined from the salt water."

I took off my watch and held it out to her. But my hands shook from the cold and my nerves. "Please don't lose it. The watch was a gift from my mother." I should pack it away myself, but I was too keyed up.

"Kat, keep it. Hide it in your purse. No one will ever know."

"No. You're right. It's safer packed." While I stuffed my watch in my suitcase, I took a deep breath feeling light-headed.

"I can do this," I said, but my voice shook.

"Yes, you can. And you will have the time of your life. Ready?" I nodded, but then Annette clapped her hands and said, "Oh, your coat is too modern. Mine will be better. We can trade back when you return."

Fine, I slipped out of mine and into hers. Annette's black sweater coat wasn't as warm as my down filled polyester jacket but it did look better with my dress. I'd packed some sweaters but didn't want to search for them now.

Tomorrow, I'll make a detailed list of what was in my suitcases while I can still remember it. If they lose anything, they'll have to reimburse me. But my personal belongings weren't a priority, and I focused on boarding the ship and the long cruise ahead.

"Annette, what about my Danish? I don't speak perfect Danish, and my accent is off."

"Your Danish is fine. In three months, you'll sound just like us. The sailors will help you out like the guy you met today."

She leaned against the car and lit a cigarette for a quick smoke. "Oh, the hoop!"

Annette grabbed it from the hatchback and put in on the pavement near her car. I stepped over it, and she bent down to help me. I lifted my blue skirt, and we tied it around my waist.

I laughed at this weird situation. Not just from fixing the hoop, but here I was wearing a bell-shaped long skirt again. At least at the ball, other women were dressed like this. On the ship, I may be the only one.

Annette inhaled on her cigarette and stared at me as if she didn't recognize me.

"I know. This outfit is pretty damn strange."

She laughed. "I'm used to it. All our clients have different unique situations. They all rave about their trips afterward.

One of these days, I'm going to let Max find me a trip."

I wanted to hear more about these other trips and something encouraging. But I knew we had to go, or the ship might set sail without me.

Annette took another deep drag on her cigarette. I wanted to tell her to stop after seeing Axel's long struggle with lung cancer. But she'd complained about trying to quit, and I was sympathetic. Tobacco addiction was supposedly harder to beat than opium.

She stamped out her cigarette and picked up a carpetbag. I lifted the other bag and regretted all the extra toiletries and books since it was so heavy.

"Are you taking some bricks along as ballast for the ship?"

"You were the one who said no electronics. Books weigh a ton not to mention toiletries in glass bottles. I'm not flying back with any of this stuff."

We walked down a narrow stone pathway towards the ship. The hoop kept my skirt off the ground so at least it wouldn't be dirty from day one. I sighed relieved no one was around to see me in this get-up. At least photos wouldn't be posted to Facebook, and everyone onboard better follow these rules too.

A samba song beat ringtone rang out. Annette said, "Oh that's my daughter's unique ring. I have to get this."

We stopped, and I was glad to put down the heavy bag and rubbed my sore arm.

Annette said on the phone to her daughter, "All right. Stay where you are. I'll be there in about twenty minutes."

"Sorry, Kat. I've got an emergency at home. The sitter had to leave, and my boyfriend can't get home. I've got to run. Can you manage?"

"Sure. I'll get onboard and talk to the captain. Get home to your family. You've done so much. See you in about three months." I felt guilty keeping her away on a Sunday.

"If you don't like it or what he says, have them call you a cab, go back to the hotel, and we'll figure it out tomorrow." We hugged goodbye, and my hoop swayed and bounced against her jeans.

"Kat, I hope you complete the entire journey. I can't wait

to hear how it all goes. We'll celebrate when you return and trade coats, but I like this one." She gave me quick, smoky smelling kiss on my cheek. "You'll be fine and have the time of your life."

I nodded hoping she was right and picked up my weighty and burdensome carpetbags. At least this physical exertion got my blood pumping with a welcome dose of bravery.

42 ~ Off-Balanced

The path ended at the waterfront, and around a slight bend, a large sailing ship with towering masts was docked in the water next to a wooden pier. That must be my clipper, and it didn't disappoint. I put my bags down wonderstruck at the site of my beautiful new home for about three months. She was dreamlike, even without the sails up. Mr. Turner would have loved to paint her. I couldn't wait to get closer to touch her and confirm she wasn't a mirage.

Onboard the ship the moonlight and lanterns illuminated the sailors moving around, and their footsteps echoed off the wooden deck. Men's voices carried in the wind, but I was too far away to make out the words. When I got closer, someone would help with my bags and escort me onboard.

Lifting my heavy bags again, I trudged onward to the pier. After dropping my carpetbags again, I rubbed my aching arms missing my wheeled suitcases. The wind picked up and rustled my skirt. The air against my bare legs felt odd since I always wore pants. I pulled Annette's coat tighter and briefly missed Axel's warm scarf. The scent of salt, dead fish, and pungent algae from the stagnant water near the shore invaded my nose. To avoid the stench, I breathed through my mouth.

Weighed down again with my carpetbags, I continued towards the ship. The pier's old wooden planks creaked and seemed so authentic to 1860. If I boarded when it wasn't so dark, it would probably look disappointedly modern and run down. After reaching the ship, intricate details carved into the wood were visible from the moonlight reflecting off the water. The re-enactors picked a beautiful ship to indulge their fantasies.

A sudden chill ran down my spine causing an involuntary shiver. To warm up, I shoved my hands in my pockets and stamped my feet. I stood on the pier next to the ship, but there wasn't a gangway. Looking around, I tried to figure out how to board. A rope ladder hung over the edge, but I couldn't climb that in a dress or with two heavy bags.

I called out, "Hello. It's Kat, Kathryn Jensen. I'm here. Ready to board."

Apparently, they couldn't see or hear me since nothing happened.

I yelled, "Permission to board, please."

Still no response. Maybe the crew was waiting for me to speak Danish, part of the re-enactment and being in character. I switched to Danish and screamed, "May I board the ship?"

As I contemplated what to do, a grinding noise accompanied the gangplank as it was lowered to the pier. I waited sure someone would walk down to the pier to help me, but no one showed. This situation was bizarre. Where was the Customer Service staff to assist with boarding? They'd hear about it later in their customer satisfaction survey.

"Thanks for nothing," I muttered in Danish now that my brain was switching over from English.

Tired of waiting, I was determined to board on my own. I inspected my options. The gangplank was at a steep angle without railings or any safety precautions. In a long dress with heavy bags to carry it wasn't going to be easy. Despite the dress code rules, I regretted leaving my tennis shoes behind for these slick soled boots.

With my right foot on the wooden plank, I pressed hard to test the stability. It didn't rock and felt sturdy enough. Some helpful wooden strips to prevent slipping were set at intervals across the plank.

I picked up my bags and started up the steep incline. I tried to ignore the water below me. If I fell in, I wouldn't drown, but it would be cold and hard to swim in this dress. To my relief, the plank didn't wobble.

As I neared the top, a young man said in Danish, "M-M-Madame, w-w-welcome." He was either nervous or had a strong stutter, and I hoped it was the former.

I didn't dare look up, not wanting to lose my precarious balance and concentration. Noise from a flurry of activity made me pause and ruined my momentum. Someone joined me on the gangway and stood by my side. The man took one of the carpetbags from me and grasped my elbow to support me, and someone else grabbed the other carpetbag. We walked the last few steps together to the deck.

I sighed in relief after boarding and looked up at him and around the ship. The man on my left who took my arm and a carpetbag was tall and in uniform, and a young boy held my other carpetbag.

I explained to them in Danish, "Sorry about being late. Unexpected delays." I was lucky to be onboard finally, and despite the boarding issues, I wanted to start out on the right foot. I was in awe at being onboard, and the lanterns and moonlight made it a surreal experience.

The uniformed sailor replied in Danish, "Welcome onboard, Madame Jensen. You arrived in the nick of time. Your trunks are here, and we hoped you would show."

He stuck his hand out, and I grasped it to officially meet. He said, "Captain Mikkel Kløve Madsen."

I smiled back dumbstruck. The captain's hand was stiff and rough, and he towered over me by about a foot. He must be over six feet tall, so I craned my neck to see his face. His face was thin, and he had a short beard, but at least he was smiling.

"Madame Jensen, you should not walk on the gangway alone. Someone will escort you on and off the ship."

I wanted to explain that I tried to get help but didn't want to start out by complaining. Besides, I was distracted by the sights and sounds on board. I'd been on cruises onboard many different ships, but this was indescribable. A real working ship from the look of the sailors and their sense of urgency.

He looked so formal and official standing there in a uniform, but I must get certain things cleared up before we left. "Captain, Sir -"

He glanced at me waiting. I was unnerved stumbling over what should be basic Danish.

"Yes, Sir. I mean Captain. I need to know. Do I have work responsibilities? Like the crew?"

"Like the crew?" The captain repeated while he monitored the sailors' activities. He looked confused by my question and shook his head. "No, Madame Jensen, you have no duties.

Sailing a ship is hard and often dirty work. Sometimes dangerous. I hope you won't be lonely or bored without your family or friends onboard."

Relief flooded over me. I didn't want him to think I'd be a demanding high maintenance passenger. "Don't worry. I won't get lonely or bored. And I don't mind helping, but I'd prefer to learn more about sailing."

Captain Mikkel chuckled. "I'd be happy to show you when we're at sea. When the weather is calm."

The captain spoke to another uniformed sailor and introduced me to Lars Hansen, another officer and the first mate. We shook hands. This time I told them to please call me Kathryn. I wasn't about to be called 'Madame Jensen' for three months by anyone.

Captain Mikkel nodded and said, "We use our Christian names among the officers. But the passengers determine how they prefer to be addressed."

The captain added, "Lars, Katrine wants sailing lessons."

I considered correcting him to Kathryn or Kat, but I had a feeling my name would be switched to the Danish version 'Katrine' pronounced 'Katrina.' Danes often called me Katrine by mistake. I felt like a different person wearing these clothes and starting this journey so I decided to let it go.

Lars laughed and said, "Happy to oblige." He excused himself to prepare for the departure.

Why did they find this so funny? I hoped I wouldn't be given a twenty-pound bag of potatoes to peel like Kathleen warned. I'd much rather help with the sailing.

Lanterns illuminated the deck in some areas. The all-male team worked in earnest handling sails and other tools. Some of the sailors were cutting ropes with knives.

The small light haired boy who helped me with my luggage came up and said in Danish, "C-C-Captain Madsen, may I h-h-help?" He looked young, not even a teenager. Maybe the captain was his father. No one mentioned kids would be on board.

The captain turned to me. "Katrine, may I present Uffe Petersen. He's a cabin boy who will help you on the journey.

Uffe, this is Madame Jensen."

I was about to tell Uffe to call me Katrine too, but that could wait. I stuck out my hand and waited for young Uffe's handshake. He hesitated and glanced at my hand and then at who nodded. Uffe grabbed my hand and crunched and pumped it as if he'd never shaken hands before. I smiled but was glad when Uffe released my throbbing hand.

Captain Mikkel spoke rapid Danish in an accent I wasn't used to, but I followed the gist of it. We were leaving soon, and I was to settle into my cabin. But this sounded like a command, not a suggestion.

"Aye, aye, sir," I said in English with a left-handed salute.

He chuckled so at least he had a sense of humor.

I followed young Uffe struggling with my heavy carpetbags and planned to assist him. But I stopped determined to see the departure from Denmark. This old sailing ship didn't have balconies or big windows. I wouldn't be able to see much from my cabin. I'd be lucky to have a small porthole in my cabin.

The captain was talking and signaling to the sailors. They raised the gangplank, and it scraped loudly against the deck. Two sailors tied it up while others readied the sails scattered around the ship for hoisting in the towering wooden masts as soon we left the pier.

"Excuse me Captain Mikkel. I would like to see the ship leave port."

"You wish to observe our departure?" He glanced at me briefly. I wondered if his eyes were blue, and his hair blonde like the stereotypical Dane but he was in the shadows. He was distracted focused on leaving the port. An old ship without engines must be difficult to sail, especially at night.

"I promise to stay out of the way."

He appraised me again, and I moved from one foot to the other and wondered why a simple yes or no took so long. Was I breaking an unwritten rule detailed in the re-enactment guide book that no one bothered to give me? Another damn Max foul-up? My customer survey will be filled to the hilt. Particularly, once I wore my Internal Audit businesswoman's hat and got into my critiquing mindset.

Uffe hovered a few feet away waiting and put my heavy carpetbags down. If he hadn't, I would have gone over to insist.

The captain nodded. "Uffe, take Madame Jensen's bags to her cabin. Then return to fetch her after we have left the Strait and are at sea."

Uffe said, "*Javel, Herr.*" A formal version of 'Yes, Sir.'

Captain Mikkel motioned for me to stand near a wooden platform covered with maps and papers. First Mate Lars stood with his hands on the ship's huge wheel. He stood stiffly on alert to guide the ship from the pier and head north.

The ropes from the dock were released, and the sails raised by the sailors caught the breeze. The wind blew against me, and my worries felt like they were blown away too. A few tears, a salty mixture of relief, happiness, and excitement, rolled down my cheeks. Now that I was finally here, I was determined to enjoy it.

Captain Mikkel stood near me and must have sensed my emotional response to the departure since he whispered, "It's always bittersweet departing from home. I'm glad you're here."

Grateful, I was tempted to give him a hug to thank him, but I told myself to stay calm. He may take it the wrong way and think I was one of those women who swooned over a man merely because he wore a uniform.

On the shoreline few lights were visible, but it was late. Danes were known for saving energy and caring about the environment. Denmark's reputation was 'green' and relied heavily on alternative and natural methods. Our ship was proudly doing its part by not using engines. Above our heads, the sails rippled and cupped the wind with a flapping noise.

The captain pointed out some sights, but I didn't recognize them. He said, "We're sailing north from the Sound to the Baltic Sea."

The land mass on our right was Sweden, and we'd soon pass the northern tip of this Danish island called *Sjælland.*

Captain Mikkel said, "Excuse me, Katrine. I must monitor the course ahead since it narrows to four kilometers."

I didn't mind his absence since I wanted to enjoy the view

alone and not be distracted by conversation. I pulled Annette's coat closer hoping there was a warmer one in my cabin. One of those freebies I could borrow. The sailors had thick jackets on with sweaters showing underneath, and I'd prefer to wear that.

Kronborg, a former Royal Castle, came into view. I'd toured the Renaissance castle, an official world heritage site, years ago. I'd even seen it several times from the water - on a Royal Caribbean cruise to Norway and the ferry to Sweden. But at night and onboard such a small ship powered only by white sails billowing above us, this was unique.

The wind picked up, and the sailors climbed higher into the masts adjusting the sails based on instructions shouted to them. What a lot of work this must be when you don't have an engine and rely on wind power. But it sure was magical.

Captain Mikkel returned to my side. "Such a beautiful castle. I never tire of seeing her, and she greets us every time. This is a narrow channel so we must be cautious."

People stood on the roof of the castle. "Is Kronborg open for tours this late at night?"

"Soldiers live there."

Soldiers? This was news to me since it was a museum, not a fort. But it must be another re-enactment.

We passed the moonlit silhouette of the castle, and now there was no turning back. I was on an adventure with months ahead of me on this old clipper ship sailing into the vast unknown. My jaw clenched with worry again.

Kronborg was famous as Hamlet's castle, the site envisioned by Shakespeare in his play. Hamlet considered major questions about what it meant to live. In high school, we'd had to memorize part of the play in high school, and a few famous lines were stuck permanently in my head.

I couldn't resist reciting, "To be or not to be - that is the question. Whether 'tis nobler in the mind to suffer the sling and arrows of outrageous fortune, or to take arms against a sea of troubles, and by opposing end them."

Captain Mikkel heard me and added in his heavily Danish-accented English. "My bounty is boundless as the sea, my love as deep. The more I give to thee, the more I have, for both are infinite."

I recognized this quote and stared at him surprised. "Isn't that what Juliet said to her Romeo?"

He didn't answer right away since he was giving First Mate Lars instructions for the crew. When he turned towards me, he touched my arm. "Yes, and Juliet did so beautifully."

I sighed in relief. I'd lugged aboard Mel's gift, a book of Shakespeare's plays, to keep me busy. And now even the captain appreciated him too.

I stole a sideways glance at him. The company, Max, or whoever selected an excellent ship and captain. He appeared to be in that state called flow when you lose yourself in something you love. He was in his element and knew how to sail and command the crew. If he was as kind and intelligent as he acted, this voyage shouldn't be too difficult even without my electronics and modern stuff.

Captain Mikkel motioned that I could stand over by the railing. I grabbed it and tilted my head back staring at the bright stars high above us. The billowing white sails caught the wind and propelled the ship and the rest of us north.

My hair braid slipped out of the rolled knot behind my head from the wind, and wisps of hair flew around my face. I reached up to hold it out of my eyes.

From studying maps at home, I knew we'd leave this channel and head to another bay, the *Kattegat*, before crossing the North Sea to the coast of England. As I watched the ship cut through the water, the clipper was living up to its name. We moved at a fast-paced clip.

Memories from the beginning of my quest reappeared as if watching a PowerPoint slideshow of my past week. The initial taste of aquavit and repeated visions of a clipper that encouraged me. Refusing to listen to all the naysayers, I'd kept at it with my exhausting computer search, help from my Dad, and the tiresome on-line questionnaire for Max.

After finding the ship, I jumped through hurdles to get medical tests and the right clothing. Even today, my doubts and fears plagued me and jeopardized the whole trip. And then

I encountered the last minute unexpected complications and difficulties boarding the ship.

Here I was on a beautiful 19th-century clipper ship headed to Asia with the wind in my face and the promise of an unforgettable adventure. Finally, I was doing something special, and what I chose to do. All those obstacles faded away. Axel and everyone I knew was left behind in the ship's rippling wake.

Going forward, I'll be more optimistic and show all the doubters and worriers they were wrong. I'll handle whatever challenges get thrown at me. Besides, the whole world was waiting for my exploration.

~ ~ ~

THAT'S IT FOR NOW

~ ~ ~

About the Author

Karen Stensgaard grew up in San Antonio, Texas and was a foreign exchange student for a year in Denmark when she tried aquavit for the first time. After completing her MBA in Texas, she moved to San Francisco and through a series of unexpected twists became an internal auditor focused on financial firms. Karen later moved to New York City and now lives in Philadelphia with her husband and cat Lucy. Aquavit is her debut novel with more stories about Kat's adventures underway.

To find out more about this book and others in the pipeline, visit her website karenstensgaard.com and sign up for updates or join her Facebook Novelist page. On Pinterest, she has created several boards related to the novel's characters and scenes.

What was the inspiration for the story?
I love to travel on ships and wake up arriving at a new port to explore just steps from the gangway. I wondered how someone would prepare for an extended re-enactment cruise onboard a 19th-century sailing ship. How to overcome challenges, the fear of traveling alone, and bad omens.

Is there a message in your book that you want readers to grasp?
Be brave, embrace life, and never give up on your dreams. Don't settle for less - wrong people, awful jobs, or miserable situations. And as I remind myself: try to enjoy the journey, not just the destination. And while I don't support overindulging, once-in-a-while a shot of Aquavit can be inspiring.

What are you working on now?
I'm finishing the entire Aquamarine Sea series. The second book should be published sometime next year.

Book Club Discussion Topics

Spoiler Alert!

Enhance your discussion with a Scandinavian aquavit tasting. But be careful, it's strong stuff! Alternatively, have a glass of one of Kat's favorite wines – a dry riesling, rosé, or viognier.

1. Kat is unhappy and wants to leave town. Is she making the right decision? Where would you go if you had two months to travel and wanted a real adventure?
2. The three men in her life – Charlie, Greg, and Matteo – all seem to care about her but not be the right guy. Should she rekindle a relationship with any of them, when she returns home?
3. After Kat gets to Copenhagen, she loses her momentum. Have you seen this happen to other women? How do you get past the fear of the unknown?
4. Elsebet insists her husband tell Kat the truth. If you knew something like this about a good friend or relative would you tell them?
5. If you were in Kat's shoes in the last chapter what would you have done?

Kat's adventures will continue in Book 2 in the Aquamarine Sea Series.

Made in the USA
Lexington, KY
31 August 2017